C0-AZH-262

Mercian Studies

Mercian Studies

Edited by Ann Dornier

Leicester University Press 1977

95873

C640485

First published in 1977 by Leicester University Press
Distributed in North America by Humanities Press Inc., New Jersey

Copyright © Leicester University Press 1977

All rights reserved. No part of this publication may be reproduced, stored in a
retrieval system, or transmitted, in any form or by any means, electronic, mechanical,
photocopying, recording or otherwise, without the prior permission of the Leicester
University Press.

Designed by Arthur Lockwood
Consultant draughtsman A.G.McCormick

Set in IBM Press Roman by Charnwood Typesetting (Leicester) Ltd
Printed in Great Britain by Unwin Brothers Limited, The Gresham Press, Old Woking,
Surrey
ISBN 0 7185 1148 4

CONTENTS

064048 5   95873

PREFACE

The papers in this volume are the fruits of a conference on Mercia held at Leicester in December 1975. All the contributions were read at the conference with the exception of Chapter 5, which was circulated among some of the members, and Chapter 9, which arose out of one of the discussions. Three of the papers delivered at the conference are not included.

The aspects of Mercia dealt with at the conference were, because of the time factor, of necessity selective. The three themes chosen correspond to the three parts into which the book is divided : political and administrative history; coinage and towns; Christianity. This resulted in the omission of two major fields : the material culture of the pagan period and the Viking impact. It is hoped that these two will be the subject of a future conference.

There has been no attempt to standardize the orthography of proper names apart from initial *ash*. Contributors have also been left to follow which convention they prefer when citing primary written sources.

Leicester, 1976   Ann Dornier

8

ILLUSTRATIONS

ABBREVIATIONS

Antiq.J.	*Antiquaries' Journal*
Archaeol.J.	*Archaeological Journal*
Ass.Archit.Socs.Rep.Pap.	*Associated Architectural Societies' Reports and Papers*
Bedfordshire Archaeol.J.	*Bedfordshire Archaeological Journal*
Brit.Numis.J.	*British Numismatic Journal*
Bull.Board Celtic Stud.	*Bulletin of the Board of Celtic Studies*
Engl.Hist.Rev.	*English Historical Review*
J.Brit.Archaeol.Ass.	*Journal of the British Archaeological Association*
J.Derbyshire Archaeol.and Nat.Hist.Soc.	*Journal of the Derbyshire Archaeological and Natural History Society*
Medieval Archaeol.	*Medieval Archaeology*
Northamptonshire Archaeol.	*Northamptonshire Archaeology*
Numis.Chron.	*Numismatic Chronicle*
Proc.Brit.Acad.	*Proceedings of the British Academy*
Trans.Lichfield and S.Staffordshire Archaeol.and Hist.Soc.	*Transactions of the Lichfield and South Staffordshire Archaeological and Historical Society*
Trans.Royal Hist.Soc.	*Transactions of the Royal Historical Society*
V.C.H.	*Victoria History of the Counties of England*
W.Midlands Archaeol.News Sheet	*West Midlands Archaeological News Sheet*
Yorkshire Archaeol.J.	*Yorkshire Archaeological Journal*

ANN DORNIER

Introduction

In 1935 R. Hodgkin wrote that ' ... the early history of Mercia is so dark that it is better to pass it by and admit the impossibility of putting together any trustworthy story.' *(A History of the Anglo-Saxons,* vol.II, 194.) No-one would dispute the fact that many aspects of Mercian history, both early and late, will always remain shrouded in obscurity, but the papers by Drs Davies, Hart and Kirby, and Charles Phythian-Adams permit one to wonder whether such total pessimism is really justified and whether it is not possible to offer at least a partial reconstruction of certain problematical areas of Mercian political and administrative history, provided its inferential nature is recognized.

The problem of the origin of Mercia is of course synonymous with the problem of the origins of the Mercian dynasty. Dr Davies considers that entries in post-Conquest sources, which she argues are based on earlier material, throw light on this matter. Her examination of the regnal lists in particular leads her to accept the tradition that the first member of the family which became the Mercian royal house - and which may originally have settled in East Anglia - to have ruled in the Midlands was Crida c.585, thus pushing back this dynasty's first appearance in the area into the late sixth century. She also puts forward the suggestion that Penda may have begun his reign as early as c.607.

The westward expansion of Mercian royal power led inevitably to encroachments upon the territory of the Welsh kingdoms, notably Powys. From his study of the relevant early Welsh poetry Dr Kirby argues that there is no hint of conflict between the Mercian rulers and their contiguous Welsh neighbours before about the middle of the seventh century - though of course there is no extant poetry of Powys during the first half of the seventh century - after which, however, border warfare was a serious factor in Welsh - Mercian relationships.

To reconstruct in its various stages of evolution the political geography of the extensive kingdom which Mercian rulers subsequently carved out for themselves in the seventh and eighth centuries is a complex task. Using principally the Tribal Hidage, which he attributes to Offa, and accepting the assumption that the medieval dioceses fossilize the seventh- and eighth-century bishoprics, Dr Hart puts forward his suggestions about the territorial boundary of the kingdom, together with its major subdivisions and the geographical location of its various peoples in the late eighth century. If, as has been suggested by Dr Davies elsewhere, the Tribal Hidage belongs to the reign of Wulfhere, one cannot of course be certain that all of the groups still existed as distinct and recognizable entities nearly a century later.

Charles Phythian-Adams has also addressed himself to the problem of the identification of Mercian administrative traditions and puts forward the idea that Rutland may perhaps be co-terminous with a primitive *regio*. It is of course sometimes possible to delineate with greater precision the smaller territorial unit of the estate at a particular period, and the main theme of the paper is that the area of Rutland was a royal Mercian estate of pre-Danish origin.

The economic history of Mercia is the subject matter of the papers by Dr Metcalf, Philip Rahtz and John Williams. Dr Metcalf's analysis of the distribution of the sceattas of Mercia during the reign of Æthelbald throws an important light on Mercian trade during that period. He argues that the issue of a royal coinage in Mercia began during Æthelbald's reign, and he points to clusters of finds which show that the use of money was greatest in the frontier areas, principally the south and east, well away from the original political heartland, and that the monetary circulation also reflects particular activities, such as the Cotswold wool trade.

To what extent the growth in trade in eighth-century Mercia resulted in the growth of urban centres is impossible to say until there has been much more excavation. In his survey of west Mercian towns Philip Rahtz deals with the slight evidence for the existence of pre-tenth-century towns in that area. He also discusses the related problem of whether or not there was any urban survival from the Roman period and he concludes that, although there was some continuity of occupation for a period on some Roman sites, it was no longer urban in character. However, one has to bear in mind in considering both these problems that only relatively limited areas have been investigated in any one town. Both Philip Rahtz and John Williams emphasize the difficulty of deciding whether or not an earlier occupation on the site of a late Mercian town is of an urban nature, particularly where the evidence recovered so far is slight.

The documentary and archaeological evidence for late Mercian towns is beyond dispute. At present most of the archaeological evidence comes from west Mercia from the eight principal towns which are the subject of Philip Rahtz's paper : Chester, Gloucester, Hereford, Stafford, Shrewsbury, Tamworth, Warwick and Worcester - although our knowledge of these sites is at present confined chiefly to their defensive circuits. By contrast, John Williams is concerned with areas within the late Saxon town of Northampton which have yielded up information on the internal layout and associated buildings, and he suggests that the impetus for these developments may have come from the Danish occupation. With the exception of Northampton there is not much archaeological information available at present about other east Mercian towns, although it is to be hoped that the results of work in progress on several other sites will shortly redress the balance.

Similarly the reconstruction of the history of the full impact of Christianity on Mercia is dependent ultimately on the work of the archaeologist, together with that of the architectural historian. This is not to belittle the written evidence that does exist, and in my own paper I have taken another look at the documentary material relating to Breedon and have put forward the suggestion that some of the properties hitherto ascribed to Peterborough belonged in fact to Breedon. In this context Alexander Rumble considers the linguistic arguments for and against my identification of *Repingas* with Repton.

The material culture is best reflected in the physical remains of these ecclesiastical centres. In his contribution David Parsons tackles the problem of the interpretation of the surviving above-ground fabric at Brixworth and his work leads him to consider whether the building sequence might not be different from the traditional interpretation. Here, as elsewhere, the different phases will probably only be really satisfactorily disentangled by excavation as well. He also reviews the other work carried out so far by the Brixworth Excavation Committee. Equally important for the reconstruction of the appearance of these sites is the substantial collection of stone carving. Professor Rosemary Cramp discusses four of the regional schools into which she divides Mercian sculpture, together with their cultural affinities, on the basis of what she believes to be the significant diagnostic features of stylistic variation.

Stylistic considerations are also the criteria which Hazel Wheeler employs in her study of the Book of Cerne. Whether or not any of the extant illuminated manuscripts are Mercian will probably always be a matter of debate, but she argues that the similarity of style between some of its illuminated pages and certain pieces of Mercian sculpture makes it extremely likely that this particular manuscript was produced in a Mercian scriptorium. It is of course even more difficult to decide whether or not a Mercian origin should be ascribed to some of the other portable objects found in a Christian context. The mobility of such objects is well known and is illustrated by the metalwork of Frankish and Irish origin at Breedon mentioned in my paper.

ANATHEMA

If any man, fretted by excess of gall, shall perversely strive to undo this bountiful deed of my liberality, not for him be a happy lot in the company of blessed spirits, but let him know for certain that when the Lord shall come to judge all mankind he will be plunged up to the neck in avenging whirlwinds of fire, unless by making salutary and sufficient amends he shall have earned the divine forgiveness beforehand.
Grant of land at Mathon, Herefordshire, by king Æthelred to Ealdorman Leofwine, 1014 (H.P.R.Finberg : *The Early Charters of the West Midlands*, 1972, 145).

Part One

Part One

WENDY DAVIES

1   Annals and the origin of Mercia

It is the aim of this paper to make a technical and essentially textual contribution, by demonstrating that there is a little-noticed corpus of material of early origin which is additional to that collected and collated in the Anglo-Saxon Chronicle but is now preserved by English post-Conquest chroniclers; and secondarily, that this material has some bearing on our understanding of the early development of Mercia. Of course, this is hardly a new suggestion, either generically or specifically. The northern annals used by Symeon of Durham have been recognized for many years (Blair 1963: 86-99), and Hart has recently pointed out the early southern annals used in the Ramsey Computus (Hart 1970: 35-8). In the case of my chroniclers, the same suggestion was made by Liebermann nearly a century ago but with reference to ninth- and eleventh-century material (Liebermann 1888: 12).

The chronicles that I have in mind are Henry of Huntingdon's *Historia Anglorum* (Arnold 1879) and the two *Flores Historiarum* of Roger of Wendover (Coxe 1841-4) and Matthew Paris (Luard 1890). I will refer to these as Henry, Roger and Matthew respectively, and as *Flores* where Roger and Matthew are identical. Henry undertook his work at the request of Alexander, bishop of Lincoln; it ran in the first instance to 1129, though he subsequently extended it to 1154. Roger of Wendover was writing at St Albans, terminating his chronicle in 1234, possibly later extending it to 1235. He died in 1236. Matthew Paris, also writing at St Albans, produced a *Flores* which ran to 1249, with later continuations. The relationship between the two *Flores* is complex, but the essentials are as follows: Roger, who wrote first, used a variety of sources to 1212/14 and then became independent; Matthew's more famous work, *Chronica Majora*, followed Roger to c.1236; Matthew's *Flores* was based on his own *Chronica*, but he corrected errors found both in Roger and in his own *Chronica*. In his second work, therefore, Matthew was making use of Roger's sources as well as Roger's own work (Vaughan 1958: 97).

The material in these chronicles which has a bearing on the early development of Mercia is of sixth- and early-seventh-century date. Before proceeding further, I should like to recall the problems of dealing with early annalistic material. Annals which refer to events of the seventh century and earlier and use A.D. dates almost invariably owe that A.D. date to some later computation. This does not mean that the record itself does not derive from a contemporary record nor that it was undated, but it does mean that the date on that original record was expressed in terms of regnal or imperial or post-consular years, of indictions, of years counted from a variety of different fixed starting points. The early annalist's problem, therefore, was to synchronize dates of records drawn from a variety of sources; correspondingly, the modern critic's problem is to unravel those synchronisms. English annals of fifth- and sixth-century date present yet a further set of problems: it is conventionally supposed that these *cannot* be derived from contemporary written records since the English were not literate until their conversion to Christianity; if so, then problems of the viability of memory must be added to those of synchronization.[1]

Now it is clear that Henry, the *Flores* and the Anglo-Saxon Chronicle (Whitelock 1961) are independent in their treatment of the late sixth and early seventh centuries. Henry only occasionally uses A.D. dates but normally uses imperial years before 449, years from the *Adventus Saxonum* between 449 and 519, and then regnal years of West Saxon followed by English kings. His regnal years cannot be deduced from the Chronicle's dates since the synchronisms vary: the battle of *Certicesford*, for example, occurs in the ninth year of Cynric, which is in accordance with 519 and 527 of the Chronicle,[2] but the taking of the Isle of Wight occurs in the thirteenth year of Cynric. Since the Chronicle places this in 530, one would expect the twelfth year of Cynric by the same synchronism. The battle of Dyrham, on the other hand, occurs in the eighteenth year of Ceawlin, again in accordance with the Chronicle's 560 and 577,[3] but Ceolric becomes king in his thirtieth year. Since the Chronicle has 591, one would expect the thirty-second year by the same synchronism. Much of Henry's actual content is directly comparable to that of the Chronicle, but the order of events diverges in the late sixth and early seventh centuries. Ceawlin, for example, dies in the same year as Ælle, three years before the Wodens Barrow battle, while Ceolric succeeds in the same year as Æthelric; in the Chronicle, Ælle dies in 588, and Æthelric succeeds in the same year, Ceolric succeeds in 591, and Ceawlin dies in 593. Further, Henry concedes victory to the British at Wodens Barrow, though the Chronicle implies victory to the English. Although, therefore, there can be no doubt that Henry frequently used at least one text of the Chronicle,[4] his late-sixth-century material cannot be derived from any extant versions of it or from their immediate archetypes.

The *Flores* use A.D. dates, unlike Henry, but both the actual dates and the synchronisms are often at variance with those of the Chronicle: Cerdic and Cynric arrive in 494 and Port in 501, where the Chronicle has 495 and 501; the Isle of Wight is taken in 528, where the Chronicle has 530. The battle of *Bedcanford* (ASC 571) is conflated with that of Dyrham (ASC 577) under the year 580. The dates and synchronisms are, further, at variance with those of Henry and cannot therefore be derived from his work or any extant versions of the Chronicle. However, since they all include much material which appears in the Chronicle with different synchronisms they must have had access to a collection of annals very similar to those which lie behind the latter, but without the synchronisms imposed by its late-ninth-century edition; they must therefore have used a collection of annals of the mid-ninth century or earlier.[5] Events from one region are invariably in the same order in all sources and it would therefore appear that it is the collation of different sets of sources which is the point of variation. For events from 449 to 519 Henry and the *Flores* are more consistent with the synchronisms of extant Chronicle manuscripts, though not absolutely so; this might suggest that the annals they were using for the sixth and seventh centuries were a collection made before the accretion of the *Adventus* and fifth-century material.[6]

Both Henry and the *Flores* also contain English material which is not to be found in the Chronicle. Moreover, the *Flores* include more of this additional material than Henry does and do not follow all of his variations. It is therefore quite clear that Henry is not dependent upon the Chronicle for all of his early English material, and that the *Flores* are dependent upon neither; they are drawing upon sources which are now lost. The relationship between the two *Flores* has already revealed the existence of such sources at St Albans in the late twelfth and thirteenth centuries. Now although the *Flores* have more English material than Henry, both *Flores* and Henry have a series of entries for the sixth century which pertain to Mercia, East Anglia and Essex. These are listed in the Appendix below. These entries are common to all three texts; they occur in the same order in all three; and in some cases, in these entries, there are close verbal connections. For 527, for example, Henry reads '...Ea tempestate venerunt multi et saepe de Germania, et occupaverunt Eastangle et Merce: sed necdum sub uno rege redacta erant. Plures autem proceres certatim regiones occupabant, unde inumerabilia bella fiebant: proceres vero, quia multi erant, nomine carent', while the *Flores* have '...Eodem anno venerunt de German[n]ia pagani et occupa [ve] runt Est-angliam, id est regionem illam quae Orientalium Anglorum regio dicitur, quorum quidam Merciam invadentes bella cum Britonibus plurima peregerunt; sed, quoniam proceres eorum erant multi, nomine carent'. For 584 all read 'Victi sunt igitur Angli et fugae dati'. Although, therefore, the chronicles themselves are not interdependent, they must in part draw upon a common source for the sixth century. Since the interest of this source was clearly midland and eastern England it is likely that it originated from some mid- or East Anglian archive and was therefore not available when the Anglo-Saxon Chronicle was compiled, at a time when East Anglia was politically controlled by the Danes. Liebermann suggested that Roger was using a lost East Anglian chronicle and other St Albans records which were the source of some of his eleventh-century material; this is by no means impossible, but since the close correspondence between Henry and the *Flores* is confined to the sixth century it is unlikely that such a chronicle was available to all three writers and it is therefore unlikely to be the common source (Liebermann 1888: 12f). In summary, therefore, we may conclude that Henry and the two *Flores* are not interdependent but that all three had access to a common source of uncertain date containing midland and eastern material about the sixth century *and* to unsynchronized collections of annals of the mid-ninth century or earlier.

It is obvious that the late sixth-century material in these chronicles has a significance beyond the purely Mercian. Kirby has already made use of the Northumbrian material in his work on early Northumbrian chronology, while the West Saxon entries badly need collating with the better-known sources for early West Saxon history (Kirby 1963: 525). This must wait. The Mercian entries are those s.a. 527, 585, 588, 594, 610 (and 629) in the *Flores*, and the corresponding years in Henry, with the addition of the regnal lists s.a. 886 in the *Flores* and at the end of Book Two in Henry, c.685. Between them, they suggest that there was invasion from East Anglia in the early sixth century; that the kingdom of Mercia began in 585 with Crida/Creodda; that the succession of kings after Crida was *Wibba* (i.e. Pipba[7]), Ceorl, Penda; that *Wibba* ruled for three years and Ceorl for ten; that *Wibba* was ruling at the time of the conversion (in Henry only); that Penda was ruling in the first year of Cynegils (*Flores*) or began to rule in the sixteenth year of Cynegils and ruled for 30 years (Henry).

The problems of assessing this material are of different kinds. Where does the material come from? Where do the dates come from? How are the particular problems of the inconsistency over Penda's succession date and the inconsistency in the *Flores* over Pipba, who has a regnal length of three years but dates of 588-94, to be resolved? I shall treat the source and dates of the late-sixth-century material first and the 527 entry, which appears to derive from a different type of source, subsequently. The *Flores* quote regnal lengths, even to the point of inconsistency. The order of events (the original material without the dates) in both Henry and the *Flores* is the same and those events consist essentially of notices of accessions and deaths. It is difficult to conceive of any source for such material other than a simple regnal list, with dates computed later. There is plenty of evidence of the use of regnal lists and of dating by regnal years in seventh- and eighth-century England (Blair 1950; Kirby 1963: 515, 523-7) and this is precisely the kind of source that one might expect in very early English contexts. If the source be simply a regnal list, this allows us to resolve the inconsistency over Pipba's dates. Given that the *Flores* is inconsistent in itself, and that the A.D. dates derive from late computations, then the regnal figure for Pipba is much more likely to be early, and right, than the dates. In fact, the year implied by Henry for Pipba's accession is 593 (the year after Wodens Barrow and the year of Æthelfrith's accession), while 597 is that implied for his death, after the coming of Augustine and before the accession of Ceolwulf (both in 597). He also comments incidentally that Pipba was ruling at the time of the conversion. These implied dates are in accordance with a regnal length of three years and some months; since it is uncommon for the months to be noted, it would in fact appear that Henry's information about the length of Pipba's reign is no different from that of the *Flores* although it is, of course, differently synchronized. The *Flores* synchronize the first year of Pipba with the year of Æthelfrith's marriage, s.a.588; it is not inconceivable that this has been confused with the first year of Æthelfrith, 593, and that the *Flores* also intended a synchronization between the accession of Pipba and that of the latter. The content of the original regnal list, therefore, would seem to have been Crida ? years, Pipba three years, Ceorl ten years, Penda ? years, with dates of 593-7 and 597-607 applied to the second and third.

The second major problem lies in the source of the dates attached to this regnal list. The absolute dates 527 and 571 in all three sources must have been deduced

before collation with imperial years and West Saxon material because both Henry
and the *Flores* agree on 527 for the influx while only Henry collates that with
Certicesford and only the *Flores* collate with the first year of Justinian; both agree
on 571 for the beginning of the kingdom of East Anglia though Henry collates this
with *Bedcanford* (ASC 571) and the *Flores* place *Bedcanford* in the same order but
later, s.a. 580. The relationship between Henry and the *Flores*, therefore, is such that
the dates are highly unlikely to have been deduced from a synchronization with
imperial years or the beginnings of imperial reigns; though the *Flores* do make
frequent reference to imperial accessions, these appear to have been added to the
material at a comparatively late stage on the model of that of the Chronicle of Ado
of Vienne (Pertz 1829), of which there was an eleventh- or twelfth-century copy at
St Albans (Ker 1964: 165). Now although no regnal length is given for Penda in the
Flores it seems most likely that the original regnal list did give it, and that the
majority of the dates were calculated backwards from the relatively well-evidenced
death-date of Penda. In order to demonstrate the viability of this suggestion, it is
necessary to begin by considering the discrepancy over Penda's dates. The length of
the reign of Penda is a well-known and much-discussed problem, and the
discrepancy between Henry and the *Flores* is but a reflection of a discrepancy in
other sources. Henry, in fact, follows a Chronicle annal (MSS. A, B and C) which
notes that Penda began to rule in 626, at the age of 50, and ruled for 30 years.[8]
Bede, on the other hand, made him rule from 633-55, i.e. 634-56[9] (Bede: 124, 354)
while the *Historia Brittonum* has a mere ten years (Mommsen 1898: 208). Two
observations seem to be necessary. Firstly, these discrepancies are less significant
than might be supposed because they seem to be reflecting the different criteria used
by different sources to arrive at significant regnal lengths. Hence, Bede saw the
death of Edwin of Deira as significant for the beginning of Penda; the *Historia
Brittonum* saw the death of Penda's brother Eowa as the significant date; while the
Anglo-Saxon Chronicle, and Henry following it, merely seem to be calculating from
the regnal length of 30 years and have neither independent evidence nor collations
for the 626 date. Secondly, the contemporary activity of Penda and his brother
Eowa is well-evidenced since the former was certainly fighting battles c.628 (ASC),
while the latter fell, as king of the Mercians, at the battle of *Cocboy* (i.e. Maserfield)
c.643 (Mommsen 1898: 208; Phillimore 1888: 158). Unless, therefore, one is
convinced of the dominance of ideas of monarchy there is no problem in viewing
the two brothers as contemporary kings. In the light of both observations, I find the
implications of the source of Henry and the *Flores* - that Penda became king c.607
and was ruling in 610 - at least as credible as the varying suggestions that he became
king in 626 or 634 or 643, provided we understand that kingship as one sometimes
shared with his brother. Moreover, when we recall that no source, early or late, has
any indication of kings intermediate between Ceorl and Penda/Eowa; that their
father died c.597; and that Ceorl's daughter was Edwin's first wife and their
marriage must have taken place very early in the sixth century; then the suggestion
becomes rather more credible than the varying later suggestions. If this be credible,
then it is at least conceivable that the Anglo-Saxon Chronicle's source noted that
Penda had a reign of 50 years from the age of 30 rather than 30 years from the age
of 50.[10] The latter suggestion is of course speculative, but the establishment of that
minor error would render the Anglo-Saxon Chronicle, Henry and the *Flores*
consistent in their view of the regnal length - and provide a source for all the early

accessions and deaths except that of Crida.

Neither *Flores* nor Henry make any statement of regnal years for Crida. There are no fragments of evidence, even corrupt ones, to suggest, therefore, that his accession date is similarly deduced by a calculation back from the accession of Pipba. Though both chronicles are often at variance in their treatment of late-sixth-century material they concur in collating the accession with the battle of *Fethanleag*. It occurs immediately subsequently. It is just conceivable that there is a real connection here and not merely a synchronic one: though Ceawlin captured many villages and countless booty, he nevertheless returned home in anger (ASC 584), perhaps because Crida emerged dominant.[11] I can suggest no other explanation for the date than the collation, and this may be coincidental. Whatever the absolute date considered significant by early writers it is nevertheless worth noting that all extant Mercian regnal lists begin with Crida and that that idea was certainly current by 886.[12] Whatever the precise date, therefore, it was an early notion that the kingdom of Mercia began with Crida.

There therefore seems every reason to suppose that a Mercian regnal list from Crida, with king lengths for Pipba, Ceorl and Penda at the least, is the source that lies behind these entries; that the dates attached to it were in the main calculated backwards from Penda's deathdate, although 585 may have been derived by collation with *Fethanleag*; that that list is credible and consistent with the indications of other sources; that list (and dates) are unlikely to be of later origin than the mid-ninth century.

The 527 entry is of a different type. In the version of the *Flores* it reads 'In the same year (527) pagans came from Germany and occupied East Anglia... some of whom invaded Mercia and fought many battles with the British; but, since their leaders were many, their names are missing'. It must be admitted that this is very unspecific, and has every appearance of a retrospective comment. There is very little in the entry itself to suggest that it is or derives from a contemporary record, but the viewpoint is quite clearly the same as that reflected in another St Albans product, the Lives of the Two Offas. In this the ancestor of the Mercian kings, Wermund, was associated with the Western Angles, an implication that the Angles formed two groups - Eastern and Western - and therefore that there was an implied connection between Mercian and East Anglian (Chadwick 1907: 118). Now both Henry and the *Flores* clearly intend the date 527, but although that date is deducible in the former from its relation to the battle at *Certicesford* the *Flores* omit *Certicesford* s.a. 527 and enter it s.a. 508.[13] (The *Flores* also omit the Chronicle's West Saxon entry s.a.519 and appear to be using a source which does not contain the well-known duplication of three early-sixth-century entries at 19-year intervals (Harrison 1971: 528-32).) The ultimate source of our 527 entry cannot therefore derive its date from a collation with *Certicesford*. Nor, as explained above, would it appear to derive it from the first imperial year of Justinian. Moreover, it is obviously not a calculation backwards by regnal years from a fixed point, since the invasions occur well before the beginning of the kingdoms.[14] A clue to its possible source occurs in a rather unexpected place, the *Flores* entry for 571. This annal refers to the end of a great cycle, 532[15] years from the passion of Christ, in the seventh indiction, in addition to noting the beginning of the kingdom of East Anglia. The reference to the end of a great cycle does not appear to derive from any chronicle which may have been available to the St Albans writers for it is, as far as I can ascertain, unique. It must, moreover, ultimately derive from some source which does *not* use A.D. dates since the synchronism is incorrect; the other dates quoted in the entry point consistently to 559, the proper end of the cycle. The most likely explanation is that the whole entry actually derives from a table for calculating Easter dates in which the beginning of the kingdom of East Anglia was noted under the final line of figures, the figures for the last year of the cycle. When collected and noted by the annalist, both figures and comment were copied out. Now all of the sources used by the *Flores* for the sixth century can be identified with the exception of those for 571 and 527; most of the Continental material, in fact, derives from the early-twelfth-century chronicle of Sigebert of Gembloux (Pertz 1844). Since there are only two entries whose source cannot be identified, and since one of those appears to derive from an Easter table, then the chances that the other derives from the same table are worth considering. The Easter table which runs for 532 years from the Passion is that of Victorius of Aquitaine, from A.D.28 to 559. Roger and Matthew, or their source, have wrongly synchronized the end of the cycle with the year 571. If our 527 entry derives from the same table, therefore, it must have been written under annal 488 of the table, i.e. A.D.515. It would of course be naive in the extreme to suggest that an entry made on a Victorian Paschal Cursus was necessarily contemporary or early, but it is highly unlikely that the table would still have been in use after the early eighth century. The table was inaccurate; this was realized in Rome as early as 501, although it continued to be used in Italy until c.550 and in Gaul until the early eighth century (Jones 1943: 67-8). It was also available in western Britain at some period before the early ninth century (Dumville 1972-4: 443-5). Recent work on early England has suggested that it was probably already being replaced by Dionysiac tables by c.660 (Harrison 1973: 113). Unless the record comes ultimately from a British source, therefore, it is unlikely to have been entered much later than c.700. There is therefore some strong reason to suppose 515 is intended as the date of invasion, and that the idea, though retrospective, is of no later than seventh-century origin.[16]

This is surprisingly consistent with information of quite different origin. The Mercian royal family of the early eighth century was known as Iclingas, descendants of Icel. Icel occurs in the early stages of the Mercian genealogy, and H.M.Chadwick pointed out some years ago by analogy that there is a strong suggestion in the term Iclingas that Icel was a leader in, or immediately subsequent to, the migration. Moreover, those members of the genealogy who come before Icel are only celebrated in Continental contexts, those who come after in Insular ones (Chadwick 1907: 15f). Since Icel is the great-grandfather of Crida, there is already some independent indication that the member of the future Mercian royal dynasty who was involved in the migration was so engaged c.510-35 (at 25 years per generation before Crida) (cf. Morris 1973: 272). There are, moreover, a few echoes of this in the distribution of material culture, if such distribution patterns can bear any relation to the movement of people, and some in the distribution of Icel place names in eastern England. Myres has pointed out that *Buckelurnen* with feet spread out from East Anglia through Middle Anglia towards the South West in the late fifth century (Myres 1969: 102), a date which many critics would prefer to call early sixth century (Morris 1974: 225-32). Pretty has recently pointed out

95873

connections between the metalwork of the Upper Avon and East Anglia from about 500 until the late sixth century (1975).

I should like to suggest, therefore, that the material that I have been discussing derives at the least from a couple of entries on a Victorian table, and from a Mercian regnal list, put together early in the Saxon period. Since the earlier sixth-century dates are common to Henry and the *Flores* it is likely that the material was already compiled with other material of predominantly East Anglian interest and that the chroniclers were not referring to the original sources. It is impossible to comment on the date of compilation, but the tradition that the Mercian kingdom began with Crida is at least as old as the late ninth century. The suggestion of this material that the settlement of Mercia sprang from East Anglia and/or from a migration which also produced settlement in East Anglia, in the early sixth century, and that the family which was to become the Mercian royal dynasty took part in that migration, is a reasonable suggestion in the light of other evidence. Further, the material provides very good evidence that kings of Mercia were noted from Crida onwards, c.585, and hence that we can certainly begin the kingdom of Mercia before Penda and the 630s, despite the current orthodoxy.

Though we may be able to refine notions about the beginning of the kingdom there remain some crucial problems. Mercia fits into a pattern of predominantly late-sixth-century beginnings among the English kingdoms, but though we may note the consistency of the pattern we still do not know who selected this period as the significant point of origin and by what criteria the selection was made. Does the late sixth century, therefore, really represent a period of change in the nature and concepts of political authority among the English, or is it emphasized by the new literacy of the seventh century: do the first kings of the late sixth century owe their prominence to the limits of early-seventh-century memory? Again, although it is quite clear that the territorial competence of the Mercian kingdom extended considerably under Penda, it is still very unclear just which areas represented the original base of the dynasty and the territorial horizons of the kings before Penda and it is not clear if either coincided with the area inhabited by the people known as Mercians. The patterns of settlement, of the ownership of property and of political ambition, have no necessary geographical coincidence although there is likely to be some relation between the latter two. These are the problems which need resolution in the coming years. Work on the origins of the kingdom may well be accelerated by a recognition of the separate nature of settlement, proprietory and political spheres: we need not look for the origins of the Mercian royal dynasty and Mercian political authority in the area of the earliest Mercian settlement. Indeed, although there is plenty to suggest an early northern focus and outlook for the people known as Mercian (Collingwood and Myres 1937: 417), the more southern and western aspect of the seventh-century Mercian kings - revealed by place-names, land grants and Penda's earliest battles (Collingwood and Myres 1937: 410; Stenton 1971: 45) - may be less inconsistent and inexplicable than has often been supposed. No-one doubts that the west Midlands became central to the operations of the Mercian kings in the course of the seventh century, but this development is very largely to be explained by the waning political capacity of the British kingdoms of the North and Midlands. It is not in itself a clue to the early fortunes of the dynasty.

APPENDIX

A. Comparative annals

ASC	Flores	Henry
571: *Bedcanford.*	571: Wffa in East Anglia. (572-6)*	12 Ceawlin: *Bedcanford.* Beginning of East Anglia, with Wuffa.
	577: Tiberius; Theodoric in Bernicia for 7.	
577: Dyrham.	578: Vortipor for 3 after Aurelius; Titilus after Wffa in East Anglia.	18 Ceawlin: Dyrham.
	579: Pope Pelagius.	
	580: *Bedcanford* and Dyrham.	
	581: Malgo after Vortipor.	
583: Maurice.	(582-3)	
584: *Fethanleag.*	584: Maurice; *Fethanleag.*	25 Ceawlin: *Fethanleag.* Beginning of Mercia.
	585: Beginning of Mercia.	
	586: Karetius after Malgo.	
	587: Sledda after Erkenwin in Essex.	
588: Æthelric for 5.	588: Æthelfrith marries; Crida dies; Wibba for 3.	30 Ceawlin: Ceawlin dies; Ceolric for 5. Ælle dies; Æthelric for 5.
	589: Birth of Sebert.	
	590: Death of Cissa.	
591: Ceol(ric) for 5 (or 6).	(591-2)	
592: Wodens Barrow.		3 years after: Wodens Barrow.
593: Ceawlin, Cwichelm, Crida die. Æthelfrith.	593: Ceawlin dies; Ceolric for 5; Ælle dies; Æthelfrith.	Next: Crida dies; Wibba; Æthelfrith.
	594: Wibba dies; Cherl for 10. (595)	
595/6/7: Augustine's mission.	596: Augustine's mission.	Mission.
	(597-8)	After Wibba, Cherl. Ceolric dies; Ceolwulf for 14.
597: Ceolwulf.		
	599: Eorpenwald after Redwald. (600)	
601: Pallium to Augustine.	601: Pallium to Augustine. (602)	
603: *Degsastan.*		7 Ceolwulf and 1 Phocas: *Degsastan.*
	603: Chester.	
604: Conversion of East Saxons.	604: Conversion of East Saxons.	
605/7: Chester.	(605-6)	9 Ceolwulf: Chester.
607: Ceolwulf against South Saxons.	607: Ceolwulf for 24.	Ceolwulf against South Saxons.
	(608-9)	
	610: Cynegils for 31; Penda etc. ruling.	
611: Cynegils.	(611-15)	14/15 Ceolwulf: Cynegils for 31.

614: *Beandun.*		4 Cynegils: *Beandun.*
616: Eadbald.	616: Eadbald in Kent; 3 sons of Sebert in Essex.	6 Cynegils: Eadbald.
617: Edwin.	617: Edwin.	7 Cynegils: Edwin.
	623: Sigeberht in Essex. 624: Eorpenwald after Redwald.	
626: Lilla; Penda.	626: Lilla.	16 Cynegils: (Lilla); Penda; 2 sons of Sebert; Sigeberht in Essex.
628: Cirencester.	629: Cirencester.	3 years after: Cirencester.

*(The *Flores* have Continental entries for the years bracketed.)

B. The additional annals
Invasion of East Anglia and Mercia (527).
Beginning of the kingdom of Essex, with Erkenwinus (527).
Wffa in East Anglia (571).
Titilus in East Anglia, after Wffa (578).
Beginning of the kingdom of Mercia, with Crida (585).
Sledda in Essex, after Erkenwinus (587).
Death of Crida, succeeded by Wibba (for 3 years) (588).
Birth of Sebert, son of Sledda (589).
Death of Wibba, succeeded by Ceorl (for 10 years) (594).
Penda ruling in Mercia, Redwald in East Anglia, Æthelbert in Kent, Sebert in Essex, Æthelfrith in Northumbria (610) (*Flores* only).
2/3 sons of Sebert in Essex, after Sebert (616; 626 in Henry).
Sigeberht in Essex, after the sons (623; 626 in Henry).
Eorpenwald in East Anglia, after Redwald (599 and 624) (*Flores* only).

C. The regnal lists
Flores, s.a. 886: 'Creodda, Wibba, Cearlus (Roger only), Penda Peada primus Christianus, Wlferus/Wlfere, Æthelfredus/Ethelred...'.
Henry: 'Primus Crida; Wibba, Ceorlus, Penda; Peda, fidem primus suscepit; Wlfhere, Ædelred' (Arnold 1879: 65).

NOTES

1. This is the current convention. Although this must normally be true, there are probably some exceptions: it is not impossible that the passage of time was noted and recorded in the pre-literate period by some such method as notches cut on sticks (Harrison 1971: 528-30); it is by no means impossible that some of the earliest English annals were originally recorded by British sources, for it is difficult to explain the orthographic peculiarities of some of the early West Saxon annals except with reference to British practice.
2. As MS. E; other MSS. have *Cerdicesleag* s.a. 527 and *Cerdicesford* s.a. 519.
3. 559 in MSS. C and F.
4. Plummer considered that Henry was using the archetype of MS. E and the actual text of MS. C (1899: 1v-1xvi).
5. The Anglo-Saxon Chronicle was compiled during the reign of Alfred (Whitelock 1961: xxi-xxiv), and most of its A.D. dates appear to have been calculated at that time on the basis of regnal lengths and years; Kirby has suggested, however, that at least some of the West Saxon dates of the seventh century must have been calculated *before* the regnal lists were compiled (1965: 17f).
6. The *Adventus Saxonum* was clearly a familiar historical concept in the eighth century; both Bede and the *Historia Brittonum* use it.
7. Both *Flores* and the regnal list in Henry employ the form *Wibba;* Henry's text uses *Wipha, Wippa* and *Wibba.* It is quite clear from the genealogies that Penda's father was Pipba/Pybba and therefore that this is the name intended here. Confusion between 'w' and 'p' was common in the copying of Old English manuscripts since the Old English letter *wen, ꝥ* i.e. 'w', was often read as 'p' by the ignorant, while a genuine 'p' was sometimes incorrectly transcribed as 'w' by those with a little knowledge.
8. This does not appear in MS. E.
9. After Kirby (1963: 516-20).
10. H.M. Chadwick argued that the Chronicle must have been incorrect on the grounds that Penda cannot have fought so many vigorous battles in old age and that his relatives by one degree were still young in the late seventh century (1907: 16f); this is a powerful argument, but it is not decisive for we cannot expect every lifespan necessarily to conform to our conventional estimates of the span of generations.
11. There is a death of a Crida recorded in the Chronicle in 593. For reasons given above, since Henry is not dependent upon the Chronicle for his late-sixth-century material it is unlikely that it is the Chronicle entry which is the reason for placing the death of the Mercian king and accession of Pipba s.a. 593. If the two notions are not interdependent, then it is possible that they are in fact corroborative: that the Chronicle Crida is the same man as the Mercian king but that he was closely involved in the battles of the West Saxon kings; hence, that the emergence of Crida c. 585 was a direct consequence of success against the West Saxon Ceawlin. The material in the prefaces to Florence of Worcester's *Chronicon ex Chronicis* similarly seems to select Crida as the significant starting point, though Florence makes no reference to the East Anglian material in his text; I should like to thank my student David Rollason for pointing out that these prefaces really form separate histories, produced earlier than the Chronicle itself, probably c.1100.
12. There is no reason to suppose that Henry's regnal list at the end of Book Two is necessarily of early origin; however, those in the *Flores* s.a. 886 would appear to have been compiled in that year or very shortly after. Kent, Mercia, East Anglia, Essex, Sussex each have lists terminating before 886 and ending with the comment that the kingdom was then transferred to the West Saxons; the Northumbrian list ends with 'Ricsius, Egbertus, Cuthredus', of whom Ricsic was in power c.873-6, Egbert c.876-?8, and Cuthred seems unknown; the area was soon taken over by the Danes. The inclusion of a number of names that are otherwise unknown, especially at the end of the lists, weighs against it being an abstract of the

previous content of the chronicles.

13. MSS. A B C E F enter *Cerdicesford/Certicesford* s.a. 508 and 519, and E also s.a. 527, where A B C have *Cerdicesleag*.

14. In fact, both *Flores* and Henry go on to note the beginning of the kingdom of Essex, but there is no need to suppose that the two consecutive entries recording invasion of Mercia and the beginning of Essex in the East Anglian source were necessarily intended to be contemporary. Since the accession of the next king of Essex is not recorded until 587 it would seem very unlikely.

15. Miscopied as 524, i.e. cccccxxiv for cccccxxxii.

16. The Victorian cycle does not appear to have been recognized as a great cycle until the seventh century. I should like to thank Miss Barbara Troubridge for pointing out that the dates 527 and 571 for the beginnings of Essex and East Anglia are also given in marginal notes to the register of Walter of Whittesley, preceding kinglists.

REFERENCES

Note ASC = Anglo-Saxon Chronicle (see below, under Whitelock)

Arnold, H. (ed.), 1879, *Henrici Archidiaconi Huntendunensis Historia Anglorum.*

Bede. *Venerabilis Baedae Opera Historica,* ed. C. Plummer, 1896.

Blair, P. Hunter, 1950. 'The Moore Memoranda on Northumbrian History', in *The Early Cultures of North-West Europe,* ed. Sir Cyril Fox and B. Dickens: 243-57.

Blair, P. Hunter, 1963. 'Some observations on the *Historia Regum* attributed to Symeon of Durham', in *Celt and Saxon,* ed. N. Chadwick: 63-118.

Chadwick, H.M., 1907. *The Origin of the English Nation.*

Coxe, H.O., 1841-4. *Rogeri de Wendover Chronica, sive Flores Historiarum.*

Collingwood, R.G. and Myres, J.N.L., 1937. *Roman Britain and the English Settlements* (2nd edn).

Dumville, D., 1972-4. 'Some aspects of the chronology of the *Historia Brittonum*', *Bull. Board Celtic Stud., 25:* 439-45.

Harrison, K., 1971. 'Early Wessex annals in the Anglo-Saxon Chronicle', *Engl. Hist. Rev., 86:* 527-33.

Harrison, K., 1973. 'The Synod of Whitby and the beginning of the Christian era in England', *Yorkshire Archaeol.J., 45:* 108-14.

Hart, C., 1970. 'The Ramsey Computus', *Engl.Hist.Rev., 85:* 29-44.

Jones, C.W. (ed.), 1943. *Bedas Opera de Temporibus* (Cambridge, Mass.).

Ker, N.R. (ed.), 1964. *Medieval Libraries of Great Britain* (2nd edn).

Kirby, D.P., 1963. 'Bede and Northumbrian chronology', *Engl.Hist.Rev., 78:* 514-27.

Kirby, D.P., 1965. 'Problems of Early West Saxon history', *Engl.Hist.Rev., 80:* 10-29.

Liebermann, F. (ed.), 1888. *Ex Rerum Anglicarum scriptoribus saeculi XIII, Monumenta Germaniae Historica, SS, xxviii* (Hanover).

Luard, H.R., 1890. *Flores Historiarum.*

Mommsen, T. (ed.), 1898. *Chronica Minora saec. IV, V, VI, VII Monumenta Germaniae Historica, AA,* xiii (Berlin).

Morris, J., 1973. *The Age of Arthur.*

Morris, J., 1974. 'Review of J.N.L. Myres, *The Anglo-Saxon Cemeteries*', *Medieval Archaeol., 18:* 225-32.

Myres, J.N.L., 1969. *Anglo-Saxon Pottery and the Settlement of England.*

Pertz, G.H. (ed.), 1829. 'Ex Adonis archiepiscopi Viennensis chronico ad a 869', *Monumenta Germaniae Historica, SS, 2:* 315-23 (Hanover).

Pertz, G.H. (ed.), 1844. 'Sigeberti Gemblacensis Chronica', *Monumenta Germaniae Historica, SS, 6:* 300-74 (Hanover).

Phillimore, E., 1888. 'The *Annales Cambriae* and Old Welsh genealogies, from *Harleian MS.* 3859', *Y Cymmrodor, 9:* 141-83.

Plummer, C. (ed.), 1892-9. *Two of the Saxon Chronicles Parallel.*

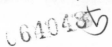

Pretty, K., 1975. 'The Welsh Border and the Severn and Avon Valleys in the Fifth and Sixth Centuries A.D.: An Archaeological Survey' (Ph.D. thesis, University of Cambridge).

Stenton, F.M., 1971. *Anglo-Saxon England* (3rd edn).

Vaughan, R., 1958. *Matthew Paris.*

Whitelock, D., with Douglas, D.C., and Tucker, S.I., 1961. *The Anglo-Saxon Chronicle.*

D.P. KIRBY

2 Welsh bards and the Border

Professor K.H. Jackson comments in his translation of Aneirin's poem, the *Gododdin*, that 'in early times the business of the professional poet, the 'bard', was not entertainment by means of narrative, but precisely to celebrate the praises of the aristocratic class in general and of his own patron in particular, (Jackson 1969: 38; cf. Ford 1974: 5ff.). He continues: 'by very ancient common Celtic custom poetry was composed in the head and without the use of writing; was recited orally to the assembled company in the chief's hall; and was handed down orally, being learnt by heart by subsequent reciters and so passed on for generations; and ... all this was fostered and practised by the institutions of 'bardic schools' in which budding poets were given an elaborate training in their profession, in oral composition of poetry, and its recitation and transmission when learnt by heart' (Jackson 1969: 60). Nevertheless, as Professor Jackson naturally concedes, bardic poems were vulnerable to corruption in the course of oral transmission, and to modernization. In the case of a piece not so regularly recited as acclaimed classics like the *Gododdin*, non-modernized, archaic forms were preserved but were often meaningless to a much later generation and written down eventually or copied in a confused and muddled manner. Where the original sense of a poem, or large parts of the poem, was lost, the problem of translation now can be a very difficult one. Moreover, the heroic eulogies and elegies of the bards, constituting essentially panegyric addressed to a leader, only allude incidentally and cryptically to events and persons, so that what is recoverable is by no means easily integrated into a known and precise pattern of events.

Gildas upbraided Maelgwn, king of Gwynedd, for, among many other personal failings, preferring to hear his own praises sung by a rascally, lying crew of

Bacchanalian revellers than to listen to the melodic voice of church music (Gildas, *de Excidio Britanniae* c.34). What Gildas is saying, in his own inimitable way, is that the praises of Maelgwn were sung, much to the king's satisfaction, by bards in his own lifetime (Foster 1965: 227), bards who did not necessarily dwell on truth so much as on a panegyrical distortion of the real facts. A fragment of bardic tradition associates Maelgwn with an attack on Dyfed (Jarman 1951: 40-4), but otherwise there seems little in later bardic lore concerning Maelgwn to commend itself as authentic, certainly not the story of the contest between the youthful Taliesin and the bards of Maelgwn. Maelgwn died c.547-9. Taliesin flourished in the last two decades of the sixth century, apparently then at the height of his professional powers, and it is unlikely that he was even born during Maelgwn's lifetime. It cannot be regarded as absolutely certain that the early poem to Cynan Garwyn (on the possible meanings of 'Garwyn' see Bromwich 1961: 318) king of Powys in the late sixth century, son of Brochfael Ysgithrog ('of the tusks'), included in the corpus of poems by Taliesin and regarded as one of the authentic poems of the late sixth century (Williams 1960: no. 1, and cf. Caerwyn Williams 1968; no. 1), really was by Taliesin (Lewis 1968; 298 n.1). If it was not, Taliesin's certain contact with Wales is unproven and he was a bard rather of the 'Men of the North'. In bardic tradition, the legendary Taliesin is even made to boast that he 'sang before a renowned lord where the Severn winds, before Brochfael of Powys who loved my muse.' While it is indeed true to say that 'These and other references make it obvious that Brochfael's exploits had kept his memory alive for centuries after his death' (Williams 1960: no.XXIX), Taliesin's association with Brochfael is surely quite unhistorical. It is indeed probable that all the bards named in the *Historia Brittonum* (Mommsen 1898) - Taliesin, Aneirin, Talhaeran, Cian and Bluchbard - belonged to the North British area only, and there is no comparable list of bards who were famous in the Welsh area at the same period. It must not simply be assumed that these early bards did travel across wide areas.

The poem to Cynan, king of Powys, is the earliest bardic piece to survive from Wales. Cynan is described as the son of Brochfael, of the lineage of Cadell, ruling, like his grandfather, Cyngen, a wide dominion, and the poem lists his battles, his military victories (for a translation, see Foster 1965: 229-30). Powys, stretching into the west Midland areas of Shropshire and Cheshire, must have been a powerful realm. What is so striking about this poem to Cynan is the absence of any reference to a battle against the English - the men of *Lloegr* - despite campaigns on a wide geographical front: in Dyfed (1.13), on the Wye (1.9), against the men of Gwent (1.10), in Brycheiniawc (1.20), and apparently even against the Britons of Cornwall (1.16). While this poem is panegyric rather than chronicled history, like all bardic poems, it nevertheless 'gives a vital glimpse of an historical situation and accordingly it can be taken as a record of the struggle of dominion and wealth among the rulers within Wales at the close of the sixth century' (Foster 1965: 230). It is concerned with Cynan's military ascendancy at the expense of other neighbouring British rulers. It betrays the limited vision which so appalled Gildas. The Anglo-Saxon advance evidently, to judge from this poem, did not impinge upon Cynan's existence. It soon did impinge on Powys, of course, for in c.616 at the battle of Chester, Æthelfrith, king of Northumbria, defeated and slew Selyf, 'Serpent in battles', son of Cynan, and put to ignominious flight a certain Brochfael whose identity is unclear: Arofan was Selyf's bard, but none of his verses have survived (Chadwick 1963b: 167-85: cf. on Arofan and other early poets, Lloyd Jones 1948: 169).

A certain weakening in the power of Powys, coinciding perhaps with the growth of a dynamic Gwynedd, may have contributed towards the propelling into the forefront of border warfare the rulers of north-west Wales. Maelgwn probably left behind him a powerful Gwynedd. Cadfan, king of Gwynedd, great-great-grandson of Maelgwn, was styled on his death, c. 630 'wisest and most renowned of all kings' (Nash-Williams 1950: 13; Alcock 1971: 224). He had given protection from Æthelfrith to the Northumbrian exiled prince, Edwin of Deira, and, according to tradition fostered Edwin with his own son, Cadwallon (Lloyd 1939: I, 183; Bromwich 1961: 339; Chadwick 1963a: 149ff.). Edwin's subsequent attack on Cadwallon in Gwynedd, once he was secure as king of Northumbria, earned him the description in Welsh tradition of 'the Deceitful'. Edwin had seized Anglesey and Man, possibly from a naval base at Chester: he was ready to embark upon 'What was the first English invasion of Wales' (Lloyd 1939: I, 183-4). Indeed, so successful was this invasion that Cadwallon, king of Gwynedd, was besieged by Edwin on the island of Priestholm, off Anglesey, and then driven into exile in Ireland c.630/2 (Lloyd 1939: I, 184-5). He returned from Ireland, allied with Penda, king of embryonic Mercia, and defeated and slew Edwin at the battle of Hatfield in 634, after which for a year he ravaged Northumbria until eventually slain by Oswald, son of Æthelfrith, at the battle of Heavenfield, near Hexham.[1]

These details are well known to historians of Anglo-Celtic Britain. Less well-known are the Welsh bardic poems describing the exploits of Cadwallon. One of these poems, *Marwnad* (Elegy) *Cadwallawn*,[2] is a battle poem, like that to Cynan of Powys, of the kind which may lie behind the catalogue of Arthur's battles in the *Historia Brittonum*. It is concerned with Cadwallon's military exploits against fellow-Britons - on the Teifi (1.26), or in the uplands of Dunawd's land (1.31) - but a number (by contrast with the poem to Cynan) relate to the conflicts with the Saxons: Cadwallon is 'a fierce affliction to his foe, a lion of hosts over the Saxons' (11.6-7), and the men of *Lloegr* 'numerous their complaints'(1.23). Battles are fought on the Severn and on the Wye and there is an allusion to the near-burning of Meigen (1.11) or *Meicen*, which Welsh tradition placed near the boundaries of Powys but which was sometimes confused with the battle of Hatfield. (Lloyd 1939: I, 186; Foster 1965: 223; Bromwich 1961: 151-2). One line (1.8), which reads

The camp of the famous Cadwallawn

on the uplands of Mount Digoll ...

may be correlated with the tradition preserved in the Welsh triads (which contain several references to Cadwallon) under the heading of the Three Defilements of the Severn: 'Cadwallon when he went to the Action of Digoll, and the forces of the Cymry with him: and Edwin on the other side, and the forces of *Lloegr* with him. And then the Severn was defiled from its source to its mouth.' The mountain of Digoll - Caer Digoll - signifies the Long Mountain in Montgomeryshire, on the opposite bank of the Severn from Welshpool, in the centre of the district called Meigen (Bromwich 1961: 182-3). Not all the engagements listed in this poem can have been fought by Cadwallon between his return from Ireland and his advance to Hatfield. Some of the conflicts may in fact reflect the advance of Edwin from the vicinity of the upper Severn which led to Cadwallon's expulsion. But, on the other hand, others may belong to the period after Cadwallon's return and to the counter-offensive against the Northumbrians. To determine which battle belongs in which period is no easy matter. Of considerable interest are the final lines (11.34ff.) of the poem, which refer to 'the plotting of strangers and unrighteous monks' and go on to say that, as the wood is dressed for summer (i.e. the campaigning season is at hand), 'let us meet around Elfed' - which could, of course, be the district of Elfed in Carmarthenshire (on which cf. Richards 1969: 66, 253), or more likely perhaps the Christian British kingdom of Elmet in North Britain, in Yorkshire (cf. Kolb 1973: 285-313). Cadwallon's father, Cadfan, probably had friendly relations with Elmet, in which region Edwin had also sought refuge when in exile (Chadwick 1963a: 151); and Edwin annexed Elmet to Northumbria by conquest in the 620s (*Historia Brittonum* c63) (Mommsen 1898). Could Elmet have been partly betrayed into the power of the Angles by British clergy in Elmet after Edwin's conversion? Did Cadwallon attempt to retrieve the loss of Elmet and did this action perhaps directly bring about Edwin's assault on Gwynedd to reduce by intimidation the risk of future Welsh intervention north of the Humber? Such questions are more easily raised than answered, but they spring naturally from the enigmatic nature of this bardic material and they at least pose intriguing possibilities for consideration.

The second poem, *Moliant* [Eulogy] *Cadwallawn*, possibly by Cadwallon's bard, Afan Ferddig, celebrates Cadwallon's victorious progress and refers to Edwin the Deceitful so directly as to make it clear that this composition is concerned with the triumphal nature of Cadwallon's return from exile in Ireland.[3] The text in its surviving relatively late manuscripts, however, is so corrupt that no professional Celticist has yet ventured upon a published translation of it. Nevertheless certain details do emerge. It was apparently composed while Cadwallon was still alive and 'certainly evokes the language, formulaic patterns and the ethos of Taliesin and Aneirin' (Foster 1965: 231). 'No-one is higher [in glory] than Cadwallon except the sky and the stars' (11.48-9). His people are the *Cymru* (11.12, 28, 40) - the earliest example of the use of *Cymru* - and their land is 'Cadwallon's land' (1.28). Cadwallon had gathered a victorious host (11.1-2) and appears to have been encamped on Anglesey (1.22) with a fleet nearby. The poet prays that the wind and waves will not help the foreign host but also will not hinder Cadwallon's army (11.6-7, 15). Presumably, just as the wind which blew Harold Hardrada across the North Sea in 1066 kept William the Bastard in Normandy, so the wind which drove Cadwallon back into Wales immobilized Edwin's ships. Cadwallon, apparently, was a hero like Maelgwn (1.23); he refused to treat with the men of Bernicia (1.24), for Edwin was a too-deceitful leader (1.25). Brave Guallauc is remembered (1.30) - and it is striking to note here that Taliesin had spoken of Guallauc as a judge 'in Elmet' (Williams 1960: no.XII) - and so is the army of great and honourable *Catraeth* (1.31), Catterick, the site of conflict between the Britons and Æthelfrith which had been celebrated by the bard, Aneirin, and which had involved primarily the men of the *Votadini*. The Northumbrian advance northwards was probably by now seriously compromising the ultimate survival of the *Votadini*, whose rulers were in all likelihood kinsmen of Cadwallon, descendant of Cunedda of Manaw Gododdin (Kirby 1974b: 1-13). To the aid of the *Votadini*, as to that of the men of Elmet, Cadwallon would no doubt wish to go, styled as he was 'luydawc Prydain' (1.29), (?) 'battle-hosted one of Britain', or 'ruler of the armies of Britain' (Foster 1965; 231) - Edwin, of course, was *bretwalda* - and (?) '(m)vneir Prydin', 'lord of Britain' (1.38). In the face of Cadwallon's army, Edwin's is depicted as retreating, if not fleeing, many being slain as they fled over the salt sea (11.46-7), with Cadwallon pursuing to *Caer Caradog* (1.36), even setting York ablaze (1.37). The poem makes no reference to the slaying of Edwin personally. If it is indeed a genuine composition from the court of Cadwallon of Gwynedd, it belongs to the very eve of Hatfield. As such it may well have been designed to encourage Cadwallon in the campaign ahead.

The death of Cadwallon at Heavenfield marked the decisive turning of the tide in the battle for North Britain. The Welsh played a part - no doubt a significant part - in the defeat of Oswald, king of Northumbria, at Old Oswestry in 643, and Cadafael, king of Gwynedd, was present at the battle of the *Winwaed* in 656, but he did not fight there: he fled, and with his flight began what Sir John Edward Lloyd called 'the age of isolation' for Wales. Wales, of course, was far from being totally isolated because of maritime links across the Irish Sea Province, but landward to the east it was hemmed in geographically by the power of a developing Mercia.

The bardic verse relating to the Welsh and border warfare has not so far concerned itself openly or obviously with the Mercians. Some of the Saxons referred to in *Marwnad Cadwallawn* might have been Mercians, but the Mercian kingdom itself was probably only forming under Penda (634-56), and Cadwallon's bards take no notice of him at all, even though for Bede Cadwallon was essentially Penda's ally. The Welsh clearly possessed a different perspective on the situation. As the Mercian kingdom stabilized under Penda, however, and expanded under Penda and his son Wulfhere (659-75), not only was it an obvious source for plunder but it was to prove a serious military threat. In the south, the Magonsaete, from the beginning or more likely eventually to become a Mercian satellite folk-group, were pushing into the Herefordshire area with serious consequences for the British kingdom of Erging (Archenfield) (Charles 1963: 85-110). The Mercian impact was felt most in Shropshire, the eastern border area, that is, of Powys. What we know of Penda and Wulfhere, successive kings of Mercia in the seventh century, bears on their conflicts with other Anglo-Saxon rulers rather than on any warfare they waged with the Britons. Indeed, one of the principal features of Penda's reign is his association in alliance with British leaders, culminating, of course, in the campaign which finished so disastrously for Penda and his British allies at the battle of the *Winwaed*. No such pattern of alliance dominates the reign of his son, Wulfhere (659-75). Rather Lloyd's 'age of isolation' was accompanied by a sustained assault on Powys. The evidence for this comes not from Anglo-Saxon sources nor even Welsh annals but from bardic verse.

In North Powys the ruling family was descended from the legendary Cadell Durnlluc ('Bright-hilt'), whom the *Historia Brittonum* (Mommsen 1898) represents in 'Excerpts' from the Book of Germanus - which there is every reason to regard as a Powys source (Kirby 1968: 49-52) - as displacing Vortigern; but Vortigern's descendants at first ruled only in South Powys in Gwrtheyrnion (implied in Kirby 1968: 54). Vortigern's descendants, it would seem, probably only moved into North Powys to rule there in the time probably of Eliseg, great-grand-father of Cyngen (Concenn), king of Powys, who erected the monument known as Eliseg's Pillar, extolling the praises of Eliseg and of Cyngen himself, the latter dying in Rome in 856. Cyngen traced his descent through Eliseg from Vortigern and recorded his family tree on the monument (Bartrum 1966: 1-3). Eliseg must date to *c*.750. But when the Book of Germanus was written, the descendants of Cadell governed Powys 'to this day' *(Historia Brittonum* cc. 32-5) (Mommsen 1898). In the bardic poem to Cynan

Garwyn, Cynan is described as of the lineage of Cadell. Cynan's father, Brochfael, was a son of Cyngen 'Renowned', and the one genealogical connection most constantly reiterated at this stage across the broad spectrum of early Welsh genealogies is that Cyngen 'Renowned' was a son of Cadell 'Bright-hilt' (Bartrum 1966: 59, 60, 63, 69, 82, 100, 107, 113). It was the Cadelling kings under Selyf, son of Cynan, who fought the Northumbrians at Chester. Cynddylan, son of Cyndrwyn, probably a Cadelling king (Bromwich 1961: 321), fought the Mercians in the later seventh century. The most valuable pieces of evidence for Cynddylan are the early bardic fragments, one of which may date him and the other of which derives from a contemporary elegy. Subsequently Cynddylan the Fair of Pengwern became a central character in a prose and verse saga, *Canu Heledd,* of which now only the verse survives, associated with a separate prose and verse saga of Llywarch Hen ('the Old'), *Canu Llywarch Hen,* which Sir Ifor Williams studied so closely.[4] According to the North British genealogies Llywarch was a kinsman of Urien of Rheged, and around his person and family is woven a theme on the affliction of Powys. The date of the Llywarch Hen saga is generally taken to be the ninth century, though, of course, it need not have been committed to writing until some centuries later. Sir Ifor Williams was of the opinion that the saga of Llywarch Hen reflected the experiences of the men of Powys in the ninth century, when the Mercians actually brought Powys under their sway in 822 or 823 and Cyngen retired to Rome as a pilgrim in 854/5.[5] Moreover, to this may be added that by the early ninth century the descendants of Vortigern, a figure despised by many in Powys, were ruling Powys. The Cadelling had gone, and their going was lamented. Probably they were finally destroyed in fighting at the time of the construction of Wat's Dyke by (?) Æthelbald of Mercia. Certainly this would accord well with the rise to power in Powys c.750 of Eliseg.

Cynddylan himself, however, probably belongs to the seventh century. A crucial stanza in the Cynddylan saga represents Cynddylan as present at the battle of *Maes Cogwy,* Old Oswestry, in which Oswald, king of Northumbria, perished, a battle deep in the heart of Powys territory at this time; indeed, it is not generally appreciated how far into Powys Oswald had penetrated and how isolated his position must have been at Old Oswestry. 'I saw armies on the ground of the field of Togwy, and the battle full of affliction; Cynddylan was an ally.'[6] There may, of course, have been more than one conflict at Old Oswestry, to which hill fort, for example, runs Wat's Dyke. But the defeat of Oswald there must have been an event much celebrated and the probability perhaps is that this is the conflict to which reference is made. If Cynddylan were present, this stanza - and it alone - fixes his *floruit.* But his warfare with the Mercians probably at this time lay in the future, in the period after the collapse of the *Winwaed* coalition and the death of Penda. Penda's death was followed by an interval of three years in Mercia before his son, Wulfhere, seized power in Mercia (Bede: *Historia Ecclesiastica* III, 24). These three years and probably those immediately following must have been very vulnerable ones for Mercia. Perhaps it is to this period that some at least of the exploits of Cynddylan extolled in *Marwnad Cynddylan,* composed perhaps by the bard, Meigant, belong.[7] This apparently contemporary elegy can be understood to signify that Cynddylan too was 'Cadelling', that is, a descendant of Cadell. The poem is of uncertain meaning in a number of lines, and does present considerable problems of interpretation, but line 15 must be read 'lord of Dogfeiling, the famed one [or 'the glory'] of the line of Cadell', which means that the ambiguous line

9 should be construed 'lord of Dogfeiling, the violent one of Cadell's line'. Dogfeiling, which name derives from Dogfael, reputed son of Cunedda, was part of the realm of Gwynedd, not Powys, but it bestrode the upper valley of the Clwyd with its centre at Ruthin and must have been very liable to fall within the sphere of influence of Powys in those early centuries. Perhaps it originally was part of Powys, subsequently annexed to Gwynedd and a genealogical fiction provided to link Dogfael to Cunedda. What is not absolutely clear is whether the 'famed one of the line of Cadell' refers to Cynddylan or to some other patron of the poet, but even were the latter the case the interest of such a Cadelling patron would hint strongly that Cynddylan was also in fact Cadelling. Cynddylan had evidently attacked Gwynedd (11.7, 15), but to the east he had launched an attack beyond *Tren* (1.22) (the river Tern in Shropshire) (Williams 1972: 149) to the 'too proud land' (Foster 1965; 232), and attacked *Caer Lwytgoed*, that is *Letocetum* or Lichfield. A tentative translation may be proposed for one stanza which is very relevant in the context of Welsh-Mercian relations at this time:

> Magnificent combat, great the booty,
> Before Caer Lwytgoed Morfael took
> Fifteen hundred cattle and five herds of [?] swine,
> Eighty stallions with their accompanying harness;
> Not a single bishop in four corners
> Nor book-holding monks were afforded protection.
> ...
> I shall mourn until I am in my poor grave.
> Cynddylan slain, praised by every generous man.

The identity of Morfael is unknown.[8] It has been suggested that this was an attack on Lichfield which was intended to avenge the slaughter of the monks of Bangor-is-coed at Chester in c.616, dating to the period between Penda's reign and Wulfhere's and to the time of the Northumbrian mission to Middle Anglia under the ill-fated Peada (Richards 1973: 146). But the missionaries did not extend their activities into Mercia until after Peada's death, and it is not certain that Lichfield was selected as the Mercian ecclesiastical centre until Chad's consecration in 669. Before that any clergy or monks at Lichfield could have been British. Might there be a parallel here between the 'unrighteous monks' of [?] Elmet and British monks in Mercia who had established a *modus vivendi* with their conquerors? The letter of Aldhelm of Malmesbury to Geraint, king of Dumnonia, reveals how hostile some at least of the Welsh were to those Britons who associated with Saxons in Wessex and then returned across the Severn into Wales. Cynddylan may have had scant sympathy for British clergy in Mercia. This early poem by Meigant, therefore, is important not only for what it records but because it reveals the substratum from which the subsequent bardic traditions about Cynddylan evolved.

Whenever precisely his raid on Lichfield took place, the aggression of Cynddylan evidently brought about a counter-offensive on the part of the Mercians, led probably by King Wulfhere. The objective was *Pengwern*, Cynddylan's centre, their purpose its destruction. *Pengwern* was destroyed and Cynddylan and his brothers slain. The memory of these events is preserved in the poems associated with Llywarch Hen. The Elegy on Cynddylan laments this British disaster:

> Cynddylan the bright buttress of the borderland, wearing a chain,
> stubborn in battle, he defended Trenn, his father's town.

How sad it is to my heart to lay the white flesh in the black coffin,
Cynddylan the leader of a hundred hosts.
The hall of Cynddylan is still tonight, after losing its
chief; great merciful God, what shall I do?
The eagle of Penngwern, grey-crested, uplifted is his cry,
greedy for the flesh of Cynddylan.
The chapels of Basa are his resting place tonight, his last
welcome, the pillar of battle, the heart of the men of Argoed ...
The white town in the valley, glad is the kite at the bloodshed of
battle; its people have perished ...
I have looked out on a lovely land from the mound of
Gorwynnion; long is the sun's course - longer are my
memories ...[9]

The Elegy is represented as part of a series of dramatic monologues by Heledd,
sister of Cynddylan, as she stands on one of the neighbouring heights and looks
down on the blazing ruin of her home (Williams 1972: 148). Heledd is clearly a
central figure in what has become *Canu Heledd,* an unhistorical saga (Williams
1972: 149), but most commentators are prepared to accept that behind these
particular verses lies a tradition of the historical destruction of *Pengwern* and the
death and burial of Cynddylan. *Trenn* is again the river Tern in Shropshire with
which Cynddylan is associated in Meigant's earlier elegy, and on this river
presumably Cynddylan made his last stand, three miles north-west of the Wrekin
upon which *Pengwern* may have been situated,[10] while *Bassa* is Baschurch, 16
miles north-west of the Wrekin. What is clear is that the river Tern was vital to him
strategically, while other place-names mentioned in passing or intimated embrace
west Shropshire and south-east Montgomeryshire (Williams 1972: 149-50) and this
was clearly the area in which Cynddylan ruled. The death of Cynddylan and the
preoccupations of Wulfhere with southern England did not terminate Mercian-
Welsh conflict. Felix's Life of Guthlac records how Guthlac, once an exile among
the Britons, was a young warrior in the time of Æthelred, king of Mercia (675-
704) and how in the days of Coenred, king of Mercia (704-9), Æthelred's nephew,
the Britons, implacable enemies of the Saxons, troubled them with pillage and
devastation.

   And indeed hostile relations persisted into the ninth century, although bardic
literature relating to historical events of the eighth and ninth centuries has not
survived. What has survived is the verse saga of Llywarch Hen. The historical
Llywarch Hen lived in the late sixth century. The saga of Llywarch Hen represents
him as seeking refuge in Wales in old age and agonizingly witnessing his 24 sons
perish successively against the Saxons. The last son, Gwen, appears to be suffering
reproach for not having fought with his brothers, and in the Elegy for Gwen his
father, Llywarch, recites how he fell keeping watch by the Llawen at the ford
(rhyd) of Forlas (Williams 1935: 1; Williams 1972: 138-9; Clancy 1970: 74-6).
Rhyd Forlas is a stream running into the river Ceiriog (Williams 1972: 150), south
of Llangollen. Few Celticists, however, would ascribe a seventh-century date to
these verses, nor even to the events they purport to record. They seem to have been
inspired rather by the disasters at the hands of the Mercians which overtook
Powys in the first half of the ninth century, and a substantial case can be made for
concluding that they sprang from the traumatic experiences of the conquest of

Powys by Mercia in 822 or 823 and the flight of King Cyngen in 854/5. The light shed here on events is really essentially impressionistic, a sense of despairing hopelessness. There is little secure historical information in these details of the alleged sons of Llywarch. If there is a historical kernel it is contained in the names of battle-sites (like *Rhyd Forlas*) and in the names perhaps of the British leaders who fell there (like Gwen). The geographical range is considerable, extending south, if the identification is correct, to the Herefordshire Frome (Williams 1972: 150).

It was at such a time that the tradition of Cynddylan, 'the bright buttress of the borderland', were being elaborated too, for Cynddylan's overthrow reflected a similar trauma. The persons responsible for patronizing this bardic material co-co-ordinated around Llywarch's sons and Cynddylan were probably Merfyn Vrych ('the Freckled'), who became king of Gwynedd in 825, and his son, Rhodri the Great, who reigned after him both in Gwynedd and Powys on Cyngen's flight. Though king of Gwynedd, Merfyn was of Powys origin on his maternal side, and the only descendant of Llywarch's kinsmen to establish a dynasty in Wales. The *Historia Brittonum* (Mommsen 1898), produced in Gwynedd in 829-30, drew on Powys traditions about Vortigern to whom it was violently hostile, citing Excerpts made from the Book of Germanus by Run, son of Urbgen (Urien), which pseudonym links the 'Excerpts' at least to Merfyn's kinsmen. There already existed among the descendants of Vortigern traditions of a St Germanus, probably derived from the cult of an original Powys saint, Garmon, for Germanus is said on the pillar of Eliseg to have blessed Vortigern's son, Britu. It was easy, if incorrect, to identify Garmon (Germanus) with Germanus of Auxerre: and his relations with Vortigern and Britu were evidently seen as essentially honourable. The Book of Germanus, presenting the saint as hostile to Vortigern, was produced between 731, by which date Bede had (probably quite mistakenly) identified Vortigern with Gildas' 'proud tyrant', and c.750, by which time Eliseg had established himself in North Powys.

Though there is not scope to develop this now (cf. Kirby 1968; 51), it seems possible to conclude that Merfyn's maternal family, intensely hostile to the descendants of Vortigern, bitterly resented their ascendancy in North Powys and their subsequent failure to protect Powys and encouraged rather anachronistic sagas of their own kindred and treasured the memory of the Cadelling princes, particularly Cynddylan, a line of princes which had fallen on the one hand before the advance of the Mercians and on the other before the rise of the kings of Gwrtheyrnion. The heroic virtues of the Cadelling highlighted by contrast the shameful ignominy of their supplanters: 'long is the sun's course - longer are my memories....'. But few Celticists also would feel that the last word has yet been said about *Canu Llywarch Hen,* and these final observations can only be tentative.

NOTES

1. *Historia Ecclasiastica* 20: III, 1-2, and cf. Kirby 1974a: 7. On the date 634 (as opposed to 633 or 632) and other dates in Northumbrian history, see Kirby 1963, 514-27.
2. Evans 1911, cols. 1043-4 (the line references given below in the text are not the marginal numbers of the edition, which are simply the numbers of the lines in the column, but the actual line of the poem which is being cited). There is a translation in Barber 1972: 98-9. Lloyd (1939: I, 182 n.89) dismissed the poem as having no relation to the Cadwallon ap Cadfan of history but rather commemorating the deeds 'of some medieval prince', but this is certainly not the view of most Celtic scholars now, who would assign it rather to a (probably) ninth-century date in its written form and regard it as indeed addressed to Cadwallon ap Cadfan. For the comments of R. Bromwich, see Bromwich (1961: 195).
3. This piece was first properly edited by Williams (1933: 23-32), and more recently from earlier manuscrips of the seventeenth century by Thomas (1970: 309-16). I have been greatly assisted by the kindness of Professor G. Gruffydd of the University College of Wales, Aberystwyth, in discussing with me the problems in any translation of the poem as it now stands. Cf. also on the poem Bromwich (1961: 294).
4. Williams 1935: cf. Williams 1932: 269-301, reprinted with additional notes by Williams 1972: 122-54. See now also, for *Canu Llywarch Hen* (but *not Canu Heledd*). Ford 1974, where the verse is translated. Ford is sceptical (pp.48ff.) about the former existence of a (now lost) prose saga, the possibility (only) of which has, he says 'passed from theory to accepted fact' (p.51).
5. Williams 1972: 151; Ford (1974), evidently under the influence of Green (1972: 1-11), is prepared to consider a date of composition later than Williams' mid-ninth century (pp.14-26) - not least the tenth century. This is always possible, but Green's 'compelling arguments' for viewing the poetry of Aneirin and Taliesin not as sixth- but as ninth- or tenth- century 'forgeries' (p.14) have now been met by Jackson (1973-4; 1-32, in particular, 1-17). A tendency also to regard Llywarch as somehow 'introduced' into the genealogies (Ford 1974: 26), presumably artificially, fails to carry much weight. The North British genealogies are more acceptable than the 'crucial genealogical information' concerning the sons and daughters of Brychan, and Llywarch's absorption into their tangled network of relationships and marriages in no way compromises the place of the historical Llywarch, Urien's cousin, in the North British pedigrees. Cf. the comment of Bromwich (1961: 431).
6. Williams 1935: 48, 242. There is a translation of this stanza by Jackson (1963: 39). Cf. Williams (1972: 149). On the indentification of *Maes Cogwy* with Old Oswestry, see Williams (1926-7: 59-62).
7. This valuable poem was first edited by Williams (1934: 134-41), and then included in Williams (1935: no.XIIII). There is a translation by Clancy (1970: 87-9), and of one stanza by Richards (1973: 143).
8. An early pedigree (Bartrum 1966: 12) associates a Morfael with Lichfield on the one hand and Glastonbury on the other: cf. Morris (1973: 243). What lies behind this association, however, remains uncertain.
9. Williams (1935: no.XI, stanzas 5, 17, 30, 40, 45, 54). There is a translation, which is here quoted directly, by Jackson (1951: 275-8), with the permission of the author and of the publishers, Routledge & Kegan Paul.
10. Richards (1973: 142). In the O'Donnell lecture for 1974-5 in the University of Wales, Professor Glanville Jones expressed a preference for Wrockwardine, near the Wrekin. Shrewsbury, by the twelfth century at least traditionally the site of *Pengwern,* is rejected as such by Richards (1969: 141). Williams retained an open mind (1972: 149-50).

REFERENCES

Alcock, L., 1971, *Arthur's Britain.*

Barber, R., 1972. *The Figure of Arthur.*

Bartrum, P.C., 1966. *Early Welsh Genealogical Tracts.*

Bede. *Venerabilis Baedae Opera Historica,* ed. C. Plummer, 1896.

Bromwich, R., 1961. *Trioedd Ynys Prydein: the Welsh Triads.*

Caerwyn-Williams, J.E., 1968. *The Poems of Taliesin* (Dublin).

Chadwick, N.K., 1963a. 'The Conversion of Northumbria', in *Celt and Saxon: Studies in the Early British Border,* ed. N.K. Chadwick, 138-66.

Chadwick, N.K., 1963b. 'The Battle of Chester', *ibid.,* 167-85.

Clancy, J.P., 1970. *The Earliest Welsh Poetry.*

Charles, B.G., 1963. 'The Welsh, their language and place-names in Archenfield and Oswestry', *Angles and Britons* (The O'Donnell Lectures), 85-110.

Evans, J. Gwenogvryn, 1911. *The Poetry in the Red Book of Hengest* I (Series of Old Welsh Texts, vol.XI).

Ford, P.K., 1974. *The Poetry of Llywarch Hen.*

Foster, I. Ll., 1965. 'The emergence of Wales', in *Prehistoric and Early Wales,* ed. I. Ll.Foster and G. Daniel, 213-35.

Gildas. *Gildae de excidio Britanniae,* ed. H. Williams, 1899 (Cymmrodorion Record Ser.3).

Green, D., 1971. 'The linguistic considerations in the dating of Early Welsh verse', *Studia Celtica, 6:* 1-11.

Jackson, K.H., 1951. *A Celtic Miscellany.*

Jackson, K.H., 1963. 'On the Northern British section in Nennius', in *Celt and Saxon,* ed. N.K. Chadwick, 20-62.

Jackson, K.H., 1969. *The Gododdin: The Oldest Scottish Poem.*

Jackson, K.H., 1973-4. 'Some questions in dispute about Early Welsh literature and language', *Studia Celtica, 8/9,* 1-32.

Jarman, A.O.H., 1951. *Ymddiddan Myrddin a Thaliesin.*

Kirby, D.P., 1963. 'Bede and Northumbrian chronology', *Engl. Hist. Rev., 72:* 514-27.

Kirby, D.P., 1968. 'Vortigern', *Bull.Board Celtic Stud., 23:* 37-59.

Kirby, D.P., 1974a. 'Northumbria in the time of Wilfrid', in *St. Wilfrid of Hexham,* ed. D.P. Kirby, 1-34.

Kirby, D.P., 1974b. 'The Kingdom of Northumbria and the destruction of the Votadini', *Transactions of the East Lothian Archaeological and Natural History Society, 14:* 1-13.

Kirby, D.P., 1976. 'British dynastic history in the pre-Viking period', *Bull.Board Celtic Stud., 27:* 81-113.

Kolb, E., 1973. 'Elmet. A dialect region in northern England', *Anglia, 91:* 285-313.

Lewis, S., 1968. 'The Tradition of Taliesin', *Transactions of the Honourable Society of Cymmrodorion,* 293-8.

Lloyd, J.E., 1939. *A History of Wales,* vol.I.

Lloyd Jones, J., 1948. 'The court poets of the Welsh princes', *Proc.Brit.Acad., 34:* 167-97.

Mommsen, T. (ed.), 1898. *Chronica Minora Saec. IV, V, VI, VII, Monumenta Germaniae Historica, AA, xiii* (Berlin).

Morris, J., 1973. *The Age of Arthur: A History of the British Isles from 350 to 650.*

Nash-Williams, V.E., 1950. *Early Christian Monuments of Wales.*

Richard, M., 1969, *Welsh Administrative and Territorial Suffixes.*

Richards, M., 1973. 'The Lichfield Gospels (Book of St. Chad)', *National Library of Wales Journal, 18:* 135-46.

Thomas, G.C.G., 1970. *'Dryll o Hen Lyfr Ysgrifen', Bull.Board Celtic Stud., 23:* 309-16.

Williams, I., 1926-7. 'A Reference to the Nennian Bellum Cocboy', *Bull.Board Celtic Stud., 3:* 59-62.

Williams, I., 1932. 'The Poems of Llywarch Hen', *Proc.British.Acad., 18:* 269-301.

Williams I., 1933. 'Hengerdd', *Bull. Board Celtic Stud., 7:* 23-32.
Williams I., 1934. 'Marwnad Cynddylan', *Bull.Board Celtic Stud., 6:* 134-41.
Williams, I., 1935. *Canu Llywarch Hen.*
Williams, I., 1960. *Canu Taliesin.*
Williams, I., 1972. *The Beginnings of Welsh Poetry: Studies by Sir Ifor Williams*, ed. R. Bromwich, 122-54.

CYRIL HART

3 The kingdom of Mercia

I shall not dwell in this paper on the origins of Mercia, which are discussed by other
contributors, nor on the later history of the territory after the coming of the Danes.
I shall confine myself instead to an account of the Mercian hegemony during the
historical period of its ruling dynasty, from Penda who rose to power in 632 A.D. to
the last king, Ceolwulf II, who disappeared into the mists of antiquity some two
and a half centuries later. Even within these limits the canvas is a large one, and the
time available allows of only the briefest impressionistic sketch. Here and there,
however, I shall sharpen the picture, by focussing attention upon particular aspects
such as the boundaries of Mercia, and the administration of the hegemony.

It is important from the outset to get it quite clear in our minds just what we
mean when we speak of Mercia. We must try to distinguish between the kingdom
ruled directly by its monarchs, and the surrounding territories over which the
Mercian kings exercised a quasi-imperial hegemony during nearly the whole of the
period under review (John 1966: 1-63; Stenton, 1970: 48-66). The outer limits of
this hegemony varied somewhat with the fortunes of the individual monarchs, but
there can be no doubt that for most of the time the Mercian kings had power over
all of England south of the Humber.

Maps of early England published in standard history books during the last
century assign to Mercia a territory which varies widely in position and extent,
according to the interpretation of the particular author. The one characteristic
shared by all these maps is that they do not attempt to delineate the boundaries of
the Mercian kingdom. Perhaps such historical materials as are available for a
reconstruction had not received sufficient attention at the time when the maps were
drawn up, but there are other possible explanations. Even today, some historians

remain doubtful if kingdoms had fixed bounds in this early period, suggesting rather that territorial limits were still in a state of flux. Others may argue that it is in any case unrealistic to try to demarcate the limits of a kingdom whose archives suffered so severely at the hands of the Danes, and whose boundaries (whether fixed or fluctuating) were obliterated, first by the Danish settlement in the last quarter of the ninth century, and then by the shiring of the Midlands some 40 years later. I hold the view however that the bounds of the Mercian kingdom remained substantially unchanged from the time of Peada, son of Penda, to the period of the Danish settlement, and that thanks largely to the works of Chadwick and Stenton we are now well placed to attempt their reconstruction.

Before doing so, we have first to consider the document known as the Tribal Hidage (Brownbill, 1925; Hart, 1971). This is a tribute list drawn up, I believe, during the second half of the eighth century, probably for Offa, the greatest of the Mercian kings, and overlord of all the Anglo-Saxon peoples with the sole exception of Northumbria. The hidage names no less than 35 different peoples, inhabiting (except for the tip of Cornwall) the whole of England south of the Humber, and assigning to each a round number of hides, these being units of assessment for taxation and other burdens. No other document illustrates so vividly the power exercised by the Mercian overlords over their subject kingdoms and principalities, and as a detailed record of historical topography the hidage has no parallel for its period in the whole of Western Europe.

Table 1 *The Tribal Hidage*

	hides		hides
Myrcna landes	30,000	Hwinca	7,000
Wocen saetna	7,000	Ciltern saetna	4,000
Westerna	7,000	Hendrica	3,500
Pec saetna	1,200	Unecung-ga	1,200
Elmed saetna	600	Arosaetna	600
Lindes farona and Heath		Faerpinga	300
feld land	7,000	Bilmigga	600
South Gyrwa	600 }	Widerigga	600
North Gyrwa	600 }	East Willa	600 }
East Wixna	300 }	West Willa	600 }
West Wixna	600 }	East Engle	30,000
Spalda	600	East Sexena	7,000
Wigesta	900	Cantwarena	15,000
Herefinna	1,200	Suth Sexena	7,000
Sweordora	300	West Sexena	100,000
Gifla	300		
Hicca	300	Addition in	
Wihtgara	600	manuscript	
Noxgaga	5,000	(erroneous)	242,700
Ohtgaga	2,000		
		recte	244,100
Addition in manuscript	66,100		

Table 1 lists these people and their assessments in the order in which they appear in the document. All except four of them (whose combined hidage amounts to less than five per cent of the total) have now been located with a reasonable degree of certainty, and as we shall see presently, there are very few places left for these unlocated pieces to be fitted in the topographical jigsaw of England in the eighth century.

Table 2 *The Mercian hegemony*

Kingdoms and principalities listed by size of assessment.

KINGDOMS AND MAJOR PRINCIPALITIES		MINOR PRINCIPALITIES AND TRIBES		
hides		*hides*		
100,000	Wessex	4,000	Ciltern saetan	
30,000	Mercia	3,500	*Hendrica*	
	East Angles	1,200	Pec saetan	
15,000	Kent		Hurstingas	
7,000	Hwicce		*Unecung-ga*	
	Westerna (=Magon saetan)		⎰ South Gyrwe	(600 hides)
	Wreocen saetan		⎱ North Gyrwe	(600 hides)
	Lindsey (with Hatfield Chase)		⎰ East Willa	(600 hides)
	East Saxons		⎱ West Willa	(600 hides)
	South Saxons	900	Wigesta	
	⎰ *Noxgaga* (5,000 hides)		⎰ East Wixna	(300 hides)
	⎱ *Ohtgaga* (2,000 hides)		⎱ West Wixna	(600 hides)
		600	Aro saetan	
*represents unlocated peoples			Elmet saetan	
			Spalda	
			Bilmigga	
			Widerigga	
			Wihtgara	
		300	Faerpinga	
			Sweordora	
			Gifla	
			Hicca	

Now let us look at Table 2 where these people are listed again, this time in descending order of hidage assessment, remembering all the time that it was upon this assessment that the tribute was raised. The 100,000 hides allotted to the kingdom of Wessex, the 30,000 to the East Angles, and the 15,000 to Kent, should be thought of therefore as a measure of the relative size of the payments (perhaps in pennies) demanded of them when a levy was raised by their Mercian overlords. Stenton pointed out that some scholars have regarded these figures as incredible (Stenton 1947: 292); but they fit in well with the payment of 30,000 (? pennies) by the Kentish people to the king of Wessex recorded in the Anglo-Saxon Chronicle for the year 694, and with the figure of 100,000 measured in land and treasure (*locren bēaga*) given by Hygelac, king of the Geats, to each of his retainers Wulf and Eafor as a reward for their prowess in battle (Beowulf, line 2995). What is important is that these arbitrary figures of the Tribal Hidage could never have represented the sum of all the hidage assessments of the individual estates within each kingdom or principality concerned. In this respect the hidage differs radically from the shire assessments of the tenth century, which represent an entirely new cadastre, quite unrelated to the taxation arrangements of the era of the Mercian supremacy.

The 7,000 hide units that follow the major kingdoms represent a standard assessment for a subject province the size of a lesser kingdom or larger principality. In heroic poetry, this was the reward given by King Hygelac to his kinsman Beowulf for his exploits overseas; with it went a hall and a *brego-stōl*, or princely throne (Beowulf, line 2195). Commonly such provinces had dynastic rulers of their own, and of the six listed in the Tribal Hidage, pedigrees survive (or can be re-constructed) for all but one of them. Moreover, North Mercia is similarly allocated 7,000 hides in Bede *(Historia Ecclesiastica,* hereafter HE, bk III, c.24). The combined assessment of the mysterious *Ohtgaga* and *Noxgaga* was likewise 7,000 hides, and the equally mysterious province of *Hendrica* was allocated a hidage of just half that sum.

One would give much to know just how it came about that this unusual figure of 7,000 was regarded as a suitable assessment for a subject province, for it fits into neither a decimal nor a duodecimal system of computation. It may have been an archaic survival from a much earlier period of Germanic society. When we come to the smaller principalities of the Tribal Hidage, however, we find clear-cut evidence of a duodecimal system, with levies of 300, 600, 900 and 1,200 hides. This is in keeping with the arithmetic of the Mercian coinage, in which 240 pennies went to the pound (Chadwick 1905: 31). Thus a levy of two pennies per hide would raise 10 pounds in taxation from a principality assessed at 1200 hides. This reinforces the conclusion, arrived at from consideration of other historical sources, that in England as well as the Continent the coinage of the eighth century was required as much for taxes as for trade (Blunt 1961). As yet, however, one must admit that we have but slight numismatic evidence that the Mercian coinage was sufficiently developed, or widely enough distributed, for the payment of tribute in this manner.

It seems that as with the larger provinces, each of these minor tribal units had its own ruling dynasty. We may discount with Plummer the claim in the Anglo-Saxon Chronicle that Wihtgar, allegedly the first prince of Wight, gave his name to the island (Plummer 1899: II, 32), but we cannot ignore Bede (HE bk IV, c.16) who tells us of Arwald, king of Wight, and his two sons who were killed by Cedwalla, king of Wessex. Later, Bede names a prince of the South Gyrwe, who married into the East Anglian royal family (HE bk IV, c.19). There is no evidence that any of these small princely houses survived later than the end of the seventh century, and most of the larger provincial dynasties became extinct during the reign of King Offa.

The imperial house of Mercia preserved within its archives genealogical tables of the ruling houses of these subject provinces. One such record, perhaps from Lichfield, survives in the original of the early ninth century (Sisam 1939). While these tribal rulers retained their ranks as kings and princes within their own territories, however, in the eyes of their Mercian overlords they were but ealdormen. Their pretensions to autonomy were firmly resisted. Clearly, a province administered by a nominee of the Mercian king would be far more effectively controlled than one ruled by its own dynastic lord. Hence the trend to limit the authority of these hereditary rulers, which culminated in the extinction of their dynasties. This development of the office of ealdorman must be regarded as one of the most important features of royal administration in the period of Mercian supremacy.

In 1971 I attempted to plot all the peoples of the Tribal Hidage on a map (fig. 1). The boundaries are only approximate, but the general picture is clear enough although parts of it are unfamiliar to modern eyes, due to the radical changes brought about by the Danish settlement. It will be seen that I have assigned the unidentified *Noxgaga* and *Ohtgaga* to what is now Berkshire, and the equally unknown *Hendrica* and *Unecung-ga* (the name is almost certainly corrupt) are placed provisionally to the north of the Ciltern saetan. It is difficult to know where else to put them.

We are ready at last to take a look at the kingdom of Mercia itself, as opposed to the subject peoples of the hegemony. In the mid-seventh century, according to Bede, it was divided by the River Trent between the North Mercians, assessed at 7,000 hides, and the South Mercians of 5,000 hides (HE bk III, c.24). One and a half centuries later the Mercian lands were assessed in the Tribal Hidage at no less than 30,000 hides. There can be little doubt that this great increase was due to the absorption into the kingdom of Mercia of small unorganized units of Middle Anglian stock, lying to the south-east of the original Mercian nucleus. Probably this expansion took place during the time of Peada the son of King Penda, who was given first the Middle Anglians and subsequently the South Mercians to rule (*ibid.*, c.21, 24). In my map I have given the name Outer Mercia to this assimilated territory, comprising 18,000 hides.

During the preparation of the present paper I embarked on a radical revision of the boundaries of the kingdom of Mercia as I had drawn them on my map of 1971, and this revised version is shown as fig. 2. It is convenient at this point to outline some of the criteria upon which one can rely when drawing these early boundaries.

It is generally accepted that the earliest diocesan boundaries were coterminous with those of individual provinces, for each kingdom and larger principality was given its own bishop. This was certainly the case, for example, with the Hwicce (diocese of Worcester), the Magonsaetan (diocese of Hereford), the East Saxons (diocese of London), East and West Kent (dioceses of Canterbury and Rochester), the South Saxons (diocese of Selsey, later transferred to Chichester), and Lindsey, whose bishop ruled from *Sidnaceaster*, probably Caistor-on-the-Wolds (Radford 1947).

Moreover, there is ample place-name and charter evidence to show that for the most part (give or take a few border villages) the diocesan boundaries, once established, did not change right down to the time of Henry VIII, except for the occasional formation of new dioceses by splitting the territories of old ones. The boundary between the dioceses of the Hwicce (Worcester) and the Mercians (Lichfield), running through Warwickshire, is a well-documented example of this continuity (Hart 1971: 149; Gover *et al.*, 1936: xvi - xvii), but in fact it will be found wherever the evidence is available for inspection. For our purpose, the most convenient map of diocesan boundaries is that of *Monastic Britain* (South Sheet), published by the Ordnance Survey in 1950, on a scale of 10 miles to the inch. This uses the accurate map of pre-Reformation dioceses published by J. Caley in volume 3 of his *Valor Ecclesiasticus*, edited in six volumes for the Record Commission in 1834.

Furthermore, when we compare these diocesan boundaries with those of the later Mercian shires (whether of Danish or English creation), we find that very often shire and diocesan boundaries coincide, forcing one to the interesting supposition

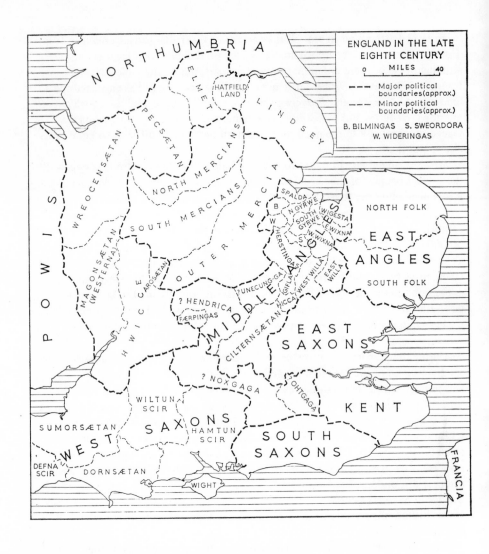

Figure. 1. England in the late eighth century: political boundaries reconstructed from the Tribal Hidage (reprinted from *Transactions of the Royal Historical Society,* 5th ser., 1971, *21*:137).

(which will be considered more fully later) that the shires formed in the tenth century were usually coterminous with kingdoms and principalities of the eighth century, or with territories formed by the amalgamation or subdivision of these early tribal units. These shire boundaries remained for the most part unchanged until the local government reorganization of 1974.

These generalizations hold good for most of the subject provinces of the Mercian hegemony. When we come to the Mercian kingdom itself, however, the situation is rather more complicated. Originally, after their conversion in the mid-seventh century, both the Mercians and the Middle Angles were placed under the jurisdiction of a single bishop (Bede, HE bk III, c.21). The site of his first *cathedra* is unknown, but it could well have been at *Letocetum*, later called Wall, the Roman station from which nearby Lichfield (literally 'the open land at *Letocetum*') derived its name. It will be recalled that Peada, the first Christian king of the Mercians, was baptised *ad Murum (ibid.)* The coincidence of names is striking, but the context of Bede's statement does not allow us to identify this place with *Letocetum*. Peada's baptism occurred in 654. The episcopal seat was established soon afterwards, and transferred to the new site at Lichfield in 669, during the reign of Wulfhere, Peada's younger brother and successor (Eddius Stephanus, *Vita Wilfridi*, c.14, 15). A decade later, however, the bishopric was divided into two, as the episcopal lists concluding Florence of Worcester's chronicle show (Thorpe 1848-9). Though reduced in size, the see of Lichfield still embraced the provinces of the Wreocensaetan and the Pecsaetan as well as the North and South Mercians; the new see of Leicester served the territory I have called Outer Mercia, and in addition the rest of Middle Anglia.

The boundary between Outer Mercia on the one hand, and the North and South Mercians on the other, is therefore relatively easy to define, for it followed the diocesan boundary between the sees of Leicester and Lichfield, and this in turn was coterminous in later years with the county boundary between Warwickshire to the west, and Oxfordshire, Northamptonshire, and Leicestershire to the east. Further north, the Leicestershire bounds march with those of Staffordshire, Derbyshire and Nottinghamshire, and this again represents part of the earlier Outer Mercian boundary. The single exception I have noted is that of Breedon-on-the-Hill, the site of an important Mercian monastery, which lay right on the diocesan boundary, and belonged first to Lichfield diocese, but later (perhaps in the tenth century) was transferred to the diocese of Dorchester with which the old dioceses of Leicester and Lindsey had been amalgamated after the Danish settlement.

The north-eastern boundary of Outer Mercia is equally well defined, for it is a safe assumption that the original diocese of Lindsey coincided with the kingdom of Lindsey, and Sir Frank Stenton postulated that this in turn was coterminous with the area settled by the Danish army based on Lincoln, which was one of the Five Boroughs (Stenton 1970: 127-137). Eventually, after the Norman Conquest, this territory became known as the Parts of Lindsey in Lincolnshire, and so it remained with limits unchanged until the local government reorganization of 1974. The boundary between Outer Mercia and Lindsey was therefore the Roman canal called the Fosse Dyke from the River Trent to Lincoln, and then the River Witham from Lincoln to The Wash.

At this point precision ends as far as the Outer Mercian boundary is concerned, for from now onwards we are dealing with a number of obscure Middle Anglian

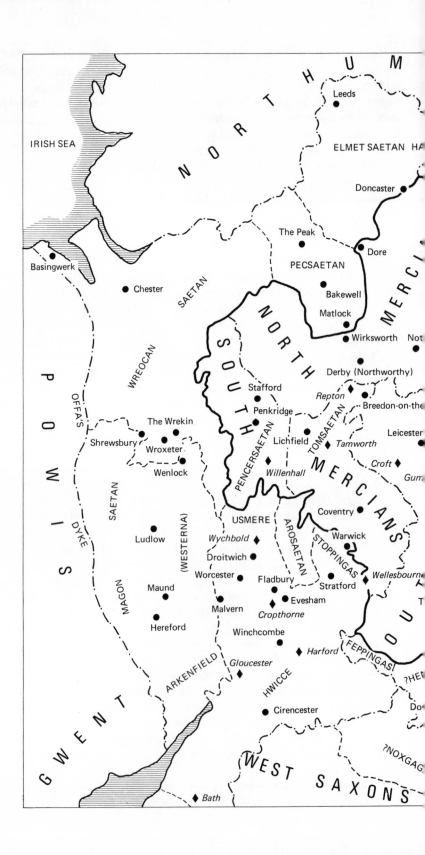

IRISH SEA

Leeds

ELMET SAETAN HA

Doncaster

The Peak

Dore

Basingwerk

PECSAETAN

Chester

SAETAN

Bakewell

Matlock

Wirksworth Not

WREOCAN

Derby (Northworthy)

NORTH

SOUTH

Stafford

Repton

Breedon-on-the

POWIS

OFFA'S

The Wrekin

Penkridge

Shrewsbury

Wroxeter

Lichfield

Leicester

PENCERSAETAN

TOMSAETAN

Tamworth

Wenlock

Willenhall

Croft

MERCIANS

Gum

SAETAN

Coventry

USMERE

AROSAETAN

DYKE

Ludlow

Wychbold

Warwick

(WESTERNA)

STOPPINGAS

Droitwich

Wellesbourne

MAGON

Worcester

Fladbury

Maund

Stratford

Malvern

Evesham

Cropthorne

Hereford

Winchcombe

Harford

FEPPINGAS

Gloucester

?HE

ARKENFIELD

HWICCE

GWENT

Cirencester

Do

?NOXGAG

WEST SAXONS

Bath

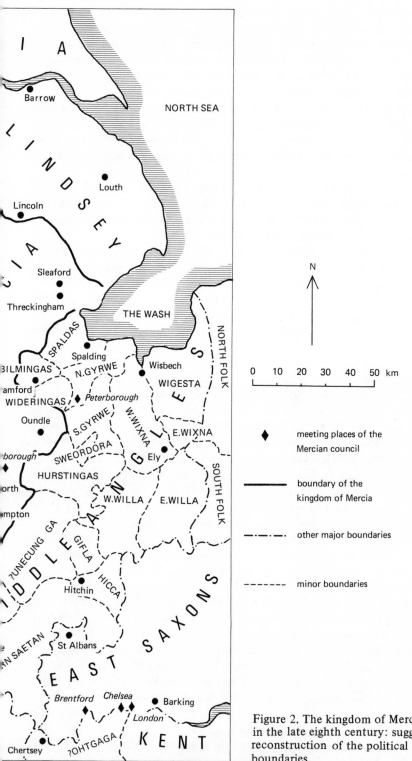

Figure 2. The kingdom of Mercia
in the late eighth century: suggested
reconstruction of the political
boundaries.

tribes, whose exact territory is difficult to establish. My map shows the coastline of The Wash as it existed in Anglo-Saxon times, coming inland as far as Boston and Spalding (Hallam 1954). One cannot be sure whether or not Outer Mercia had direct access to The Wash south of the Witham outlet. Spalding was presumably the capital of the Spaldas, a folk assessed at 600 hides in the Tribal Hidage, but the precise boundaries of this people have yet to be reconstructed. Along its eastern border, Outer Mercia marches with the territories of the Spaldas, the Bilmingas, the Wideringas, the Gyrwe, and the Hurstingas, in that order, the line of the modern map running roughly from Sempringham to the west of Stamford, then down along the Northamptonshire border to somewhere east of Irthlingborough. It could well be that those parts of the later shire of Northampton lying to the north-east of Watling Street and south of the River Welland were formed from two or more self-contained regions of Outer Mercia (Hart 1970); if so, the present Northamptonshire border from Fotheringhay to Stony Stratford may preserve the line of the original Outer Mercian boundary with the Middle Angles.

Towards the south the Outer Mercian boundary is even more conjectural, due to our inability to locate the *Hendrica* and the *Unecung-ga*. I have shown it running roughly from Buckingham to Bicester. After this, it may have marched with the boundary of the Feppingas to the north-east of Charlbury. The Hwiccean boundary is then joined, and since this is now represented by the diocesan boundary of Worcester, we know that it ran northwards between Banbury and Shipston-on-Stour, until the territory of the South Mercians was reached near Radway.

Having completed (albeit with a bit of a scramble) the perambulation of Outer Mercia, we turn our attention to the North Mercians; before attempting to locate their bounds, however, it is useful to consider for a moment the later history of their territory.

The coincidence in the Midlands of parts of the later county boundaries with parts of earlier diocesan boundaries has important implications for our knowledge of the settlement by the Danes of the territory of the Five Boroughs, recorded in the 'A' version of the Anglo-Saxon Chronicle under the year 877 (Plummer 1899). The most clear-cut example of this coincidence is the territory of the Danish army based on Lincoln, which seems to have been exactly coterminous with the territory of the ancient kingdom and diocese of Lindsey. One is driven by this to postulate that the territory that became Nottinghamshire formed a distinct part of the ancient territory of the North Mercians, having its own local administration, based on Nottingham, before the Danish settlement. Similarly, in Outer Mercia, the territories of the later counties of Leicestershire and of Northamptonshire (north-eastwards of Watling Street and south of the River Welland) appear to have formed distinct administrative regions in the period of the Mercian supremacy. In other words, it seems likely that the Danes did not create new administrative boundaries when they settled the territory of the Five Boroughs; instead, each army took over the territory of a pre-existing administrative unit, either a whole kingdom (as with Lindsey) or a subdivision of a province (as with Nottinghamshire within North Mercia, and with Leicestershire and part of Northamptonshire within Outer Mercia). This fits in nicely with the fact that another division of the great army of the Danes settled the whole territory of the ancient East Anglian kingdom.

Armed with this useful concept, let us return to the task of delineating the territory of the North Mercians. Bede tells us that they were separated from the

South Mercians by the River Trent, and on my map this common boundary is shown stretching from Stoke-on-Trent in the west to Repton in the east. Since I believe that the North Mercians occupied the whole territory of the later shire of Nottingham, I have assumed that the entire southern and eastern section of the Nottinghamshire county boundary represents the limits of the original North Mercian people. To the north, we know from contemporary evidence that North Mercia reached as far as Dore (Plummer 1899, s.a. 825 (*recte* 827), and 942), so it must have incorporated those parts of the modern West Riding of Yorkshire lying to the south of the River Don, which may well have formed the original boundary between Mercia and Northumbria at this point.

Unfortunately, there is no space here to pursue in detail the intriguing subject of the origin of the various dyke earthworks round the outer borders of the Mercian hegemony as it existed in the mid-seventh century. I would suggest however that the earthworks known as the Becca Banks and the Roman Rig near Leeds were thrown up (or perhaps refurbished) by the Northumbrians to resist the Mercian advance at the time of the Battle of Winwaed (655 A.D.), and that the Roman Ridge north of Sheffield, the Nico Ditch south of Manchester, and the Grey Ditch south of Eyam were all used by the Northumbrians for the same purpose at a slightly later date. In general, these dykes have to be considered together with the East and West Wansdykes thrown up against the Mercians by the West Saxons, and the whole series of Cambridgeshire and Norfolk dykes dug against the Mercian incursion by the East Angles. The lengths of these dykes appear to have increased progressively as they were constructed in the seventh and eighth centuries. The earlier dykes defended routes of penetration, but the later ones demarcated considerable lengths of frontiers. Clearly, the Mercians had good precedents to work on when they themselves built first Wat's Dyke and later Offa's Dyke against the Welsh.

Returning once more to the North Mercian boundary, we cannot be sure of the line along which it marched with the south-western limits of the ancient kingdom of Elmet, but I would hazard that it coincided with the northern parts of the original diocesan boundary of Lichfield, which in turn is represented today by the north-eastern border of Derbyshire. The north of modern Derbyshire was occupied however by the Pecsaetan, who were a people distinct from the North Mercians, as the Tribal Hidage shows; but just where the border between the two territories lay must remain a matter of doubt. I have shown it running southwards through Chesterfield down to Belper, then westwards towards Ashbourne, then north-westwards towards Macclesfield, until the border between Derbyshire and Cheshire is reached.

On this analysis, the North Mercians occupied what we now think of as Staffordshire north of the River Trent, Derbyshire except for the Peak District, the whole of Nottinghamshire, and a small part of the West Riding of Yorkshire to the south-east of the River Don. The capital of all this territory was undoubtedly Derby, called originally *Northworthig* (Campbell 1962: 37) to distinguish it from *Tamworthig* (Tamworth), the capital of the South Mercians.

Finally, we come to South Mercia, whose bounds with North Mercia and Outer Mercia we have considered already. The western and south-western boundaries remain to be defined. The English settlement of Cheshire was largely completed by the time of King Penda (Dodgson 1967), and there can be little doubt that together with North Shropshire it lay within the ancient bounds of the Wreocensaetan, and that the north-western boundary of South Mercia is now represented by the western border of Staffordshire. South-westwards, the limits of South Mercian territory ran along the boundary between the dioceses of Lichfield and Worcester, and can be established in great detail from the evidence of place-names and charters (Hart 1971: 149; Gover *et al.*, 1936: xvi-xvii). It cuts across modern Warwickshire, leaving Warwick itself on the Hwiccean side of the boundary.

Before leaving this topic of the internal boundaries of the Mercian kingdom, I should mention that it now seems possible to delineate fairly closely the territories occupied by the Tomsaetan and the Pencersaetan, who were the two most important of the tribal units forming the South Mercian peoples. It has long been known that the land of the Tomsaetan stretched from Breedon-on-the-Hill southwards along the valley of the River Tame to the boundary of King's Norton, south of Birmingham (Gover *et al.*, 1936: xvii-xviii). Tamworth, the Mercian capital, and Lichfield, the seat of the principal Mercian bishopric, both lay within its territory, which formed therefore the very heartland of Mercia and was ruled by its own ealdorman. One may now suggest that the northern and western parts of South Mercia were settled by a large tribe named the Pencersaetan, who occupied the valley of the River Penk, with Penkridge (Brit. *Pennocrucium;* OE *Pencric*) for their capital. Both Stafford and Wolverhampton lie within this area, and the boundary of the Pencersaetan appears to have marched with that of the Tomsaetan along a line running northwards from King's Norton towards the River Trent, leaving Lichfield within the tribal area of the Tomsaetan, and Cannock with the Pencersaetan.[1]

I want now to turn away from topography, and take a brief glance at the Mercian dynasty. In the first of the pedigrees (pp. 55 and 57) the 12 kings of Mercia in historical times from Penda to Ceolwulf I are numbered. These kings span two centuries, and all are descended from Pybba the father of King Penda. When Peada's brother Wulfhere died in 674 his son Cenred was probably still a minor, for the kingdom passed first to Wulfhere's brother Æthelred, and only then to Cenred, and subsequently to Æthelred's son, Ceolred. When Ceolred died in 716 there appears to have been no eligible descendant of King Penda ready to take the throne, and Æthelbald, an exile descended from a collateral branch, took over.

To establish his right, Æthelbald had to go back for four generations along his family tree, but he possessed a strong personality, and his reign was a stable one. When he died 40 years later, evidently without heirs, the kingdom was seized by a pretender named Beornred, whose relationship to the dynasty is not clear. He was deposed by Offa, the most famous of the Mercian kings, whose pedigree has to be traced back through five generations to reveal the legitimacy of his claim.

With Offa, the Mercian dynasty reached its apogee. He ruled all England south of the Humber with an authority never achieved by his predecessors, and not to be repeated until the reign of Edgar two centuries later. He exercised considerable ruthlessness in securing his objectives. The greatest of these was to ensure the uncontested succession of his son Ecgfrith after his death. His method was to kill off all possible rival claimants to the throne. It was poetic justice that in doing so, Offa was undoubtedly responsible for the eventual extinction of his dynasty, and the resultant crumbling of Mercian power during the following century; for his son Ecgfrith survived him by only a few months, and died without producing an heir of

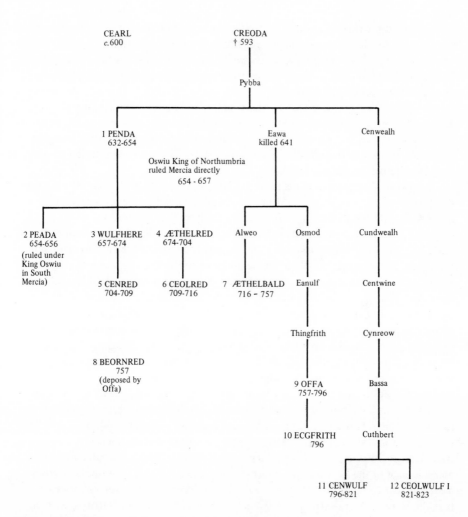

Kings of Mercia in capitals, numbered in order of succession.

Pedigree I. *The Mercian dynasty in historical times*

his own. Alcuin wrote truly in 797: 'That most noble young man (King Ecgfrith) has not died for his own sins, but the vengeance for the blood shed by the father has reached the son. For you know very well how much blood his father shed to secure the kingdom of his son. This was not a strengthening of his kingdom, but its ruin.' (Whitelock 1955: 787).

After Ecgfrith's death, therefore, there had to be the most extraordinary hark-back over eight generations before a suitable claimant could be found in the person of Cenwulf. It is as if in modern times one had to hunt through the royal pedigree right back to George III to find a descendant with a legitimate claim to the throne, were Elizabeth II to die without heirs.

Cenwulf was succeeded by his brother Ceolwulf I, but after his death the country was thrown once more into confusion, for again there was no obvious successor. Beornwulf took the throne, but his place in the dynasty is unknown. I have suggested a possible pedigree (pedigree 2) but it is quite tentative, and from this point onwards one cannot do more than guess at the titles of the various claimants. Inevitably, the insecurity of the reigning house was reflected in its lack of authority to rule the kingdom, and every time the ruling monarch died Mercia faced the threat of anarchy. At one point (in 829) the whole kingdom fell into West Saxon hands, but the situation was retrieved swiftly by one Wiglaf, who upon taking power had married his son into the Mercian royal house to help secure his title. It was therefore a much weakened Mercia that the Danes encountered during their raids of the mid-ninth century, and no doubt this helped towards their eventual decision to settle the eastern part of the kingdom.

I would like to pass on now to a short account of some features of the Mercian court and administration. It is well known that few documents other than charters survive to illustrate the period of the Mercian hegemony, but it would be a mistake to assume from this silence that Mercian administration was rudimentary. Archaeologically, we have secure evidence from Sutton Hoo of the splendour and magnificence of the East Anglian court (Bruce-Mitford, 1974), and similarly from Yeavering for Northumbria (Wilson 1957: 148-9).There is no reason to suppose that the Mercian *bretwaldas* of the two succeeding centuries were satisfied with any less elaborate an establishment. After the conversion, what they lost in pagan ostentation was more than compensated for by the increased organizational opportunities afforded by the services of a literate clergy, which also brought them into close contact with the expansionist pretensions and luxurious habits of the Merovingians. To maintain a style of living on this scale must have required great wealth drawn from the subject provinces of the hegemony, and this in turn must have involved the maintenance of an administrative machine of some sophistication.

We see this reflected in the remarkably advanced (though apparently restricted) coinage, a subject discussed in Chapter 5. We meet its consequences again in the dyke constructed by Offa to ward off the Welsh. Nothing like it had been seen in England since the time of the Romans, and it was indeed unparalleled for the period anywhere north of the Alps. The organization required for setting up this great earthwork must have been of a scale and efficiency approaching that needed for the erection of the pyramids of Egypt. Equally impressive must have been the arrangements for maintaining and policing the dyke and its stockade.

The great kings of Mercia had imperial pretensions over their hegemony (John 1966: 1-63), and it could even be that Charlemagne, with whom Offa dealt on equal

The Kings   *A suggested pedigree*

8 BEORNRED 757

13 BEORNWULF 823-825

14 *LUDECAN 825 - 827

15 *WIGLAF 827 - 840

16 BEORHTWULF 840-852

17 BURGHRED 852-874 (exiled)

18 CEOLWULF II 874-(877 x 883)
   (puppet set up by the Danes
   to rule Western Mercia)

*Place in the dynasty unknown,
 and not conjectured here

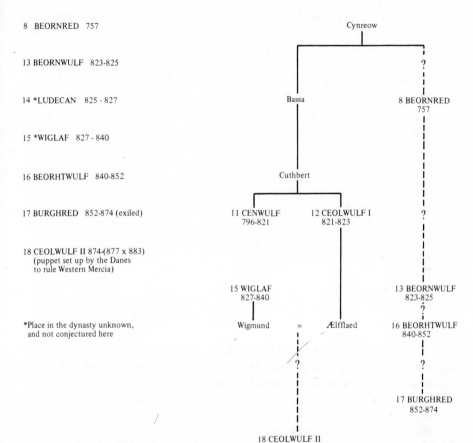

Kings of Mercia in capitals, numbered in order of succession.

Pedigree 2. *The last kings of Mercia*

terms, found his own path towards acceptance of the imperial Roman title eased by Offa's example (Levison 1946: 121-5). There is much to suggest that Offa in turn sought to model his administration on that of Charlemagne's court, which ceased to be wholly peripatetic at this period, and became centred at Aachen. Tamworth had been a royal residence - possibly the principal royal residence - as early as 691, if not before (Stenton 1970: 182 n.2). Sometime later, probably in the mid-eighth century, a defensive dyke was dug to enclose the site, so forming what the Anglians called a *worthig*, and from then onwards its name was changed from *Tomtun* to *Tomworthig* (Gould 1968-9: 37-8). Charters provide evidence that at least from 781 onwards, the Mercian kings kept the great festivals of Christmas and Easter regularly at Tamworth[2] and that (in the ninth century, if not earlier) a permanent treasury was maintained there for the receipt of royal dues (CS 436). Some, at least, of the royal archives may have been kept there, for on occasion land charters written elsewhere were brought to Tamworth for ratification at the Christmas court (Hart 1975: 69).

From 742 to 825 there are records of 21 ecclesiastical councils of the Southern province, presided over by the Mercian kings acting in their capacity as *bretwaldas*, and there is little doubt that these gatherings were held annually in the late summer or early autumn, at places along the Thames valley near London.[3] The custom appears to have been initiated at the Council of Hertford in 673, when it was laid down 'placuit omnibus in commune, ut kalendis Augustis in loco qui appellatur Clofaeshooh semel in anno congregemur' (Bede, HE bk IV c.5).

We have a picture therefore of an annual royal progress between Tamworth and London, which is quite different from the account of wars and devastation which is all that is recorded in the Anglo-Saxon Chronicle. This is not to say that the king did not travel widely over his domains in time of peace, but such perambulations were fitted in between his regular periods of residence at Tamworth and London. At other times the court might stay at abbeys as far apart as Bath, Repton, and Peterborough, and we have records of repeated visits to the royal vills of Wychbold, Cropthorne, Gumley, Barrow, and *Werburgh wic*.[4]

All the rulers of his subject provinces were required by Offa to attend him at court, and he treated them as his territorial deputies, or ealdormen. They were given precedence in accordance with their rank, and charters list them as *subreguli, principes,* and *duces* (e.g. CS 205). Individual *subreguli* had their own *prefecti* beneath them (CS 213-4), and men of this rank appeared occasionally at the Mercian court. So, of course, did the thegns, but they were rarely considered of sufficient account to witness royal charters. A butler travelled with the court (*pincerna*, CS 232), and no doubt many lesser royal officials; charters could be issued from the court while staying at royal vills (CS 432) as well as monasteries (CS 454). A reeve protected the imperial interests in London (CS 171), and a number of tax-gatherers were kept there to collect the royal tolls on ships (CS 177, witnessed by *panti thelonarii*).

There was at least some royal control over the quality of exported goods, for the lengths of cloth were regulated (Whitelock 1955: 43). Within the hegemony, taxes were raised on products such as salt (Finberg 1961: 90-1). Careful provision was made for the reception at Mercian abbeys of messengers and ambassadors travelling to and from both home and foreign royal courts (CS 416, 434; Hart 1975: 68). Justice was administered by reeves at the royal vills (CS 357), with major causes reserved for the king's presence. Food rents from surrounding estates were also payable at the royal vills (CS 273), and each of the larger landholders had obligations to provision the royal huntsmen, their servants, horses, birds of prey and hunting dogs (CS 450, 489). By the mid-eighth century, King Æthelbald had regularized the arrangements for landowners in the western parts of the hegemony to undertake repair of bridges, causeways, and defences of nearby *burhs* (Brooks, 1971: 83), and some time later similar provision was made for lodging and feeding armies engaged in expeditions against the Welsh (CS 489).

Much has been written about the conditions and obligations of land tenure under the Mercian kings, but the extraordinary fact is that for the period before the Danish settlement, the texts have survived of only two authentic royal charters booking land within the Mercian kingdom itself, as opposed to the subject kingdoms of the hegemony. They are dated 675 x 691, and 848, and both are preserved in the Peterborough *Liber Niger* and relate to its daughter cell at Breedon-on-the-Hill (CS 454, 851). We are unable therefore to do more than speculate on the terms upon which lay magnates held land within the kingdom of Mercia.

This lack of evidence can arise from one of two circumstances. Either there was no bookland at all for other than ecclesiastical holders, and hence no charters were issued, or alternatively there was bookland, in which case all records have perished, due presumably to destruction by the Danes. A case has been well argued for the former circumstance (John 1966: 22), but I am inclined to favour the second solution, which ties in with the lack of surviving Mercian law codes (although Offa is known to have issued at least one code, referred to in the Introduction to Alfred's Laws, 49.9), and with the dearth of Mercian chronicles and narrative sources for the period of the supremacy. With a few doubtful exceptions (Kuhn 1957), practically nothing written at a date earlier than the tenth century has survived from Lichfield, and nothing at all from Leicester, nor from any monastery within the Mercian kingdom, although charters are known to have been drawn up at Repton (CS 454). There is a similar lack of evidence from Lindsey, and from the territories of the East and Middle Angles, except for a few charters whose texts survived at Peterborough. All this can be blamed on the Danes, and the argument is strengthened greatly by the survival of much precious material at Worcester, well outside the Danelaw.

Our historical evidence is therefore scanty, but all that has survived points in the same direction. The Mercian *bretwaldas* did much to weld together their subject provinces to form a unified English state, and in doing so they developed many of the features that were to characterize royal administration in England during the succeeding centuries. Indeed, it can be argued that the very name of England owes its adoption and survival to the Mercian hegemony; had the West Saxon dynasty held the power instead of the Mercians in the eighth century, we might well be living today in Saxonland.

Postscript. It was not until I had completed this paper that through the kindness of Dr Wendy Davies I was able to read the important article entitled 'The Contexts of the Tribal Hidage: Social Aggregates and Settlement Patterns' which she contributed jointly with Hayo Vierck in 1974 to *Frühmittelalterliche Studien* 8: 223-93. This opens fresh fields for debate, but after careful perusal I see no reason to modify my own views to any radical extent.

ACKNOWLEDGMENTS

I would like to thank A. G. McCormick for drawing fig.2.

NOTES

1. This interpretation of the tribal area of the Pencersaetan arises from a re-examination of the bounds of CS 455, a Worcester charter dated 849, whose text is preserved in Heming's Cartulary (Finberg 1972: 15-16). The boundary clause relates to five hides within the Hwiccean diocese, comprising parts of Cofton Hackett, King's Norton, Hopwood, and Alvechurch. It is clear that the perambulation commences on the northern border of this territory, somewhere to the west of Icknield Street. At this point the estate boundary coincides with the boundary between the Worcester and Lichfield dioceses, and therefore between the principality of the Hwicce and the province of South Mercia. The boundary starts at the landmark between the Tomsaetan and the Pencersaetan. Since the Tomsaetan are known to have been a Mercian people, it has been assumed in the past that the Pencersaetan must have been Hwiccean, i.e. that their territory lay in what is now Worcestershire. This clearly will not do, for Cofton Hackett and Alvechurch are situated at the headwaters of the River Arrow, and must have belonged therefore to the Arosaetan, one of the Hwiccean peoples listed in the Tribal Hidage; next to them lay the Stoppingas of the Wooton Wawen region. Probably the perambulation commences therefore at the point where the bounds of all three tribes met, with the Arosaetan to the south, the Tomsaetan to the north-east, and the Pencersaetan to the north-west. (The bounds of CS 1312 commence at a similar triple landmark, see Hart 1975: 95). The bounds of CS 455 were first examined by G.B. Grundy in *Transactions Birmingham and Warwickshire Archaeological Society*, 1927, *52:* 54-60, but more work on them is needed. In the bounds, *straet* = Icknield Street; *heathlege* = Headley Heath in King's Norton; *colle* = the River Cole; *Hopwudes* = Hopwood in Alvechurch; *Crawanhyll* = *Croweshull* in the 1299 survey of Hopwood in the Red Book of Worcester (P.R.O.).
2. All surviving Mercian charters dated Christmas or Easter were ratified at Tamworth. These are, for Christmas CS 239 - 40 (781), CS 350 (814), CS 432 - 3 (841), and CS 450 (845); for Easter CS 259, a forgery based on a genuine text (790), CS 326 (808), CS 430 (840), and CS 492 (857). Other charters dated from Tamworth do not record the time of year - CS 293, 455, 488.
3. Councils presided over by Mercian kings were held at Brentford in 780 (CS 236) and 781 (CS 241); at Chelsea in 799 x 802 (CS 201), 785 (CS 247-8), 787 (CS 251), 788 (CS 254), 789 (CS 255-7), 793 (CS 267), 796 (CS 280-1), 801 (CS 302) and 816 (CS 358); at *Aclea* in 801 (CS 445), 804 (CS 313), and 805 (CS 322); and at *Clofesho* in 742 (CS 162), 747 (CS 174), 793 x 796 (CS 274), 794 (CS 269), 798 (CS 291), 803 (CS 309, 310), 824 (CS 378-9) and 825 (CS 384). The only Councils for which a full date is recorded were held in September 747 (CS 174), 22 September 780-1 (CS 236), 6-12 October 803 (CS 308-310), 27 July 816 (CS 358), and 30 October 824 (CS 378-9).
4. Bath in 796 (CS 278) and 864 (CS 509); Repton in 848 (CS 454); Peterborough in 765 (CS 196); *Crogedena* in 809 (CS 328). Wychbold on 19 March 815 (CS 353) and 1 September 831 (CS 400); Cropthorne in 780 (CS 235-6) and 814 (CS 432); Gumley in 749 (CS 178) and 775 (CS 209, 210); Barrow in 743 (CS 165) and on 25 November 814 (CS 348); *Werburghwic* at Whitsun 823 (CS 313) and in 840 (CS 152, confirmation).

REFERENCES

Note CS = *Cartularium Saxonicum* (see below, under Birch)
Bede. *Venerabilis Baedae Opera Historica,* ed. C. Plummer, 1896.
Beowulf, ed. A.J. Wyatt and R.W. Chambers, 1933.
Birch, W.de Gray, 1885-93. *Cartularium Saxonicum.*
Blunt, C.E., 1961. 'The coinage of Offa', in *Anglo-Saxon Coins,* ed. R.H.M. Dolley.

Brooks, N., 1971. 'The development of military obligations in eighth and ninth century England', in *England before the Conquest,* ed. P. Clemoes and Kathleen Hughes.

Brownbill, J., 1925. 'The tribal hidage', *Engl.Hist.Rev., 40:* 497-503.

Bruce-Mitford, R., 1974. *Aspects of Anglo-Saxon Archaeology.*

Chadwick, H.M., 1905. *The Origin of the English Nation.*

Dodgson, J. McN., 1967. 'The English arrival in Cheshire', *Transactions of the Historical Society of Lancashire and Cheshire, 119:* 1-37.

Eddius Stephanus. *Vita Wilfridi,* ed. W. Levison, 1913, *Scriptores Rerum Merovingicarum,* vi (Berlin).

Finberg, H.P.R., 1972. *The Early Charters of the West Midlands.*

Gould, J. 1968-9. 'Third report on excavations at Tamworth', *Trans. Lichfield and S. Staffordshire Archaeol. and Hist.Soc., 10:* 32-42.

Gover, J.E.B., Mawer, A., Stenton, F.M., and Houghton, F.T.S., 1936. *The Place-Names of Warwickshire.*

Hallam, H.E., 1954. *The New Lands of Elloe* (University of Leicester Dept of English Local History Occasional Paper, First Series, No.6).

Hart, C.R., 1970. *The Hidation of Northamptonshire* (University of Leicester Dept of English Local History, Occasional Paper, Second Series, No.3).

Hart, C.R., 1971. 'The tribal hidage', *Trans.Royal Hist.Soc., 5th ser., 21:* 133-57.

Hart, C.R., 1975. *The Early Charters of Northern England and the North Midlands.*

John, E., 1966. *Orbis Britanniae.*

Kuhn, S., 1957. 'Some early Mercian manuscripts', *Review of English Studies, 8:* 355-74.

Levison, W., 1946. *England and the Continent in the Eighth Century.*

Plummer, C., 1899. *Two of the Saxon Chronicles Parallel* (2 vols).

Radford C.A. Raleigh, 1947. 'A lost inscription of pre-Danish Age from Caistor', *Archaeol.J., 103:* 95-9.

Sisam, K., 1939. 'Anglo-Saxon royal genealogies', *Proc.Brit.Acad., 39:* 287-348.

Stenton, F.M., 1947. *Anglo-Saxon England* (2nd edn).

Stenton, F.M., 1970. *Preparatory to Anglo-Saxon England* (collected papers of F.M.Stenton, ed. Doris Mary Stenton).

Thorpe, B., 1848-9. *Florenti Wigorniensis monarchi chronicon ex chronicis* (2 vols, English Historical Society).

Whitelock, D., 1955. *English Historical Documents,* vol.I.

Wilson, D.M., 1957. 'Excavations at Yeavering, Northumberland', *Medieval Archaeol., 1:* 148-9.

CHARLES PHYTHIAN-ADAMS

4 Rutland reconsidered

Perhaps the most necessary but least easy task for the local historian is to account for the origins of the locality which he is studying. Unlike the specialist in one of the branches of pre-Conquest studies, he cannot confine himself to a particular excavation, the intricacies of diplomatic or even a specific theory on, for example, the problem of continuity. His starting point is the given locality itself, whether or not the evidence available for its analysis is rich or uneven. Yet the effort has to be made, and made synoptically, since as many as possible of the evidential fragments of the puzzle need to be brought into some sort of coherent relationship. In particular the local historian has to depend to a greater extent than might be thought proper on the evidence of the map and the older boundaries described upon it.[1] It is thus all the more important that each link in the argument should be open to inspection, especially by the relevant experts in their various fields. It is too easily, and, regrettably, too frequently done, to make sweeping assertions in the space of a few short paragraphs which consequently skim over the major difficulties. Hopefully, therefore, although the arguments which follow may not command acceptance, at least their detailed presentation may call attention to the very difficult general principles involved in such an analysis.

The origins of Rutland present problems of a unique complexity that is appropriate to its singular position in the shire-system of England. The compact area of the modern district, which only acquired county status late in the twelfth century (Ramsey 1908: 167-71), was, as is well known, still territorially divided at the time of Domesday (see fig. 3). The northern, carucated half, which alone was called *Roteland* (a term which I shall use hereafter to distinguish it from Rutland as a whole) was divided into two wapentakes, and was fiscally accountable to

Nottinghamshire. In 1066, as Sir Frank Stenton demonstrated 70 years ago, it was, and had been for some time, the dower of the late Anglo-Saxon queens (Stenton 1908: 135-36). The southern portion of Rutland, by contrast, comprised a hidated area known in Domesday as Witchley hundred or wapentake, which formed the northernmost part of Northamptonshire (Stenton 1908: 121-22; 1909: 11).[2]

Two alternative causes of this division have been proposed. Stenton tentatively suggested that *Roteland* had been formerly another wapentake of Northamptonshire which was presumably detached from its mother-territory when it became dower land (Stenton 1908: 136 n.30). More recently, Cyril Hart has put forward another solution to the puzzle. He claims that Rutland as a whole was probably once an integral unit of a larger territory that also included the parts of Kesteven to the east, and which was dependent upon the Danish borough of Stamford. Within this district of 'Stamfordshire', he ascribes the partitioning of Rutland to the activities of King Edward who, after the submission of Stamford in 918, is said to have assimilated the southern hundred of Witchley to what was then, or soon after was to become, his new county unit of Northamptonshire (Hart 1970: 13, 27-8; 1973: 138-40).

For both these scholars, the issue hinges ultimately on what each perceives as the antique fiscal arrangements common to the two halves of Rutland. For both writers, the interpretation depends on the acceptance and extension of Horace Round's famous thesis on the archaic nature of the Northamptonshire ploughland (Round 1902: 258-69). According to this theory, the Domesday hidation of that county which, at manorial level, frequently stands in some varying but regular relationship to the number of ploughlands enumerated, indicates a calculated reduction of fiscal liability from a time when the hundreds had each represented one hundred actual hides. In other words, the term 'ploughland' (itself a nineteenth-century shorthand term for the phrase *terra est x carucis*) is taken to represent the re-naming of an older hide or carucate, the reduction in the fiscal liability of which is broadly charted at an intermediate stage, by the Northamptonshire geld-roll. In the case of Rutland, both Stenton and Hart have seen close similarities between the regular groupings of ploughlands in respectively duodecimal or septimal arrangements which each has claimed as common to both parts of the district. For Stenton, the duodecimal character of the 'assessments' of both the Domesday *Roteland* and Witchley could be closely paralleled by a similar arrangement discovered by Round in north-eastern Northamptonshire. This relationship seemed to corroborate the evidence of a writ of Edward the Confessor concerning *Roteland*, but which was addressed nevertheless to the Northamptonshire authorities (Stenton 1908: 123-6, 135). For Hart, only in the two halves of Rutland were ploughlands also arranged in sevens: *ergo*, Rutland was *not* originally a part of Northamptonshire (Hart 1970: 27-8).

This is not the place to embark upon a detailed critique of Round's theory, but two general and fundamental objections to it must be made. First, a perceptibly regular ratio between two given quantities surely does not prove that one quantity is necessarily of vastly older origin than the other: it implies only that one quantity was almost certainly calculated from the other - a very different proposition.[3] Second, it is an extraordinary fact that Round's assertions with regard to the artificiality of the ploughland unit have been accepted at their face value with, it would seem, no attempt at questioning their basis. Yet even a superficial

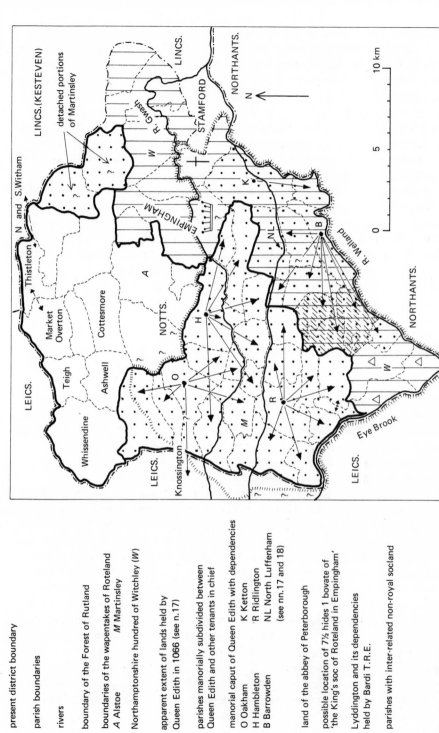

present district boundary

parish boundaries

rivers

boundary of the Forest of Rutland

boundaries of the wapentakes of Roteland
A Alstoe
M Martinsley

Northamptonshire hundred of Witchley (*W*)

apparent extent of lands held by
Queen Edith in 1066 (see n.17)

parishes manorially subdivided between
Queen Edith and other tenants in chief

manorial caput of Queen Edith with dependencies
O Oakham   K Ketton
H Hambleton   R Ridlington
B Barrowden   NL North Luffenham
                (see nn.17 and 18)

land of the abbey of Peterborough

possible location of 7½ hides 1 bovate of
'the King's soc of Roteland in Empingham'

Lyddington and its dependencies
held by Bardi T.R.E.

parishes with inter-related non-royal socland

Figure 3. Rutland in 1066.

examination of the Northamptonshire Domesday reveals again and again that in a
large number of cases - half the total entries which can be so tested - the number
of ploughlands given equates exactly with the figures for demesne and peasant
ploughs combined. A ranking of all the counties for which the relevant information
is available, indeed, demonstrates that Northamptonshire was second only to
Cambridgeshire in its equivalence per entry of ploughs and ploughlands.[4] Whatever
else this may imply, it certainly does not indicate an archaic unit of assessment. On
the contrary, it is far more reasonable to infer that in this case the numbers of
ploughlands had been calculated comparatively recently - possibly at the time when
the reductions recorded in the Northamptonshire geld roll were made.[5]

These general criticisms hold good in respect of Rutland. Of the 18 entries which
provide complete information on the number of ploughs in the Northamptonshire
half, ploughlands are matched exactly in eight cases, while for the remaining
entries concerned, the difference between the two quantities is never more than 1½.
In Alstoe wapentake, out of 12 entries, only two match exactly (or possibly three
out of 11 cases, if one obvious amalgamation is allowed),[6] but in only two further
cases is the difference between the two quantities more than 1½. Indeed, when that
wapentake is divided into its two component fiscal hundreds along the lines
suggested by Stenton, one of these contained 42 ploughlands as against 43 teams.
In the case of the other hundred, much of the difference between the 42
ploughlands and 58½ teams recorded may be explained by the distorting effect of
the single exceptional entry for Cottesmore (Stenton 1908: 122).[7] It would be
remarkable indeed if an archaic assessment (perhaps instituted one or even two
centuries earlier by the Danes) still corresponded so closely to current agricultural
realities.

It is thus clear that this ingenious but essentially unprovable thesis cannot be
used to claim an archaic link between *Roteland* and Northamptonshire. The
evidence of the actual units of assessment, of course, indicates exactly the
contrary. Domesday, for example, specifically records that the carucation of
Roteland had not changed since the Conquest: each entry states that the T.R.E.
holder 'habuit ... x carucatas terrae ad geldum'. The light imposition of that
carucation and the recurrence in Alstoe of four assessments at 3 carucates and one
at 1½ might well suggest that that wapentake at least had had its duodecimal
carucation conceivably halved at some unknown date before 1066. In Witchley
hundred, by contrast, it is known that by 1086 a reduction of 60 per cent [that
is, from 200 hides to 80 (actually 76)] had been secured since its initial hidation,
40 per cent of which had been effected *since* the Conquest. Hence the 2, 4, 8 and
16-hide units of Domesday theoretically represent the remnants of original
decimal groups of 5, 10, 20 and 40 hides respectively. From an unknown date
before the Conquest, therefore, the two halves of Rutland had used totally
different systems of assessment.[8]

It is thus to other indications that we must look for an explanation of Rutland's
curious development. The Domesday *Roteland*, for example, was politically
identified with Danish territory and in particular that of the Five Boroughs. Like
Leicestershire, Derbyshire, Nottinghamshire and Lincolnshire, it was carucated
with its wapentakes subdivided into fiscal and, in the absence of evidence to the
contrary, very possibly judicial and military hundreds.[9] It appears in Domesday
before Lincolnshire and Yorkshire, and after Derbyshire and Nottinghamshire with

their combined shire-court. Its geld was collected by the sheriff of Nottingham and the hundredal subdivisions of its wapentake of Alstoe had been closely integrated at some date with two of Nottinghamshire's wapentakes (Stenton 1908: 126-7) - a carefully calculated arrangement, which can hardly have been later than the carucation of the areas concerned. Like the Five Borough counties, its fiscal assessments were recorded as T.R.E., while its tax liability per vill was similar to that in Derbyshire and Nottinghamshire (Stenton 1905: 294; 1906: 208). Finally, while there are no entries duplicated under Northamptonshire, eight out of 12 entries for Alstoe are repeated almost exactly in the Lincolnshire section of Domesday.

For the southern half of Rutland, earlier evidence still implies that what the Northamptonshire geld roll shows once to have been the *double* hundred of Witchley, had long comprised the furthest extent of Northamptonshire's jurisdiction. The County Hidage (which probably reflects the situation between c.990 and c.1010) only makes sense if the 32 hundreds there ascribed to Northamptonshire included the double hundred of Witchley (Maitland 1960: 527). That this connection may have been older still is to be inferred from a somewhat ambiguous entry in the *Anglo-Saxon Chronicle* for 917. There we hear of the submission to King Edward of Earl Thurferth, the *holds,* and 'all the army which belonged to Northampton, as far north as the Welland' (Whitelock 1955: 197). This curiously limiting phraseology seems to imply, even if it does not prove, what Professor Stenton and Canon Taylor both independently suspected: that a further section of Northampton's territory, beyond the Welland to the north, did not then submit (Stenton 1909: 11 n.3; Taylor 1957: 20 n.2). If so, it is unlikely that this was within the territory of the army of Leicester, and in view of the later evidence, the area of Witchley hundred thus represents the likeliest situation. Whatever the exact date when the connection between Witchley and the territory of Northampton was first established, however, there is evidence enough from well before the time of Edward the Confessor's writ to indicate the northern limits of that shire's fiscal and military responsibilities.

This problem of *Roteland's* relationship to Witchley raises another question which, although implicit in Hart's idea regarding 'Stamfordshire', has never been fully examined: does Domesday inadvertently disguise the original extent of *Roteland?* The map, for example, shows the later Rutland as a compact territorial unit almost entirely encircled to the north of the river Welland by a continuous boundary. The only intrusion is the anomalous peninsula of Lincolnshire on which Stamford is situated to the east - a matter which will receive attention below. In the wider context, it is noteworthy that not only was Rutland to become at some unknown date a discrete ecclesiastical unit comprising the medieval rural deanery of Rutland, but well before the district aspired to county status, it was to be treated administratively as a sub-divided whole known as 'Rutland' even as early as 1129-30 (Ramsay 1908: 167-8). Unless then there was *already* a well-established association in the minds of contemporaries between the northern and southern parts of the district, it is difficult to account for this extension of a topographically restricted name to part of a neighbouring county.

These suspicions are amplified on turning to evidence from the Conquest period. Edward the Confessor's writ of 1064 x 5 which notified the grant of *Roteland* to St Peter's Westminster, also reserved to Queen Edith a life interest in the area, out of which she was to enrich the monastery. Taken in conjunction with Domesday, this evidence implies at first sight no more than that Edith received the profits of the Domesday *Roteland*, although her *demesne* lands (appropriately sub-divided into church sokes which, later at least, came into the hands of Westminster) were restricted to only one part of that district, the wapentake of Martinsley (Harmer 1952: 359, 514-5). But Domesday further reveals that Edith had very probably controlled as well practically all the adjacent area to the south and south-east of Martinsley; that is, a large part of the Northamptonshire hundred of Witchley.[10] Since Edith did not possess even a single manor in either Alstoe to the north or the Northamptonshire territory to the immediate south of the Welland, it is difficult not to believe that this whole compact area once represented a unified royal estate. It is thus significant that this territory equated very closely with Rutland's share of what became known - again before county status was achieved - as the royal forest of Leicestershire and Rutland. Although the royal holdings in Witchley had been eroded manorially by the time of Domesday, the combined area of Martinsley and the relevant parts of Witchley corresponded too closely with the later forest bounds of Rutland's share for this to have been accidental (Page 1908: 253; McKinley 1969: 265). It may well be relevant in this connection that the only vill in Witchley hundred which was both adjacent to the Domesday *Roteland* and divided by the course of the later forest boundary was specifically distinguished in the Great Survey. Although situated in Northamptonshire, 7½ hides plus one bovate out of Empingham's 14 hides and one bovate were said to belong to 'the king's *soc* of *Roteland*' (Page 1908: 142).

It is not at all impossible, therefore, that the area which later comprised the forest of Rutland once represented the extent of the royal *demesne* with which the Anglo-Saxon queens were endowed: an endowment indeed that was specifically linked by Gaimar with Rockingham - another later hunting area to the immediate south (Gaimar 1889: 4139). In the early twelfth century, Henry I may well have been continuing an earlier tradition when he also granted in dower a substantial part of Witchley within the forest bounds to Queen Maud, the *caput* of whose estates was at Barrowden (Page 1931: 170). Perhaps significantly, however, Barrowden was held from her at farm for a time by William d'Albini, who later in 1129-30 in his capacity as a justice of the forest also accounted to the Exchequer for Rutland as a whole (Page 1931: 168, 1). For a parallel situation seems to stand revealed at the time of Domesday. In 1086, Queen Edith's lands in Witchley (apparently including Barrowden) were also held at farm, by Hugh de Port, whose main territorial interests lay in Hampshire and included parts of another hunting region, the New Forest (Page 1908: 140; Round 1900: 423-4 and map between 488 and 489). Hugh's profits from the Rutland area must have derived in part from sources other than those of agriculture, since in two at least of these manors he does not seem to have received the profits of their labour services. On the contrary, Domesday states explicitly that the men of these manors were 'to labour at the *king's* work, which the reeve shall command [my italics]'. Hugh, moreover, was burdened with extraordinary administrative duties. When in 1080-7 the king commanded the conveyance of the *Roteland* churches of Uppingham, Wardley and Belton with their lands, tithes and chapels to Westminster, he addressed his writ, unlike Edward the Confessor, not to the shire court of Northampton, but to the Bishop of Lincoln, Hugh de Port 'et omnibus ministeriis suis ac fidelibus, Francis et Anglis, de Snotingham scire' (Dugdale I, 1817: 301; Davis 1913: no. 275). Now the Bishop of Lincoln is hardly likely to have been a member of the shire court of Nottingham, which lay in the diocese of York, while there is no evidence at all to suggest that Hugh de Port was ever sheriff of either Nottinghamshire or Northamptonshire, in neither of which counties did he hold any land.[11] It appears more probable that he was so addressed in his capacity as farmer of Edith's lands in Witchley. By virtue of this position, it would seem, he also witnessed the confirmation grant of the other *Roteland* churches to Westminster, and moreover, was personally directed by the King to seise the abbey of the tithes of *Roteland* (Dugdale I, 1817: 30; Davis: nos. 381, 382). Although Domesday is silent on the matter, it may well be wondered whether in these circumstances Hugh farmed all the Queen's manors in the 'forest' area, including her demesne lands in Martinsley. It is difficult otherwise to account both for his executive powers across a county boundary and also for the reference to ministers and liegemen in Nottinghamshire, a description which seems best explained as applying to *Roteland.*

While the evidence is not conclusive, such facts as there are point to a Rutland which, although administratively divided between Nottinghamshire and Northamptonshire at the time of Domesday, still retained something of a former, wider identity because of the royal hunting area that blurred the boundary between the two counties. If Martinsley is thus seen as but a part of that privileged area, much of which lay in Witchley, this goes a long way towards explaining the address of the Confessor's writ to the Northamptonshire authorities, at a time when the district was not at farm.

And there are other pointers which suggest that the county division severed a pre-existing unity (see fig. 5). It is an awkward and indeed overlooked fact that although the *Roteland* churches and dues granted to Westminster are traditionally taken to have included only those within the church sokes of Martinsley, yet in later times, while that interpretation is generally confirmed, there is nevertheless one significant exception. Amongst the several parts of Martinsley still owing dues to the abbey in 1291 is listed a part of Bisbrooke, which in 1086 was situated unambiguously within the Northamptonshire hundred of Witchley (Record Commission 1802: 66). The link must have been of considerable antiquity, for there is no other documentary trace of that connection with Westminster (Page 1931: 178). Another possible indication of the artificial nature of the county boundary lies in the contradictory situation of the place-name Edith Weston. Weston, as it was originally known, was evidently one of the berewicks which pertained to Queen Edith's Martinsley manor of Hambleton (Page 1931: 68) and yet it lay not to the west, but more or less south-east of the manorial *caput.* If, as seems to be generally accepted, place-names which include a descriptive directional element are taken as later subordinate settlements, then Weston's name can hardly have resulted from its relation to another Hambleton berewick, Normanton, which is the only possible candidate available, and from which it stood anyway in a more southerly position. In the absence of evidence for deserted village sites to the east of Weston, therefore, it might be suggested that its name derived originally from its westerly and subordinate position in respect of the royal manor of Ketton in Witchley hundred (Beresford and Hurst 1971: 202; Brown 1975: 7-8). In later times, indeed, the two settlements shared Witchley heath, the name of which gave that hundred its name (Page 1931: 62, 257). A more positive and undeniably archaic link across the county boundary is that which once existed between Luffenham and Luffwick. As Cox has shown, both places clearly took their names from the same eponymous *Luffa*. Separated by the intervening parish of Lyndon, in 1086, Luffenham lay in Witchley while Luffwick must have pertained to Manton in Martinsley (Cox 1971: 679).

It may be added finally in this connection, that Domesday alone is responsible for the usual interpretation with regard to the limited extent of *Roteland*. Yet if, as the County Hidage seems to demonstrate, Witchley hundred had been absorbed into Northamptonshire at the very least eight decades before, the silence of Domesday concerning what appears to have been once a wider entity is not in the least surprising.

But if these arguments go some way towards meeting Hart's suggestion that Rutland as a whole was once a part of 'Stamfordshire', the evidence for an early connection between the borough and the district has still to be explored (see fig. 4). It is a well-known fact that, apart from Empingham, the only place specifically mentioned in Domesday as pertaining to *Roteland* outside its bounds was a part of the *royal* borough of Stamford. There Queen Edith had possessed 70 messuages which 'iacuerunt in *Roteland*' (Foster 1924: 10). Taken by themselves, these holdings might imply only that the queen, or perhaps one of her predecessors, had come into possession well after a time when the local Danish autonomy was unchallenged - certainly later than 918, and as possibly, after 942. But the additional fact that 2½ carucates of the surrounding lands which were appurtenant to these messuages also lay in *Roteland* arouses the suspicion that the connection was of greater antiquity. Moreover, the church of St Peter, Stamford, with a further 2 messuages and a ½-carucate of land belonging to it, was the daughter church of Hambleton at the heart of Martinsley wapentake (Page 1908: 140b; Foster 1924: 10). On the Domesday evidence, indeed, St Peter's has the strongest claim to have been the mother church of Stamford. For when the enigmatic Portland, which was entered after the adjacent royal estate at Casterton in the Northamptonshire folios, is - as Round suggested - added to the territory of Stamford, it becomes clear that St Peter's parish covered three times the area comprising the parish of its nearest rival All Saints', that is 1½ carucates as opposed to a ½-carucate (Round 1902: 277-8). Indeed, of all the royal land outside Stamford in 1086, 3 carucates certainly, and possibly 4 (if the St Peter's holding in Portland is included) out of only 5⅔ carucates in all, lay, and probably long had lain, in Rutland - despite the fact that most of Stamford town was now situated in the recently created county of Lincoln (Taylor 1957: 24). This suggestion derives considerable support from the evidence of the map, where the territory of Stamford (which was largely occupied by the late combined parishes of St Peter and All Saints) may be seen to intrude otherwise inexplicably into the south-eastern corner of modern Rutland.[12] The boundary in fact seems to indicate a political re-adjustment at an unknown date.

It is thus hard to accept this arrangement as the product of a later imposition of Anglo-Saxon control, when a more obvious solution would have been to place Stamford unambiguously *outside* Lincolnshire or the territory of the Five Boroughs.

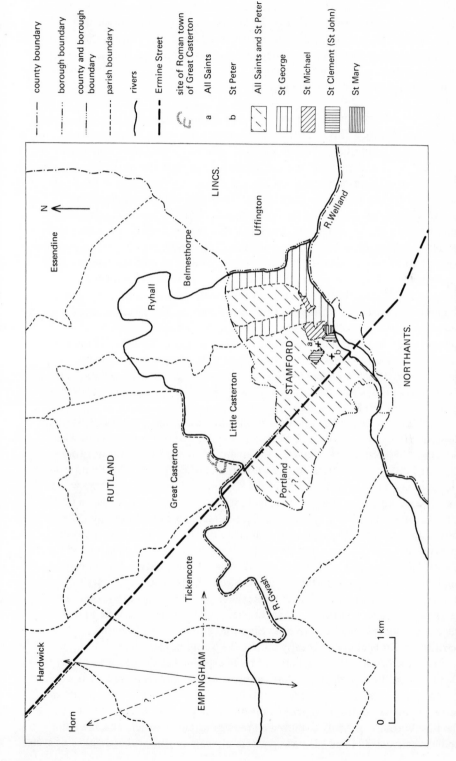

Figure 4. Parish and other boundaries of Stamford and its environs *(after Rogers 1972 and the Ordnance Survey).*

It is even more difficult to accept when St Clement's parish, from where there is
archaeological evidence which might indicate Danish occupation (Rogers 1972:
60 n.2), provides a suggestive clue to the possible location of the original Danish
burh. Its church's significant dedication; the compact regular shape of the parish;
and the indication that it was carved out of the surrounding and hence pre-existing
territory or territories of St Peter's and All Saints', all imply, even if they cannot
prove, Danish settlement and control from the periphery of an earlier English
town.[13]

Only excavation can decide these finer points, but if Stamford originally arose
on Rutland territory, this is far from agreeing that this district and Kesteven
together once comprised a shire of Stamford created by the Danes. Quite apart
from the fact that there is no direct evidence for the existence of the Mercian shires
before the closing years of the tenth century - let alone any hint as to the prior
existence of 'Stamfordshire' - there is no proof at all, without the aid of the
archaic ploughland thesis, that the double hundred of Witchley had ever been
subjected to a Danish system of carucation. As has previously been discussed, the
Roteland of Domesday had the closer connection with Stamford, yet if it ever had
been a part of 'Stamfordshire', it is difficult to see why its geld was later
supervised so inconveniently from distant Nottinghamshire and not from
Lincolnshire.[14] Place-name evidence, furthermore, reveals a marked thinness of
Scandinavian settlement throughout this entire district. Though a number of names
in *by* are to be discovered within a few miles of Rutland's boundary in
Leicestershire and Lincolnshire, there is no trace of any in Rutland. Within the
district there are 11 names in *thorpe*, all apparently comprising only minor
secondary settlements. Of the six compounded with Scandinavian names, five
were situated in the area least connected with Stamford - the double hundred of
Witchley (Cox 1971: 637 *et passim*).

In all of these circumstances, the evidence of Æthelweard's chronicle is surely
decisive. There we hear how in 894 Ealdorman Æthelnoth went to York where,
in Campbell's version, 'he contacted the enemy, who possessed large territories in
the kingdom of the Mercians, on the western side of the place called Stamford.
This is to say, between the streams of the Welland and the thickets of the wood
called Kesteven by the common people' (Campbell 1962: 51). As Stenton (1909:
10-12) demonstrated long ago, the district so described clearly corresponds
closely to the area of Rutland, the topography of which is shaped by the course
of the waterways that flow into the Welland: the Eye brook, the Chater and the
Gwash. Whether one accepts Stenton's view that in this passage Æthelweard is
implying a connection with the ravages of Sigeferth *piraticus*, or inclines to the
more neutral phraseology of Campbell's rendering of 'non parva territoria pandunt'
as simply implying possession, the fact remains that here is a clear-cut statement
demonstrating the separation of both Stamford and Kesteven from the
territory of Rutland at a very early date in the Scandinavian period.[15]

But if the origins of Rutland are not to be explained as the outcome of early
Danish connections with either Northampton or Stamford, is it possible to account
for its unique development? There seems little alternative but to suggest that the
early temporary control by *York* Danes of a district in the emergent territory of
the Five Boroughs possibly fossilized a pre-existing entity which, at some point
perhaps between 894 and 917, was deliberately partitioned - either *de novo* or even

along already established lines - between two other Danish interests both *independent* of Stamford.[16]

The artificial superimposition of this division at a time which must have antedated the mid-tenth century grant of the area to Queen Ælfthryth (Harmer 1952: 515, 551), is vividly illustrated by the differential social developments evident in the two resulting halves of the district (see fig. 3). For the boundary between them cuts right across what has been suggested as the original demesne lands of the Anglo-Saxon queens, which estate must therefore have comprised a discrete block of territory long before it was so granted. Of this area in 1086, Martinsley alone appears unaffected. With its archaic system of manors and berewicks[17] and the almost total absence of sokemen, it seems to represent an estate structure of some antiquity. In the relevant part of Witchley by contrast, there are indications that an earlier, simpler organization has been eroded. In particular, the important manor of Barrowden, with its five and possibly nine dependent members, bears all the signs of having once been a topographically discrete entity,[18] clearly indentifiable on the map, and very similar in structure to the component manors and berewicks of Martinsley. In this case, however, any former unity was in process of fragmentation. A fraction of Barrowden itself and parts of five of its members were controlled by other tenants-in-chief in 1086. Witchley as a whole, moreover, contained no fewer than 113 sokemen as against only two in Martinsley, and three on half a carucate in Alstoe. The vast majority of these were resident on royal manors or were within the royal jurisdiction.[19] In an area so lightly settled by the Danes - if the place-name evidence is a true indicator in this respect - it is thus difficult to regard these sokemen as of Scandinavian descent. Indeed, if the foregoing arguments carry any weight, the division of a once discrete area (which resulted in a marked absence of sokemen in the north, but their proliferation in the south) strongly implies that in the latter district, where the royal territory was undergoing rapid manorial dismemberment, Sawyer's view (1971) of the matter may hold good. There the sokemen may well have represented the descendants of those fortunate English peasants who had been released from their previous territorial allegiances by the accident of Danish domination. Reference has already been made to the evidence for a somewhat greater Danish presence in Witchley than in the northern area. It is a curious additional fact that of the 23 Domesday entries relating to mills in Rutland as a whole, no fewer than 16 were valued in units of the Danish ora, and of these 14 were situated in Witchley.

The conjunction of all the circumstances so far discussed has further implications. Despite the administrative control later exercised over *Roteland* itself by Nottingham with its Danish fiscal system, the former emerges into the light of history as a very English district in the midst of Scandinavianized territory. The possibility at least that *Roteland* represented the remainder of the larger district of Rutland which had been the property of the Mercian kings long before the Danish invasions cannot be dismissed. Indeed the unique character of the area, and its early separation from the coalescing territory of the Five Boroughs, might even suggest that its survival could have been the product of a deliberate arrangement between the Danes of York and Ceolwulf of Mercia in the bargaining that took place in 877 or at some time thereafter.[20]

Speculative as such theories inevitably must be, they at least take account of the

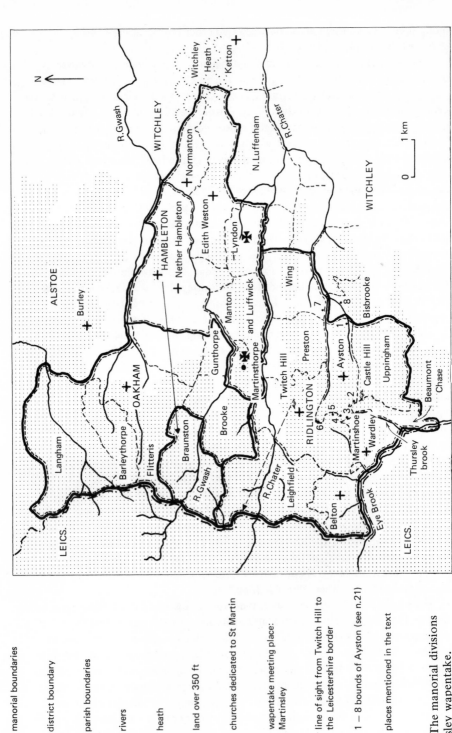

Figure 5. The manorial divisions
of Martinsley wapentake.

	manorial boundaries
	district boundary
	parish boundaries
	rivers
	heath
	land over 350 ft
✠	churches dedicated to St Martin
●	wapentake meeting place: Martinsley
▼----	line of sight from Twitch Hill to the Leicestershire border
1 – 8	bounds of Ayston (see n.21)
+	places mentioned in the text

discordant and hitherto ignored elements in the puzzle. There are, moreover, some signs that Rutland did once comprise a pre-Danish administrative unit. Certainly the place-name evidence suggests that its western boundary was a frontier of considerable antiquity (see fig. 5). Situated on the scarp of one of the most impressive hills in the east Midlands, overlooking the boundary with Leicestershire, lies Wardley, a name which probably betokens 'a look-out clearing'. To its north-east, in the neighbouring parish of Ridlington, was Twitch Hill, another look-out place with an uninterrupted view towards the present boundary of Leicestershire (Cox 1971: 682). In the valley below lay Belton, once an ecclesiastical dependency of Wardley (Page 1931: 31) - a name which it has been found difficult to interpret with confidence, though two alternative solutions fit a frontier situation: whether the name refers to a farmstead beside a warning beacon, or if it be associated with 'a space' or 'interval' in wooded country, thus implying perhaps a stretch of no-man's land (Smith 1965: 26-7; Ekwall 1960: 35; Cox 1971: 687). Further north, along the Rutland boundary towards Oakham, lay the park of Flitteris, which Cox interprets as 'a brushwood region of disputed ownership' (1971: 695). In a frontier context, it is relevant to note finally the siting of the only probable heathen place-name in the region. The bounds of the Ayston charter of 1046 refer to Thursley brook, which, in an area practically devoid of Scandinavian settlement seems thus to refer not to a Danish personal name, but more probably, as Cox suggests, to a grove dedicated to Thunor (1971: 675). A re-working of Professor Finberg's analysis of the charter bounds, indeed, strongly suggests that the brook took its name from part or all of the wooded area which in Norman times became Beaumont Chase, and alongside which it ran.[21] The stream flowed into the Eye brook, the ancient line of the Rutland boundary, thus indicating that Thursley was situated in a classic position for a boundary shrine. It may well be relevant also in this connection, that the pre-Conquest church of neighbouring Wardley was dedicated to the seventh-century East Anglian saint, St Botolph, whose dedication, for reasons unknown, is commonly associated with ancient boundary lines.[22] But what is significant about this grouping of English frontier names on the western side of Rutland is that they clearly do not relate to what was surely the most likely direction of a Scandinavian threat: from Lincolnshire or Stamford. Rather it looks as though they originate from a period when it was necessary for one of the many small peoples of the Middle Angles to demarcate their territory from aggressive neighbours in the area of the later Leicestershire.

It is consequently not beyond the bounds of possibility that Rutland once comprised one or even conceivably two *regiones* controlled by such a division of the Middle Angles. If so, the royal *caput* may well have been Hambleton rather than Oakham. Even as late as Domesday, the former emerges as the most important manor of *Roteland*. Its church, not that of Oakham, was the mother church of St Peter's, Stamford. The churchlands pertaining to Oakham, Hambleton and Stamford, and held by Albert the Clerk, seem to have lain largely in Hambleton,[23] while that manor boasted three *Roteland* churches as opposed to Oakham's one. In 1066 Hambleton also had the highest valuation or farm in the district - 12 pounds more than either Oakham or Ridlington; while its total value, when the lands of Albert the Clerk are included, was equivalent to the farm of the whole of Alstoe wapentake (Stenton 1908: 128). In 1086, it contained the only

functioning mill in Martinsley, and when this is taken in conjunction with the
Domesday inference that the Oakham demesne was not yet fully tilled, it might
seem that the royal hall at Oakham was in fact a quite recent development.[24]
Oakham, indeed, with the prescriptive market and the gaol which are first revealed
in post-Conquest sources (Page 1931: 7, 8, 13), betrays all the
characteristics of a royal *tūn* from which the king's reeve operated. As with the
topographical relationship between the 'king's *tūn*' of Kineton and the palace at
Wellesbourne in the Warwickshire *regio* of the *Stoppingas*, it was appropriately
situated at a little distance from the royal *caput*.[25]

Hambleton, by contrast, occupied a commanding hill-top site - from which it
took its name - overlooking the vale of Catmose and Oakham below, and possibly
stood in some sort of relationship to a similarly sited *būrh* at Burley-on-the-Hill
across the valley (Cox 1971: 650). Above all, the manor of Hambleton probably
contained the meeting place of Martinsley wapentake, and in doing so, may well
have dominated an area with very ancient connotations (Page 1931: 58).
Martin's wood or clearing appears to have been situated in the Hambleton
berewick of Martin's/thorp or *stoc* (both alternatives are first found in medieval
times: (Cox 1971: 679), where also stood a church dedicated to St Martin
(Page 1931: 84). Two and a half miles to the east, Lyndon church was
similarly dedicated; while three miles to the south-west, the great spur on the
west of which Wardley is situated, was known in 1046 - and probably long before -
as Martin's *hōe*. The least that might be inferred from this would seem to be that
a large tract of territory, without parallel elsewhere in this part of the Midlands,
was topographically associated with a pre-Danish dedication.[26]

But if the outlines of a case can be made for the possible existence of an early
administrative unit in this area, it is still true that all the evidence so far adduced
relates essentially to the district described as *Roteland* in Domesday. From this
area, furthermore, comes the only information about the possible extent of the
territory controlled by the eponymous *Rota*. For if the area of Martinsley perhaps
represented the archaic core, to the north, the two adjacent parishes of
Whissendine and Teigh in the wapentake of Alstoe (see fig. 3) alone contain minor
names which indicate the existence of '*Rota's* moor' (Cox 1971: 646). There thus
remains a possibility that the Danish partition of Rutland roughly perpetuated a
pre-existing sub-division of the district.[27]

In view of its English name, it is not impossible that the double hundred of
Witchley was once a pre-Danish administrative unit of the kind elucidated by
Cam (1963: 91-105). The name was apparently derived from the once wooded
area which lay astride the division of East and West Witchley. Though the first
element of the name may be yet another unrecorded O.E. personal name, or even
an O.E. by-name meaning 'chest or trunk' (Cox 1971: 684), there is something to
be said for the traditional interpretation, accepted most recently by Smith and
Hart, that it refers in fact to a wood or clearing of the *Hwicce* (Smith 1965: 42;
Hart 1971: 138n.). The first recorded version of the name (rendered as
Hwicceslea - Robertson 1956: 234) appears less than a century after the main
territory of the *Hwicce* had ceased to exist as an administrative entity.[28]   Such
folk-names, as Ekwall showed, when found outside the primary areas of settlement
concerned, clearly demarcated the aberrant situation of such districts from those of
the other peoples surrounding them. In this case, the identification is marginally

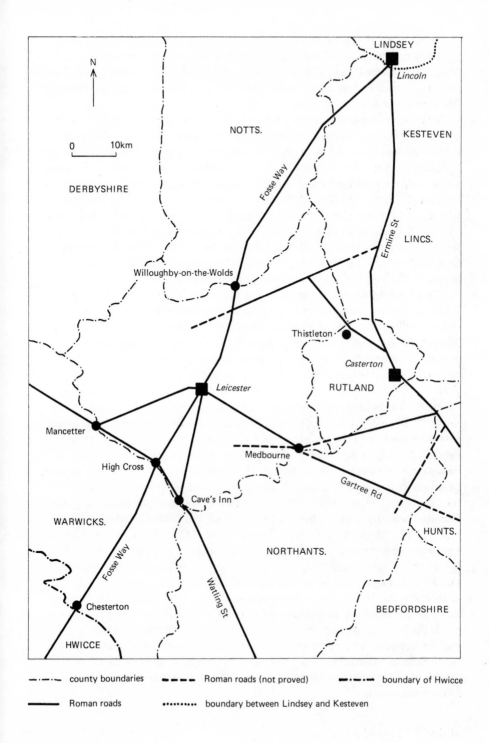

Figure 6. The relationship of select Roman settlements to the Roman road system and later administrative boundaries.

strengthened by the fact that the only place-name parallel nearby is to be found, curiously enough, some 20 miles to the south at Whiston in present-day Northamptonshire (Hart 1971: 136, 138n.). The possibility that Witchley had once been a detached enclave of the *Hwicce,* however, remains no more than surmise. The evidence is too inconclusive.

Nevertheless, whether the artificial partition of Rutland was Scandinavian or earlier, an even more ancient origin for the discrete character of this district as a whole remains a distinct possibility. The conjunction of heavy Roman settlement, federate remains and a number of both early Anglo-Saxon cemeteries and place-names, might well suggest a case of continuity.[29] Within the district, Bonney's findings for Wessex (1972: 168-86) may be closely paralleled by the manner in which Ermine Street cuts through the possibly pre-existing edge of Empingham's territory and that of its adjacent and possibly once dependent neighbours (see fig. 4).[30] On the periphery of Rutland there are two further indications which fit so well with a whole series of similar coincidences in the midland region generally that they are unlikely to have been accidental.

It is a remarkable fact that in a number of cases, at the point where Roman roads cross ancient administrative boundaries, there are to be found planted Roman settlements some of which may well have contained markets (see fig. 6). Where the Fosse Way cuts across the probable line of the principality of the *Hwicce* in Warwickshire lies a Roman settlement at Chesterton.[31] Where all but one of the probable Roman roads radiating outwards from Leicester cleave through the county boundary are similar settlements: at Mancetter, High Cross, Caves Inn, Medbourne; and to the north, Willoughby-on-the-Wolds - once a Celtic shrine.[32] In Lincolnshire, Lincoln itself is sited at the point where Ermine Street cuts the boundary of the ancient kingdom or sub-kingdom of Lindsey. In the case of Rutland, where a branch of the Ermine Street runs across the district boundary, there was situated a Roman settlement at Thistleton near what appears to have been a re-used boundary shrine on the frontier of the *Coritani* and the *Catuvellauni* (Lewis 1966: 84, 93-4). Finally, in view of the probability that Stamford was carved out of the territory of Great and Little Casterton, it looks very much as though the substantial Roman town of Great Casterton occupied a similar situation commanding the southern boundary of Rutland (see fig. 4).[33] It may be suggested, therefore, that unless we are to assume, most improbably, that all these major boundaries were later deliberately drawn to include the areas surrounding the ruined remains of important Roman sites, it is more likely than not that the boundaries in question were of very much greater antiquity. In other words the Romans, perhaps strategically, planted these settlements on pre-existing frontiers - whether major or minor. Since Rutland fits so neatly into this wider midland pattern, it could well be that the origins of the district should be sought, not in the administrative reorganizations of the tenth century, but over a millennium earlier.[34]

ACKNOWLEDGMENTS

I would like to thank Dr Barrie Cox for allowing me to quote so freely from his thesis, and Margery Tranter for both drawing the maps and many helpful comments.

NOTES

1. It must be emphasized that boundaries are used below only to indicate the approximate situation of ancient divisions. In well-wooded or sparsely populated areas, it is clear enough that in early times districts were probably divided from each other by broad strips of no-man's land or inter-commonable territory.
2. For the possibility of an earlier wapentake system in Northamptonshire, see Chadwick 1963: 199-200.
3. Two recent discussions of the ploughland restrict its enumeration to 1086: Moore 1964: 124; and Harvey 1975: 187-9.
4. The relevant figures are supplied in Darby 1954 and succeeding volumes.

Plough teams and ploughlands
County percentages of entries (which may be so tested) where teams are more than, equal to, or less than ploughlands.

	Excess	*Equal*	*Deficient*
Cambridgeshire	2	69	29
Northamptonshire	12	50	38
Warwickshire	24	28	48
Leicestershire	26	23	51
Rutland: Witchley	24	24	52
Staffordshire	22	22	56
Huntingdonshire	20	17	63
Lincolnshire	42	16	42
Rutland: Alstoe	57	21½	21½
Nottinghamshire	73	15	12
Derbyshire	71	13	16

5. The exceptions comprise those royal estates from which demesne ploughs appear to have been omitted. These entries are, however, included in the table above.
6. Burley and Alesthorp, which together (2 + 1 carucates) comprised a three-carucate unit within the continuous surrounding boundary of the same parish.
7. Cottesmore is credited with 12 ploughlands but 24 ploughs. It may be added that Martinsley has been omitted from this discussion because of its manifestly artificial assessment which reflected its specially privileged status.
8. A close inspection of the Rutland Domesday evidence suggests that both hides and carucates had possibly been calculated on the basis of a surviving framework of earlier estates, from ploughlands arranged in slightly rounded regular groups.
9. For the policing and judicial functions of the Lincolnshire hundreds see Stenton 1924: xv.
10. Domesday is ambiguous in that the catalogue of the king's ancient demesne lands in Witchley do not end with a *separate* paragraph stating that 'Queen Edith held these lands'. Instead, this statement follows on immediately from the entry for Luffenham (wrongly ascribed to *South* Luffenham in Page 1908: 140b) and Sculthorp. Both Stenton (1908: 133) and Round (1902: 273), however, accepted the wider ascription of this phrase, the position of which in the text may be explained by the fact that the Domesday scribe wished to fit it in at the foot of the column in question.
11. William of Cahaignes appears to have been Sheriff of Northamptonshire at this time (Davis 1913: nos. 288b, 383, 476). For Nottinghamshire, see Stenton 1906: 240 n.2a.
12. The hamlet of Bradcroft (Rutland) appears in later times to have been taxed as pertaining to Stamford, from where it lay to the west (Rogers 1965: 49-50). Part of Uffington, Lincolnshire, was taxed in 1086 'as belonging to the manor of Belmesthorpe' (Rutland) (Foster 1924: 176 no. 56, 4). Uffington also appears to have contained the only manor outside Stamford to have been connected with the burgesses (Foster 1924: 127 no. 27, 35).

13. References to Stamford by historians usually imply that its urban character was the outcome of the Danish occupation. But there is no evidence to suggest that it might not have achieved this status before. Indeed, the reference by Æthelweard implies that it was already significant in 894, and unlike Derby, it was not re-named by the Danes. Topography and place-name evidence also suggest that the settlement perhaps migrated eastward from the area nearer to the Ermine Street ford from which, in my view, Stamford probably took its name originally. St Peter's church, which was situated to the west of the medieval borough, might thus mark a logical early step in this eastward development.

14. That it was simply an area of special royal privilege is hardly a rational explanation for this extraordinary arrangement. A positive action or decision deliberately severing *Roteland* from neighbouring 'Lincolnshire' and 'the royal borough' of Stamford is strongly implied.

15. The name Kesteven, with its suffix indicating a Scandinavian meeting place (Ekwall 1929: 36-7), certainly implies that the district might have been a Danish creation, but there is nothing to indicate that O.E. 'Rōta's land' was of similar origin. Stenton's view (1908: 136) that the district might be equated with the wapentakes of Fram*land* and Ave*land* nearby, has been superseded, since in each of these two cases the suffix represents a corruption of O. Scand. *lūndr* or grove. The problem of defining a likely period for the possession of Rutland by the eponymous Rōta remains insoluble. Cox (1971: 646) has pointed out that the name is to be also found in the hybrid Ratby in Leicestershire, so it is not necessarily early. Hart (1973: 127 n.6, 133) has drawn attention to an ealdorman of south-east Mercia called Æthelstan 'Rota' who witnessed charters between 955 and 970, but from at least 964, when Ælfthryth married Edgar, and hence probably from before, Rutland must have been in royal hands.

16. There is perhaps a danger that scholars are reading back too far in time the later evidence for the confederation of the Five Boroughs which is first mentioned only in 942 (Whitelock 1955: 202). The early conflict with Wessex was largely in the hands of the Danes of York and East Anglia, and there is nothing to suggest united action by the armies of the Five Boroughs. On the contrary, the Danes of Leicester, at least, joined forces with those of Northampton on at least two occasions, 913 and 917 (Whitelock 1955: 194, 196).

17. There is no reason to disagree with the usual interpretation that Oakham's five berewicks comprised Longham, Brooke, Egleton and Gunthorpe (Page 1931: 10), though there was an additional connection across the Leicestershire boundary with *soc* land (but not church *soc* land) pertaining to Oakham in Knossington (Page 1907: 309a). The seven berewicks of Hambleton probably comprised Nether Hambleton (a D.M.V. which I identified in 1968, and which is currently being excavated by the Rutland Field Research Group), Braunston, Normanton, Lyndon, Martinsthorpe, Manton and Edith Weston. The connection between Market Overton (anyway separately enumerated under Alstoe in Domesday) and Hambleton is far too late to carry conviction (Page 1931: 68, 141-2). Braunston was a detached chapelry of Hambleton (Page 1931: 36), and a study of its situation on fig. 5 is a further indirect confirmation of the suggestion made below with regard to the probable earlier superiority of the manor of Hambleton over its neighbour Oakham. The boundaries imply that the latter may well have been carved out the greater territory of the former. (In later times, Clipsham and Pickworth, to the east of the district, together comprised a detached portion of Martinsley, but as neither is mentioned in Domesday, it is impossible to allocate them to any one manor in the wapentake.)

The seven berewicks of Ridlington must have been Ayston, Belton, Leighfield, Preston, Uppingham, Wardley and Wing (Page 1931: 92). It may be added that for the reasons suggested on p.75. Belton and Wardley were probably ancient settlements, while Uppingham is clearly an early place-name. If the bounds of Ayston (re-interpreted in n.21 below) are any guide, moreover, it is very likely that the Æthelstan who probably gave it its name, and to whom the already existing *tūn* (Kemble 1846: 784) was granted in 1046, had in fact re-named it. 'Thornham brook', which divided Ayston from Uppingham, can hardly have referred to the latter settlement, so it is distinctly possible that the name 'Ayston' replaced an earlier *hām*.

18. The parts of Barrowden in Domesday were Seaton, Thorpe, Morcott, Bisbrooke, with Glaston and South Luffenham (incorrectly described as North Luffenham in Page 1908: 140). To these should also certainly be added Pilton (Page 1931: 211). If, moreover, the Barrowden complex was of considerable antiquity, then it may once have embraced also North Luffenham and Sculthorp, both of which were held as one separate manor by the king in 1086 (for the situation of Sculthorp, see Brown 1975: 20). The continuous boundary which delimits the eastern parts of the two Luffenhams, and the process of fission implied by their names, would seem to indicate that both had once comprised a single unit.

19. The only sokemen unconnected, on the basis of surviving evidence, with past or present royal manors in 1086 were to be found at Ryhall (four sokemen). At Tolethorpe, there were eight, but the king had the *soc* of the manor. At one manor of Empingham there were 14, but this was within 'the king's *soc* of *Roteland*'. Both Tickencote (with eight) and Horn (one) had once probably formed outliers of the Empingham estate (see n.30 below). The Countess Judith's manor at Glaston also included three sokemen, but this clearly represented a fragmentation of an earlier royal dependency of Barrowden (see p.73 and n.18 above).

20. This suggestion depends on Campbell's rendering of 'pandunt' (above, p.72). Since *Æthelweard* (*passim*) usually employs the verb 'vastare', or its like, when he refers to ravaging, I incline to Campbell's commonsense translation. This also does less violation to the chronology of that chronicle than Stenton's interpretation, because Sigeferth's visitation is clearly dated to the *previous* year, 893. If 'possession' of the area is thus implied, this might well be related back to the famous entry in the Anglo-Saxon Chronicle for 877 which states that 'in the harvest season the army went away into Mercia and shared out some of it, and gave some to Ceolwulf' (Whitelock 1955: 179).

21. Kemble 1846: no. 784. Professor Finberg's interpretation in Hart 1966: 108-9 is clearly wrong. 'Wing ford' can hardly have been on the road between the parishes of Preston and Uppingham, as opposed to a road to Wing. Nor is it likely that a bound went from this ford 'to' what Finberg was then obliged to take as the same stream ('Thornham Brook') as that which the ford had already crossed a mile further up. The slight triangular deviation of the parish boundary to touch the northern edge of castle hill (which took its name from a post-conquest motte and bailey castle), which Finberg takes to be 'Martin's-hoe', finally, bears all the signs of a later adjustment.

    An alternative solution (see fig. 5) which fits the local topography more naturally is as follows. 'Wing ford': (884015) (bound 7) where they only road in the area to Wing (and appropriately enough from Ayston) crosses a brook, to the north of what looks like a later addition to Bisbrooke parish between the confluence of two streams which flow from west to east. 'Thornham Brook' (bound 1): the southerly stream of these two, which still coincides with a small section of the southern boundary of Ayston for a third of a mile south-west of 882008. 'Thursley Brook' (bound 2): having followed Thornham Brook westwards and then the parish boundary, the only possible stream is that which cuts that boundary at 849007. 'Martin's hoe' (bound 3) was thus the point where the boundary crosses the ridge at 844009; 'Holbrook' (bound 4) was probably the dried-out water course, which ran eastwards 15 yards in from, and parallel to, the parish boundary from about 845013; the 'Brock holes (bound 5)

may have been at the still surviving, unploughed kink on the boundary at
845015; and the 'Red Way' (bound 6) was (as in Finberg's version) the lane to
Ridlington starting at 844019, that soon crosses the un-named stream further
down which 'Wing ford' is sited.

22. The church of Belton was granted as it had been held T.R.E. in 1080-7
(Dugdale 1817: 301). Other dedications to St Botolph on ancient boundaries
seem to include Shepshed (near the division between the *Tomsaeten* and the
Middle Angles); Burton Hastings in Warwickshire - again on the early frontier of
Mercia (which I hope to discuss on another occasion); and, near the limits of the
eight hundreds of Oundle, Longthorpe and Helpston.

23. 'The same Albert also has of the king the church of Ocheham and of Hameldun
and of St Peter of Stanford as much as belongs to the same churches in (ad)
Hambleton with the neighbouring lands.' (Page 1908: 140).

24. 'There the King has 2 ploughs (belonging) to the hall and nevertheless there can
be 4 other ploughs' (Page 1908: 139).

25. An analysis of this area is in preparation.

26. St Botolph is known to have dedicated a church to St Martin (Arnold-Forster,
189a: II, 54). In this region, the dedication is usually found in close association
with Roman roads: in Northamptonshire, St Martin's in Stamford Baron on
Ermine Street; and at Welton and Litchborough near the Watling Street; in
Leicestershire, at Leicester itself and, on the road to Mancetter, at Desford,
Peckleton and Stapleton. Clearly such dedications have to be viewed with
caution, but in the case of Rutland, the fact that St Martin appears to have been
associated with topographical features suggests a long-standing connection. The
association was first suggested by Finberg in Hart 1966: 109.

27. Smith (1970: ii, 283) makes the interesting suggestion that the first element of
'Uppingham' might indicate 'a look-out platform', an interpretation which fits
neatly with the similar frontier names discussed on p.75 and the elevated
position of Uppingham on the southern boundary of Martinsley.

28. The *Hwicce* had an ealdorman as late as 997 (Napier and Stevenson 1895: 111-
12).

29. For an up-to-date survey of the archaeological material see Clough 1975 (I am
grateful to Miss Ann Dornier for the opportunity to see this in typescript); for
place-names in *hām* see Cox (1971: 634-5), who also correlates Clipsham,
Greetham and Luffenham with Roman or sub-Roman sites (cf. Cox 1973: 29-
30).

30. Bonney 1972: 168-86. Empingham (7½ hides plus 1 bovate, + 4 hides + 2½
hides) and Horn (2 + 1 hides) and Tickencote (3 hides less 1 bovate) together
comprised a neat 20-hide unit in an area continuously described by the
surrounding boundary. 'Horne field' lay in Hardwick, a dependency of
Empingham (Page 1931: 242). The fragmentation of what here appears
to have been a very ancient estate was early. Horn, or part of it, had been
already granted away to Sempringham before 852 (Hart 1966: 107).

31. The ancient diocesan boundary of Worcester. It may be significant that the
scatter of coinage associated with the *Dobunni* does not extend much further to
the north-east than this point (Ordnance Survey 1967: 30).

32. In the case of Tripontium, the Roman road from Leicester is not certain
(Margary 1967: 217). The Cave's Inn area is nevertheless situated at the junction
of the county boundaries of Leicestershire, Warwickshire and Northamptonshire.
For *nemeton* names see Powell 1959: 138-40.

33. The *territorium* of a town of this size would have been fairly substantial. Great
and Little Casterton were clearly once a single unit and the continuation
southwards of the eastern boundary of the latter into the outskirts of Stamford
indicates a connection of some antiquity (Rogers 1972: 61). In Domesday,
Portland, which quite possibly refers to the territory of Stamford that protrudes
north-westwards on the other side of the Ermine Street, is entered immediately
after Casterton (Page 1931: 141a).

34. For the scatter of pre-historic artifacts see Brown 1975: *passim*.

REFERENCES

Note T.R.E. = Temporis Regis Edwardi

Arnold-Forster, F., 1899. *Studies in Church Dedications, or England's Patron Saints*.

Beresford, M.W., and Hurst, J., 1971. *Deserted Medieval Villages*.

Bonney, D., 1972. 'Early boundaries in Wessex', in *Archaeology and the Landscape*, ed. P.J.Fowler, 168-186.

Brown, A.E., 1975. *Archaeological Sites and Finds in Rutland: A Preliminary List* (University of Leicester: Department of Adult Education).

Cam, H., 1963. 'Early groups of Hundreds', *Liberties and Communities in Medieval England*, 91-106.

Campbell, A.(ed.), 1962. *The Chronicle of Æthelweard*.

Chadwick, H.M., 1963. *Studies on Anglo-Saxon Institutions* (New York).

Clough, T. McK., 1975. 'Rutland', in *A Guide to the Anglo-Saxon and Viking Antiquities of Leicestershire including Rutland*, by T. McK. Clough, Ann Dornier, R.A. Rutland (Leicester Museums publication).

Cox, B., 1971. 'The place-names of Leicestershire and Rutland' (Ph.D. thesis, University of Nottingham).

Cox, B. 1973.'The significance of the distribution of English place-names in *Hām* in the Midlands and East Anglia', *Journal of the English Place Name Society, 5:* 15-78.

Darby, H.C. (ed.), 1954 and subsequently. *The Domesday Geography of England*.

Davis, H.W.C., 1913. *Regesta Regum Anglo-Normannorum 1066-1154*.

Dugdale, W., 1817. *Monasticon Anglicanum: A New Edition Enriched ...* by J. Caley, H.Ellis, and B. Bandinal, vol.I.

Ekwall, E., 1929. 'Etymological notes', *Studia Neophilologica, 2:* 36-7.

Ekwall, E., 1960. *The Concise Oxford Dictionary of English Place-Names*. (4th edn).

Foster, C.W. and Langley, T. (eds.). 1924. *The Lincolnshire Domesday and the Lindsey Survey* (Lincoln Record Society).

Gaimar, G., 1889. *Lestorie des Engles solum Translacion Maistre Geffrei Gaimar*, ed. T.D. Hardy,(Rolls Series)

Harmer, F.E. 1952. *Anglo-Saxon Writs*.

Hart, C.R., 1966. *The Early Charters of Eastern England*.

Hart, C.R., 1970. *The Hidation of Northamptonshire*.

Hart, C.R., 1971. 'The Tribal Hidage', *Trans. Royal. Hist. Soc.*, 5th ser. 21: 133-57.

Hart, C.R., 1973. 'Athelstan 'Half King' and his family', *Anglo-Saxon England, 2:* 115-44.

Harvey, S., 1975. 'Domesday Book and Anglo-Norman governance', *Trans. Royal Hist.Soc.*, 5th ser., *25:* 175-93.

Kemble, J.M.(ed.), 1846. *Codex Diplomaticus Aevi Saxonici*.

Lewis, M.J.T., 1966. *Temples in Roman Britain*.

Maitland, F.W., 1960. *Domesday Book and Beyond* (paperback edn).

Margary, I.D., 1967. *Roman Roads in Britain*.

McKinley, R.A., 1969. 'The forests of Leicestershire', in *V.C.H. Leicestershire* II: 265-70.

Moore, J.S., 1964. 'The Domesday teamland: a reconsideration', *Trans. Royal Hist. Soc.*, 5th ser., *14:* 109-30.

Napier, A.S., and Stevenson, W.H. (eds.), 1895. *The Crawford Collection of Early Charters and Documents now in the Bodleian Library*.

Ordnance Survey, 1967. *Map of Southern Britain in the Iron Age*.

Page, W. (ed.), 1907. *V.C.H. Leicestershire* I.

Page, W. (ed.), 1908. *V.C.H. Rutland* I.

Page, W. (ed.), 1931. *V.C.H. Rutland* II.

Powell, T.D., 1959. *The Celts*.

Ramsay, J.M. 1908. 'Political history to 1625', in *V.C.H. Rutland* I: 165-84.
Record Commission, 1802. *Taxatio Ecclesiastica Angliae et Walliae Auctoritate P. Nicholai IV c.A.D. 1291.*
Robertson, A.J., 1956. *Anglo-Saxon Charters.*
Rogers, A., 1965. 'Medieval Stamford', in *The Making of Stamford,* ed. A. Rogers, 34-57.
Rogers, A., 1972. 'Parish boundaries and urban history', *J. Brit. Archaeol. Ass., 35:* 56-63.
Round, H.R., 1900. 'Domesday Survey', in *V.C.H. Hampshire* I.
Round, H.R., 1902. 'Domesday Survey', in *V.C.H. Northamptonshire* I.
Sawyer, P.H., 1971. *The Age of the Vikings.*
Smith, A.H., 1965. *The Place-Names of Gloucestershire, IV.* (English Place-Name Society).
Smith, A.H., 1970. *English Place-Name Elements* (English Place-Name Society).
Stenton, F.M.H., 1905. 'Domesday Survey' , *V.C.H. Derbyshire* I: 293-355.
Stenton, F.M.H., 1906. 'Domesday Survey', *V.C.H. Nottinghamshire* I: 207-88.
Stenton, F.M.H., 1908. 'Domesday Survey', *V.C.H. Rutland* I: 121-36.
Stenton, F.M.H., 1909. ' Æthelweard's account of the last years of King Alfred's reign', reprinted in *Preparatory to Anglo-Saxon England,* ed. D.M.Stenton, 1970, 8-13.
Stenton, F.M.H., 1924. 'Introduction', in *The Lincolnshire Domesday and the Lindsey Survey,* ed. C.W. Foster and T. Langley (Lincoln Record Society).
Taylor, C.S., 1957. 'The origin of the Mercian shires', in *Gloucestershire Studies,* ed. H.P.R. Finberg, 17-45.
Whitelock, D., 1955. *English Historical Documents c. 500-1042.*

Part Two

Part Two

D. M. METCALF

5   Monetary affairs in Mercia in the time of Æthelbald

After the deaths of Wihtred of Kent and Ine of Wessex, Mercia rose under Æthelbald (716-57) to a dominant position among the Anglo-Saxon peoples south of the Humber, a position which was maintained throughout the reign of Offa (757-96). The coins of Offa, particularly his portrait coins, are justly famous, but it should be appreciated that the great majority of them belong to the last ten years or so of his reign. Before that, he was able to strike coins on only a very limited scale, and only (on the conventional view) in east Kent. The swift expansion of the currency into the Midlands, that is, largely into Mercian territory, late in Offa's reign and under Coenwulf, should not mislead us into supposing that a money economy had previously been unknown there. The monetary 'boom' of the 780s represented a recovery from a recession in the 740s and 750s, and in the middle of Æthelbald's reign the coinage had circulated even further into the Midlands than it did at the end of the century. In the second quarter of the century the coins in use were not silver pennies but silver sceattas, which until c.730-5 had much the same intrinsic value as the later penny, but which suffered rapid debasement in the 740s. Rigold's researches have established that the earliest types of sceattas, from the years c.680-725, belong decisively to east Kent and the Thames estuary (Rigold 1961). The excavations at Southampton have shown equally clearly that certain other types belong to *Hamwih*, and doubtless they were struck there (Blunt 1954; Addyman and Hill 1968). Other varieties are from East Anglia - possibly from a coastal mint such as Ipswich. But what about Mercia? We know from archaeological evidence that sceattas circulated there, but were any struck there, or were they all brought in from the south and the east?

Rigold was the first to establish a serious chronology for the sceattas, and he was able to dismiss out of hand the attribution by earlier students of certain inscribed sceattas to Mercia. Those with a runic inscription reading *Pada* are emphatically not attributable to Peada, prince of the Middle Angles under Penda and king or sub-king of South Mercia under Oswiu. Also it is problematic whether the runic 'porcupines' reading Æthiliræd in boustrophedon can be given, as they are in the *British Museum Catalogue* (Keary 1887), to king Æthelred of Mercia - even though the three known provenances for them, all east Kentish, do not necessarily rule it out.

What has emerged only recently, and following on from Rigold's revisions, is the possibility of attributing a series of types of sceattas to Æthelbald of Mercia (Metcalf 1966a). The evidence for this claim is still tenuous, and it may be helpful to non-numismatists to have the nature of the arguments made clear. There are perhaps eight distinct lines of argument, of which the first two bear on the dating of the coins. One is the hoard-evidence, including grave-finds from Kent, Essex, and Yorkshire, and including also Continental hoards (Rigold 1961, 1966). The other is analysis of the metal contents of the sceattas, which reveals the progressive stages in their declining silver contents, and allows many of the different types to be arranged roughly into a relative chronological order. Third, the provenances of stray finds (and hoards) show the regions to which particular sceatta types or styles belong, although of course coins were often carried from one region to another and one must also come to terms with imitation, which can confuse the distribution-patterns. To decide which coins are imitative involves, fourth, arguments about style, which are best conducted on the evidence of as many specimens as possible, since sceattas were mass-produced objects, and what one is looking for essentially is the stylistic regularity which comes with mass production. Many specimens are needed, also, for a fifth line of argument, namely metrology, since average weights and the distribution-curve around an average are statistical measures. Sixth, and when all these other arguments have been explored, one may begin to speculate on the significance of the pictorial designs chosen for the coins. Seventh, *all* the coin evidence has to be accommodated into a unified view. There are over a hundred varieties of sceattas (Keary 1887; Hill 1953), and room has eventually to be found for all of them. Eighth, any hypothesis to interpret the coins has to be fitted against the historical background. It may merely agree with what is already known, or it may lead to some surprising conclusions; but it has to be tried against the ideas of historians and archaeologists. Of these eight arguments the fourth, concerning style, often seems crucial in the present state of our knowledge, because where there are only two or three specimens extant of a particular variety, the interpretation of their styles is problematic and many of the other arguments are not viable.

Even before the death of Bede, Æthelbald had established some kind of supremacy over the southern English kingdoms. At the height of his political power, two or three mints were striking coins of the same design or related designs (Metcalf and Walker 1967; Metcalf 1972). Æthelbald took control of London probably in 731 or 732, and he seems thereafter to have had one mint in London and another further west, perhaps in south Mercia, i.e. the Oxford region, both striking sceattas with a standing figure of the king as their principal type (see fig. 7). This standing figure is often shown holding two long crosses, and

Figure 7. King Æthelbald of Mercia: the two main styles of 'bird and branch' sceattas, struck c.730-5. Left, the western (South Mercian?) style; right, the eastern, 'London', style. (Composite drawings, enlarged x 3.)

has been misconstrued in the past as a bishop. But he wears a *cynehelm*, the helmet-crown of the Anglo-Saxon kings; and in a related design he holds a falcon (Metcalf 1976b). The absence of an inscription, in contrast with the conspicuous name and royal title on the coins of Offa, has contributed also to an idea that the sceatta coinage was not under royal control. This view seems equally misleading. At *Hamwih* the representation of the Mercian king on the coinage appears to have been judged politically unacceptable, but the same 'bird and branch' reverse design was used: a diplomatic step, perhaps, in the direction of a unified coinage. It was coupled first with a more neutral obverse, consisting of a scutiform design, and subsequently with a so-called 'Wodan' design similar to one favoured in Frisia.

Several Midlands issues of sceattas show a dual distribution pattern. They are found in the region for which they were struck, and also in the emporia of the Wantsum Channel in east Kent, but not much in between. Cross-channel trade was the principal motor of the money economy in the eighth century, and the relatively very large numbers of coins found there show that merchants transacted much business at Channel ports such as Fordwich, Richborough, Reculver - and, of course, London and Southampton. The coins also suggest that, during the second quarter of the eighth century, merchants were travelling inland, for example to and from south Mercia and the Channel ports, or to and from the Cotswolds and the Channel ports. One must suspect that Mercian wool was entering international trade (Finberg 1957). No doubt a range of other commodities was exchanged too.

The idea that before the tenth century or thereabouts coinage was not much used as money in the normal sense, but merely for royal donatives and similar prestige purposes, can be rejected from the evidence of the sceattas themselves. In the various official series, large numbers of dies were cut, and the volume of issue of a substantive type was measured in hundreds of thousands of coins. The output of primary sceattas of Types A and B, which can be estimated more accurately than most because of a higher survival-rate, may be put at 2 to 3 million coins (Metcalf 1965a, 1967). The implications for the history and archaeology of eighth-century Mercia deserve consideration.

The ability of a medieval ruler to strike coinage depended on the availability of bullion. Coinage and money were virtually synonymous in the eighth century, and the size of the currency was limited by the supply of silver. Some of this may have come from silver mining, but it likely that the main supply came from Gaul and the Rhinelands, as a balance of payments surplus in the form of Merovingian or Frisian coins. In England the supply of silver ran out in the second quarter of the eighth century. Stocks dwindled, and, in an attempt to maintain a viable currency, Æthelbald and other rulers debased the coinage metal. They even resorted to expedients such as the addition of tin to whiten what had become a poor, coppery alloy (Metcalf and Walker 1976). Nothing that they could do was effective, and the English currency simply vanished throughout the Midlands, lingering on for a few years, perhaps, in London and the Channel ports. Into this monetary 'vacuum' there penetrated a few early Carolingian coins, which would not have been allowed in more normal times. In Frisia the recession was never so complete. Æthelbald must have been perfectly well aware of the advantages of a flourishing money economy based on trade - for example in the tolls and taxes which it brought into the royal treasury. Offa must have been equally aware of salient political and economic facts that were well within the memory of his advisers, and indeed within the memory of much of the adult population. Had either Æthelbald or Offa been able to foster or re-establish a Mercia currency in the 750s or 760s, one may be sure that they would have done so. In the event, Offa had to wait for the slow revival of commerce in east Kent in the 770s (Metcalf 1966c, 1974a).

There is little evidence for the use of sceattas during Æthelbald's reign in the northern and western parts of Mercian territory. One hesitates to be definite, as new finds are coming to light year by year, and may gradually modify the picture. But they are unlikely to shift the balance much towards the north and north-west. Places such as Tamworth and Lichfield were not - if the pattern of coin finds is at all to be relied on - centres of monetary circulation, even though they were seats of political and ecclesiastical power. Again, there are no sceattas, for example, from Droitwich and its area, in spite of the known importance of the salt workings in the time of Æthelbald. Similarly, no eighth-century coin finds are recorded from the Welsh border or from the line of Wat's Dyke (constructed probably in the time of Æthelbald) or Offa's Dyke (Stenton 1970: 357-63), such as one might perhaps have expected if coinage were in any way linked with defensive disbursements.

Where then are the coins found? There is a thick scattering of sceatta finds in the area below the Chiltern scarp, roughly the frontier zone of Greater Mercia (i.e. including Middle Anglia) (Chevenix-Trench 1973) - with a particular concentration in the immediate vicinity of Dunstable and Houghton Regis, and Totternhoe (see fig. 8). Dunstable seems to have been the main centre for this region until its function was taken over by Bedford in the late ninth or tenth century (Matthews 1962 and 1963: Baker 1970). Presumably the coins are there because the Watling Street route through the Chilterns to St Albans and London intersects the Icknield Way at Dunstable (Cox 1923: 164-6; Stenton 1970: 241-2; Margary 1973: 173-5). Between the crest of the Chilterns and London, by contrast, there are very few finds of sceattas. This may be partly because the area was still under-settled and thickly wooded in the eighth century (Morris 1962). This contrast, incidentally, is repeated for Offa's pence, for a topographical analysis of which the economic and monetary background is likely to have been in many aspects similar to that of two generations earlier. There are more eighth-century coin-finds from Dunstable and its immediate vicinity than from any other place in Greater Mercia. From the time of Offa, but not of Æthelbald, there are also finds from a more southerly route through the Chilterns by way of High Wycombe (Head 1974). Secondly, there are a good many finds from Cambridge and its immediate region - more specifically to the south-west of Cambridge; both sceattas and pennies. They are perhaps marginal to a consideration of Mercian monetary affairs, but again, one wonders whether they might not be seen in the context of a frontier zone between Middle Anglia (through a corridor delimited by the Fens - see fig. 8) and the East Anglian and East Saxon kingdoms. Thirdly, there is a concentration of finds in the area of Oxford, Abingdon, and Dorchester-on-Thames - once again, the southern frontier zone of Mercia, and again, a pattern that is repeated among the early pennies. Fourthly, a clear case of the topographical significance of a find of sceattas is provided by two coins from Winteringham, on the south bank of the Humber near the crossing-point of Ermine Street, or more

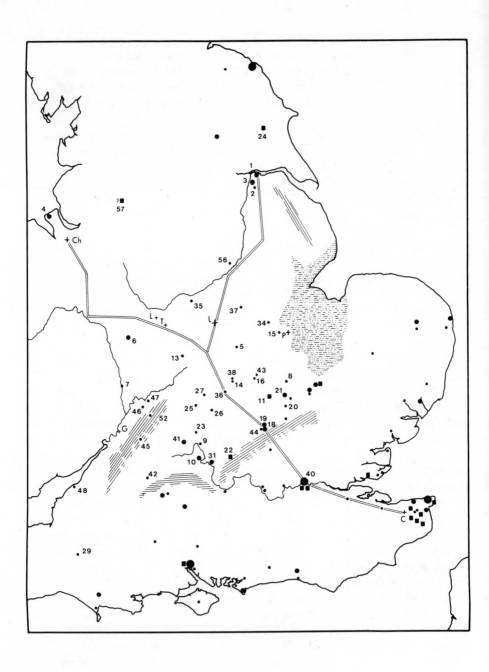

Figure 8. Finds of sceattas in England. The map is intended to show *all* finds of sceattas in England. Finds within or close to Greater Mercia are given the same numbering as in the text.

1	Winteringham
2	Crosby
3	Normanby
4, 33	Meols
5	Dingley
6, 12	Compton
7	Worcester
8	St Neots
9	Binsey
10, 30	Abingdon
11, 17	Bedford
13	Coventry
14	Hunsbury
15	Castor
16	Wollaston
18, 50	Dunstable
19, 32, 53	Houghton Regis
20	Langford
21, 28	Sandy
22	Aston Rowant
23	Tackley
24	Garton-on-the-Wolds
25	Banbury
26	Brackley
27	Chipping Warden
29	Ilchester
31, 39, 51	Dorchester-on-Thames
34	Stamford
35	Breedon-on-the-Hill
36	Eastcote
37	Saxby
38	Northampton
40, 54, 55	London
41, 49	Shakenoak
42	Wootton Bassett
43	Irchester
44	Totternhoe
45	Chedworth
46	Sedgeberrow
47	Badsey
48	Portishead
52	Temple Guiting
56	Southwell
57	Manchester
	Repton (not on map)

•	single finds
●	2 or more separate finds at a locality
⬤	numerous finds
■	hoards or grave finds

exactly of the 'Middle Street' ridgeway a little to the west, into Yorkshire (1). Also in the north-west corner of the old kingdom of Lindsey there are finds from Crosby (2), of a 'plumed bird' sceat, and from Normanby, where one sceat was found in 1970 and another in 1976 (3). The Normanby finds may reflect another routeway, crossing the Trent to pass from Greater Mercia into Northumbria; and all five may be in some sense 'frontier finds' analogous with those from the Dunstable area. There is a Northumbrian sceat from Caistor in Lincolnshire, which is however a little later in date, and falls outside the scope of this survey.

Finally, very late in the sceatta series, in the 740s or 750s, there is a group of finds from Hwiccian territory, again with the standing figure of Æthelbald as their design (Metcalf 1976b). Apart from these groupings, there are scattered finds mostly in the eastern parts of Greater Mercia, to which no topographical significance can at present be attached.

There are eighth-century parallels for the concentration of coinage at the frontiers of a realm - for example Dorestad, as a point of entry into the Carolingian kingdom, was an emporium with an extremely active mint, where merchants bringing in foreign silver coinage were undoubtedly required to have it converted into the official Carolingian currency (Hess 1962). A similar requirement helps to explain the importance of the Canterbury mint in this country over many centuries. It is too soon to say how closely, if at all, these analogies might be relevant to the concentrations of coin finds on the eastern, northern, and southern borders of Greater Mercia, but the idea should be borne in mind because it could very much influence one's assessment of Mercian monetary affairs, one way or another, as new finds come to light.

The earliest silver currency in Mercia, antedating Æthelbald's reign, consisted of 'porcupine' sceattas, together with English and Frisian primary sceattas. We know that great quantities of 'porcupines' were struck in Frisia, while other sub-varieties can be attributed as English, but they are all extraordinarily difficult to date (Metcalf 1966b), and there are many examples, not in standard and therefore recognizable styles, whose place of origin is still conjectural. These unfortunately include most of the Mercian finds. We do know, however, that the 'porcupines' are mostly of good silver (Metcalf and Hamblin 1968). The regular English varieties (see fig. 9) are exceptionally pure - 97-8 per cent silver - and they are presumably contemporary with Rigold's 'primary series' A and B and with the best of the runic coins. These three groups all belong to east Kent, London, and Essex, where grave-finds suggest that 'porcupines' were largely excluded from the currency. 'Porcupines' seem, nevertheless, to have been a widely-accepted coinage elsewhere in England in the decades around 700. Finds are scattered throughout Wessex and Northumbria as well as Mercia, and they reach surprisingly far west in comparison with Æthelbald's coins. Two separate finds from Meols on the Wirral peninsula (4), both imitative, point to the use of money in coastal trade in the Irish Sea (Bu'Lock 1960). One which seems to be Frisian was found before 1712 in a woad-ground at Dingley, Northants. (5). There are other examples from Compton, Staffs.(6); from Worcester, the Hwiccian bishop's seat (7); and from St Neots priory (8). The Crosby (Scunthorpe) find has been mentioned above. Further to the south and east, 'porcupines' have been found in Binsey (near Oxford) (9) and at or near Abingdon (10); and a group of three obtained in Bedford is presumably a local find (11).

Figure 9. 'Porcupine' sceattas, of the 'VOIC' and 'plumed bird' varieties.

Figure 10. The primary series of sceattas, Types A and B.

Figure 11. Type BIIIB and *BMC* Type 37.

When there are so many 'porcupines' from Mercia, it might be thought that there is a case for reinstating the Æthilræd 'porcupines' as issues of Æthelred of Mercia (674-704). If one were to be found in Mercia, the question might be re-opened.

It is not yet possible to analyse the likely origins of the Mercian 'porcupine' finds in relation to their provenances. Presumably many of them were imported into the region. That is certainly true of the roughly contemporary Primary A and B (see fig. 10) and related runic (R1 and R3) sceattas, which make up the majority of the early finds from the Chiltern region. They originate variously from Kent, Essex, or Frisia. They seem not to have penetrated as far as the 'porcupine' type, although there is one specimen from Compton, Staffs. (12), and one or possibly two from Coventry (13). One, of Type B, which is however imitative, was found within the ramparts of the iron-age hill fort of Hunsbury, just south of Northampton (14). Others come from Castor, Northants. (15), Wollaston, Northants. (16), Bedford (17), Dunstable (18), Houghton Regis (19), and Langford (20). From Sandy there is an example of Type B, probably imitative (21). The large and important Aston Rowant hoard (Kent 1972; Glendining 1975) of about 300 sceattas (22) contained a high proportion of Frisian coins as well as some English, and has been dated to c.710. It may have been a traveller's hoard, for many of the Frisian coins are of varieties rarely found in England. Another Frisian coin, of *BMC* Type 31, possibly rather later in date, has been found at Tackley (23) in Oxfordshire on the line of Akeman Street.

The numerous finds of sceattas of good silver contents cover quite a long period, say, 30 or 40 years. Even so, they suggest that there was an abundance of coinage widely distributed through Mercia in the reigns of Æthelred, Coenred, and Ceolred. The coins from the succeeding period of 20 or 30 years are, in total, about as numerous, but they can be assigned to four or five short phases on the basis of their silver contents, and thus there are fewer in each group. The alloy declined progressively from over 90 per cent to under 20 per cent silver.

The earliest coins for which a Mercian attribution is now proposed (see fig. 11) were introduced probably a few years after the deposit of the Aston Rowant hoard, and copied the design of the Kentish Primary series B. They are designated BIII B. Unlike the Kentish BI coins, which are heavily concentrated in east Kent, BIII B is scattered in a wide arc through the Midlands and beyond. It was originally suggested that this was the result of coastwise diffusion from east Kent (Rigold 1961), but too many of them are inland finds for their distribution to be interpreted in that way. Rather, their origin was in Mercia, and from there they were carried to the coast (Metcalf 1966a). The same argument applies to *BMC* Type 37, the style of which (fig. 5) indicates that it is from the same mint as BIII B. It is no doubt a little later in date, and reflects the mint's branching out into using its own designs. A scarce type also from the BIII B mint, apparently, is *BMC* Type 60 (Metcalf 1966a); but a die-similarity with BIII C has been pointed out (Rigold 1961), which would make Type 60 late rather than early in relation to BIII B, and possibly derivative. The combined list of find-spots includes Garton-on-the-Wolds, E. Yorks. (24), Winteringham, Banbury (25), Brackley (26), Chipping Warden (27), Sandy (28), Ilchester, Somerset (29), and (recently) Repton (B III B). At least two of these are contemporary counterfeits, with base metal cores.

The 'bird and branch' coins (fig. 7) have been dated to shortly after Æthelbald took control of London, i.e. after 731/2. There are two distinct styles, one eastern and one western, and the available coins in the western style (see fig. 12) are slightly heavier and more accurately adjusted in weight. It is this combination of stylistic and metrological evidence which affords the main grounds for the interpretation of the coins. Finds from Abingdon (30) and Dorchester-on-Thames (31) are the evidence for recognizing one of the two styles as south Mercian. Among finds in the 'London' style is one from Houghton Regis (32). In the 'south Mercian' style there is a unique 'bird and branch' coin, Type 63, with a bust as its obverse type and the tantalizing but so far unexplained inscription ARIP (Hill 1953). Roughly contemporary with this phase of the Mercian currency is a coin of *BMC* Type 7 from Meols (33). Of a similar date there are two finds of *BMC* Type 9 (a 'porcupine' derivative inscribed +LEL) from Stamford, Lincs. (34) and from the hill-fort monastery site of Breedon, Leicestershire (35). These two Mercian finds are the only English provenances so far recorded for Type 9. A basically similar coin inscribed MONITASCORVM comes from Eastcote, Northants. (36). A coin of quite another variety, *BMC* Type 41a, is reported from a cemetery at Saxby, Leics. (37), and one of Type 3a (imitative) from excavations in the castle area, Northampton (38). Type 35, an imitative type which mules Type 3a with the 'bird and branch' design, has been found at Dorchester-on-Thames (39). From London, at a date when it was already under Mercian control, Roach Smith records an imitative coin muling the 'bird and branch' reverse with a Southampton obverse (40).

The same two styles of coinage, again on different weight-standards, can be recognized in a group of related types (see fig. 13) which have rather lower silver contents of around 70 down to 50 per cent - *BMC* Types 20, showing the king holding up a bowl or chalice, and 32, 33, and 42, the 'wolf' and 'hound and tree' sceattas (Metcalf and Walker 1967). Their probable date is c.735-40. There are finds from the Shakenoak excavations near Witney (41), and (just beyond the southern frontiers of Mercia) from near Wootton Bassett (42) and at Walbury Camp, an iron age hill-fort on the Hampshire Ridgeway. An alleged find from Oxford rests upon a confusion of the evidence (Metcalf 1976b). Type 20 is recorded from Irchester, Northants. (43). In similar style, there is a unique and remarkable coin recently discovered near Walbury Camp, showing the kneeling figure of a bowman.

At about this date, or possibly a little earlier, the numismatic connexion between *Hamwih* and south Mercia seems to have been interrupted by the intrusion of a typologically unrelated coinage showing two standing figures, with a monster on the reverse, *BMC* Type 41b (see fig. 14). It has a Wessex distribution: Old Sarum, Walbury Camp, and a second find from near Walbury (Metcalf 1976b). An imitiative, 'eastern style' specimen of the same type was found not long ago at Totternhoe (where there is a large hill-fort on the Ridgeway) near Dunstable (44). One wonders whether some of these finds from the vicinity of hill-forts could be connected with territorial disputes between Mercia and Wessex in the 730s (Hogg 1975; Fowler 1971; Hill, forthcoming).

The silver contents of the sceattas fell further still in another group of related types which can, once more, be divided stylistically and on grounds of provenance between more than one mint. *BMC* Types 12-19, which repeat the standing figure of Æthelbald, include a few coins inscribed E LVNDONIA, and these have been

Figure 12. King Æthelbald, on a 'bird and branch' coin found at Dorchester-on-Thames.

Figure 13. *BMC* Types 20, 32 (Shakenoak find), and 42.

Figure 14. *BMC* Type 41b.

found in two hoards from the Thames at London. The most consistent style among these types, however (see fig. 15), making up only a minority of the coins in the Thames hoards, accounts for nearly all the finds of Types 12-19 outside London. They show a strikingly West Country distribution: Chedworth (although not the villa site) (45); Sedgeberrow (46) and Badsey (47), both localities near Evesham; Portishead, on the Bristol Channel near the end of the Wansdyke (48); and two separate finds from the Shakenoak excavations (49) - both of which, incidentally, contain significant amounts of tin, and show a general decline in quality (fig. 15). All these places fall within or close to the territory of the Hwicce, a sub-kingdom annexed to Mercia and under Æthelbald's control (Metcalf 1976a; Metcalf and Walker 1976).

What seems to be the earliest coin in the 'Hwiccian' series is related by its legend to the Badsey find, and is probably by the same hand (see fig. 16). It is a copy of the preceding 'wolf' type. The reverse design is a lateral reversal of the version on which the wolf is shown with legs (e.g. *BMC* 151), rather than as a wolf-headed torc. The obverse carries a legend, which is an unusual feature, and mirror-reversal is the key to its interpretation. The first two letters in front of the face can only be C Y , and the natural interpretation is that they stand for *Cyning*. The third letter, V , may be an N that has lost a down-stroke. The letter behind the head is problematic, but it is very carefully cut. One may guess that it is an illiterate die-cutter's rendering of the cursive m which is regularly used in the later eighth century as the abbreviation for *Merciorum*. The Badsey find (fig. 16, and cf. also fig. 15) copies the inscription, but loses the C; it reproduces the Y and the incomplete m (without lateral reversal), and fills in the middle of the legend with borrowed letters to give a resemblance to the current E LVNDONIA series.

There are very few other Mercian finds attributable to this final phase of the sceatta currency. Those few comprise an East Anglian runic sceat (mature R2) from Dunstable (50), and a similar coin from Normanby (3); a coin of Type 23a var. from Dorchester-on-Thames (51); and a group with 'wolf-whorl' reverses. There are three main 'wolf-whorl' types, and it would seem that they repeat the essentially simple monetary pattern of the 'bird and branch' issues. The whorl reverse, that is to say, is coupled with the standing figure of the king (*BMC* Type 23e); with the scutiform obverse (Type 48); and with a sphinx (the so-called 'female centaur', Type 47) (see fig. 17). The more neutral scutiform type again belongs to Southampton (where it has been found), and the sphinx has been attributed to the East Saxon kingdom (Metcalf 1976b). Type 23e has been found in a grave at Temple Guiting (52) in the Cotswolds. Type 47 is recorded from Houghton Regis (53), and there are two specimens (one in very inferior style) from London (54), from where also there is an imitation of Type 15b (55).

This concludes the survey of sceatta finds from Mercia and its borders. For the sake of completeness one may add that there are sceattas of which the types are not recorded, from a villa site at Southwell, Notts. (56), and, conjecturally, from Long Sutton, Lincs. An alleged hoard from Manchester may have consisted of some other kind of coins, not sceattas (57).

In the 740s the connexion between monetary circulation in Mercia and trade - in this case trade in Cotswold wool - emerges rather clearly. In earlier phases of the sceatta currency there is nothing specific from which to argue, except that the coin finds are concentrated in the eastern and southern frontier zones of the

Figure 15. The London series, in the 'Hwiccian' style. On the right, a late coin, from Shakenoak.

Figure 16. Imitative coin inscribed *Cyn m* (centre), its 'wolf' prototype (left), and the Badsey find, with related inscription (right).

Figure 17. The three 'wolf-whorl' types: Southampton (left), Mercian (centre), and East Saxon (right).

Mercian empire. Overall, it is the evidence of recession and expansion, and of contacts between the Midlands and east Kent, which show that the use of money was primarily a consequence of interregional trade, and not, for example, of military expenditure. From the date when Æthelbald began to strike a Mercian coinage, somewhere about 715-20, a majority of the finds from Mercia belong to a sequence of related types: B III B, Types 60, 37, 63, 23b/d, 20, 32-3, 42, and finally 12-19. Through the later part of this sequence there is evidence which points to two mints, one conjecturally in south Mercia and the other presumably in London. Money was carried from Mercia to London and east Kent, and even across the Channel, and was thought worth imitating. It seems to have been carried from Mercia to *Hamwih* to a much lesser extent. There are still many points at which our knowledge of the Mercian currency is sketchy and uncertain, and what has been set out here should be taken as a working hypothesis, based unfortunately on only a couple of hundred surviving specimens. But it should not be doubted that coinage was issued and circulated under royal control, and in total quantities measured in hundreds of thousands, essentially in connexion with trade.

INVENTORY OF SCEATTAS FOUND IN OR NEAR MERCIA: SOURCES

(1)   Metcalf, Merrick and Hamblin 1968: 21, analyses Sc.1 and Sc.2. Found by
      Mr Henry Brumby in the garden of the late Admiral Dudding, Silver Street,
      Winteringham. Coins now in Scunthorpe Museum. For Romano-British and
      late Roman finds from Admiral Dudding's garden, and for a detailed
      discussion of the topography, see H. Dudley, *Early Days in North-West
      Lincolnshire* (Scunthorpe, 1949), 129 and the map on 130, and also 147ff.
(2)   Picked up during May 1949 on blown sand on the Old Park Farm (Atkinson's
      Warren), Grid Ref. 8792 1303. Dudley, *Early Days,* 234; Metcalf, Merrick
      and Hamblin 1968: 22, analysis Sc. 3.
(3)   *SCBI Mack* 341, 'a London-connected' design with northern associations,
      picked up by a farmer on his land at Normanby in 1970; Glendining, 20 July
      1976, lot 510, an East Anglian sceat of Type R2, published in Metcalf 1976b.
(4)   The coins are illustrated in *Transactions of the Historical Society of
      Lancashire and Cheshire,* 1865-6: 215f., and 1867-8: 113-15. The first, 'in
      excellent preservation', weighed only 7 grains, and was of the general type of
      Numis. Chron., 1966, pl. XV, 10. The second, weighing 17 gr., was a VOIC coin
      ibid., pl. XV, 7, but with an annulet in the central part of the obverse, which
      suggests that it is an imitative production (Metcalf 1966b: 195).
(5)   Morton 1712: 532; Metcalf 1976b.
(6)   Metcalf and Hamblin 1968: O.132. It is not clear from the sale catalogue
      whether this might be the Compton 2 miles w. of Wolverhampton, or
      Compton 5½ miles w. of Stourbridge.
(7)   *SCBI Midlands* 65; also *Transactions of the Worcestershire Archaeological
      Society,* 1968-9: 106-15.
(8)   *Proceedings of the Cambridge Antiquarian Society* 1966: 33-74. I am
      indebted to Mr J. G. Pollard for the information that the coin, now in the
      Fitzwilliam Museum, (CM-13-1965) weighs 1.24 g. and is cf. *SCBI Fitzw.* 238
      (VOIC variety).
(9)   Metcalf and Hamblin 1968: 0.131; Metcalf 1966b: 194 and pl. XVI, 43.
(10) Metcalf 1966b: 194 and pl. XVI, 42.
(11) *Ibid.,* pl. XVI, 31-2 and 37; Metcalf and Hamblin 1968: 37; see also n.16 below.
(12) Ashmolean Museum, 0.96 g. Rigold classification A3.15a.
(13) *SCBI Midlands* 63. I am indebted to Mr A. Davis, the Director of the Coventry
      Museums, for the information that the earliest recorded owner of the coin
      was H. M. Pratt. It was later in the City Guild Museum (which was opened c.
      1914). A (similar) coin shown in the British Museum in 1911, and said to have
      been found in Coventry, could have been this same one. Sutherland 1942: 18.
(14) I am indebted to the finder of the coin for details, and also to Mr W.R.G.
      Moore, of the Northampton Museum, for his help. The coin is closest to BII,3
      but with a pseudo-legend of dots on the reverse, and other features not proper
      to BI. Published in Metcalf 1976b.
(15) Type A. Hill 1949-51.
(16) Type R1x.
(17) Frisian Runic (*BMC* Type 2c). Sutherland 1942: 11 s.v. 'Uncertain'.
(18) Apparently two different coins: (1) R3, with head *left* - see *Numis. Chron.,*
      1852: 94-5. (2) Sotheby 17 Nov. 1913, lot 154 (P.W.P.Carlyon-Britton, ex
      Rashleigh, found 1851, 'portions of extremely degraded bust to right', and
      weighing only 9 gr.
(19) Early R2, or possibly R1z. Rigold 1961. Formerly loaned to Letchworth
      Museum.
(20) Early R2, head left with radial strokes. Sutherland 1942: 11 (but it is not
      certain that this is the Langford in Beds.)
(21) F.Latchmore in *Numis. Chrom.,* 1897: 248; Sotheby 14 March 1898: 172.
(22) Kent 1972. Found in Grove Wood. A further parcel from the hoard has
      subsequently been brought forward by the finders.

(23) Metcalf 1976c.
(24) Rigold 1961.
(25) Metcalf 1965b, 1976c.
(26) A coin in the Northampton Museum, 'probably found at Brackley': *SCBI Midlands* 66. BIII CI, ii in Rigold's classification, i.e. from the same obv. die as a coin in the Cimiez hoard, but a different reverse.
(27) From the Black Grounds, i.e. the old site of the town. *J.Brit.Archaeol. Ass.* 1847: 346, where the coin is described as cf. Ruding, pl. I, 17. This is a coin of the scarce variety BIII C, but the likelihood is that it was taken as a sufficiently close illustration of the more plentiful B III B. Note, however, the find 'probably' from nearby Brackley.
(28) Sotheby 14 March 1898: 174.
(29) Sotheby 19 July 1917: 52.
(30) Metcalf 1972.
(31) *Ibid.*
(32) *Seaby's Coin and Medal Bulletin* 1973: 441. I am indebted to Mr R. Hagen of the Luton Museum for a photograph of this coin.
(33) Hill 1952-4. Analyses show silver contents for Type 7 around 70 per cent.
(34) *SCBI Fitzw.* 248.
(35) I am indebted to Miss Ann Dornier for details of this coin from her excavations.
(36) *British Museum Quarterly* 1952: 54; Hill 1953.
(37) Baldwin Brown, *The Arts in Early England,* vol. III: 109.
(38) I am indebted to Mr John Williams and to Miss Marion Archibald for their help over this coin.
(39) Hill 1953.
(40) Smith 1848-80: pl. XLIV, 7.
(41) Metcalf and Walker 1967.
(42) Metcalf 1976b.
(43) Sotheby 14 March 1898: 172 (not Type 17!).
(44) Metcalf 1974b.
(45) Metcalf 1976a.
(46) *Ibid.*
(47) *Ibid.*
(48) Grinsell 1970; Metcalf 1976a.
(49) Walker 1970; Metcalf 1976a; Metcalf and Walker 1976.
(50) Rashleigh sale cat. Sotheby 21 June 1909: 23. Found 1851. (Cf. n.18.) Rigold 1961. Fineness may have been around 50 per cent - cf. analyses 0.74-6.
(51) Better described as a mule between Types 41 and 15-16. Metcalf 1972: 62, nn 47-8.
(52) Carson 1964.
(53) *Transactions of the East Hertfordshire Archaeological Society,* 1937-9: 232; 1940-4: 154-61.
(54) Smith 1848-80: pl. XLIV, 7, 9.
(55) *Ibid.:* pl. XLIV, 8.
(56) *Transactions of the Thoroton Society,* 1966: 41. I am indebted to Mr Charles Daniels, the excavator, for the advice that the coin was mislaid while out of his keeping, and that its present whereabouts is unfortunately unknown.
(57) Sutherland 1942.

REFERENCES

Note BMC = *British Museum Catalogue*(see below, under Keary)
  SCBI = *Sylloge of Coins of the British Isles*(see below, under British Academy)

Addyman, P.V., and Hill, D.H., 1968., 'Saxon Southampton: a review of the evidence, I', *Proceedings of the Hampshire Field Club*, 25: 61-93.

Baker, D., 1970. 'Excavations in Bedford, 1967', *Bedfordshire Archaeol. J., 5:* 67-100.

Blunt, C.E., 1954. 'Saxon coins from Southampton and Bangor', *Brit. Numis. J., 27:* 256-62.

Bu'Lock, J.D., 1960. 'The Celtic, Saxon, and Scandinavian settlement at Meols in Wirral', *Transactions of the Historical Society of Lancashire and Cheshire, 112:* 1-28.

British Academy: *Sylloge of Coins of the British Isles.* fasc.1, P. Grierson, 1958, *The Fitzwilliam Museum Cambridge, pt. 1;* fasc.17, A.J.H. Gunstone, 1971, *Midlands Museums;* fasc.20, R.P. Mack, 1973, *R.P. Mack Collection.*

Carson, R.A.G., 1964. 'Two interesting site finds', *Brit. Numis. J., 33:* 171.

Chevenix-Trench, J., 1973. 'Coleshill and the settlements of the Chilterns,' *Records of Bucks., 19:* 241-58.

Cox, R.H., 1923. *The Green Roads of England* (2nd edn).

Finberg, H.P.R., 1957. 'Some early Gloucestershire estates', in *Gloucestershire Studies*, 1-16.

Fowler, P.J., 1971. 'Hill-forts, A.D. 400-700', in *The Iron Age and Its Hill-forts*, 203-13.

Glendining 1975. *Auction Catalogue*, 13 March 1975, lots 211-42.

Grinsell, L.V., 1970. 'A sceatta from Portishead, Somerset', *Brit. Numis. J., 39:* 163-4.

Head, J.F., 1974. 'An important early valley route through the Chilterns', *Records of Bucks., 19:* 422-8.

Hess, W., 1962. 'Geldwirtschaft am Mittelrhein in karolingischer Zeit', *Blätter für deutsche Landesgeschichte, 98:* 26-63.

Hill, P.V., 1949-51. 'The "standard" and "London" series of Anglo-Saxon sceattas', *Brit. Numis. J., 26:* 251-79.

Hill, P.V., 1952-4. 'The animal, "Anglo-Merovingian", and miscellaneous series of Anglo-Saxon sceattas', *Brit. Numis. J., 27:* 1-38.

Hill, P.V., 1953. 'Uncatalogued sceattas in the national and other collections', *Numis. Chron., 6th ser., 13:* 92-114.

Hogg, A.H.A., 1975. *Hill-forts of Britain.*

Keary, C.F., 1887. *A Catalogue of English Coins in the British Museum, Anglo-Saxon Series.*

Kent, J.P.C., 1972. 'The Aston Rowant Treasure Trove', *Oxoniensia, 37:* 243-4.

Margary, I.D., 1973. *Roman Roads in Britain* (3rd edn).

Matthews, C.L., 1962. 'Saxon remains on Puddlehill, Dunstable', *Bedfordshire Archaeol. J., 1:* 48-57.

Matthews, C.L., 1963. *Ancient Dunstable.*

Metcalf, D.M., 1965a. 'How large was the Anglo-Saxon currency?' *Economic History Review, 2nd ser., 18:* 475-82.

Metcalf, D.M., 1965b. 'An eighth-century find at Banbury', *Oxoniensia 29/30:* 193-4.

Metcalf, D.M., 1966a. 'A coinage for Mercia under Æthelbald', *Cunobelin, 12:* 26-39.

Metcalf, D.M., 1966b. 'A stylistic analysis of the 'porcupine' sceattas', *Numis. Chron., 7th ser., 6:* 179-205.

Metcalf, D.M., 1966c. 'Artistic borrowing, imitation, and forgery in the eighth century', *Hamburger Beiträge zur Numismatik, 6:* 379-92.

Metcalf, D.M., 1967. 'The prosperity of north-western Europe in the eighth and ninth centuries', *Economic History Review, 2nd ser., 20:* 344-57.

Metcalf, D.M., 1972. 'The "bird and branch" sceattas in the light of a find from Abingdon', *Oxoniensia 37:* 51-65.

Metcalf, D.M., 1974a. 'Monetary expansion and recession: interpreting the distribution-patterns of seventh- and eighth-century coins', in *Coins and the Archaeologist,* ed. J. Casey and R. Reece (British Archaeological Reports, 4), 206-23.

Metcalf, D.M., 1974b 'Sceattas found at the iron-age hill fort of Walbury Camp, Berkshire', *Brit. Numis. J., 44:* 1-12.

Metcalf, D.M., 1976a. 'Sceattas from the territory of the Hwicce', *Numis. Chron., 7th ser., 16:* 64-74.

Metcalf, D.M., 1976b. 'Notes on sceatta finds', *Brit. Numis. J., 46:* (forthcoming).

Metcalf, D.M., and Hamblin, L.K., 1968. 'The composition of some Frisian sceattas', *Jaarbook voor Munt - en Penningkunde, 55:* 28-45.

Metcalf, D.M., Merrick, J.M., and Hamblin, L.K., 1968. *Studies in the Composition of Early Medieval Coins.*

Metcalf, D.M., and Walker, D.R., 1967. 'The "wolf" sceattas', *Brit. Numis. J., 36:* 11-28.

Metcalf, D.M., and Walker, D.R., 1976. 'Tin as a minor constituent in two sceattas from the Shakenoak excavations', *Numis. Chron., 7th ser., 16:* 228-9.

Morris, J., 1962. 'The Anglo-Saxons in Bedfordshire', *Bedfordshire Archaeol. J., 1:* 58-76.

Morton, J., 1712. *The Natural History of Northamptonshire.*

Rigold, S.E.R., 1961. 'The two primary series of sceattas', *Brit. Numis. J., 30:* 6-53.

Rigold, S.E.R., 1966. 'Id., Addenda and corrigenda', *Brit. Numis. J., 35:* 1-6.

Smith, C.R., 1848-80. *Collectanea Antiqua.*

Steane, J., 1974. *The Northamptonshire Landscape.*

Stenton, F.M., 1970. *Preparatory to Anglo-Saxon England.*

Sutherland, C.H.V., 1942. 'Anglo-Saxon sceattas in England: their origin, chronology and distribution, *Numis. Chron., 6th ser., 2:* 42-70.

Walker, D.R., 1970. 'Another early Saxon coin from Shakenoak', *Oxoniensia, 35:* 106-7.

PHILIP RAHTZ

6 The archaeology of West Mercian towns

SCOPE OF PAPER

This paper discusses the archaeological evidence that has been recovered from West
Mercian towns. It makes no claim to be an exhaustive study. Most of the evidence
described is of recent origin, much of it of the last decade. No attempt is made to
relate the archaeological evidence to historical, topographical, numismatic or other
sources, which can only be done by intensive studies of each town; or to the major
dynastic, diocesan and settlement problems discussed at the conference. No such
survey has yet been done for any Mercian town except Worcester (Barker 1970),
though topographical and historical summaries with maps are available in the
Historic Towns Atlas for Hereford and Gloucester (Lobel 1969). Surveys are
currently in progress for Shrewsbury (M. Carver), Stafford (J. Walker), and
Gloucester (C. Heighway); a comprehensive survey of West Midland towns is in
preparation by J. Crickmore for the West Midlands Rescue Archaeology Committee.
Nor have I attempted to list all earlier finds such as coins, pottery, or metal objects.
Although these are archaeological evidence, they are mostly from unstratified
contexts. They would of course be mapped in detailed studies, and are indeed
crucial elements of such surveys as those of Cambridge and Norwich.

   The geographical definition of Mercia is clearly difficult, as the papers in
this volume show. I have restricted my survey to the eight principal towns of
Western Mercia, from Gloucester to Chester. The towns I have examined
are fortunately those which have yielded the best archaeological evidence,
including Hereford and Offa's capital of Tamworth. I have, however, included
all West Mercian towns in fig. 18, which is derived from the O.S. *Map of Britain*

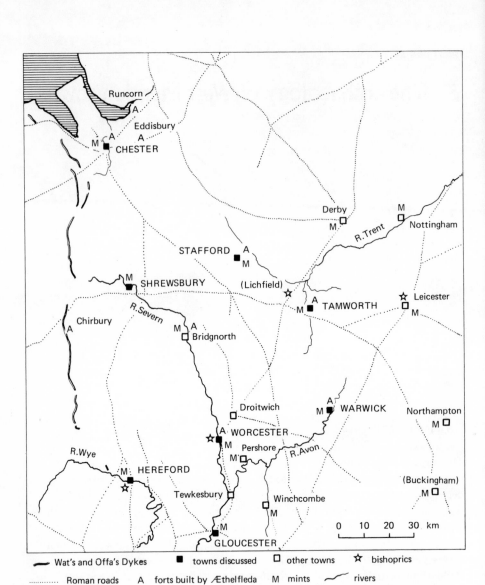

Figure 18. West Mercian towns.

before the Norman Conquest, with symbols indicating some attributes selected by the O.S. I have strayed outside the narrow time limits properly attributable to Mercia and considered all urban evidence from late Roman to the eleventh century.

In the context of this conference I have thought it most useful to try to illustrate the ways in which archaeological evidence can illustrate different aspects of *urbanism.* I have not therefore embarked on any discussion of the fortresses of Æthelfleda and Edward, except where these coincide with urban nuclei. It seems more appropriate too to consider the evidence under topics, rather than town by town. These topics are really in the nature of an agenda for future work. For most of them, the archaeological material is painfully thin, but discussed under these headings will at least indicate the gaps, and especially the extreme imbalance between evidence for urban institutions, buildings, streets, the economic and social environment in which they flourished - and the defences which encircled them. The latter figure more prominently in the archaeological record both because they have been massive enough to inhibit later destruction and because they have always been especially attractive to archaeologists.

TOPICS CONSIDERED

My topics have been chosen to explore the central problem of urban archaeology: what do we mean by urban in an archaeological sense? Is there such a thing as urban archaeological evidence independently of historical definitions of the town in which it is found? If not, can archaeological evidence help the historian to quantify the extent of urban development or the balance between, say, rural and urban activities? All my topics are, I think, subjects which the historian would consider relevant to urban studies based on written sources. They are as follows:

Roman or other pre-Mercian origins
Pre- or proto-urban features
Defences and the definition of urban status and town size
Street plans
Ecclesiastical buildings or structures in an urban context
Public and private buildings
Domestic features and finds
Industrial or craft activity
The environment and human population
Extra-mural settlements
Relations with extra-mural world - local
                                       - inter-regional
                                       - international
The evidence for most of these can be dismissed in a few words. They are subjects nevertheless to which archaeology has contributed useful material in other places.

ROMAN OR OTHER PRE-MERCIAN ORIGINS

There are Roman urban origins for Gloucester, Worcester and Chester. In none of these can continuity of urbanism or even of occupation be clearly demonstrated. At Worcester deep soil above the Roman ditch in Lichfield Street was remarkably clean (Barker 1970: 18). At Chester, a Roman building seems to have been 'squatted in' in the tenth or eleventh century (Thompson 1969: 13). At Gloucester the evidence now points to continuity. Contrary to earlier interpretations of a thick barren layer between late Roman and late Saxon levels (e.g. Hurst 1972: 67), recent soil analysis by Bridgewater has shown that this layer is disturbed throughout (Hurst 1974: 23). In Heighway's excavations recently completed at Westgate Street, a remarkable sequence has been demonstrated. Very late in the Roman period there was a major reorganization of the town centre. Buildings flanking the north side of the *via principalis* were knocked flat and levelled over; a small wooden hut was built over the debris. A large area was then heavily metalled, sealing shell-gritted pottery, and destroying the water-pipe system. After only slight silting of hollows in this metalling, there were several phases of timber buildings with no pottery in a thick organic layer, which continued until the twelfth century (information from C. Heighway, November 1975). Clearly, however, the former existence of the Roman town, or the continuing existence of the defences, was the major factor in the establishment or restoration of an urban nucleus in these places, even if through a primarily royal or ecclesiastical intermediary status.

Some kind of Roman settlement is indicated archaeologically at Hereford (Shoesmith 1974 and forthcoming), where there are several Roman altars. These and other re-used material may indicate a Roman religious or military focus before the establishment of the town, palace, or bishopric in the seventh or eighth centuries (Lobel 1969, Hereford: 1), or the material may have been brought from nearby Kenchester. A Hereford origin seems probable, as altars are not very suitable building material, and there is also some Roman pottery.

At Stafford, the 1975 excavations demonstrated progressive reclamation of a marshy area in Roman times which may indicate concentrated settlement nearby (information from M. Carver).

Some Roman finds are recorded from most other West Mercian towns, but they do not necessarily indicate anything more than rural settlement, or re-use of Roman material in Saxon contexts. In these cases the towns must be considered as creations *de novo* (but not necessarily in an urban sense) in the seventh or later centuries, for political, ecclesiastical, military, or economic reasons.

PRE- OR PROTO-URBAN FEATURES

Assessment of the reasons for these new foundations or for redevelopment of earlier sites will rely on detailed topographical and historical studies, and it is only rarely that archaeology can produce direct or indirect evidence concerning town origins, such as the 'Germanic' finds in later Roman Winchester which led Biddle to his major hypothesis about its English origins. No such stratified finds of early material yet suggest a similar model for any of the towns we are now considering, though there is early 'Germanic' material from the Kingsholm suburb of Gloucester (Hurst 1975: 290-4).

The only such historical model that may be suggested concerns the origins of Shrewsbury. In this area it may be possible to demonstrate a series of urban or administrative nuclei. The earliest is the Iron Age hill-fort of the Wrekin. *Viriconium* (Wroxeter) represents the new Roman city, and the buildings currently being excavated by Barker may be the latest urban phase of its development, in the fourth century or later: a sub-Roman but by no means a negligible complex. The English settlement of the area is 'late', to judge by the absence of pagan burials in the area.

Its political or administrative nucleus may be the newly-discovered timber halls at
Atcham, north of Wroxeter (St Joseph 1975). Their close similarity to those at
Yeavering and Millfield (Hope-Taylor, forthcoming) may indicate not only a
seventh-century date, but also perhaps Northumbrian associations. Close by the new
site, on the banks of the Severn, is the pre-Conquest church of Atcham which was
dedicated at least as early as 1075 (the date of the baptism of Ordericus Vitalis) to
St Eata, a name known otherwise as that of the abbot of Melrose, later bishop of
Lindisfarne and Hexham (d.686). This may suggest some mission to the area from
the Church of Northumbria.

Shrewsbury may represent the reversion, in this nuclear sequence, to a defensible
hill-top position within a loop of the Severn, a few kilometres from Atcham. Carver
suggests (Carver, forthcoming) that there were originally four settlements here, of
Biforgatam, North Foriet, Rumaldesham and *Altus Vicus* on the high ground where
the castle later stood (fig. 19). In some area as yet unknown, the possible *burh*
defences presumably enclosed part of this area.

It is indeed difficult to demonstrate that any features and finds *are* pre-urban. At
Hereford (Shoesmith forthcoming) there are structures and finds beneath the western
defences which clearly antecede them, but they may be outside some inner circuit
defining a smaller urban nucleus, or inside a wider line which has subsequently
contracted. These are two corn-drying ovens of L-plan. Their walls include two
re-used Roman altars and other stones, some with Roman mortar adhering to them,
though they are packed with clay. The only finds were an iron knife and a little
charcoal and burnt grain. A post-Roman date was also suggested by a radiocarbon
determination centering on 761. The presence of two such structures may indicate
more than rural activity. They may perhaps be associated with the royal or
ecclesiastical nucleus postulated in the cathedral area (cf. Lobel 1969, Hereford).
It may seem fortuitous that they were found beneath the later defences, but recent
analysis by Shoesmith of the sequence in Victoria Street suggested that this is not
the case. They are directly overlaid by a building, bounded on its west side by a very
small ditch and bank which presumably comprise its property boundary. This
subsequently seems to determine the line of the later defences (fig. 20).

Further south, excavations in Berrington Street located further features, which
may be contemporary or may be of the next phase (see below). A metalled surface
was surrounded by a layer of re-used stone with some associated post-holes. There
was a little abraded Roman pot and tile in this level, but fortunately there was also
a coin of Alfred of c.900. Insufficient of the level was available for excavation to
determine whether it had any linear relationship to the later defences.

At Tamworth (Gould 1968, 1969; Sheridan 1973a and b) there are two definable
phases of Saxon banks or ditches. The later one is plausibly identified with the
defences built by Æthelfleda in the early summer of 913. The earlier phase has been
defined at three points in the circuit. At Brewery Lane it was first located as a ditch
c.2m wide and c.1.3m deep, with possible timber features behind it (Gould 1968;
18 and fig. 2). At Lichfield Street it was again found beneath the western gateway of
the *burh* (Gould 1969: 34-5), c.2.6m wide and c.1.6m deep, apparently continuing
through the southern side of the western gateway as later established in the
Æthelfledan circuit. Here there were indications also of possible timber features
behind it, and a series of stake-holes at various angles in the ditch sides. These
Gould thought might have held pointed stakes, or the basis of a thorn barrier. What

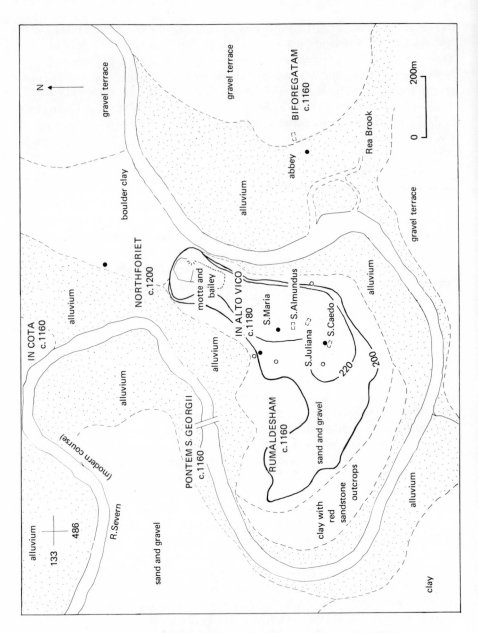

Figure 19. Late Saxon/Early Medieval Shrewsbury *(by courtesy of Martin Carver).*

Figure 20. Hereford: building under western defences *(by courtesy of R. Shoesmith).*

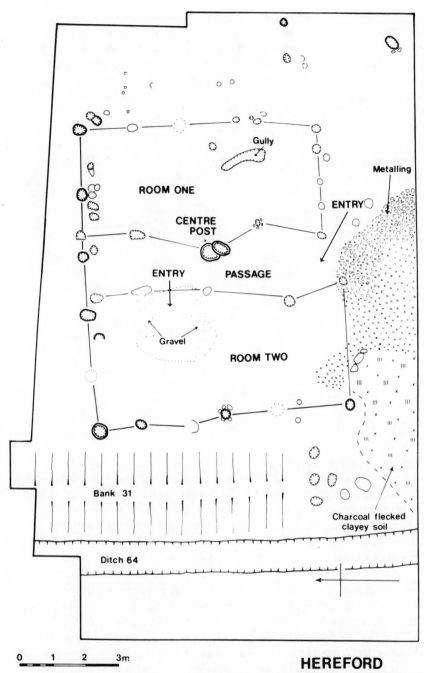

ROOM ONE

Gully

Metalling

CENTRE
POST

ENTRY

ENTRY

PASSAGE

Gravel

ROOM TWO

Bank 31

Charcoal flecked
clayey soil

Ditch 64

| 0 | 1 | 2 | 3m |

○ Posthole: < 10cms. into natural
◔ " " 10 ≤ 20 " " " "
◑ " " 20 ≤ 30 " " " "
✵ " " > 30 " " " "
⊙ " " : Hypothetical

**HEREFORD
VICTORIA STREET**

Period 2

TIMBER BUILDING
POSSIBLE DESIGN

was probably the same feature was recorded by Wainwright in 1960 (Sheridan 1974b: 39 and fig. 1) on the northern side. Some linear feature is thus definable on at least the north and west sides of the later *burh* circuit. While this could be the first definition of an urban nucleus, Gould is inclined to interpret it as an enclosure of the royal palace from which Offa issued two charters in 781; if he is right then it was clearly this palace complex and its defensive boundary which determined the location and extent of the later *burh*.

The possible site of the palace was explored by Young in 1968 (note in *Medieval Archaeol. 13*, 1969: 239). In a complex and difficult waterlogged area he found ditch and timber features. A primary ditch 1.3m wide and 1m deep was silted before a second ditch 5m wide and 2m deep was cut south-east of and parallel to it; the latter was completely silted by the twelfth century. Behind the second ditch to the north-west were numerous timber slots which may represent the strapping at the base of a rampart. In the ditch itself were saplings, and a destruction level of large preserved dressed timbers, preserved wattle-work, and building material: roofing slates, tiles, and painted wall-plaster. There was no associated pottery, but a radiocarbon determination from one of the timbers centred on 409, which may of course be earlier than the felling or construction date. Even so, and allowing for the full limit of statistical deviation, this can hardly be as late as Offa. Either these structures are pre-Offan or he was re-using older timber and perhaps Roman stonework. This is clearly an area which must be given high priority in future work; in particular we would in the present discussion like to know the relationship of these features to Gould's pre-urban circuit, to the postulated tenth-century defences, and to the watermill discussed below.

DEFENCES AND THE DEFINITION OF URBAN STATUS AND TOWN SIZE

The creation of defensive earthworks may be seen as at least offering the security or nucleation in which urban features might be established. Clearly some Mercian forts were more related to past or potential development than others. Hereford or Tamworth can hardly be compared with Chirbury or Eddisbury either in the function of the defences to any existing mercantile or other nuclei, or to the expectation that urban features would develop within them.

Apart from the evidence discussed above, we can only speculate on the existence of proto-urban conditions which may have been associated with royal or ecclesiastical nuclei. It is clear, however, that in all cases where late Saxon urban status can be demonstrated, the fortifications were central in the pattern of subsequent urban development, even if this was delayed for several decades.

The Roman defences were available at Gloucester and Chester, and possibly at Worcester. At Gloucester, where no evidence of *burh* defences has yet been found, the Roman walls of c.1510m may have been utilized with very little alteration, and Hurst believes (1974: 13; 1972: figs. 1,2) that it was within them that the late Saxon town developed, together with its street plan (see also Heighway 1974: 9). This view was not shared by Lobel (1969, Gloucester: 3) who suggests that the later Saxon nucleus lay at least partly outside the Roman defended circuit in the area between them and the Severn, perhaps in the area of the Roman *vicus*. There may have been urban development in both areas; but

Hurst has demonstrated at Berkeley Street that the Roman north-western wall could have survived until the eleventh century, when Berkeley Street was laid across its levelled line, probably at a similar time to that of the establishment of the Norman St Peters Abbey across the north corner of the Roman defences.

At Worcester, the post-Roman town (and indeed the Roman one) remain elusive (Barker 1970). Early post-Roman activity may have been restricted to areas, around the later cathedral, where two burials, possibly of early Christian, pre-English date were recently found (Barker 1974: 146), with radiocarbon determinations centering on 536 and 585. A coin of Phocas (c.609) is said to have been found in the same area under the later Castle Mound (Barker 1970: 39).

There are no datable archaeological finds to locate the area or limits of the *civitas* referred to as early as 690-700 (Clarke and Dyer 1970), the *burh* of 884-901, or Bishop Waerfrith's *haga* of 904. Worcester is assessed at 1200 hides in an addendum to one manuscript of the Burghal Hidage (Hill 1969: 90). The entry for this and Warwick seems to be added later than the main list of Wessex *burhs* (Hill 1969: 92; Brooks 1964: 87-8). The formula which links hidation to the upkeep of the wall, and thus to its length, of 1 man: 1 hide: 4.125ft (1.258m) which has been tested so successfully in Wessex (Hill 1969: 90-1) may not of course apply to Worcester and Warwick. The hidage figure for the former is indeed close to that for the whole shire as later recorded in Domesday Book (1189 hides), and is unique in its correlation with the 12 hundreds of the shire (information from C.C. Dyer).

Barker (1970: 39) did attempt to apply the Wessex formula to Worcester, and showed that the resulting hypothetical defensive circuit of 1650 yds (c.1510m) was intermediate between the Roman wall length and the later medieval one, and might therefore be sought between their respective perimeters. Such a position is indeed appropriate for features seen in the south-east corner of Worcester east of the Cathedral. At Lich Street Barker's ditch (d) (1970; fig. 7) lay outside the Roman ditch and was therefore a candidate for some element of the Saxon defences. In the Sidbury area, Susan Hirst recently recorded data revealed in a large cutting made behind the thirteenth-century wall for a new road scheme. Immediately above Roman extra-mural iron-working debris and buildings were two banks of clay. The earlier was c.5m wide and followed the orientation of Roman features. At an angle to this was a secondary bank sealing eleventh to twelfth century sherds. This new alignment was that of the thirteenth-century wall, the construction trench of which cut through all the bank layers.

Further north in 1971 in the area of King Charles House, Bennett (1973) also found evidence of a pre-1150 bank and ditch, which he thought might be the Saxon defences. Analysis of all the data from these cuttings (Hirst 1976), and further work in the Sidbury area planned for 1976, may suggest a circuit for the *burh* defences.

For Chester, there is no Burghal Hidage figure, but Cheshire is assessed in Domesday at the same figure as the Burghal Hidage figure for Worcester of 1200 hides, and in its entry for Chester reads 'For the repair of the city wall the reeve was wont to call up one man from each hide in the county'; Hill (1969: 92) points out that this sounds like the application of the same formula as that for Wessex in the Burghal Hidage, and that the length thereby calculated of 1650 yds (c.1510m) is not inconsistent with the 'land walls' of Chester in the eleventh century. These Hill estimates at c.1710 yds (c.1560m) (1969: 92, n.32), though the length of the Roman fortress walls are nearer 2000 yds (c.1830m) (see Thompson 1969: fig. 4, incorporating earlier work).

Excavations at Chester, on the line of the western side of these defences in Linenhall Street, have located evidence of a post-Roman re-fortification of the Roman rampart (Thompson 1969). At one point Thompson found a mass of sandstone masonry set in clay, apparently rectangular in plan. This was associated with a length of flat-based ditch cut into the rampart. A little further north were a series of deep square post pits set in a narrow gully. Thompson suggested these represent Æthelfleda's defences, the stone feature a gate-tower on the north side of an entrance, and the pits and gully what he calls the 'standard defensive arrangement' of a palisade. (Similar features had been seen some years ago 160m to the south (*Journal of Roman Studies*, 36, 1946: 138, fig. 12), and interpreted in a similar way, but Thompson (1969: 3) has reasons for discounting this earlier evidence).

Warwick is also included in the Burghal Hidage addendum with the figure of 2404 hides, a figure which is not rounded up to the nearest hundred (Hill 1969: table I and p.92). Klingelhofer (1976) has pointed out that if the Burghal Hidage formula was applied to Warwick on the basis of this figure the resultant circuit of c.3300 yds (c.3020m) would be greater than that of the Warwick hill-top or the greatest expansion of the medieval town (c.2000 yds, c.1830m). He postulates a smaller area for Æthelfleda's *burh* of 914 centred on the junction of Jury, High and Church Streets with a length near to that of Worcester and Chester's proposed 1650 yds (c.1510m). He accordingly suggests that the Burghal Hidage figure is wrong, a scribal error, which does not of course necessarily follow. But his suggestion is given some support by the fact that Warwickshire's Domesday assessment is indeed only slightly different from that for Chester and Worcester, at 1138 hides. The lower figure is also given in the County Hidage figure for Warwickshire of 1200 hides.

Klingelhofer's hypothesis remains to be tested by excavation. The only possible archaeological evidence of a pre-medieval rampart was in fact seen outside his suggested area, just inside the medieval wall in Market Street (Powell 1965). In a restricted area here was seen a layer of spade-cut blocks of clay and turf apparently cut from a marshy area, and similar in appearance to the bank seen in Worcester in November 1975. This lay directly on Roman and Neolithic levels, and was sealed by an early metalling of Market Street which yielded no datable finds.

At Tamworth, the line of the presumed Æthelfledan wall has been sectioned on three sides of the circuit, the fourth being the river Anker where perhaps no defence was needed (Gould 1968, 1969; Sheridan 1973a and b). On the west side the 5m-wide rampart was of turf revetted with clay (Gould 1968: 18-20) and integrated with systematic timbering, reconstructed by Gould as a stepped platform and breastwork, 6m wide (1968: fig.4). Outside this was a berm 6m wide, and then a ditch c.2m wide and 2m deep. The north and east sides were similar, where sectioned by Wainwright (Sheridan 1973b), Sheridan (Sheridan 1973a), and Sherlock (unpublished, photographs in Tamworth Museum), except that no such systematic timbering was seen, and there were additionally many stones incorporated in or on the rampart, which may have been collapsed stone facing; there was also evidence of some timber revetment on the back of the bank

(Sheridan 1973b: fig. 1). A coin of 979 found by Wainwright in primary metalling at the back of the bank (Dolley in Sheridan 1974b: 42-4), sealed by material apparently from the collapsed rampart, is not inconsistent with an Æthelfledan attribution.

Gould also located the western gateway of Tamworth (Gould 1969), where from a forest of post-holes he was able to reconstruct the gateway and the relationship to the rampart he had already found. Further north in Orchard Street, Sheridan located the same line of the western defences, with a possible tower set into its front (note in *Medieval Archaeol. 17*, 1973: 149). The circuit thus defined at Tamworth, and the most complete in this west Mercian series is c.1600 yds (c.1460m).

Hereford (Shoesmith 1974 and forthcoming: Lobel 1969, Hereford) provides the most complex series of defensive works, with at least two pre-Conquest phases above the pre-defensive features discussed above. At each end of the western defences a small gravel rampart was seen in several places. This is later than the source of the radiocarbon determination centering on 761 mentioned above. It could be the western limit of the levels in Berrington Street which yielded a coin of Alfred (above, p.111), which would suggest an eighth-century date; or it might seal them, which would give a *terminus post quem* of c.900. If the latter were the case then this rampart might be that of the *burh* which existed by 914.

There is, however, a major turf and clay rampart on top of this, for which a tenth-century date seems probable on the basis of pottery evidence, and the preferred hypothesis is that this is that of the 914 *burh*, allowing the gravel rampart to be perhaps earlier than the Alfred coin and of eighth-or ninth-century date, conceivably built by Offa after the Battle of Hereford in 760 (cf.Lobel 1969, Hereford: 3).

The turf and clay rampart above this has been seen in cuttings through the western defences and in the south-east corner at the opposite side of the circuit (fig. 21). The rampart was consolidated with a timber revetment at the rear. In the south-east corner of Hereford at Cantilupe Street the whole rampart survived. Originally there was at the front a wall of round posts 1m apart, supporting horizontal members. Before this had rotted, but after it had begun to collapse outwards due to the pressure of the bank, a mortared stone wall 2m thick with a timber breastwork was added to the front, which is the most substantial defensive stone wall yet found in an Anglo-Saxon context. 4m behind this was a smaller stone wall built into the rampart, 75cm thick.

As we have seen this rampart is later than c.900 and in its original form is believed to be of early tenth-century date. A radiocarbon date centering on 615 from the branches is not very helpful in this context. The date of the stone wall is not clear. Earlier hypotheses about the Hereford sequence suggested that the next phase in the defences, a massive gravel rampart derived from a big ditch, was built by Harold Godwinson after the Welsh sacked Hereford in 1055. Recent work has, however, shown that in the south-east corner of the town at least, the gravel rampart was deposited at the same time as the building of the thirteenth-century wall. Here therefore it is possible that the stone wall represents Harold's strengthening of the early tenth-century defences, though the time-gap of a century and a half may seem too great for the survival of the original timber front. The whole sequence is currently being reconsidered by Shoesmith.

Figure 21. Saxon *burh* wall (tenth-eleventh century) at Cantilupe Street, Hereford: medieval wall and construction trench in foreground *(photograph: Derek Evans, Hereford).*

At Shrewsbury the presumed Saxon defences have not yet been located, though on topographical grounds they should be within the area of high ground within a loop of the Severn, as discussed above. Recent excavations have shown that the pre-Conquest levels of Shrewsbury have been virtually swept away by medieval and later development.

At Stafford, the most neglected of the west Mercian towns, there is still no positive evidence of the defences of the *burh* of 913. All the evidence for Stafford is currently being assessed by Jill Walker. She will postulate a circuit of c.1500 yds (c.1370m) based on the inner street plan network and the evidence of an early seventeenth-century map, with later extensions to the south-east, where the 1975 excavations took place (see p. 122 below).

Even though the size and perimeters of most of the town are still uncertain, it is clear that the defences of the four which can reasonably be defined are very similar in size, comparable to Radford's concept for Wessex of an 'Alfredian or immediately post-Alfredian norm,' of a rectangular layout of rather less than 100 acres (40 ha) (Radford 1970: 99; cf. Biddle and Hill 1971). The outline plans in fig. 22 show that this is also true of at least two of the new towns, and of the two Roman forts which were adapted in late Saxon times. They may enable predictions to be made about the extent and shape of the other four towns, the outlines of whose defences are still speculative.

STREET PLANS

The present and earlier street plans have been considered by others in all West Mercian towns. Although they are, strictly speaking, archaeological artifacts, I do not propose to discuss them in this paper. Elements of them have been believed to be of late Saxon date in some cases, e.g. by Klingelhofer for Warwick (1975), Hurst for Gloucester (1974: 13), Barker for Worcester (1970: 39), and Petch and Strickland (1975: 3) and Thompson (1969), for Chester. No streets are so far dated archaeologically, except the possible intervallum roads. That at Tamworth is represented by metalling found by Wainwright in 1960 (Sheridan 1973b), in which he found the coin of 979 (above, p. 117). There are similar metalled areas at the rear of the Hereford defences, which are more likely to be continuous intervallum roads rather than areas of metalling with some other function.

ECCLESIASTICAL BUILDINGS AND STRUCTURES IN AN URBAN CONTEXT

The only possible Saxon church to be excavated within a West Mercian town is that of St Bertelin in Stafford (Oswald c.1960). Timber-slots of a wooden church were found, and a large burnt wooden object, thought to be the remains of a buried cross. A radiocarbon determination from the main body of this wood centred on 1180, but two other samples of loose charcoal which seem also to have been part of the cross yielded two determinations centering on 830 and 845 (*Radiocarbon, 13*, 1971: 152-3). The context and the sampling are both the subject of much confusion. Some of the burials in the area seem to be pre-Conquest, and include possible charcoal burials.

At Hereford (Shoesmith forthcoming) a cemetery has been excavated in the area of Castle Green in the south part of the Saxon circuit. The graves include eight

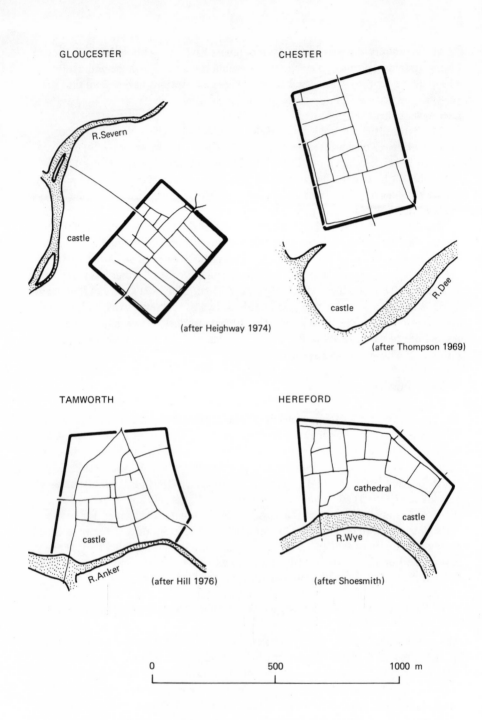

GLOUCESTER

R.Severn

castle

(after Heighway 1974)

CHESTER

R.Dee

castle

(after Thompson 1969)

TAMWORTH

castle

R.Anker

(after Hill 1976)

HEREFORD

cathedral

castle

R.Wye

(after Shoesmith)

0   500   1000 m

Figure 22. West Mercian *burh* defences.

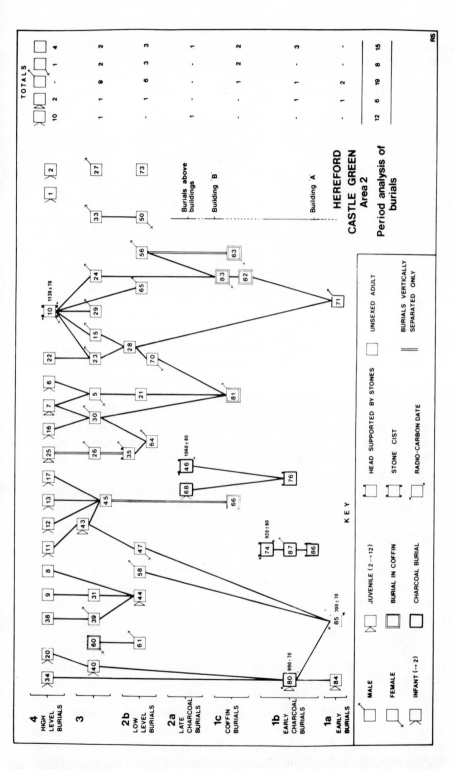

Figure 23. Castle Green, Hereford: grave sequences *(by courtesy of R.Shoesmith).*

charcoal burials, one of which is secondary to a stone building, which may be a church of the seventh or eighth century. Radiocarbon dates for the burials extend from the eighth to the eleventh centuries (fig. 23).

PUBLIC AND PRIVATE BUILDINGS

Apart from the possible Tamworth 'palace' mentioned above, which may in any case be pre-urban, no other public buildings or structures have been identified archaeologically. This is hardly surprising since no large areas have yet been excavated in the central area of any West Mercian town. For the same reason and because of the vastly greater disturbance encountered behind the defences, few buildings of any kind have been located. At Tamworth, Meeson (*Medieval Archaeol. 15,* 1971: 133, and pers. comm.) has located parts of large post-hole and timber-slot buildings of pre-tenth-century date, including a possible sunken-featured building, in a complex sequence, which ends with two phases of a late pre-Conquest bank, which is unrelated to the defences already discussed.

At Hereford the building over the corn-dryers has already been mentioned, which, although re-defensive, may still be urban in some sense. At Berrington Street Shoesmith found parts of timber buildings of two periods, the earlier associated with the coin of Alfred, the later with Chester ware, behind the tail of the probably Æthelfledan rampart. At Stafford (information from M. Carver) the 1975 excavations found an area delineated from marshy levels by a preserved wattle fence. This was earlier than Chester-type pottery. Its relationship to any defensive circuit remains uncertain, though it is probably well outside.

Only at Gloucester have substantial indications of late Saxon buildings and features within the presumed *burh* circuit of the Roman walls been found. Three phases could be defined at Southgate Street (Hurst 1972: 58, figs. 18-19). Buildings had walls of squared vertical and horizontal planks (Hurst 1972: 61), or wattle-revetted turf walls (Hurst 1972: 61), with floors of blue Lias clay and stone hearths; there were also wattle fences and pits. Further extensive domestic buildings and features have recently been found at Westgate Street (information from C. Heighway).

DOMESTIC FEATURES AND FINDS

Other domestic features are as usual more common. Pits, some at least of which are likely to be latrine pits, have been found in several towns as follows: Stafford (3 pits, two with structural features) (inf. M. Carver); Warwick (several, one with a coin of Canute, one with a coin of Edward the Confessor) (*Medieval Archaeol. 13,* 1969: 241; inf. H. Mytum, 1975); Chester (a tenth-century pit) (Petch and Strickland 1975: 6); Shrewsbury (several, including a cess-pit with 18 stake-holes around it, either a fence or a framework for a wooden cover) (*Medieval Archaeol. 17,* 1973: 149); Tamworth (one or two), (inf. R.A. Meeson).

Domestic finds include pottery, which does not however occur in more than very small quantities until the later tenth or eleventh centuries. Uncertainty about the dating of pottery is the main reason why the dating of Mercian urban features is so vague. The wide dating of 'tenth-eleventh century' embraces the possible time-range of a group of fabrics, including Stamford ware and what it is proposed (by M. Carver) to call West Midlands Early Medieval Wares (WMEMW). This comprises

Chester Ware and variants which have been found at Chester (in three separate areas, including the central fortress: Thompson 1969: 13), Hereford, Tamworth, Shrewsbury and Stafford (see below). Other finds include wooden vessels or objects from Tamworth mill (Rahtz and Sheridan 1972) and Gloucester (Hurst 1972: 61); leather from Gloucester (Hurst 1972: 61); bone objects from Hereford (Shoesmith forthcoming), and other finds, which need not be enumerated here.

INDUSTRIAL OR CRAFT ACTIVITY

Industrial or craft activity is one of the key attributes which may be considered in an urban context. The Hereford corn-dryers have already been discussed. Iron-working debris, with slabby limestone possibly used as a flux, is reported from late Saxon pits at Warwick (Haldon 1976). The amount of pottery of the Stafford variant of WMEMW recovered in 1975 (10-20,000 sherds) suggests a ceramic industry in the area. The sherds are believed to be the waste from a mis-firing. It is perhaps in this context that the Tamworth watermill should be discussed (Rahtz and Sheridan 1971). It is dated to the eighth century by four radiocarbon dates and may thus be earlier than anything which could be defined as urban at Tamworth. The mill is of the horizontal type; the structure is of high quality craftsmanship, as are the fittings and millstones (see figs. 24, 25). Of especial interest is the main bearing; this is of a high quality steel (Trent 1975), though no comparative figures are yet available. In the absence of any other data from an English horizontal mill, it is difficult to answer the questions, 'was the mill of exceptional quality, and was it thus likely to be associated with a royal or aristocratic nucleus? Was its output appropriate to the needs of a farm complex, a royal household or retinue, a rural community, or a town? Was it serving the direct needs of any community or was it an instrument of economic wealth and oppression, as mills were in later centuries?' Further research may elucidate some of these problems. Meanwhile we cannot say whether the Tamworth mill was associated with the adjacent area in which Young found such impressive material, or with early urban development in Tamworth.

ENVIRONMENT AND HUMAN POPULATION

Charcoal burials, which elsewhere are characteristic of the late Saxon period (e.g. at Winchester) have also been found in excavations in the last century at St Chads and Abbey Foregate, Shrewsbury (information from M. Carver), and at Stafford and Hereford (above, p. 119) and more recently in Worcester (*Medieval Archaeol. 15*, 1971: 135; this reference does not mention charcoal, but P. Barker tells me the burials include some with charcoal). These graves have provided the only human skeletal material in these towns, apart from a skull found in rubbish deposits in Stafford in 1975 (information from M. Carver).

Animal bones have been found in most of the contexts discussed in this paper, but no analytical comments are as yet available.

Other environmental evidence includes turf, leaves and other organic material from Young's excavation in Tamworth (*Medieval Archaeol. 13*, 1969: 239), cereal grains and impressions from the mill, and mosses (possibly for caulking) from the mill-pool. These were identified as coming from fairly open grassland habitats; one

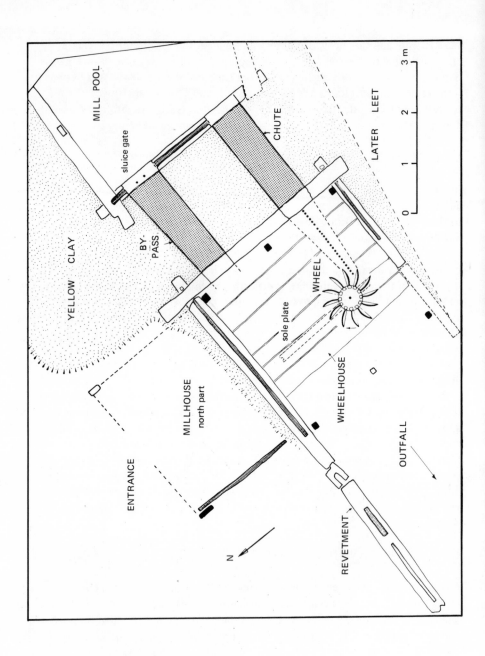

Figure 24. Tamworth Saxon watermill, diagrammatic plan.

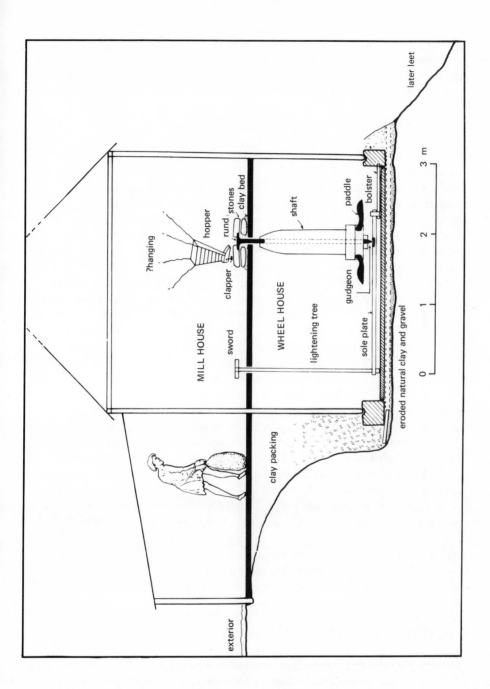

Figure 25. Tamworth Saxon watermill, diagrammatic section N-S.

was associated with areas of over 300m above O.D. and may have come from the Peak District. The stump of an alder tree was found *in situ* in a late Saxon context at Gloucester (Hurst 1972: 58). Work is in progress from organic deposits in Gloucester, Hereford and Stafford.

EXTRA-MURAL SETTLEMENTS

The criterion used above in defining certain features as pre-urban was whether they could be shown to antedate the defences. This is not a conclusive argument as they might be within some other undiscovered urban circuit. Similarly, the same problem arises with extra-mural features; in relation to what walls are they extra-mural? Not only may they be within some larger circuit which has later contracted to leave them outside the gates, but they may in fact be within earlier urban nuclei which did not become the major ones in later years.

With these reservations there are several discoveries of settlement traces outside the defences of West Mercian towns. At Hereford, occupation at least as early as the tenth century was found in 1975 south of the River Wye stratified beneath the Rowe Ditch line of defences, which now seems to be medieval. At the other end of the town, beyond its north-west corner, ditches which seem to be of boundary properties of tenth-century or earlier date were followed by tenth-or eleventh-century buildings which were associated with metal-working. The whole complex was crossed by a massive gravel rampart which represents an extension of the town in the mid-eleventh century or later. At Chester there is evidence in Lower Bridge Street, in recent digging, for ploughing of an area between the fifth and ninth centuries; this is followed by the construction of two timber huts in the late ninth century, and then by two rectangular timber structures with 'very substantial foundations' (Petch and Strickland 1975: 7). In both towns these seem to represent settlement spreading out beyond original defences, in the case of Hereford probably along one of the exit roads.

At Gloucester, at St Oswald's Priory, a western apse has recently been excavated which is secondary to a church, believed to be that built in 909 (Heighway 1975). In another suburb, at Kingsholm, there is sub-Roman occupation and burial on the Roman military site, and late Saxon timber buildings, including a hall, which may be part of the late Saxon palace (Hurst 1975). At Stafford, it is likely that the pottery and other features found in 1975 were part of a south-eastern suburb or industrial area.

RELATIONS WITH EXTRA-MURAL WORLD

Little can be said about relations between town and rural hinterland that is based on archaeological evidence. The corn-dryers at Hereford, it is presumed, were drying cereals of three kinds from areas outside any urban or pre-urban nucleus, perhaps in a context of some urgency, as has been suggested of some late Roman corn-dryers built into villa rooms - to get the grain in before it was stolen. The evidence for ploughing outside Chester may be related to the food-needs of the town. Animal bones may be evidence of local stock-raising, but this could have been done within the urban circuit.

The main evidence for local trading or inter-regional contact will be pottery.

Work is proceeding by Alan Vince and Elaine Morris both to isolate locally-made wares from those foreign to the area, and to define the variants of the WMEMW and assess their production centres. These oxydized fabrics seem to be restricted to West Mercia. From rather further afield, Stamford ware has been found in Tamworth, Warwick, Stafford, Hereford, Shrewsbury and Gloucester, impressive evidence of the spread of this ceramic into the west. Winchester ware has been found at Gloucester (Hurst 1972: 44) and possibly at Hereford.

More distant imports are sherds of probable French origin in what is probably a late tenth-century context at Hereford; and sherds of possibly Carolingian pottery from the Tamworth mill and from Meeson's excavation in the town centre, which are currently being compared with those from *Hamwih* at Southampton. These may complement the evidence of several Niedermendig lava quern stones which were used in the Tamworth mill. Were these the 'black stones' referred to by Charlemagne in his famous letter to Offa? This also refers to the export of cloth from Offa's realm.

CONCLUSION

It has been possible in this paper to find in these towns some archaeological evidence for each of the selected topics, however dubious its interpretation may seem to be. It is remarkable that very little of it would have been available if a conference on Mercia had been held in 1955, or even in 1965. If the present accumulation of data continues we should be able to make statements about the history of Mercian towns by the end of the century which will be as impressive as those for Winchester or York. The data is in the ground. We must ensure either that it stays there for future Mercians, or is recovered when development necessitates the destruction of the levels in which it lies.

ACKNOWLEDGMENTS

I should like to acknowledge the help given by the following who have provided details of unpublished work: M. Carver, J. Crickmore, C. Heighway, D. Hill, S. Hirst, D. Petch, R. Shoesmith, J. Walker, and C. Young. Carver and Shoesmith have also kindly supplied figs. 19, 20, 21 and 23.

REFERENCES

Barker, P. (ed.) 1970. 'The origins of Worcester', *Transactions of the Worcestershire Archaeological Society*, 3rd ser., *2:* 7-116.

Barker, P., and Cubberley, A.L., 1974. 'Two burials under the refectory of Worcester Cathedral', *Medieval Archaeol. 18:* 146-8.

Bennett, J., 1973. 'Interim report on the 1973 Worcester City Wall excavations', *Worcestershire Archaeological Newsletter, 12:* 4-8.

Biddle, M., and Hill, D., 1971. 'Late Saxon planned towns', *Antiq. J., 51:* 70-85.

Brooks, N., 1964. 'The unidentified forts of the Burghal Hidage', *Medieval Archaeol. 8:* 74-90.

Carver, M.O.H., forthcoming. Monograph on Shrewsbury based on his recent work there.

Clarke, H.B., and Dyer, C.C., 1970. 'Anglo-Saxon and Norman Worcester: the documentary evidence', in Barker 1970: 27-33.

Gould, J., 1968. 'First report of the excavations at Tamworth, Staffs., 1967 - the Saxon defences', *Trans. Lichfield and S. Staffordshire Archaeol. and Hist. Soc., 9:* 17-29.

Gould, J., 1969. 'Third report on excavations at Tamworth, Staffs., 1968 - the western entrance to the Saxon borough', *Trans. Lichfield and S. Staffordshire Archaeol. and Hist. Soc., 10:* 32-41.

Haldon, R., 1976. 'The Stables, Castle Lane, Warwick', *W. Midlands Archaeol. News Sheet, 18:* 39.

Heighway, C.M., 1974. *Archaeology in Gloucester* (Gloucester District Council).

Heighway, C.M., 1975. *Gloucester* (CRAAGS Reports from the Region, duplicated MS. 25 September 1975).

Hill, D., 1969. 'The Burghal Hidage: the establishment of a text', *Medieval Archaeol., 13:* 84-92.

Hill, D., forthcoming. *Anglo-Saxon Towns.*

Hirst, S., 1976. 'Worcester City Wall, 1975', *W. Midlands Archaeol. News Sheet, 18:* 53-5.

Hope-Taylor, B., forthcoming. *Excavations at Yeavering* (Dept. of the Environment Research Report, H.M.S.O., forthcoming 1977).

Hurst, H., 1972. 'Excavations at Gloucester 1968-1971, first interim report', *Antiq. J., 52:* 24-69.

Hurst, H., 1974. 'Excavations at Gloucester 1971-1973, second interim report', *Antiq. J., 54:* 8-52.

Hurst, H., 1975. 'Excavations at Gloucester, third interim report, Kingsholm 1966-75, *Antiq. J., 55:* 267-94.

Klingelhofer, E., 1975. 'Evidence of town planning in late Saxon Warwick', *Midland History, 3 no. 1:* 1-10.

Lobel, M.D. (ed.), 1969. *Historic Towns*, vol. I, sections on Hereford and Gloucester.

Oswald, A., c.1960. *The Church of St. Bertelin at Stafford* (City of Birmingham Museum and Art Gallery, undated).

Petch, D.F., and Strickland, T.J., 1975. *The Implications of Redevelopment for Archaeology in Chester* (Grosvenor Museum, Chester, MS).

Powell, B., 1965. Note in *W. Midlands Archaeol. News Sheet, 8:* 9.

Radford, C.A.R., 1970. 'The later pre-Conquest boroughs and their defences', *Medieval Archaeol., 14:* 83-103.

Rahtz, P., and Sheridan, K., 1971. 'Fifth report of excavations at Tamworth, Staffs., 1971 - a Saxon water mill in Bolebridge Street - an interim note', *Trans. Lichfield and S. Staffordshire Archaeol. and Hist. Soc., 13:* 9-16.

Sheridan, K., 1973a. 'Sixth report of excavations at Tamworth, Staffs., 1971 - a section of the Saxon and medieval defences, Albert Road', *Trans. Lichfield and S. Staffordshire Archaeol. and Hist. Soc., 14:* 32-7.

Sheridan, K., 1973b. 'Seventh report of excavations at Tamworth, Staffs. - a section through the northern defences excavated by Dr. F.T. Wainwright in 1960', *Trans. Lichfield and S. Staffordshire Archaeol. and Hist. Soc., 14:* 38-44.

Shoesmith, R., 1974. *The City of Hereford, Archaeology and Development* (WEMRAC, Birmingham) (bibliography to 1974).

Shoesmith, R., forthcoming. *Hereford Excavations* (in preparation as monograph).

St Joseph, J.K., 1975. 'Air reconnaissance: recent results, 39', *Antiquity., 49:* no. 196, 293-5 and pl. xxiii.

Thompson, F.H., 1969. 'Excavations in Linenhall St., Chester 1961-2', *Journal of the Chester and North Wales Archaeological Society, 56:* 1-21.

Trent, E.M., 1975. 'Examination of bearing from Saxon water mill', *Historical Metallurgy, 9. no. 1,* 19-25.

JOHN WILLIAMS

7 The early development of the town of Northampton

Soon after the Norman Conquest Northampton was a town of between 291 and 301 houses and 36 waste plots rendering a farm of £30 10s. (£30.50) (DB 219), a figure which had trebled by the second quarter of the twelfth century (Pipe Roll 31, Henry I). Other sources confirm the impression of a fairly prosperous shire town.

The written evidence for earlier Northampton, however, is comparatively scarce and the picture must be built up from an amalgam of documentary and archaeological sources. For the period up to A.D. 1000 we have to rely almost entirely on archaeological evidence.

The earliest reference to Northampton occurs under the year 913: 'the army from Northampton ... rode out' (ASC). More illuminating, however, is the reference for 917 which states: 'And Earl Thurferth and the holds submitted to him [Edward] and so did all the army which belonged to Northampton as far north as the Welland' (ASC). It has been reasonably argued that this establishes Northampton as the Danish administrative centre for an area stretching as far north as the present boundary of the shire (Ryland III: 1; Hart 1970: 12) This arrangement continued into the Late Saxon period; it is interesting to note that in the time of Æthelred II an Ealdorman named Ælfric bought land in the assembly of all the army at Northampton (CS 1130). The 'heres gemote' must be seen as the continuation of a Danish legal or administrative system.

In 1010 Northampton is referred to as a 'port' (ASC), testifying to its position as a market centre. By this time Northampton was also a mint. Blunt and Dolley (1971) established that coins were minted at Northampton from the reign of Eadwig; they did not, however, deny earlier minting, noting rather the substantial areas in eastern and central England for which no mint signed coins of

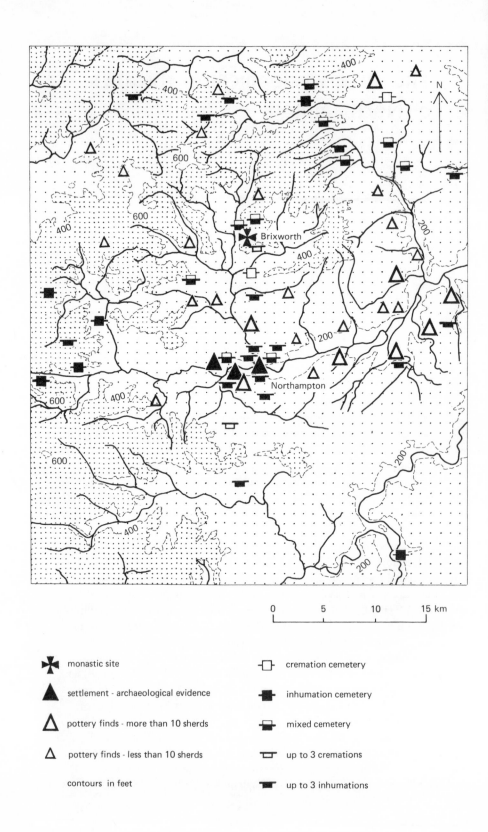

monastic site

settlement - archaeological evidence

pottery finds - more than 10 sherds

pottery finds - less than 10 sherds

contours in feet

cremation cemetery

inhumation cemetery

mixed cemetery

up to 3 cremations

up to 3 inhumations

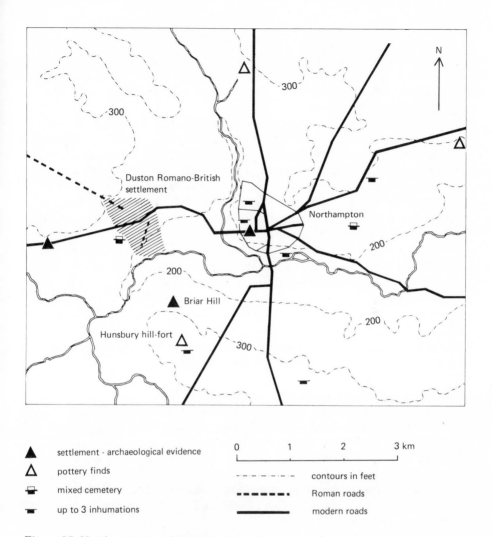

Legend:

▲ settlement - archaeological evidence

△ pottery finds

⬒ mixed cemetery

▬ up to 3 inhumations

0   1   2   3 km

contours in feet

Roman roads

modern roads

Figure 27. Northampton and its environs.

Figure 26. Distribution of Early and Middle Saxon material in the Upper Nene basin. (This figure is based on information collected from Meaney 1964; 'Archaeology in Northamptonshire in 19...', in *Bulletin of the Northamptonshire Federation of Archaeological Societies, 1-8,* 1960-73, and *Northamptonshire Archaeol., 9-10,* 1974-5; Jackson, Harding and Myres 1969; unpublished information from Messrs A.E.Brown, P.Everson, D.Hall, R.Moore and P.Woods; Ordnance Survey record cards; and the results of fieldwork and excavations by Northampton Development Corporation staff.)

Æthelstan are known.

Such is the documentary evidence. The archaeological evidence is discussed in two parts: first, the consideration of Northampton as the continuing focal point of its region over a long period of time stretching back into the prehistoric era, and second, the examination of Saxon levels in excavations recently conducted within the medieval town of Northampton.

Northampton is a natural centre of communications (figs. 26 and 27). Firstly, the river Nene gives access to the heart of the Midlands from the east coast and it is probable that early settlers arriving from the Continent penetrated inland up the river. Secondly, it is a natural crossing place of the Nene for north-south routes. Grimes argued that the Jurassic Way, a prehistoric trackway from the South-West to Lincolnshire, crossed the Nene at Northampton (1951: 149). Indeed, the obstacle which the Nene provided and the importance, therefore, of the control of the crossing is well demonstrated by the recent problems of traffic congestion on South Bridge across which all north-south traffic through Northampton is funneled. The Iron Age hill fort at Hunsbury, in a strong tactical position south of the river, commanded both north-south and east-west routes. About half a mile north of Hunsbury a causewayed camp is currently being excavated. Dating to between the fourth and second millennia B.C., it has similar advantages of position, but the significance of this is debatable since our understanding of the function of such sites is at the present time so minimal. It should be noted, however, that there is an extremely dense flint scatter immediately across the Nene to the north at Duston.

It was at Duston again that a settlement grew up in Roman times, quite possibly from an initial military origin. The site, probably some 20 acres in area, was extensively quarried for ironstone in the last century but recent excavations in a much disturbed area suggest a fairly open but regulated settlement positioned at the junction of roads arriving from Towcester, *Bannaventa* and Irchester. Although it is on the north side of the river, Duston again controlled the river crossing and the east-west route. Occupation seems to have continued at least up to the end of the fourth century, to judge from coin evidence and two typically late Roman burials containing prone and decapitated bodies.

The distribution of Early Saxon cemeteries and other find spots is interesting. Admittedly it is equally a plot of ironstone quarrying, school, hospital and road building, but nonetheless with the intensity of development over the last century and the extensive fieldwork by local archaeologists, the pattern emerging cannot be entirely fortuitous. Settlements appear to have been fairly regularly positioned along the spring lines of the river valleys and a particular concentration of sites is noticeable around Northampton. These include two mixed cemeteries and several small groups of inhumation burials. Besides the evidence from Northampton itself, which is discussed later, settlement sites include 4 *Grubenhäuser* on Briar Hill and a large sunken floored dwelling at Upton, the excavated remains at both sites probably being only parts of larger settlements. Several pottery scatters have also been noted.

The concentration of Early Saxon burials around Northampton needs examination. Myres has drawn attention to the apparent grouping of cemeteries around Roman towns, presumably indicating the presence of *laeti* and *foederati* (1969: 74ff.). Cam (1963: 7), following Fox (1923: 242 ff.), admittedly before the present theories of foederate settlement had developed, laid more emphasis on the early Saxon presence at Cambridge as part of the later development of the town. Most interestingly, Biddle has recently argued that the concentration of Early Saxon cemeteries around Winchester, while reflecting initial foederate settlement, also possibly demonstrates that Winchester perhaps contained within its walls in the sixth - seventh centuries the seat of an emergent royal power (1972:237ff.).

If one considers cemetery distribution over the country as a whole, it seems fairly common that Early Saxon cemeteries, whilst to some extent related to Roman settlement, are grouped round many later towns and major settlements of both Roman and non-Roman origin and certainly the distribution of material around Northampton suggests that for some reason it was a focal point in the Early Saxon period. The modern road network radiating out from Northampton, possibly partially in existence by the Early to Middle Saxon period, only emphasizes the position of Northampton as a continuing focus of its region geographically, economically and politically.

Thus Northampton - and here I include sites within a two-mile radius of the present centre, all of which have the same strategic advantages of position though variously tactically disposed - is either a continuous or at least regularly recurring focal point for its region from prehistoric times. The realization of this is most significant in that Northampton has generally been considered as a Midland shire town originating in the late Saxon period.

I turn now to the excavations in the centre of Northampton. As mentioned in the preceding remarks the following statement can only be regarded as provisional as one of the two major sites, Northampton Castle, is currently (1976) still being excavated and the results of the other, St Peter's Street, have not been completely processed prior to definitive publication. The phasings given here for St Peter's Street differ in some respects from those previously published (Williams 1974) and represent the most probable development at our present state of knowledge. Further modification, however, may well be necessary. It should be noted also that later disturbance is not marked on the summary plans which are therefore valid only as positive indicators of the presence of a particular period.

St Peter's Street (see figs. 28 and 29) is situated adjacent to St Peter's Church in the extreme south-west of the medieval town and in the south-west quarter of what Lee (1954) regarded as the original Saxon settlement. In 1973-4 a large area was stripped revealing fine evidence of a medieval double street frontage overlying earlier Saxon remains.

The earliest feature on the site (Phase I) was a ditch (see figs. 30, 31) approximately 4m wide by 1.5m deep, apparently enclosing the area where St Peter's Church now stands. The ditch is at present undated. The close proximity of the ditch and church is most interesting; it must be noted, however, that it was probably completely silted up by the end of the seventh century and, furthermore, Dr John Evans feels that the snail assemblage from the ditch is more likely to be prehistoric than later (in Williams 1977).

A timber building (see figs. 30, 32) of posts set in a continuous slot was constructed over the top of the ditch (Phase II). Further timber buildings of post-hole construction, found to the north of St Peter's Street, were probably also of this period. Great problems, however, were encountered during excavation. No floor levels as such were found and the timber slots and post-holes showed up as

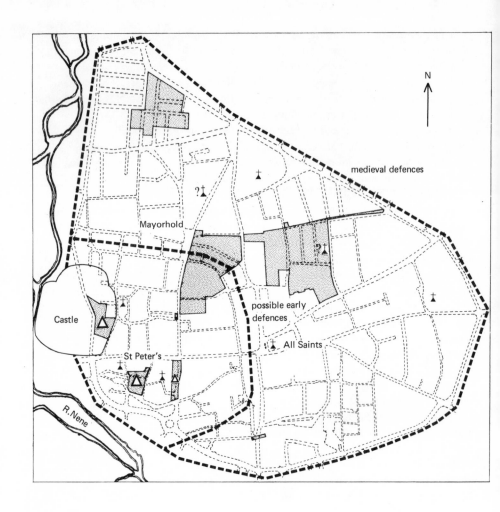

N

medieval defences

Mayorhold

Castle

possible early
defences

St Peter's

All Saints

R.Nene

□ sites excavated or
closely watched

△ pottery finds - more than 50 sherds

△ pottery finds - less than 5 sherds

✝ medieval churches

0   100   200   300   400   500 m

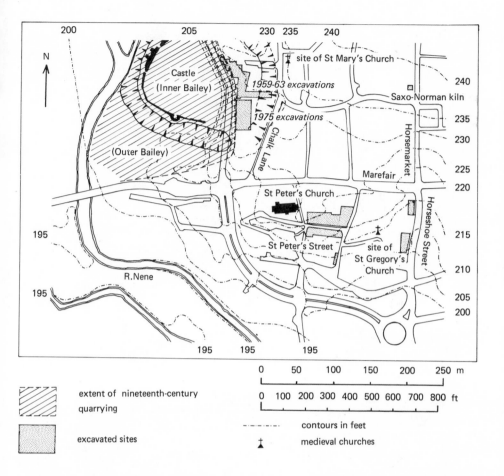

Figure 29. South-west Northampton.

Figure 28. Saxon Northampton in relation to the later town. Areas marked as 'excavated or closely watched' are those where the absence of Early or Middle Saxon material would be significant because of quantity of material recovered.

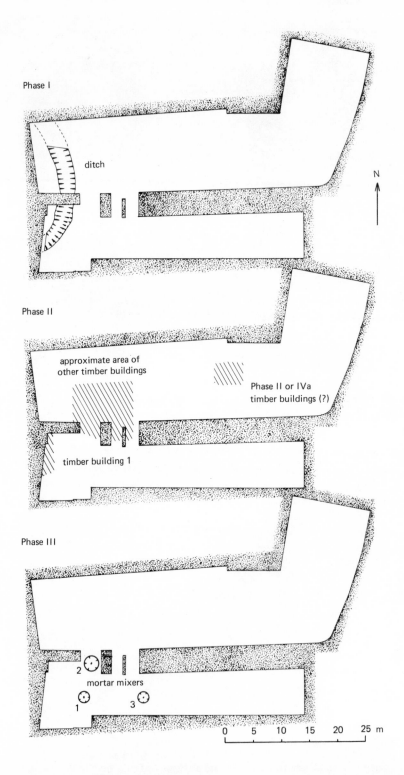

Figure 30. St Peter's Street, Phases I-III.

Figure 31. St Peter's Street: the early ditch *(photograph: Northampton Development Corporation).*

Figure 32. St Peter's Street: Phase II timber building overlying the early ditch with mortar mixer 1 bottom left *(photograph: Northampton Development Corporation).*

extremely subtle changes of texture rather than colour and some features first identified as cutting through the weathered ironstone bedrock may in fact have cut through the silty sands associated with the mortar mixers of Phase III. Finds were comparatively few and consisted in the main of very small sherds of black gritty pottery most characteristic of Early or Middle Saxon wares.

Certainly after the building over the ditch, and possibly others, were no longer in use, three mechanical mortar mixers made their appearance at the west end of the site (see fig. 30). Before discussing their historical significance, it is appropriate to digress and consider certain technological aspects. The mixers were represented by circular solidified masses of mortar. Mixers 1 (fig. 32) and 3 were 2m in diameter while Mixer 2 was approximately 3m across. All three were shallow bowls cut down into the underlying ironstone bedrock, all had a substantial central post-hole and Mixers 1 and 2 had clearly been lined with wattlework; the evidence for wattlework in Mixer 3 was not conclusive. Mixer 1 had a series of concrete and mortar deposits, the aggregate in the concrete being local limestone, but the crucial evidence for reconstruction came from Mixer 3 (figs. 33, 34, 35).

Beneath the limestone and mortar fragments and sand of the 'destruction' layers was a solidified mass of mortar. Running across the centre of the bowl was a ridge cut by the large central post-hole and what appeared to be small square post-holes. Parts of the top layer of mortar were chipped away leaving the post-holes still in position in section. The top layer separated from the underlying mortar as along a plane of cleavage and in the underlying mortar level a series of grooves could be seen cut concentrically around the central post-hole. From the evidence it is clear that wooden paddles of some sort, suspended from a beam, were being rotated round a central axis, presumably to mix mortar. The central ridge was probably formed where the final mix congealed against the stationary paddles and the various layers of concrete and mortar left in the bottom of all the mixers were almost certainly the unused residue from various workings. Tests are being carried out on the composition and other aspects of the mortar.

Finds associated with the mixers again include tiny fragments of black gritty pottery of Early or Middle Saxon date. At the present time it is impossible to be more precise in dating these pottery fabrics than to assign them to the post-Roman pre-Saxo-Norman ceramic horizon. Radiocarbon dates of ad 640±90 - A.D. 670± 95 (HAR-1246) and ad 650± 60 - A.D. 680±65 (HAR-1245) have been obtained from bone associated with the destruction of the mixers.

One possible parallel exists for the mixers, namely Building A at Monkwear-mouth (Cramp 1969: 34ff). Building A was much disturbed by later graves but it seems possible that it was originally circular, in which case it would have been c.3.5m in diameter or slightly larger than the largest of the Northampton examples. Wattlework would appear to have been present round the perimeter and grooves were recorded in the mortar surface which were concentric with the projected circumference of the structure. A stone-packed post-hole underlying the central grave could have been part of the mixer but it is located c.0.25m off centre. Additionally the dating of the Northampton and Monkwearmouth examples seems to tally very closely.

I have argued elsewhere that the presence of the three mixers at Northampton testified to the presence of a stone building large enough to require large quantities of mortar and that in the Middle Saxon period such structures were only erected as a result of royal or religious initiative (Williams 1975: 344). If the corrected radiocarbon dates are true absolute dates and the mixers thus some 100 years earlier than originally thought, and if the Monkwearmouth Building A is accepted as a valid parallel, the case for an early religious presence in Northampton is probably strengthened. The mixers are less than 50m from St Peter's Church and excavations currently in progress (January 1976) only some 10m east of St Peter's Church are uncovering large quantities of mortar similar to that from the mixers and at a consistent point in the stratigraphy. The most likely solution therefore is that there was an early ecclesiastical building on the site where St Peter's Church now stands. Such a presence possibly even suggests royal patronage or at least a gift of land from a royal estate.

Over the top of the mixers was a spread of sand and mortar. Subsequently in the area of the mixers themselves there was apparently no activity for many years but to the north of St Peter's Street there was evidence for at least two phases of activity: a gully possibly associated with post-holes and a series of posts cut through the silted-up gully (see fig. 36). The problems of establishing exactly to which level individual post-holes belong has been discussed already with reference to the earliest features and the same problems are still present with regard to the levels now under discussion. From the evidence recovered it is unclear whether the gully and post-holes are elements of a structure or simply demarcate land divisions. The few small sherds of pottery are still of the same hard hand-made gritty fabric noted previously. Bone collected from the fill of the gully has produced a radiocarbon date of ad 840 ± 80 - A.D.870 ± 85 (HAR-1244). A sceat was found on an associated surface and a silver penny of Berhtwulf (A.D.839-852) can be fairly confidently assigned to the level immediately overlying the gully. (The Berhtwulf penny was unfortunately discovered on the spoil heap but the organization of spoil disposal at the time of excavation was such that the attribution is almost certainly correct.)

The site then underwent a major change with a considerable intensification of activity clearly demonstrated by a dramatic increase in the quantities of artifacts of all types, a change of pottery styles and a sequence of timber buildings of great complexity. The pattern of development is probably not as simple as first envisaged and we are as yet a long way from completely sorting out this period of the site's history.

A major problem concerns the establishment of St Peter's Street as it now exists, a problem aggravated by the circumstances of the excavation. The areas on either side of the street were excavated first with subsequently limited trenching through the street itself. Local erosion of the early street surfaces further complicated matters. Bearing in mind these difficulties, and therefore with the proviso that the following may be modified prior to final publication, the sequence would appear to develop as follows.

In Phase IVb (see fig. 36) at the west end of the site a succession of rectangular timber post-hole buildings were associated with a metalled surface (fig. 37). The buildings to the north of the surface were roughly aligned east-west but various sub-phases to the south changed orientation during the phase. Moving east, rectangular timber buildings were arranged east to west on either side of a metalled surface possibly running parallel to the later street but somewhat to the south (fig. 37). At the east end of the site were four *Grubenhäuser* randomly disposed

Figure 33. St Peter's Street: mortar mixer 3 from north before removal of upper layer of mortar. The east-west ridge, central post-hole and 'paddle holes' can be seen *(photograph: Northampton Development Corporation).*

Figure 34. St Peter's Street: mortar mixer 3 from south after removal of upper layer of mortar apart from section retained along ridge. 'Paddle holes' perfectly aligned with some of the concentric grooves cut into the lower mortar layer are visible *(photograph: Northampton Development Corporation).*

Figure 35. St Peter's Street: mortar mixer 3, close-up of western half of central ridge as in fig. 34. Note the grooves cut by the paddles showing not only in plan but also in the stepped section *(photograph: Northampton Development Corporation).*

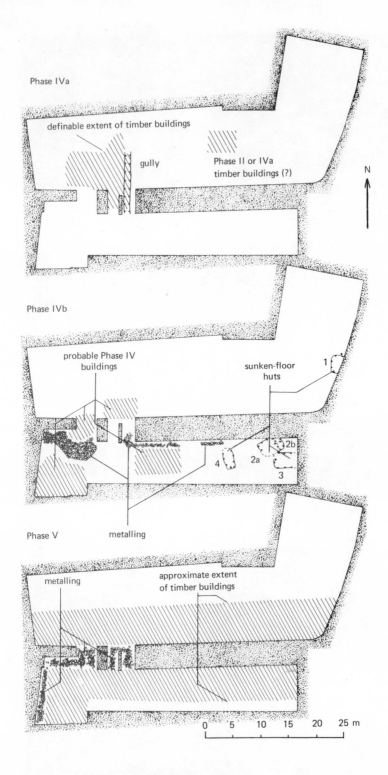

Figure 36. St Peter's Street, Phases IVa-V.

Figure 37. St Peter's Street: Phase IVb (?) timber building overlying mortar mixer 3 (top right). Note the metalled surface in the foreground *(photograph: Northampton Development Corporation).*

Figure 38. *Grubenhäuser* 2 and 3. Note replacement post, left foreground *(photograph: Northampton Development Corporation).*

(fig. 38). If the metalling in the central area is the same as that further west there is possibly an elementary street but a rather irregular one.

Phase V involves the establishing of St Peter's Street as a street along its present line with rectangular timber buildings on either side of it (see fig. 36).

The phase IV and V timber post-hole buildings were all simple rectangular structures with post-holes fairly closely set. The *Grubenhäuser* were rectangular hollows c.4m by 2m with a single internal post-hole placed centrally at each end of the hollow.

The *Grubenhäuser* should probably not be considered in isolation but be seen rather as an integral part of the settlement organization which Addyman (1973:70; 1972), following Radford's earlier ideas (1957), has indicated is common to the whole of the Saxon period both in Britain and the Continent; sunken-floored huts do, however, appear to have been less common in the Late Saxon period (Addyman 1972: 302). Whilst West Stow (West 1969) and North Elmham (Wade-Martins 1969; 1970) show this association most clearly, St Neot's (Addyman 1973) is the most valid parallel, being of similar date to Northampton.

The presence of large quantities of pottery differing in form and fabric from earlier material has already been noted. The main groups are, first, Northampton ware, a hard sandy fabric similar to Stamford ware and in typical Saxo-Norman forms (Williams 1974) and, second, the limestone gritted St Neot's-type wares again in typical Saxo-Norman forms. Additionally there are up to 50 sherds of grey wares and red painted wares probably imported from North France. Imported wares also occur on the Castle Site and their general significance is discussed later. A radio carbon date of A.D. 760±70 - A.D. 780±80 (HAR-1225) has been obtained from a charcoal soil sample from one of the *Grubenhäuser* the date is probably rather early. The earliest coins from this phase were two Edmund Memorial pennies; both were from pits not too closely linked with the structural sequence. A stratified penny of Æthelstan was also recovered. It would seem that the Phase IV buildings were probably in existence at the latest soon after A.D. 900 and the Phase V street was possibly eleventh-century. The significance for the development of Northampton as a whole is considered later.

Let us now consider the Northampton Castle site. The castle itself was largely quarried away in the nineteenth century to make way for a railway goods terminus (Sharp 1882; Law 1880; Scriven 1880), but the limited area of the inner bailey which survived was excavated in the early 1960s by Alexander *(Medieval Archaeol., 6-7* (1962-3): 322f; *8* (1964): 257f; *9* (1965): 191). The present excavations are examining an area 40m by 20m beneath the inner bailey bank, now surviving to a maximum depth of ½m and in some places completely removed by Victorian town development. As all excavated levels are beneath the castle bank, they are clearly eleventh-century or earlier. The 1975 summer season was largely concerned with reaching pre-Castle levels; major work on these levels is currently continuing. It is appropriate to comment that in spite of periods of inclement weather when the site became a veritable morass, the results obtained from winter digging far surpass those of the summer season. Post-holes represented by subtle changes of colour and texture could be seen in areas where none were visible in the summer, even with constant spraying. It would appear from experience of this and other sites around Northampton that greater consideration should be given to the winter digging of those sites where archaeological traces are so ephemeral, if much information is not to be lost. Some general comments can however be made on results to date from the Castle excavations.

Firstly, Early or Middle Saxon gritty pottery occurs over the whole of the site and so far about 150 sherds have been recovered including four stamped pieces. Secondly, there are extensive deposits of Saxo-Norman pottery, again including imports. Plans of several Late Saxon rectangular post-built structures are emerging; while some post-hole alignments seem roughly north to south, at least one building is set at an angle. Also at least one sunken-floored hut has been identified. Metalworking in the area is probably indicated by the presence of crucible fragments. A pit has interestingly produced another St Edmund Memorial penny, again dating to c.A.D.900. During the nineteenth-century destruction of the Castle, six pennies of Edward the Elder and three Edmund Memorial pennies were recovered as well as later Saxon issues (Sharp 1882: 246; Rigold 1959).

Other excavations have produced some evidence relevant to the present discussion. The possible remains of a Saxo-Norman kiln producing Northampton ware were found in Horsemarket (Williams 1974). In Horseshoe Street pits containing Saxo-Norman wares have been found and three sherds of Early or Middle Saxon pottery were also recorded. Saxo-Norman pottery has also been found to the east of Horsemarket and at the bottom of Bridge Street, but although odd sherds have been found in other excavations, the volume is so small as to be totally disregarded here.

Before trying to synthesize the documentary and archaeological evidence we have been considering, I would like to recall briefly Lee's theories of the origins and development of Northampton argued solely from topographical details (Lee 1954). He proposed quite convincingly that Bath Street, College Street and Kingswell Street on the one hand and Bridge Street, the Drapery, Bearwood Street and Scarletwell Street on the other fossilized the intra-mural and extra-mural streets of the eastern and northern perimeter of an early, perhaps Saxon, defensive system, the river defining the western and southern boundaries and Marefair, Gold Street, Horsemarket and Horseshoe Street forming the main axial streets of the town (fig. 28). Markets would have grown up outside the gates and this again is reflected in the squares at All Saints and the Mayorhold. Subsequent expansion of the town saw the town walls re-erected along the line of St George's Street, The Mounts, Cheyne Walk and Victoria Promenade.

Taking the evidence as a whole it seems reasonable to isolate two main periods of activity: the Early and/or Middle Saxon and the Late Saxon. Pre- Saxo-Norman pottery is found in quantity over an area so far defined as stretching at least 250m north-west to south-east (fig.29). A few sherds have been found c.100m further east. This earliest activity is thus apparently concentrated at the extreme south-west of the town, making the most use of the defensive possibilities afforded by the ironstone spur overlooking marshy ground and the river to the south and west. Occupation does not seem to have been particularly intensive. If the dating of the mixers in the late seventh century is correct, there is little to show on St Peter's Street for the next 150 to 200 years. Obviously the later the mixers, the less this is a problem. It should be noted that the alignment of the clearly identified pre-mixer building at the west end of St Peter's Street and the post-mixer north-south gully and associated post-holes respects the main north-south/east-west alignments of the later town. Where the pre-Saxo-Norman material on the Castle site fits into the scheme of things we cannot as yet say. Thus the possibly ecclesiastical stone building suggested by the mortar mixers seems to indicate at least an intended long occupation which is not supported otherwise from St Peter's Street, and the Castle site evidence still remains to be interpreted. Perhaps there is an actual break in continuity between the Middle and Late Saxon periods but at the moment it is preferable perhaps to think in terms of a constant nucleus, with subsidiary settlement shifting through time in its immediate vicinity. The nucleus would seem to be the hypothetical stone church, but should we consider the settlement purely ecclesiastical or as a centre of a royal or thegnly estate?

The dramatic intensification of activity in the Late Saxon period has already been described, but what is the context for the change? Two aspects should be considered, namely the form of the development and the related chronology. Following Biddle and Hill's exposition on Late Saxon planned towns (1971), current thinking seems to be dominated by town planning, organized growth and the economic impetus provided by Alfred and Edward the Elder. Certainly, elements of Northampton's topography have a planned appearance, notably Lee's main east-west and north-south axial streets. St Peter's Street also lies parallel to Marefair. The axial streets are, however, as Lee demonstrated, the main north-south and east-west routes through Northampton. As far as St Peter's Street is concerned the Period V street, probably eleventh-century, has the appearance of organization and planning but the Period IV street, if street it is, is most irregular while following a general east-west direction. Similarly the associated buildings are irregularly disposed. At the present time there is also no clear evidence of regular planning on the Castle site.

We can now consider the absolute chronology. The Danish army of Northampton submitted to Edward in 917. The coin evidence seems to suggest there was already by 917 increasing activity in Northampton and the early radiocarbon date from the *Grubenhaus* should not perhaps be entirely discounted. So far six St Edmund Memorial pennies have been found in Northampton including three stratified examples found in association with Saxo-Norman wares. Marion Archibald is of the opinion that the Northampton pennies may well have been deposited before A.D. 917 rather than later (personal communication) although obviously it is impossible to be certain in such matters. Certainly in the Morley St Peter's hoard dated to c.A.D.925-927 only 19 Edmund Memorial pennies were present out of some 900 coins, and that from a site close to where the coins were probably produced (Dolley 1958; Blunt 1974: 54). Moreover the small size of the coins, contrasting with the larger later issues of Edward and his successors, is not conducive to a high survival rate.

Thus Saxo-Norman and St Neot's type wares may be present in Danish contexts and since these and the pre-Saxo-Norman wares are not associated archaeologically in excavations in Northampton, it seems right to query whether the introduction of wheel-thrown wares into Northampton is due to Scandinavian influence. The Scandinavians were largely aceramic in their homeland but this would not prevent the movement of pottery or indeed potters as part of the general economic boost they gave to Western Europe through their trading activities. On balance, therefore, it is quite possible that it was during the Danish occupation of Northampton that the settlement began to blossom. Certainly from c.A.D.900 ($\pm$ 25 years) there was a dramatic increase in the number of buildings and pits present on the excavated sites. Industry is witnessed by the manufacture of Northampton ware and the finds of iron slag, crucibles and worked horn, and some form of foreign contact is demonstrated by the presence of imported pottery and possibly hones from Scandinavia. Mr Richard Hodges has identified three probable red burnished sherds of a North French type which occurs on the Continent before A.D.900, and some grey wares of pre-Conquest date probably from the area between the Seine and the Rhine. Thirteen sherds of red painted wares, possibly from the Beauvais area - pottery which starts to appear on the Continent by A.D.900 if not earlier - have also been found.

Hodges has recently indicated that whereas imported wares of this period found on the south coast of England are predominantly of North French origin, those on the east coast are more usually from the Rhine area (Hodges 1976). The significance, firstly of the mere presence of Continental wares in Northampton, particularly in view of the relative absence of such material from other inland sites, and secondly of the predominance of North French types, must obviously be considered. There are, however, many dangers in building elaborate trading or other connections on the basis of less than 50 sherds from, say, some 150 years.

By the time of the Norman Conquest, Northampton was probably truly urban and filled the area enclosed by Lee's early defences, but how early the eastern half of the area was occupied we cannot say, since thankfully little development has taken place here in recent years.

Some general points about early urban development are here relevant. First, in referring to Northampton I have deliberately avoided the word 'town', before the eleventh century, and I will here omit discussion of what constitutes a town, allowing a fairly wide definition. Although it is quite probable that the settlement at Northampton was developing at least some urban characteristics even from Middle Saxon times, nothing we have excavated dating to before the Norman Conquest justifies in its own right such a term. 'Nucleated settlement' and 'focal point' would all be valid descriptions for the archaeological evidence and probably for most of the period we have been looking at. Looking generally at the growth of urban centres, there is a danger of transferring a later urban character into an earlier site when the earlier site is of inferior status. For example, no one to my knowledge has suggested that West Stow (West 1969) or Chalton (Addyman and Leigh 1973) was a town, but if those sites had been found beneath a major medieval centre, I am sure the cry would have been one of urban continuity not of settlement continuity. Moreover, in talking of planning in towns let us try to differentiate between what is called 'structure planning' and what is called 'development control': one is design *ab initio;* the other is fitting a structure or other feature into a pre-existing framework.

In summary then, Northampton can be regarded as a focal point for its region from prehistoric times. In the south-west quarter of the town there was a settlement from at least Middle Saxon times of sufficient status to be building in stone. Northampton became a centre for the Danish army in the late ninth century and the archaeological evidence probably testifies to a dramatic increase of activity in that period. During the subsequent Late Saxon period, Northampton continued to grow economically and politically. However, as indicated above, these present comments can only be regarded as provisional, and I hope that the further work currently taking place will elucidate at least some of the problems.

Postscript

Excavations in the Autumn of 1976 immediately to the east of St Peter's Church seem to have confirmed the presence of the postulated Middle Saxon church. Stone foundations were interpreted as the east end of a church and associated mortar and wall rendering matched material from the 'mixers'.

Further radiocarbon determinations perhaps suggest that the 'mixers' and the church belong to the eighth rather than the seventh century.

ACKNOWLEDGMENTS

I wish to acknowledge the generous financial provision and support provided by Northampton Development Corporation and the Department of the Environment for archaeological work in the Northampton area; without this the present paper could not have been written. Additionally, Northampton Borough Council contributed to the St Peter's Street excavations. Thanks must also be given to all staff and volunteers who have assisted in excavation and post-excavation work, in particular to Mr Michael McCarthy who has done invaluable work on the pottery and contributed several general points.

REFERENCES

Note DB = Domesday Book (see below, under Ryland)
       ASC = Anglo-Saxon Chronicle (see below, under Whitelock)
       CS = *Cartularium Saxonicum* (see below, under Birch)
Addyman, P.V., 1972. 'The Anglo-Saxon house: a new review,' in *Anglo-Saxon England, I*, 237-307.
Addyman, P.V., 1973. 'The village or township at St Neots', *Proceedings of the Cambridge Antiquarian Society, 64:* 45-99.
Addyman, P.V., and Leigh, D., 1973. 'The Anglo-Saxon village at Chalton, Hampshire: second interim report', *Medieval Archaeol., 17:* 1-25.
Biddle, M., 1972. 'Winchester: the development of an early capital', in *Vor- und Frühformen der europäischen Stadt im Mittelalter*, ed. H. Jankuhn, W. Schlesinger and H. Steuer (Göttingen), 229-61.
Biddle, M., and Hill, D., 1971. 'Late Saxon planned towns' *Antiq. J., 51:* 70-85.
Birch, W. de Gray, 1885-93. *Cartularium Saxonicum.*
Blunt, C.E., 1974. 'The coinage of Athelstan 924-39 A.D. - a survey', *Brit. Numis. J., 42:* 35-140.
Blunt, C.E., and Dolley, M., 1971. 'The mints of Northampton and Southampton up to the time of Edgar's reform', in *Mints, Dies and Currency*, ed. R.A.G. Carson, 91-100.
Cam, H.M., 1963. *Liberties and Communities in Medieval England.*
Cramp, R., 1969. 'Excavations at the Saxon monastic sites of Wearmouth and Jarrow', *Medieval Archaeol., 13:* 21-66.
Dolley, R.H.M., 1958. 'The Morley St Peter treasure trove', *Numismatic Circular*, May 1958, 113-14.
Fox, C., 1923. *The Archaeology of the Cambridge Region.*
Grimes, W.F., 1951. 'The Jurassic Way across England', in *Aspects of Archaeology in Britain and Beyond*, ed. W.F.Grimes, 144-71.
Hart, C.R., 1970. *The Hidation of Northamptonshire* (University of Leicester, Department of English Local History, Occasional Papers, 2nd ser. no. 3).
Hodges, R.A., 1977 (forthcoming). 'Some early French wares in the British Isles: an archaeological assessment of the early French wine trade with Britain', in *Pottery and Economic Archaeology*, ed. D.P.S. Peacock.
Jackson, D.A., Harding, D.W., and Myres, J.N.L., 1969. 'The Iron Age and Anglo-Saxon site at Upton, Northants', *Antiq. J., 49:* 202-21.
Law, E.F., 1880. 'The ruins of the old Castle, Northampton', *Ass. Archit. Socs. Rep. Pap. 15:* 198-203.
Lee, F., 1954. 'A new theory of the origins and early growth of Northampton', *Archaeol. J., 110:* 164-74.
Meaney, A., 1964. *A Gazetteer of Early Anglo-Saxon Burial Sites.*
Myres, J.N L., 1969. *Anglo-Saxon Pottery and the Settlement of England.*
Radford, C.A.R., 1957. 'The Anglo-Saxon house: a review and some parallels', *Medieval Archaeol.,1:* 27-38.
Rigold, S.E., 1959. 'Finds of St Edmund Memorial and other Anglo-Saxon coins from excavations at Thetford', *Brit. Numis. J., 29:* 189-90.
Ryland, W., et al. (eds.), 1902-37. *V.C.H. Northamptonshire.*
Scriven, R.G., 1880. 'The earthwork on the site of the Castle at Northampton', *Ass. Archit. Socs. Rep. Pap. 15:* 204-10.
Sharp, S., 1882. 'Description of antiquities found on the site of the Castle at Northampton', *Ass. Archit. Socs. Rep. Pap. 16:* 243-51.
Wade-Martins, P., 1969. 'Excavations at North Elmham 1967 - 8: an interim report', *Norfolk Archaeology, 34:* 352-97.
Wade-Martins, P., 1970' 'Excavations at North Elmham 1969: an interim report', *Norfolk Archaeology, 35:* 25-78.
West, S.E., 1969. 'The Anglo-Saxon village at West Stow: an interim report of the excavations 1965-8', *Medieval Archaeol.,13:* 1-20.

Whitelock, D., with Douglas, D.C., and Tucker, S.I., 1961. *The Anglo-Saxon Chronicle.*

Williams, J.H., 1974. 'A Saxo-Norman kiln group from Northampton', *Northamptonshire Archaeol., 9:* 46-56.

Williams, J.H., 1975. 'Northampton', *Current Archaeology, 46:* 340-8.

Williams, J.H., 1977 (forthcoming). *Excavations in St Peter's Street, Northampton* (Northampton Development Corporation Archaeological Monograph, No. 2).

Part Three

ANN DORNIER

8 The Anglo-Saxon monastery at Breedon-on-the-Hill, Leicestershire

It is appropriate that at a conference on Mercia held in 1975 there should have been a paper on Breedon because 675, exactly 1300 years ago, is the traditional, though not necessarily the correct, date for the founding of the Anglo-Saxon monastery at Breedon.

The site is on a hill which dominates the surrounding countryside: it has a commanding view in all directions and conversely can be seen from several miles away. It was no doubt for this reason that a hillfort was constructed here in the Iron Age (Kenyon 1950: 17-82; Wacher 1964: 122-42). Stray finds of pottery, tiles and coins, ranging from the first to fourth centuries A.D., point to continued use in the Roman period, although the nature of the occupation is unknown.[1] There is as yet no evidence of any activity in the fifth and sixth centuries. In the seventh century a monastery was founded, which is the subject of this paper. In the twelfth century an Augustinian Priory was established, a cell of Nostell in Yorkshire, which remained in being until the Dissolution (Hoskins 1954: 8-9). From the sixteenth century onwards the church remained the parish church of the village which had grown up at the foot of the hill.

About two-thirds of the hill has now been quarried away (fig. 39). The only structures that can be seen today are sections of the Iron Age ramparts and the church, of which the base of the tower is Norman and the rest is medieval and later, although it may incorporate reused stones from the Saxon monastery. All that survives from the Saxon period are the sculptural fragments which have either been rebuilt into the internal fabric of the church or cemented into the floor.

The purpose of this paper is to assemble together all that is known of the Saxon monastery, namely the documentary and archaeological evidence, excluding the

Figure 39. Breedon-on-the-Hill, Leicestershire *(photograph by courtesy of J. G. Shields).*

sculpture which Rosemary Cramp discusses in Chapter 11.

WRITTEN SOURCES

To quote Bishop Stubbs from another context, ' ... all the materials, which are known to exist, are few in number and need only a little criticism to make them still fewer' (Stubbs 1862: 236). It was Stubbs in fact who first gave serious consideration to the early documents relating to Breedon in an article on Peterborough material (Stubbs 1861: 193-211). Whilst accepting the authenticity of some of the entries, he considered others as either spurious or wrongly ascribed. Subsequently Stenton restated the case for accepting these early charters and convincingly rehabilitated some of those sources which Stubbs had dismissed (Stenton 1933: 313-26).

I begin with a consideration of these early written sources, selecting various points for comment.

I. Anglo-Saxon Chronicle, Laud MS.(E) s.a. 675 (Plummer 1892: 37)

Grant by King Æthelred of lands, including Breedon, to St Peter's monastery, Medeshamstede (Peterborough).

Although this entry is considered to be an interpolation, probably of the twelfth century, it is based on the memoranda which Stenton maintained were themselves likely to be based on authentic records no longer extant (Stenton 1933: 313-26). However, it rather looks as if all the supposed grants of Æthelred have been placed in the first year of his reign to give them the greatest possible antiquity, so that the date is suspect.

II. Charter 675 x 691 (CS 841)

Grant by princeps Friduricus to St Peter's, Medeshamstede, of 20 manentes called Briudun for the foundation of a monastery to further the spread of Christianity. Hedda, a priest of Medeshamstede, appointed abbot.

This charter, together with the two immediately following, lies between 675 and 691 because of the inclusion of Æthelred, who began his reign in 675, and bishop Saxwulf who died in 691.

Friduricus, the lay patron, may be the same person as the ealdorman who witnessed a charter in 704 (CS111). If this is so, the grant is unlikely to be as early as 675. He may also be the St Frethoric mentioned by Hugh Candidus as being buried at Breedon, if that entry is reliable (Mellows 1941: 60).

Hedda was a distinguished ecclesiast in his day who acquired at least two properties for his monastery (see below) and may also have established offshoot foundations at Bermondsey and Woking (Stenton 1933: 319-20). He is probably identical with the Hedda who became bishop of Lichfield in 691 (Stubbs 1861: 204). He apparently dedicated Guthlac's church at Crowland (Stenton 1947: 49). He cannot be the same man as the Hedda of Medeshamstede mentioned in the Anglo-Saxon Chronicle (Plummer 1892: 115) and by Hugh Candidus (Mellows 1941: 23), as the latter lived about a hundred years later. It is possible that this Hedda never really existed and that the Hedda of Breedon was wrongly adopted by Peterborough at a later date.

III. Charter 675 x 691 (CS 842)
Grant by Friduricus to Hedda of 31 *manentes* called *Hrepingas.*

Stubbs suggested that this must lie within the Hundred of Repington, that is to say the Repton area (Stubbs 1861: 203). This suggestion seems either to have passed unnoticed or to have been ignored. Ekwall identified it with Rippingale, Lincolnshire (Ekwall 1964: 388). Stenton was not happy with this as he considered it too far away, but he offered no alternative (Stenton 1933: 319). Subsequent writers have opted for Rippingale with a question mark (Hart 1966: 99; Sawyer 1968: 473). It seems to me, however, that the Repton area is likely to be the correct identification. Etymologically the association is acceptable, as Rumble makes clear in Chapter 9. *Repingas* is a tribal/ territorial designation which perhaps is being employed rather loosely to describe a place (in the territory) of the *Repingas.* This raises the interesting possibility that it is the original grant of land on which the monastery at Repton was then founded. Weight is added to this suggestion by the fact that in another documentary source (see below, p. 159) *Repingas* is clearly a monastery. If the identification with the Repton area is correct, there is no known candidate other than Repton itself. It is true that Repton is known as *Hrypandun/Hrypandune* in the eight century (Ekwall 1964: 385), but a change in name or a dual nomenclature cannot be ruled out.

IV. Charter 675 x 691 (CS 843)
Grant by King Æthelred to Hedda of *Bredun* of 15 *manentes* called *Cedenan ác.*

Cedanan ác, or *Cedenac,* as it is written in the Anglo-Saxon Chronicle (Plummer 1892: 37), poses a problem. The shorter form would translate as *Cadda's oak* (Hart 1966: 99). It has been tentatively suggested that this property is Cadney, Lincolnshire (Sawyer 1968: 473), although etymologically this is unlikely. Stubbs considered that it may have been somewhere in Charnwood Forest, north-west Leicestershire (Stubbs 1861: 203).

V. Bede, H.E. v, 23 s.a.731 (Colgrave 1972: 558)
Tatwine, a priest of *Briudun* in the province of Mercia, became archbishop of Canterbury.

VI. Anglo-Saxon Chronicle, Laud MS.(E) s.a.731 (Plummer 1892: 45)
Tatwine, a priest of *Breodune* in Mercia, became archbishop of Canterbury.

As these two entries are virtually identical I will deal with them together. It is generally assumed that it must be the Leicestershire Breedon that is intended as it is described as being in Mercia, whereas the Worcestershire Bredon was within the territory of the Hwicce. This is probably a fair assumption, although by the third decade of the eighth century the term Mercia might well be used as a blanket description of those lands which had more or less been absorbed by Mercia proper.

VII. Charter 848 (corrected from 844) (CS 454)
Grant by King Berhtwulf and *princeps* Humbert of certain immunities to abbot Eanmund for his monastery at *Breodune,* to be observed by the *principes* of the *Tomseti.* In return for these privileges the monastery gives, among other things,

land at *Stanlega* and *Bellanforde* to Berhtwulf.

Humbert is clearly an ealdorman of the *Tomseti*. He witnessed several charters relating to Greater Mercia in the 840s to 860s (CS 434, 450, 513), and is probably the same Humbert who was granted land at Wirksworth by the abbess of Repton (CS 414).

As Breedon was within the territory of the *Tomseti* it presumably lay within the bishopric of Lichfield rather than Leicester.

It has been suggested that *Stanlega* is Stanley, Derbyshire (Hart 1975: 68). *Bellanforde* has not been identified. There is no record as to how and when Breedon acquired these properties.

VIII. Charter 966 x 967 x 972 (CS 1283)
Grant by King Edgar to bishop Æthelwold, and after him to the *ecclesia* at *Breodone* in perpetuity, of 3 *cassati* at *Æbredone*, 3 *cassati* at *Wifeles Ðorpe*, 4 *cassati* at *Ætheredes dun* and 3 *cassati* at *Digtheswyrthe*.

Wifeles is Wilson and *Digtheswyrthe* is Diseworth, both of which are in the immediate vicinity of Breedon (Stenton 1910: 78). The identification of *Ætheredes dun* is uncertain, but it has been suggested that it may be Atterton (Sawyer 1968: 241).

Two matters arise from these documents which merit further consideration. First, Stenton maintained that the properties listed in the Peterborough memoranda must have belonged to Medeshamstede itself, otherwise they would not have been preserved in the Peterborough muniments (Stenton 1933: 315). That is to say, the properties acquired by Hedda were intended for Medeshamstede and not Breedon. I would suggest that this need not necessarily be the case and that it is much more likely that they have been credited erroneously to Medeshamstede at a later date. Nowhere in the two charters relating to *Repingas* and *Cedenan ác* is it stated or hinted that they were granted to Medeshamstede. Even if Hedda remained in some senses a monk of that place, these properties were given to him in his capacity as abbot of Breedon.

As a result of the upheavals brought about by the Viking raids, monastic possessions were often transferred to other monasteries in the hope of preventing their destruction. It is not inconceivable that Medeshamstede acquired documents properly belonging to another monastic centre, notwithstanding its own eventual destruction by the Danes, and that some of the properties itemized in such records eventually found their way into the list of Medeshamstede's possessions. Alternatively, if Medeshamstede kept a record of the affairs of its daughter foundation, Breedon, in its initial stages in the seventh century, it is extremely likely that, either deliberately or inadvertently, any Breedon property so recorded would be incorporated in Peterborough material.

It is probably not without significance that Breedon and the two properties mentioned above occur in a block in Hugh Candidus: *'Bredun, Hrepingas, Cedenac'* (Mellows 1941: 20). There is also another block in Hugh Candidus, in the section on monasteries supposedly founded by Medeshamstede, which may be another instance of the incorporation of Breedon material: *'ad Bredon et ad Wermundeseya et ad Repingas et ad Wochingas'* (Mellows 1941: 15). The monasteries of Bermondsey and Woking were under the authority of an abbot Hedda at about the right date for Hedda of Breedon (CS 133). This could be a list of Breedon and its own three dependencies or offshoot foundations in the seventh century.

Second, turning to Breedon in the late Saxon period, it is generally assumed that it was sacked by the Vikings. There is no evidence that this was so, although it is hardly likely to have escaped the notice of the Danes, particularly when they wintered at Repton in 874/5. Whether or not it was temporarily abandoned, the church was clearly in existence in the late tenth century. The wording of Edgar's charter makes it clear that when he granted Æthelwold land at Breedon the church was functioning, and that it was not the church and its property that were granted, but some other land which was to pass to the church after his death. There is nothing in the charter to suggest that he refounded a monastery that had lain waste up to that time. If it were a refoundation one might perhaps expect a reference to the fact and, more important, a confirmation of privileges.

The Dedication

Stubbs, when writing about Bredon, Worcestershire, states *en passant* that the Leicestershire Breedon was dedicated to St Peter (Stubbs 1862: 246). He cites no authority for this and I have been unable to locate any reference. It is possible that the existing dedication to St Mary and St Hardulf is not the original seventh-century one, in which case St Peter is a very likely candidate in seventh-century Mercia. Nevertheless the present dedication may well go back to the Anglo-Saxon period. Churches were sometimes dedicated to the Virgin Mary. She may have become increasingly popular from the late eighth century onwards, as Rosemary Cramp indicates in her paper (p. 218). However, it is also true that she was added to existing dedications in medieval times (Arnold-Forster 1899, II: 42).

St Hardulf presents difficulties. According to Hugh Candidus the remains of *'sanctus Ærdulfus rex'* were interred at *Bredun,* together with those of St Cotta, St Benna and St Fretheric (Mellows 1941: 60). If this is correct Ærdulf was probably the Northumbrian king (Haerdulf on his coins) whose floruit was c.800. He may have acquired a reputation for sanctity on the occasion he is supposed to have risen virtually from the dead, at Ripon. However, there is no evidence of his being buried at Breedon, nor any tradition linking him with the area, apart from his association with Alkmund whom he is supposed to have murdered - and his invasion of Mercia in 801 - events which would hardly make him an appropriate choice for veneration[2] (Arnold-Forster 1899, II: 325-7). There was an Ærdulf who was a king of Kent, and three known bishops of that name, but there is nothing to link any of them with Breedon. According to a Life of St Modwena, based on material from Burton-on-Trent, there was an anchorite at Breedon by the name of Hardulf traditionally associated with St Modwena (Kenney 1968: 369; Kerry 1895; 49-59). One cannot be sure, however, that this is historically reliable. Moreover, the anchorite is anonymous in the earliest extant text and the name Hardulf only occurs in a later, fifteenth-century compilation (Wayne 1970: 7), so that it may have been borrowed from Breedon rather than the other way about. Hardulf could perhaps have been a lay patron who gave generously to the monastery at some time. Finally one has to consider the possibility that St Hardulf was adopted in the early medieval period at Breedon because of Hugh Candidus' statement and that there is

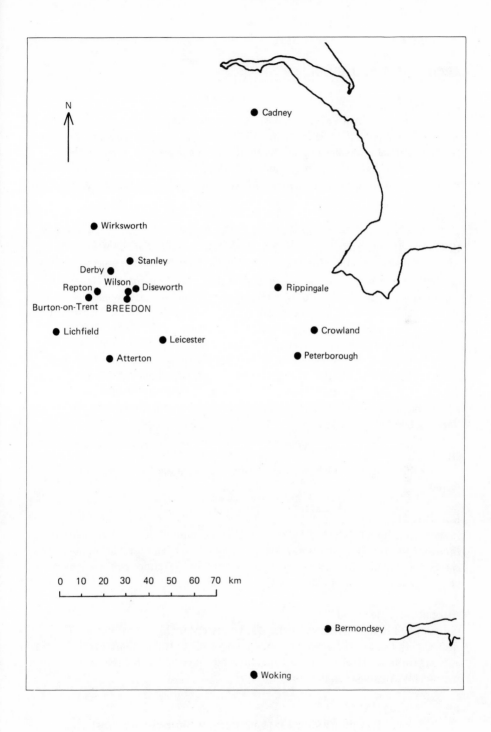

Figure 40. Map of places cited in the text in the section on 'Written Sources'.

no historical basis for the dedication.

ARCHAEOLOGICAL EVIDENCE

Structural Remains

No structural remains of the monastery have been found *in situ* as yet. Lumps of *opus signinum* and a few tile fragments which may be of Saxon date, recovered as residual material in medieval levels during the 1975 excavations, point to the existence of an Anglo-Saxon building to the north of the church (fig. 39). The only other displaced structural fragments which are recognizable are the friezes and slabs.

Burials

There was a cemetery to the east of the church (Kenyon 1950: 22-24; Meaney 1974: 144-45; Leicestershire Museums' Records). Owing to the absence of grave goods from all save one of the burials, in which at least one of the objects is Saxon (see below), it is impossible to be certain that they are Saxon in date. However, the similarity between all the burials for which there are records available, together with their east - west orientation, suggests that they are early Christian. The bodies were laid in shallow graves in rows running north - south. With the exception of one crouch burial, they were laid extended on their backs with the hands crossed over the pelvis. Some of them appear to have had cairns over their heads and shoulders. One burial contained iron nails which may have come from a coffin (Kenyon 1950: 24). Associated with some of the burials were pieces of wood which may have been the remains of coffins or wooden gravemarkers (Meaney 1964: 145).[3]

Metalwork

Only those objects which, without doubt, belong to the Saxon period are included.

Ring (fig. 41, 4)
(unpublished burial) (Meaney 1964: 145; Leicestershire Museums' Records)
Bronze with overlapping ends. Comparable types have been found in Anglo-Saxon graves, for example Chessell Down (Meaney 1964: 95-7), although these appear to be pre-seventh century in date, non-Christian and female.

Attachment plate (fig. 41, 3)
(unpublished burial) (Meaney 1964: 145; Leicestershire Museums' Records)
Bronze with faint traces of wood/bone on underside.[4] It may therefore have been a fitting for box/casket. As it was found in same grave as the ring (see above) it is presumably Anglo-Saxon in date.

Brooch (fig. 41, 2)
(unprovenanced) (Wilson 1960: 135; Leicestershire Museums' Records)
Bronze equal-armed bow brooch with ribbed bow and circular terminals, each decorated with four punched concentric circles. Iron rivet in one of terminals clearly driven through after circles were punched.

This brooch is of seventh/eighth-century Frankish manufacture. There is no

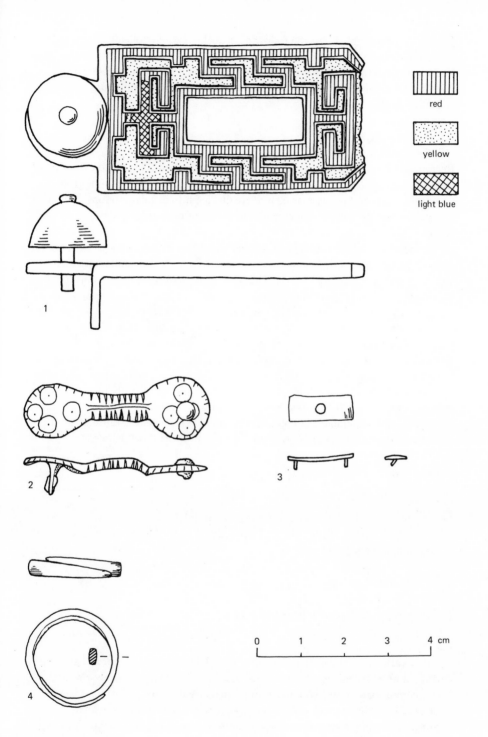

red

yellow

light blue

0   1   2   3   4 cm

Figure 41. Metalwork: 1. buckle/clasp; 2. brooch; 3. attachment plate; 4. ring.

published exact parallel, but the following brooches exhibit collectively the same characteristics in form and decoration: Conlie (Hübener 1972: 227 and Abb. 2/6), Nantes Museum (*ibid.*: 230 and Abb. 2/7), Rotterdam Museum (*ibid.*: 230 and Abb. 1/8), Cologne Museum (*ibid.*: 240 and Abb. 18/8) and Dombourg (*ibid.*: 228 and Abb. 24/3).

Buckle/clasp (fig. 41, 1)
(1975 excavations)
Rectangular bronze plate with dome-head rivet at one end fixed on to extension of main plate by bronze pin and at this end of plate deep prongs projecting from underside; other end of plate broken. Plate divided into angular cloisons filled with red, yellow and light blue enamel, with exception of open rectangular area in centre.

The only parallels to this type of angular enamelled cloisonné metalwork are the early Christian objects traditionally considered to be of Irish manufacture of the eighth century (Henry 1956: 83-4). The buckle plates of one of these objects, the Moylough belt shrine, is strikingly similar in general appearance to the Breedon plate (Henry 1963: pls. 30 and 31). On analogy with the Moylough plates one can infer that the central rectangular area was filled with a panel made as a separate piece, perhaps also decorated with a Celtic triskele motif, and that the extended broken end of the plate originally carried the buckle loop or tongue. Moreover, the depth of the prongs suggests that it is unlikely to have been worn, but would rather have been attached to a back plate that would have allowed for the thickness of a hollow casing for a belt. It is just possible that it is a book clasp, but, if so, there are no known comparable examples of this date. On balance, therefore, it would seem that this is a buckle plate from an eighth-century Irish belt shrine.

Coins

Cenwulf
(unprovenanced) (Leicestershire Museums' Records)
No descriptive details of the coin are recorded and its present whereabouts is a matter of speculation.

Sceat: porcupine derivative
(1975 excavations)
Eighth-century *BMC* type 9, inscribed + LEL.[5]

Pottery
The treatment of the pottery has been kept deliberately brief, for to have embarked upon a detailed archaeological discussion of its problems would have been inappropriate in this volume. Two particularly difficult groups have been omitted: one which may be either Iron Age or Saxon and the other which, although occurring in an early medieval context, may in origin be Saxo-Norman.[6]

Saxon
1. (unprovenanced) (Myres 1969: 158-9, no.475) (fig. 42, 1). Small biconical carinated vessel with slightly everted rim in well-fired reduced sandy fabric.

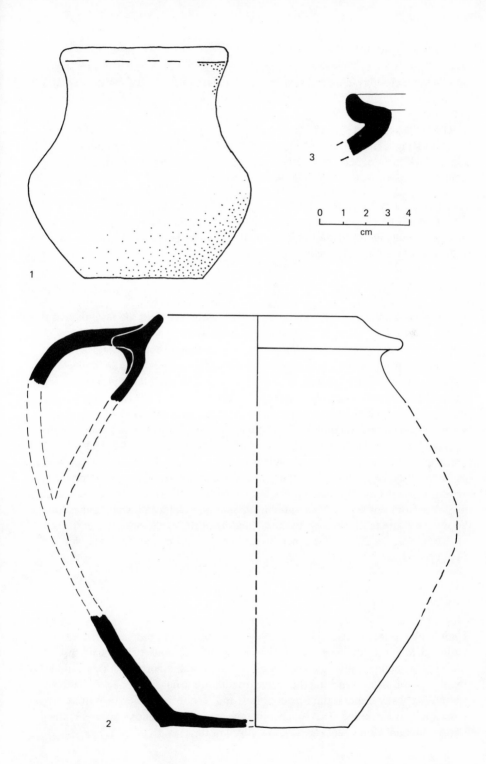

Figure 42. Pottery: 1. biconical vessel *(after Myres);* 2. imported jug *(drawn by Lynn Dyson Bruce);* 3. French import?

2. (1975 excavations)
Body sherd, approx. 2mm across, fairly hard reduced sandy fabric with rare shell and quartz inclusions, tempered with organic material (chopped grass/straw/chaff).

Imports
1. (1975 excavations) (fig. 42, 2)
Jug with flanged rim and strap-handle in fine well-fired reduced sandy fabric with glossy black surface. Made in Northern France/Belgium in eighth/ninth century. Belongs to *Hamwih* class 13/14 Blackwares.[7]

2. (1975 excavations) (fig. 42, 3)
Two rims in whitish sandy fabric. Tenth-century French manufacture? - similar to examples found at Southampton[8] (Platt and Coleman-Smith 1975: 123, no. 858), though not petrologically identical.[9]

SUMMARY

Breedon was founded as a daughter house of Medeshamstede in the seventh century. It lay within the territory of the *Tomseti* and was established explicitly to carry out missionary work in the surrounding area. Under its first bishop, Hedda, it acquired various properties. He may also have set up dependent houses. It had obtained other lands by the mid-eighth century, at which date it surrendered them in return for exemption from certain secular burdens. The sculptural material indicates that there was also a rebuilding or extensive additions in the eighth-century (see Chapter 11, p.194). Its fate during the Viking incursions is unknown: the documents are silent and none of the archaeological material can be dated with sufficient precision to be able to determine whether or not it was abandoned during the ninth century. In the late tenth century the church, if not the monastery, was operative, at which date it was granted some estates. One or two of the sculptural fragments may date from this period.[10] At present there is no evidence of what happened between the late tenth century and the founding of the medieval priory in the twelfth century, although it is generally assumed that it functioned as the Norman parish church.

ACKNOWLEDGMENTS

I would like to thank J.G. Shields for supplying the aerial photograph (fig. 39), Catharine Millar for drawing the metalwork (fig. 41), Rosemary Woodland for drawing the map (fig. 40), and classifying and drawing the pottery (figs. 42 and 43), Lynn Dyson Bruce for making the reconstruction drawing (fig. 42, 2), R. Rutland for putting at my disposal the Breedon finds and records in the Jewry Wall Museum, Leicester, and Josephine Dool for enabling me to see the Breedon material in the Derby Museum. Other debts are acknowledged in the text.

NOTES

1. Finds: Jewry Wall Museum, Leicester; Derby Museum; private possession; 1975 excavations.
2. Alkmund is associated with Derby, where an Anglo-Saxon church was dedicated to him.
3. It has not been possible to obtain any information from the excavator which might clarify the matter.
4. Information from G. Morgan.
5. Identified by J.C.P.Kent
6. These will be discussed in the report on the 1975 excavations.
7. Identified by Richard Hodges.
8. Identification suggested by John Wacher.
9. Analysis by Dr D. Williams.
10. David Wilson in a private communication (Leicestershire Museums' Records) suggested that there may be some tenth-century work and David Parsons argued during the Conference for a tenth-century date for the Angel.

REFERENCES
Note BMC = British Museum Catalogue (see below, under Keary)
    CS   = Cartularium Saxonicum (see below, under Birch)
Arnold-Forster, F., 1899. Studies in Church Dedications (3 vols).
Birch, W. de Gray, 1885-93. Cartularium Saxonicum.
Colgrave, B., and Mynors, R.A.B., 1972. Bede's Ecclesiastical History of the English People.
Ekwall, E., 1964. The Oxford Dictionary of English Place-Names.
Hart, C.R., 1966. The Early Charters of Eastern England.
Hart, C.R., 1975. The Early Charters of Northern England and the North Midlands.
Henry, F., 1956. 'Irish Enamels of the Dark Ages and their Relation to the Cloisonné Techniques', in Dark Age Britain, ed. D.B.Harden, 171-88.
Hoskins, W.G. (ed.), 1954. V.C.H. Leicestershire II.
Henry, F., 1963. Early Christian Irish Art.
Hübener, W., 1972. 'Gleicharmige Bügelfibeln der Merowingerzeit in Westeuropa', Madrider Mitteilungen, 13: 211-69.
Keary, C.F., 1887. A Catalogue of English Coins in the British Museum, Anglo-Saxon Series.
Kenney, J.F., 1968. The Sources for the Early History of Ireland: Ecclesiastical.
Kenyon, K., 1950. 'Excavations at Breedon-on-the-Hill, Leicestershire, 1946', Transactions of the Leicestershire Archaeological and Historical Society, 26: 17-82.
Kerry, C., 1895. 'Saint Modwena and "The Devill of Drakelow" ', J. Derbyshire Archaeol. and Nat.Hist.Soc., 17:49-59.
Meaney, A., 1964. A Gazetteer of Early Anglo-Saxon Burial Sites.
Mellows, W.T., 1941. The Chronicle of Hugh Candidus.
Myres, J.N.L., 1969. Anglo-Saxon Pottery and the Settlement of England.
Platt, C., and Coleman-Smith, R., 1975. Excavations in Medieval Southampton.
Plummer, C., and Earle, J., 1892. Two of the Anglo-Saxon Chronicles.
Sawyer, P., 1968. Anglo-Saxon Charters: An Annotated List and Biography.
Stenton, F.M., 1910. Types of Manorial Structures in the Danelaw (Oxford Studies in Social and Legal History II, ed. P.Vinogradoff).
Stenton, F.M., 1933. 'Medeshamstede and its Colonies,' in Essays in Honour of James Tait, ed. J.G.Edwards et al., 313-26.
Stenton, F.M., 1947. Anglo-Saxon England.
Stubbs, W., 1861. 'On the foundation and early Fasti of Peterborough', Archaeol. J., 18: 193-211.

Stubbs, W., 1862. 'The cathedral, diocese and monasteries of Worcester in the eighth century', *Archaeol. J. 19:* 236-52.

Wacher, J.S., 1964. 'Excavations at Breedon-on-the-Hill, Leicestershire, 1957', *Antiq.J., 44:* 122-42.

Wayne, K., 1970. 'In honour of S.Hardulph', *Leicester Cathedral Quarterly, 7:* 6-9.

Wilson, D.M., 1960. 'Medieval Britain in 1959: Pre-Conquest', *Medieval Archaeol., 4:* 134-9.

ALEXANDER RUMBLE

9 'Hrepingas' reconsidered

The suggestion, made by Ann Dornier in Chapter 8, that the so-far unidentified colony of Medeshamstede (Peterborough Abbey) called *Repingas* by Hugh Candidus in the twelfth century (Sparke 1723: 12; see Stenton 1970: 185) is a reference to the Anglo-Saxon church at Repton, Derbyshire, is important and deserves further discussion. The same place, spelt *Hrepingas,* is also mentioned in memoranda copied into a twelfth-century cartulary of Peterborough Abbey (Davis 1958: no.754), which were judged by Sir Frank Stenton on internal evidence to be accurate records of late seventh-century land-grants (Sawyer 1968: nos. 1803-6, particularly 1805; see Stenton 1970: 181-4).

The establishment of *Hrepingas* as an earlier or alternative name for the place now known as Repton depends on three things: (1) whether the first element of the two names is identical; (2) an explanation of the significance of two alternating but associated names for the same place; and (3) the historical likelihood of *Hrepingas* being at or near Repton rather than at or near another place whose name may contain the same first element but which is located in another part of the country.

(1)   The foundation of any argument associating the names *Hrepingas* and Repton is the assumption that they do both contain the same first element. The accepted etymology of Repton (*Hreopa dune* 755 (c.900) - Cameron 1959: 653) is that it represents a compound of (the genitive of) the OE folk-name *Hrype* or *Hreope* with OE *dūn* 'a hill' to give a name meaning 'the hill of the *Hrype* or *Hreope* people.' It should be particularly noted that there seem to have been two OE forms of the folk-name both accepted in the Anglo-Saxon period. Of the two forms, *Hreope*

occurs most frequently in the recorded spellings for Repton (Cameron 1959: 653), while *Hrype* has more frequency in those for Rippon, Yorkshire, the other major place-name definitely containing the element (in the dative plural; see Smith 1961: 164-5, where the few *Hreope* spellings were however attributed to Old Northumbrian influence). The origin of this archaic folk-name is obscure but its possible association with the OE personal-name *Hryp* found in the East Anglian royal genealogy (Sweet 1885: 640; Smith 1961: 165) is worth mentioning in the context of the mixed provenance of the several Germanic peoples whose alliance came to form the kingdom of the Mercians (Stenton 1971: 38-48). The appearance of the *Hrype* or *Hreope* as a recognized people at Ripon in Northumbria as well as in the Midlands at Repton suggests an early date for the establishment of their separate tribal identity. The question whether they were also associated in some way with the name *Hrepingas* must now be considered.

Recorded spellings of the name *Hrepingas* are found as follows:

Hrepingas 664(12) B22 (Sawyer 1968: no. 68; Medeshamstede confirmation-charter), 675 x 692(12) B842 (Sawyer 1968: no. 1805; memorandum of grant to Hædda, abbot (of Breedon)), 680(12) ASC(E) s.a. 675 (Clark 1970: 121; Sawyer 1968: no.72; grant to Medeshamstede), *Repingas* 12 HC (list of Medeshamstede colonies).

Of the above records, Sawyer 1968: no. 1805 is the most authentic. Sawyer 1968: nos. 68 and 72 are spurious, in that they are not what they claim to be, but may incorporate earlier material now lost (Stenton 1970: 180). Hugh Candidus (HC) was also working from similar lost sources (Stenton 1970: 185). Thus although none of the above spellings survive in sources written before the twelfth century they may have been copied, more or less accurately, from earlier documents which have not been preserved. Of the two spellings, *Hrepingas* and *Repingas,* the former is probably nearest the spelling in the lost exemplars but may not have been totally unchanged by the twelfth-century copyists. The analogy of the spelling of Breedon, Leicestershire, which occurs in B22 (Sawyer 1968: no. 68) and HC as *Bredun* and in ASC(E) s.a. 675 (Sawyer 1968: no. 72) as *Bredune* may be quoted here. In OE Bede (c.890) the same place is spelt *Breodun* (Ekwall 1960: 62). If a name usually spelt *Breodun* in the Anglo-Saxon period can appear in the above twelfth-century sources as *Bredun(e),* then a spelling *Hrepingas* in the same sources could represent an original OE form *Hreopingas.* Such a spelling could represent an OE folk-name formed by the addition of the suffix *-ingas,* either to the earlier folk-name *Hreope* on its own or to a contracted form of a place-name, such as Repton, containing *Hreope* as its first element. The alternative significance of such formation is discussed below.

(2)   If *Hrepingas* comes from *Hreope* + *-ingas* it reflects the obvious difficulty, shown in the spellings for Repton and Ripon (Cameron 1959: 653; Smith 1961: 164), which the Anglo-Saxons had in declining the archaic element *Hrype* or *Hreope* and in remembering that it was in origin a folk-name. Because they had forgotten its derivation they felt free to treat it as an indeterminate element denoting a district, as in the form *Hrypsetna cirican* c.890 for Ripon (Smith 1961: 164) where OE *sæte* 'settlers' has been added to the name *Hrype* to give *Hrypsæte,* which would be a compound analogous to *Hreopingas,* being the addition of an element denoting a community to the older simplex folk-name *Hrype* or *Hreope.* However, it must be stated that if *Hrepingas* does represent such a formation it

need not necessarily refer to the *Hreope* or *Hrype* who were settled at Repton rather than to another group settled elsewhere.

In my opinion, an equally likely origin for the name *Hrepingas,* if the first element is the same as, or associated with, that of Repton, is that it is an elliptical name formed by adding an *-ingas* suffix to a place-name, such as Repton, which had *Hrype* or *Hreope* as its first element. *Hrepingas* could thus represent an elliptical form of **Hreopaduningas,* meaning 'the (religious?) community at Repton' (see Smith 1956: 302 s.v. *-ingas* 7(d) for such formations). An analogous name would be *Berclingas* to denote the religious community at Berkeley, Gloucestershire (Smith 1964: 211-12). *Hrepingas* could also however represent a similar elliptical name based on any other place-name, besides Repton, which contained *Hreope* or *Hrype* as its first element.

(3)   The name-form *Hrepingas* seems therefore to be capable of more than one possible association with the element *Hrype, Hreope,* found in Repton. A name-form of itself, however, cannot ever positively assert to which particular place it refers. Actual identification of a spelling with a place must always rely on the study of the documentary context of the name-forms and the historical likelihood of the record referring to one place rather than another. The tentative identification by Eilert Ekwall (1960: 388) of *Hrepingas* as Rippingale, Lincolnshire, although formally possible, is historically less likely than its identification as Repton, with its Anglo-Saxon church and relative proximity to Breedon, Leicestershire, with which *Hrepingas* is associated in the Medeshamstede charters and memoranda. Stenton (1970: 185 n.3) rejected the Rippingale identification on grounds of its distance from Breedon. Other place-names including Ripon (mentioned above), said to contain the folk-name *Hrype, Hreope,* are all in Yorkshire (Riponshire, Ripley and *Ripestic;* Smith 1961: 77, 101 and 177) and should therefore be rejected on similar grounds.

Thus a reconsideration of the onomastic possibilities of the name *Hrepingas* does tend to support the suggestion that it could be identified, or at least associated, with Repton in Derbyshire, an identification which is quite likely from what historical evidence survives.

REFERENCES

Note ASC(E) = Anglo-Saxon Chronicle, text E (see below, under Clark)
       B   = Birch (see below)
       HC   = Hugh Candidus (see below, under Sparke)
       OE   = Old English
       OEBede = Old English version of Bede's *Historia Ecclesiastica*
Birch, W. de Gray, 1885-99. *Cartularium Saxonicum* (3 vols and index).
Cameron, K., 1959. *The Place-Names of Derbyshire*, 3 (English Place-Name Society, XXIX for 1951-2).
Clark, Cecily, 1970. *The Peterborough Chronicle 1070-1154* (2nd edn).
Davis, G.R.C., 1958. *Medieval Cartularies of Great Britain, a short catalogue.*
Ekwall, E., 1960. *The Concise Oxford Dictionary of English Place-Names* (4th edn).
Miller, T., 1890-8. *The Old English Version of Bede's Ecclesiastical History of the English People* (Early English Text Society, 95-6, 110-11).
Sawyer, P.H., 1968. *Anglo-Saxon Charters, an annotated list and bibliography* (Royal Historical Society, Handbook no. 8).
Smith, A.H., 1956. *English Place-Name Elements*, 1 (English Place-Name Society, XXV).
Smith, A.H., 1961. *The Place-Names of the West Riding of Yorkshire*, 5 (English Place-Name Society, XXXIV for 1956-7).
Smith, A.H., 1964. *The Place-Names of Gloucestershire*, 2 (English Place-Name Society. XXXIX for 1961-2).
Sparke, J., 1723. *Hugonis Candidi, Coenobii Burgensis Historia* in *Historiæ Anglicanæ Scriptores Varii e codicibus manuscriptis nunc primum editi.*
Stenton, F.M., 1970. *Preparatory to Anglo-Saxon England being the collected papers of Frank Merry Stenton*, ed. D.M.Stenton, 179-92: 'Medeshamstede and its colonies' (first published 1933).
Stenton, F.M., 1971. *Anglo-Saxon England* (3rd edn).
Sweet, H., 1885. *The oldest English texts* (Early English Text Society, 83).

DAVID PARSONS

10 Brixworth and its monastery church

INTRODUCTION

The long-term investigation of All Saints' Church, Brixworth, is one of a number of projects being sponsored by the Brixworth Archaeological Research Committee, and is intended ultimately to embrace the following areas of study, which are similar to those outlined by Taylor (1973).

(1)   a new and thorough reappraisal of the standing fabric, including the preparation of accurate ground plans and elevations, critical inspection of the masonry and structural analysis, petrological identification of the wide variety of building stones used, and laboratory examination of select building materials, especially bricks and mortars;

(2)   a re-examination of all published and unpublished documentary material referring to the church, including the evidence from earlier excavations and especially the accounts of the nineteenth-century restorations, archaeological observations in the course of the work, and drawings of the church both before and after the restorations (Fletcher (1974) has shown how profitable and how essential the latter will be); and

(3)   extensive excavation both within the church and in the churchyard, not only to elucidate the structural history of the church itself but to shed light on the monastery as a whole; the exterior excavations will be preceded by a graveyard survey of the kind described by Jones (1976).

This paper attempts to report and to make some assessment of the progress of a number of these lines of investigation, but it will be appreciated that at this stage of the Committee's activity any statement must be regarded as provisional.

THE SITE

The clear implication of the second item in the programme outlined above is that there is much information lying fallow and unregarded; the value of such information is likely to be variable, and it all requires critical re-assessment to determine what is useful and what may be discarded. Two such pieces of information are the Brixworth estate map of 1688 (the property of the late Sir Gyles Isham, but preserved at the Northamptonshire Record Office, where its reference number is 1555), published as an unnumbered plate in Pavey (1902); and some field-name evidence listed in Pavey (1906) but discussed in the earlier paper. Pavey made certain assumptions about the information furnished by the map and by the field-names (followed in the latter case by Davis 1962), and since they are potentially of some importance for the study of the monastery it is as well to re-examine them and the evidence on which they were based.

The 1688 map shows a linear feature running east - west just north of the church. Pavey interprets this as an 'entrenchment' and draws attention to the Latin caption in the field called 'Behind the Church' immediately to the north. This he prints as *ager cum cessat marubii ferox* (1906: 584). The rendering of the last word is clearly incorrect, possibly due to a printing error; it should read *ferax*, as Pavey surely knew, since he translated the label 'the ditch or bank where the horehound grows freely'. His translation of *ager* is hardly correct, however, and was presumably based upon his preconceived notion about the nature of the feature to the north of the church. The sense of the caption is 'when the field lies fallow [it is] thick with *marrubium* (presumably *M. vulgare* = white horehound)'. One would hardly expect a bank, much less a ditch, to be described as lying fallow; the caption surely refers to the whole field. This information is of some importance for the botanical history of the site, and may have significance in relation to the cultivation of a monastic herb garden in the early medieval period, as my colleague Miss Ann Conolly has pointed out to me, but it does not seem to be relevant to the superficial archaeology of the site.

What then is the correct interpretation of the feature which Pavey called an 'entrenchment'? The evidence of the map is a little ambiguous. The drawing of the feature seems to follow the convention otherwise used to indicate roads or major paths, though this also appears to be used on occasion to represent a boundary hedge, for example on the north-eastern limit of the parish. It is therefore not clear whether the feature is a road or path or whether it may be tentatively identified as some kind of earthwork after all, if only a hedge bank. Pavey made another reference to a ditch, which may have given him the idea for his mistranslation (as I think) of *ager:* 'until lately, a ditch of some size extended from the Market Harborough and Northampton Road, and passing the church, bore down towards the site near the present Spratton Station. The only remaining traces of this ditch are to be found in the boundary between the Glebe Allotments and the land once worked for ironstone, as well as in the boundary of "Linch Lane" ' (Pavey 1902: 442). This statement is made in connexion with a garbled reference to Saxon finds west of the church, which presumably refers to the mixed cemetery known as Brixworth II (Meaney 1964: 187). If this is correct, then the station concerned must be Brixworth, not Spratton, and the direction taken by the ditch to the west of Station Road (called Lutterworth Road in 1688) must have been roughly north-west, not south-west as suggested by Pavey's description. It is otherwise impossible that the ditch should

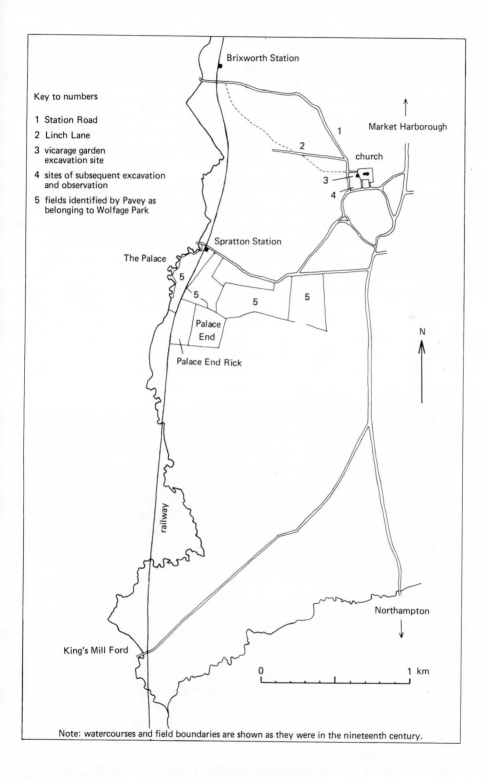

Key to numbers

1 Station Road
2 Linch Lane
3 vicarage garden
  excavation site
4 sites of subsequent excavation
  and observation
5 fields identified by Pavey as
  belonging to Wolfage Park

Brixworth Station

Market Harborough

1

2

church

3

4

Spratton Station

The Palace

5

5

5

5

Palace
End

Palace End Rick

N

railway

Northampton

King's Mill Ford

0   1 km

Note: watercourses and field boundaries are shown as they were in the nineteenth century.

Figure 43. Sketch map of western part of Brixworth parish.

cross Linch Lane, which runs west from Station Road at SP 746713, a little further north than the point of intersection between the road and the feature under discussion (fig. 43). The explanation of that feature on the map may be the continuation of Pavey's ditch east of Station Road since the reference to Glebe Allotments indicates that it must have passed the church to the north. It must be pointed out, however, that the map shows no continuation of any feature drawn in an appropriate convention *west* of Station Road, though a simple dotted line follows the approximate route described by Pavey, as here amended. On later maps a footpath to Brixworth station takes the same line.

There can therefore be no certainty about the feature on the map, and it might seem a very tenuous piece of evidence to resurrect. The reason for its potential importance is that by the time Pavey was writing the relevant area had been extensively quarried for ironstone, so that it was - and is - impossible to verify the evidence visually or archaeologically (unless the feature was close enough to the church to lie within the main churchyard: there is so far no evidence for this). It is therefore the only evidence we have for any kind of a boundary to the north of the church, whether this was the monastic boundary, the boundary of an earlier enclosure or a more recent churchyard boundary; and it should be noted that even if one is unable to believe in Pavey's ditch, a road or path is equally likely to indicate a boundary line. The point is of sufficient importance for further study and observation to be devoted to the precise location of the feature and to the determination, if possible, of its exact nature and date.

It is tempting, however, to accept the ditch hypothesis in view of recent archaeological evidence to the west of the church (fig. 44). In 1972 excavations adjacent to Station Road in the former vicarage garden under the direction of Paul Everson revealed what appears to be the western limit of the monastic site (Everson 1973a; a full report is expected in *J. Brit. Archaeol.Ass.*). A deep north - south ditch on the western edge of the site contained in its upper fill a few sherds of St Neots, Stamford and Northampton wares, while the site as a whole yielded a quantity of unstratified and unassociated sherds of pre-Conquest date. Mike McCarthy, who is studying the pottery from the site alongside that from Northampton and other sites in the county, writes of this material: 'Although there were few rims or other features diagnostic of particular forms, the fabrics, chiefly black and gritty with a small quantity of Ipswich-type ware and grass-tempered sherds, indicate an Early to Middle Saxon date for the collection as a whole' (private communication). The site appears to have been occupied, therefore, in the Anglo-Saxon period, and the ditch is provisionally interpreted as the *vallum monasterii*. Subsequent excavation on properties to the south of this site failed to locate any continuation of the line of the ditch, though observation during the building of the new vicarage confirmed it adjacent to the area excavated in 1972 (Everson 1973b, 1975). Earlier excavations immediately outside the churchyard south perimeter had not identified any similar feature on that side of the church. There is therefore at present no knowledge of the extent of the monastic site to south-west, south or east.

It is perhaps advisable to exercise a little caution in accepting the 1972 ditch as belonging necessarily to the Anglo-Saxon monastery. A recent paper has drawn attention to the dangers of assuming a monastic character for bank-and-ditch complexes where there is no direct evidence (Burrow 1973). In the case of Brixworth

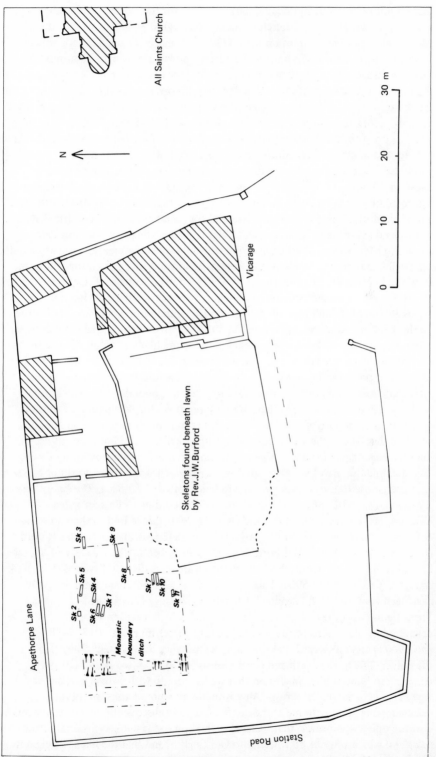

Figure 44. Brixworth: plan of 1972 excavation *(after Everson).*

there is not only the slight documentary evidence for the existence of a monastery, noted by all writers on the church including the Taylors (1965: 108), but the additional suggestive presence on the 1972 site of unaccompanied burials which appear to mark the western limit of a cemetery previously recognized around the former vicarage. It is unlikely that a cemetery so close to the church should be other than the monastic burial ground. This does not, however, *prove* the monastic nature of the ditch, which could in accordance with Burrow's dictum be that of a pre-monastic, possibly secular, enclosure. The conclusion in Everson 1975 that the ditch is monastic depends upon the assumption that the monastery was founded before the radiocarbon date for the ditch of c.700. Since the only literary source for the monastery can hardly be regarded as unimpeachable evidence this assumption may be open to question. Though it is not likely on the basis of available archaeological evidence, the possibility must be borne in mind that the Saxon monastery at Brixworth reused a pre-Saxon site. There is plenty of evidence for such a procedure in Celtic Britain and Ireland (Thomas 1971: 32-5), and not a few Anglo-Saxon monasteries are known to have been established in redundant military enclosures, e.g. Reculver and Bradwell in Saxon shore forts of the Roman period and Breedon-on-the-Hill in an Iron Age hill fort (Taylor and Taylor 1965: 503-5, 91; Thomas 1971: 43; Cramp 1974: 33). The elevated position of the church at Brixworth makes it a not impossible site for a hill fort, though the possible relationship between the feature on the 1688 map and the ditch found in 1972 (approximately at right angles to each other) might make a Roman period enclosure a more likely possibility. In terms of tangible evidence, the amount of residual material found by Everson was negligible, so that this point can be discussed only in very general terms until there has been systematic excavation of the churchyard or some neighbouring site, which should settle once and for all whether there was any pre-monastic occupation of the area.

The possible nature of any forerunner of the monastery in the Saxon period, which in the light of the 1972 excavation is the likeliest period of previous use of the site, is intriguing in view of the second cluster of evidence recorded by Pavey: 'Surrounding the site of a house called *Wolfage,* which is shown on a map of 1688 to have been close to then existing ruins, are fields called *The Palace, The Palace End Rick,* and *The Palace Meadow,* as well as a mill, according to Bridges called *Kingesmulne'* (Pavey 1902: 442; Bridges 1791: 80). 'Palace End' is shown on the 1688 map and is field 617 on the parish map of 1846 (Northamptonshire Record Office no. 3014); 'King's Mill Ford' is also shown in 1688. 'The Palace' and 'Palace End Rick' do not appear on the 1688 map but are identified by Pavey as fields 614 and 616 in 1846 (1906: 590). 'Palace Meadow' is not mentioned again, but may have been confused with 'Meadow' listed under Wolfage Park as field 613 *(ibid.).* These fields (with the exception of 'The Palace', which has been largely destroyed by alterations to the stream bed) are parcel numbers 7017, 5418, and 3900 (part) respectively on the 25-inch Ordnance Survey map. They flank the railway line to the north and south-east of SP 735703 (see fig. 43). It is tempting to jump to the conclusion that we have to do with a royal site, and to argue an Anglo-Saxon date for it. Alex Rumble, to whom I am grateful for discussing this point with me at the conference and subsequently by correspondence, is of the opinion, however, that 'palace' in this context is unlikely to derive from *palatium,* which was not borrowed into Old English, and that the likeliest origin is Old French/Middle English *palis, paleis* = palisade. Indeed, the 1688 map shows

Palace End adjacent to the apparently enclosed area of Wolfage Park, probably the centre for the eponymous manor first mentioned in 1509 (Salzman 1937: 151). The fields listed by Pavey (1906) are all adjacent to those he identified as belonging to Wolfage Park. There is not the slightest difficulty, therefore, in accepting Rumble's suggestion for the origin of these field names. Other less salubrious interpretations were offered in discussion at the conference. Of these the derivation from Latin *palus* = marsh, bog, seems unacceptable; though possible for the field(s) near the stream, it is hardly likely to have applied to those further to the south-east, which lie on rising ground bisected by the 300-foot contour; further, derivations from this source might be expected to build on the stem *palud-*, but in any case the map's draughtsman was something of a Latinist, and may be relied upon to have penetrated such an etymology, had it existed, and to have written a Latin label or an English paraphrase for the area concerned.

There are a few shreds of evidence which might favour a literal interpretation of 'palace': the indisputable existence of a king's mill (the ford is at SP 733680); the royal holding of the manor at Domesday; and the granting of Brixworth church as a prebend to Salisbury Cathedral by Henry I in 1102 (Pavey 1902: 447), a gift confirmed by Henry II (Salzman 1937: 157). The last, and the transfer of the manor to common hands, indicate that royal interest in the parish declined soon after the Conquest, so that any site which might be identified as royal is likely to belong to the Anglo-Saxon period. It may also be noted that Hart suggested for quite other reasons that Brixworth may have been a royal vill from the time of Edward the Elder (1970: 28-9), and that Davis took account of the 'palace' names when postulating the identity of Brixworth and *Clofesho*, where church councils were held in the eighth and ninth centuries (1962: 71). Though the possibility of identifying a royal site in the parish, with attendant implications for the monastic foundation and its site, is an exciting one, there is little justification for doing so on the basis of the present evidence. D.N.Hall tells me, however, that field-walking has identified an extensive Middle Saxon site in this general area, and this clearly warrants further investigation.

THE CHURCH FABRIC

Structural analysis

New and repeated critical examination of the fabric by eye and by measured drawing may be expected to lead to new interpretation or to new working hypotheses on which to base further investigation. Two examples of this process must suffice here.

It has been noted above (p. 173) that one of the Committee's preliminary tasks has been the preparation of accurate plans and elevations. The raw data produced by the new ground survey (which is not yet ready for publication) have drawn attention to an area already known to be of potential significance, but where previous plans have diverged markedly, as for example that in Salzman (1937: 153) and that in the Taylors' corpus (1965: 110, fig. 49). The former shows a clear misalignment at the west end, where the west walls of nave and tower do not stand at 90° to the main church axis. The Taylors also show the irregularity, but in a less exaggerated form. The new survey confirms the misalignment, and when complete will show its precise extent reliably for the first time; it is therefore possible now to discuss the anomaly with greater confidence. The survey also seems to indicate that the tower north and south walls are not at right angles to the nave west wall, though they have been shown as such on previous plans. The frequently suggested explanation, 'poor setting out', is hardly good enough here, since the building is otherwise fairly regular, and the most useful hypothesis at the moment appears to be that the west walls and the remainder of the nave may be of different dates. If this should prove to be so, then the nave is presumably secondary to its west wall, since the west respond of the south arcade is not significantly truncated in comparison with that on the north, while the proportions of the north arcade suggest that it may have been adjusted to fit a slightly longer east - west space than that available for the south arcade. If the north and south walls of the tower prove to run parallel to the main axis of the church, then it may become necessary to regard them as tertiary (a case can already be made out for their being secondary to the west walls concerned). Thus the west wall of the tower and the west wall of the nave may belong to an earlier narrow building running north - south, perhaps a narthex, to postulate the least unlikely of a number of possibilities. An original narthex later converted to a tower is no new suggestion (cf. Taylor and Taylor 1965: 109), but the possible sequence west walls/nave/tower north and south walls is. This is of fundamental importance to the chronology of the structure and must be borne in mind in future investigations, especially excavations around and within the west end of the church. The significance of this possible sequence for the interpretation of other parts of the building will be mentioned below (p. 181). A further observation may be held to lend some support to this hypothesis. A local preliminary study of the distribution of specific building materials has shown a great contrast between the heavy concentration of brick in the south wall of the nave and the almost total absence of it from the adjacent part of the west wall (fig. 45). The full and precise significance of this observation is not yet clear, but one possible explanation of the anomaly is that the two walls are not of the same build. It also serves to emphasize that the distributions of the building materials are not random, a point reinforced by the next paragraph, and that the projected petrological study of the masonry is likely to contribute significantly to the interpretation of the standing structure.

Similar evidence may be seen elsewhere in the nave south wall, particularly in the arcade piers, where it complements the purely structural evidence. The second and third piers from the west show an interesting distribution of building materials, with the brick not being used below a clearly marked level except for the jamb linings; these linings are straight-jointed vertically to the core of the piers below this level, and this is particularly noticeable on pier three (see fig. 47). This suggests that the apparently straightforward building sequence may have to be rethought. The non-brick, mainly granite, pier cores may represent the ends of north - south walls between a continuous line of south porticus (normally assumed for Brixworth in contrast to open aisles, especially since Jackson and Fletcher 1961); these must therefore have become embedded in a south arcade wall wholly or partly secondary to themselves. Alternatively, the brickwork may represent a rebuilding, perhaps an enlargement, of early openings into the porticus.

A second point of interest in the south arcade is the irregular, non-radial laying of the bricks which serve as arch voussoirs. This is a familiar technique in Anglo-Saxon church architecture, discussed in some detail by Baldwin Brown (1925: 66-7, 424-5). Lord Fletcher has kindly pointed out to me in a private communication that several fifth- to sixth-century churches in Rome and elsewhere in the Empire exhibit the same technique, for example Santa Maria Antiqua and the original (domestic) parts of Santi Giovanni e Paolo. The latter is illustrated by Mâle (1960: 185, pl. 27). If it is typical of the Roman examples, their irregularity can hardly be said to be of the same order as that of many Anglo-Saxon arches, and it seems that the latter still require some explanation. In any case, the south arcade at Brixworth displays a feature which makes it outstanding even in an Anglo-Saxon context. The interior of the easternmost arch head has, like its companions, concentric lines of brick following the outer contour of each ring of pseudo-voussoirs (see fig. 48). Following the inner of these two lines up from the western (right-hand) springing of the arch, it will be seen that the bricks take a false line tangential to the extrados of the arch, and run off almost vertically until the correct line is re-established by the sixth brick in the sequence. Directly above the false line, a considerable wedge of fairly well-coursed small masonry, which appears to belong to the main run of the walling (though it is impossible to be certain, because the spandrels and upper walling are plastered) divide the only partially complete outer ring of pseudo-voussoirs from the complete inner ring. It is unlikely that such 'mistakes' could occur in an arch built up organically with the wall in which it is set, neither can they be satisfactorily explained as surface decoration after the completion of arch construction: such an explanation might account for the errant bricks, but not for the wedge of stonework. Either feature is conceivable, however, if one allows the possibility of the arcade arch having been fitted into a wall in ruinous or unstable condition. The irregularity of the 'voussoirs' also becomes immediately comprehensible in the context of arch insertion. It should be noted that many of the brick arches elsewhere in the church (i.e. not in either nave arcade) are perfectly well constructed, or at least vastly superior to the nave arcades. This is not the first time that attention has been drawn to the irregularities of the arcade arches; Hamilton Thompson made similar observations over 60 years ago and came to similar conclusions. Describing the arch heads of the nave arcades he wrote: 'These rings, with their outer circumscribing semicircles are very largely composed of Roman bricks, but thin slabs of local oolite have also been freely used in a manner which suggests a reconstruction of the arches after a period of ruin, in which new stone-work was used where the supply of original bricks failed' (Thompson 1912: 505).

There is, then, some evidence both internally and externally that the south arcade may prove to be secondary to the wall in which it stands. Elevation drawings of individual building material distributions, and in particular a stone-by-stone drawing *without* the brick, might prove very instructive on this point. Alternatively or additionally, the main fabric of the nave side walls may be secondary to the west end, as discussed briefly above, so that there is the possibility of a fairly complex building sequence overall, which must be considered on the occasion of future investigations. A very brief, speculative account of the somewhat far-reaching implications of the study of structural evidence at Brixworth was attempted by Parsons (1972), unfortunately without illustrations.

Scientific investigation
The fact that the church fabric at Brixworth contains so much brick means that there is an additional opportunity for research, since the building material itself can be subjected to scientific analysis. The potential of the study of bricks in standing

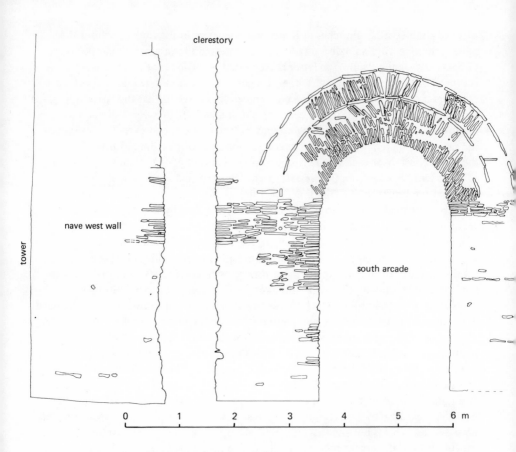

Figure 45. Brixworth, All Saints Church: elevation of south-west bay of nave arcade and adjacent west wall, showing position of bricks.

Figure 46. Brixworth, All Saints Church: the south arcade from the south-west. The arrows indicate the positions of the piers shown in detail in figs. 47a and b. The broken white line shows the extent of the walling illustrated in fig. 45.

a

Figure 47. Brixworth, All Saints Church: south arcade, details of piers: a. the second pier from the west; b. the third pier from the west.

b

structures of this age was appreciated in Germany before the Second World War, when some brick-built Carolingian churches were investigated and samples of their brick fabric subjected to analysis (Wagner 1933-8). The samples were thin-sectioned and examined in polarized light, which enabled two distinct clay sources for the Carolingian bricks to be identified; the Carolingian and post-Carolingian bricks were distinguished, however, largely on the basis of the grain size of their sand inclusions. The Brixworth bricks have not so far been thin-sectioned, since they appear mostly to have been made from the local chalky boulder clay, which is such a heterogenous material that source identification is unlikely to prove possible. The preliminary investigation has proceeded along somewhat different lines.

Everson's 1972 excavation (see above, p. 176) produced many fragments of brick, one of which, from the fill of the ditch, was submitted to the Oxford Research Laboratory for Archaeology and the History of Art for a thermoluminescent determination. The provisional reply 'probably Saxon' encouraged the Committee to consider seriously the possibility, not previously given much credence, that the bricks (or at least some of the bricks) in the church fabric might also be of Anglo-Saxon date. The Committee therefore welcomed the suggestion that Mr Everson should provide comparative samples from the church fabric for analysis by the Oxford Laboratory; in addition to assisting with the interpretation of the excavation, the additional determinations might shed some light on the architectural history of the church. A list of 15 key locations was drawn up. In the event it proved possible to sample at only eight of these points. Conventional TL techniques proved inadequate because of the presence of foreign chemicals introduced in the course of conservation work on the church fabric. Further tests using another method have so far produced results for four of the eight samples:

Sample number	Location	Provisional date-range
PBS 5	A south arcade arch head	A.D. 200 - 600
PBS 8	West door of the nave	A.D. 1400 - 1600
PBS 9	Triple opening between tower and nave	A.D. 750 - 1050
PBS 15	Blocked north door of choir	A.D. 700 - 1000

In the first place it is interesting to have confirmation of the presence of at least one brick almost certainly of the Roman period, and of two further bricks of clearly Anglo-Saxon date. At present one can only speculate on the precise significance of PBS 8!

The most interesting result is the apparent similarity in date between PBS 9 and 15. If it should prove that these samples are actually contemporary and this is confirmed by further sampling, then there would be a scientific basis for regarding the west wall of the nave as earlier than the body of the church, since the triple opening in it is by any standards a secondary feature. The dating of PBS 5 will come as no surprise to most people, though it does nothing to resolve the problem of the immediate source of such Roman bricks as there are in the church fabric; excavation in the 1960s did not confirm the expectation that the nearby villa site was their place of origin (Woods 1967: 7). The Roman date of the sample is irrelevant to the chronology of the church if one regards it as reused material. Only if one wishes

Figure 48. Brixworth, All Saints Church: south arcade interior, detail of easternmost arch head.

to insist upon a standing Roman building reused as such is the determination at all embarrassing in connexion with the arguments above about the chronology of the south arcade. However, there is little justification for drawing any conclusions from only four determinations and without any discussion of the dating method employed or the precise significance of the date brackets. On the basis of these and the next four determinations it will have to be decided whether to complete the preliminary programme of 15 samples, and then whether conclusions are justified or more widespread sampling indicated.

In order not to interfere more than necessary with the superficial appearance of the church, sampling was carried out by removing whole bricks from the wall, taking a piece from the innermost corner of each, and replacing them in the same position. This procedure made it possible to extract samples of mortar from the core of the wall at the same time, and these were submitted to Dr F.W.Anderson for inspection. The results of his preliminary examination are summarized in the following table:

Sample number	Location	Characteristics						
PMS 1	South-west quoin of nave	–	–	L	Lm	–	–	
PMS 2	Levelling courses of tower south wall	–	–	L	–	–	–	
PMS 3	Horizontal course in a south arcade pier	C	–	–	Lm	–	–	
PMS 5	A south arcade arch head	C	–	–	–	P	S	
PMS 6	Head of tower south door	C	–	–	–	–	–	
PMS 8	West door of the nave	C	–	L	–	–	–	
PMS 9	Triple opening between tower and nave	C$^+$F	L	–	P	–		
PMS 15	Blocked north door of choir	–	–	–	–	–	–	

KEY

C	=	charcoal fragments	P	=	pebbles of ? quartzite
F	=	flint fragments	S	=	shell fragments
L	=	calcined limestone or chalk	+		indicates that PMS 9 had a
Lm	=	ochreous laminae suggesting an original clay content			noticeable amount of charcoal, some fragments of which bore plant impressions

Anderson also reported that the sand content of the samples showed no significant variations, with an average grain size of 0.5 - 0.6mm, only slightly larger than the norm for present-day mortars. In general he saw the samples forming two groups, those with and those without chalk or calcined limestone. This grouping does not seem to have any particular significance, and in view of the comparatively recent date of brick sample PBS 8, which might have led one to expect a markedly different type of mortar in this position from those in apparently Saxon parts of the fabric, the usefulness of the data obtained may be doubted. It may be, however, that further quantitative analysis may reveal significant differences not apparent in a simple listing of the ingredients. At the same time, Anderson drew attention to PMS 5, the only sample to contain shell fragments; it also contained the coarsest sand. It may ultimately prove to be significant that the one remarkable sample comes from a feature which it has been argued may be an insertion.

Once again, the limited number of examples does not allow any firm conclusions. The opportunity will be taken when further work is done on the fabric to extract more mortar for analysis, at least up to the originally projected number of fifteen samples. It may be possible then to assess whether to proceed with a plan to sample the whole fabric at regular intervals by extracting cores.

CONCLUSION

Some progress has been made in the long-term research project on Brixworth church, though so far there are not a great many tangible results. This account has attempted to indicate some of the lines of approach and has suggested a possible outcome in some cases. Where this amounts to an interpretation, it must be regarded as personal and extremely provisional, and as no more than a working hypothesis to be discarded when it has outlived its usefulness.

ACKNOWLEDGMENTS

I am grateful to the many colleagues, some of whom are mentioned in this paper, who have given information to the Committee or to me personally, or who have discussed specific points with me. I am particularly indebted to Paul Everson not only for permission to refer to his excavations in advance of publication but also for kindly supplying the original of fig. 44. It goes without saying that any errors of fact or interpretation in this paper are mine and not his.

M.R. McCarthy of Northampton Development Corporation Archaeological Unit kindly supplied me with a brief preliminary report on the pottery from the vicarage garden excavation; his study of the Brixworth material will be published not only in the site report but in the unit's forthcoming volume on the St Peter's Street excavations in Northampton, where he will discuss early medieval pottery from the county as a whole. Finally I am grateful to the Rev. J.N. Chubb and the Brixworth Parochial Church Council for their kind co-operation in allowing the investigations reported here to take place.

REFERENCES

Bridges, J., 1791. *History and Antiquities of Northamptonshire*, vol. 2.
Brown, G.B., 1925. *The Arts in Early England*, vol. 2: *Anglo-Saxon Architecture* (2nd edn).
Burrow, I.C.G., 1973. 'Tintagel - some problems', *Scottish Archaeological Forum, 5:* 99-103.
Cramp, R., 1974. 'The Anglo-Saxons and Rome', *Transactions of the Architectural and Archaeological Society of Durham and Northumberland, 3:* 27-37.
Davis, R.H.C., 1962. 'Brixworth and Clofesho', *J. Brit. Archaeol. Ass.* 3rd ser., *25:* 71.
Everson, P., 1973a. 'Brixworth, Site 1', *Northamptonshire Archaeol., 8:* 17-8.
Everson, P., 1973b. 'Brixworth, Sites 2 and 3', *Northamptonshire Archaeol., 8:* 19-20.
Everson, P., 1975. 'Brixworth', *Northamptonshire Archaeol., 10:* 164.
Fletcher, Lord, 1974. 'Brixworth: was there a crypt?', *J. Brit. Archaeol. Ass.,* 3rd ser., *37:* 88-96.
Hart, C., 1970. *The Hidation of Northamptonshire* (University of Leicester, Department of Local History, Occasional Papers, 2nd ser., no. 3).
Jackson, E.D.C., and Fletcher, E.G.M., 1961. 'Excavations at Brixworth, 1958', *J. Brit. Archaeol. Ass.,* 3rd ser., *24:* 1-15.
Jones, J., 1976. *How to record Graveyards.*
Mâle, E., 1960. *Early Churches of Rome.*
Meaney, A., 1964. *Gazetteer of Early Anglo-Saxon Burial Sites.*
Parsons, D., 1972. 'Brixworth, Church of All Saints', *Bulletin of the Northamptonshire Federation of Archaeological Societies, 7:* 39-40.
Pavey, A.K., 1902. 'Some notes on the parochial history of Brixworth', *Ass. Archit. Socs. Rep. Pap., 26.2:* 441-8.
Pavey, A.K., 1906. 'Further notes on the parochial history of Brixworth: field names, etc.' *Ass. Archit. Socs. Rep. Pap., 28.2:* 575-92.
Salzman, L.F. (ed.), 1937. *V.C.H. Northamptonshire* IV.
Taylor, H.M., 1973. 'Archaeological investigation of churches in Great Britain', *Antiq. J., 53:* 13-15.
Taylor, H.M. and J., 1965. *Anglo Saxon Architecture.*
Thomas, C., 1971. *Early Christian Archaeology of North Britain'.*
Thompson, A.H., 1912. 'Brixworth Church', *Archaeol. J., 69:* 505-10.
Wagner, W., 1933-8. 'Die petrographische Baustoffuntersuchung als Hilfsmittel zur Klärung der Geschichte historischer Bauten', *Jahrbuch für Volks-und Heimats forschung Hessen Nassau,* 1933-8: 202-9.
Woods, P., 1967. 'Brixworth, Lodge Leys Field', *Bulletin of the Northamptonshire Federation of Archaeological Societies, 2:* 7-8.

ROSEMARY CRAMP

11 Schools of Mercian sculpture

In this paper I shall use the term *Mercia* to refer to Greater Mercia, but should perhaps define further my use of the term 'school'. In attempting to sort out hundreds of works of art or craftsmanship there are of course various levels of attribution one might hope to reach in producing chronological and stylistic divisions:

(a)   Attribution to a known artist, and to datable divisions of his life's work. This is not applicable here since we have no named sculptors and no documentation of individual works in the pre-Viking period.

(b)   Attribution to a school deriving from a central known figure, whose methods, designs and iconography are copied, or completed. These too are linked to a man's life's work, and are not applicable for the same reasons as (a).

(c)   Attribution to 'schools' which imply time/place divisions not linked with known individuals. This type of attribution is normal for folk art. This is my aim in this paper, but only with the most tentative model, since there is no sculpture datable by absolute or external means. We know something of the dates of Christian foundations on sites which have produced such work, but these often give a *terminus post quem,* too early to be relevant. Moreover, there are cases when one feels that one master was responsible for a group of carvings, and yet one cannot make such an attribution.

(d)   Attributions in which temporal differences are given socio-political affiliations. Some refer to the crudest temporal divisions - Roman, Anglo-Saxon, Carolingian. Some, involving both methods (d) and (e), are attempting to say more: Mercian, Northumbrian. The implication of this type of attribution is that political divisions produce stylistic differences. It is assumed that political power creates individual combinations of contacts, patronage and opportunities. I shall largely assume this to be true, but will stress as I have done elsewhere, that there seems validity in the view that, in the period late seventh to early tenth century, individual monastic houses, diocesan organization, or even royal patronage, created focal points of influence. Nevertheless, the least subjective view is to make divisions according to modern areas, e.g. west Midlands, east Midlands, south Yorkshire. Having said that I shall attempt to relate the sculpture to some political and social divisions of the past, and will assign a series of dates by analogy.

(e)   Crude temporal divisions - eighth century, ninth century - arrived at by composite consensus, putting together all types of artifacts: manuscripts, metalwork and sculpture, and trying to achieve a period fit and internal chronology. In the Anglo-Saxon period divisions by centuries are singularly inept because significant events usually happened in the middle of centuries, from the mid-fifth and mid-sixth centuries to the mid-eleventh. Therefore it must be realized that any of the dates I am so misguided as to give in the present discussion are mere refuge points to prevent one from feeling lost.

Since there are some 400 fragments which occur within the area of Greater Mercia which might be considered I will suggest at the outset that there are, in the simplest terms, certain groups in which marked resemblances exist:

1.   Groups of friezes and panels of architectural sculpture, from Fletton, Castor, Peterborough, Breedon.

2.   Peak District crosses and sarcophagi centred on Bakewell, with a strange outlier at Rugby.

3.   A west Mercian (?Hwiccan) group of crosses centred on or beginning at Gloucester, but embracing later an area from Hereford to Gloucester.

4.   An Anglian group with links between Lincolnshire and Derbyshire, based perhaps on earlier Anglian models.

5.   A southern English group which relates West Saxon and Mercian crosses and architectural sculpture from Wolverhampton to Winchester.

6.   A late western group which spreads through Cheshire to the Peak District, developing out of earlier styles in that area.

7.   A central and eastern group of crosses which spreads from Derbyshire, Leicestershire, Northamptonshire and into Bedfordshire, possibly growing out of Danelaw material.

8.   A group of grave covers mainly of Barnack stone, found in Leicestershire, Lincolnshire, Northamptonshire, Norfolk.

Here I only intend to discuss groups 1 to 4, and will roughly assign them to the period before the early tenth century, when Mercia was still a meaningful political entity. Groups 5 to 8 I have discussed recently in outline elsewhere, and do think they lie most happily in the period c.900-1100 (Cramp 1972 and 1975). Finally in this preliminary statement I must stress the 'social' difference between the type of sculpture which is a part of church decoration and that which is found on crosses and grave covers. The two co-exist but do not develop at the same speed.

In many seventh-century foundations where one might expect sculpture, one does not find it. For example at Peterborough there is only one interlace capital and one wall slab. Brixworth has no early architectural sculpture, but similarly there is nothing from Lichfield, Repton, Gloucester or Worcester, which are demonstrably late seventh- or early eighth-century foundations. This does not mean to say that such

Figure 49. Map: findspots cited in the text.

work did not exist: the strange tentative cross shaft with a style II-type animal at Brixworth makes one cautious.

However, I think we must agree with Kendrick, if we use comparative stylistic evidence, that the earliest Mercian sculpture does not appear until after the mid-eighth century or, as he puts it, the end of Offa's reign, 757-96 (Kendrick 1938: 64). Now Kendrick sees the earliest groups as dependent on Northumbrian traditions - 'a direct continuation of the Northumbrian series' - i.e. the Peak District crosses, though he does say that the figure style has 'its own Midland character'. He does not say how that character was developed. I think that there is just as good a case to be made for the primacy of the architectural sculpture (my group 1), which I see as a comparable but later development to the friezes and panels at Northumbrian centres such as Monkwearmouth/Jarrow and Hexham.

The ultimate inspiration for the strip friezes of Breedon must be seen in the decoration of Near Eastern churches such as those in the monastery of Apa Apollo, Bawit, in particular in the south church (Torp 1971: plans 1 and 2 and pl. 31). It is true that the tradition of friezes with animals and abstract ornament had been known in England since the late seventh century (Cramp 1974). Nevertheless there is a liveliness, a difference in stone cutting technique and an individual iconography which sets these Midland friezes apart from other sculpture and seems to initiate new traditions. The deep confident undercutting and the use of the drill could well indicate the importation of stone masons, but as we will see most parallels one can find are with late eighth-, early ninth-century manuscripts, both in England and on the Continent. It is impossible to say whether the motifs arrived through manuscripts, or whether both are drawing on East Christian models. First, however, let us define the range of material at Breedon.

On the narrow friezes (Clapham 1928: nos. 1 and 18), the plant scroll shows two types of organization, one a simple spiraliform scroll with trumpet bindings, and the other a crossing medallion scroll with trumpet bindings. I use the term 'simple spiraliform' when the internal strand curls around once, and the term 'spiraliform' when this curls more than once. Because of the trumpet bindings these can merge one into the other.

In the first type (fig. 50), the volutes contain hollow-cut heart-shaped leaves; hollow-cut trefoils or scooped leaf whorls; and round modelled berry bunches. The bindings are triple V-shapes. The formula used is also varied: e.g., we see in the length of the frieze a leaf, trefoil, berry three times; then leaf, whorl, berry, trefoil; then seven doublets of leaves and trefoils; then berry, trefoil, berry, whorl, with the berry bunches becoming noticeably more diminished. Small hollow-cut curling leaves, ivy leaves and occasionally berries spring from the interior of the volute and act as space fillers. Only three times does there spring a fruit from the trumpet binding. All the stems are median incised.

The medallion scrolls are formed from two strands of equal thickness which pass over and under and from each trumpet binding alternately throw off two stalks which hook-link within the medallion volute, or stems which branch across and outside the volute to act as space fillers. Occasionally there is a squared off frond leaf. The terminations are hollow-cut leaves, hollow trefoils and rounded berry bunches. Each stem is median incised and the bindings are cleverly rounded. This scroll with two crossing stems of equal thickness is like the Bawit scroll, as are also the leaf whorls (Torp 1971: pl. 31).

The form of the simple spiraliform scrolls is closely paralleled on the inhabited scrolls. There are five fragments of inhabited simple spiraliform scroll which clearly go together (four are shown in fig. 51). Each trumpet sprouts two finer volutes which encircle a creature, part of whose body extends beyond the volute. Details of the scrolls are difficult to determine but there are clearly hollow-cut leaves. On one fragment a naked human figure straddles a scroll and faces a bird with a rounded head which is back to back with another bird. There are also two long-necked quadrupeds, two pairs of centaurs and two more struggling human figures (Clapham 1928: pl. XXXIII, figs. 1 and 2).

It is possible that this group merges into a sequence of which three fragments survive in which double scrolls spring from a common root with a stiff stalk divider and are linked to the next pair by a hollow heart-shaped leaf (fig. 52). This includes four lively horsemen with lances (Clapham 1928: pl.XXXI, fig. 1); panels of pelta, trumpet spirals and interlace; and three birds pecking at grapes. These have long sinuous necks, long heads with a flying plume and long curving beaks. In the next sequence the trumpet volutes are more rectangular, rather as if the stiff leaf dividers and trumpets have been combined. Each leaf frame encloses a stiffly-striding quadruped with leaf-tipped tail and small cat-like head. Their bodies are lightly marked, one with a spiraliform hip-joint (Clapham 1928: pl.XXXIII, fig. 3).

Finally there is a sequence of panels in which birds, beasts and humans are similarly divided by panels of abstract ornament, as in a manuscript border. One (fig. 53a) has a panel of interlace, then a worn panel of casually-disposed animals, leaping, pawing and neck rubbing. Their heads are cat-like with drilled eyes and pricked ears as in some of the inhabited scrolls. The upper parts of their bodies are covered by lank fur and their legs, shown in lively attitudes, are as spindly as the plants behind them. They are separated from the next panel by a panel of key-patterning of which about half is lost (Clapham 1928: pl.XXXII, fig. 1).

Equally casually disposed against a plant background is a group of birds. One is a magnificent striding cock in profile; a three-quarter faced bird; and what may be a small hen (headless) ducked in between them; another little hen sits behind, whilst behind her is another cock with upswept tail and a bird with wings displayed (fig. 53a). Their tail and wing feathers are naturalistically depicted but their bodies are speckled with concentric rows of dots. The leaves in the plant background with their hollow pointed or heart shapes are of the same family as the other inhabited scrolls. In another length of frieze (unfortunately much worn) there is a bird of the long-necked type (see fig. 52) divided by a panel of key patterning from quadrupeds of the Insular dog type which is shown in profile and running with its head turned back to snatch at a fruit bunch (fig. 54a). The background plant scroll has a type of veined leaf of the form surmounting the stiff stalks. The panel is not complete but another section with what seems to be the same leaf and quadruped pattern is discernible in another worn fragment (fig. 54b). Finally and most originally there are the remains of three human figures picking fruit (Clapham 1928: pl. XXXII, fig. 1). They are all shown as naked (or nearly naked) like the spearman. One appears to be seated, one possibly kneeling, and one standing. Escaped from the confines of the repeating scrolls, these men, birds and beasts have a freedom which reminds one of early Scythian art (*From the Land of the Scythians:* plate 31, no. 171).

The East Christian origins of the vine scrolls are clear. The delicate undulating

Figure 50. Breedon, Leicestershire: vinescroll friezes.

a

c

d

Figure 51. Breedon, Leicestershire: inhabited spiraliform trumpet scrolls.

c

d

Figure 52. Breedon, Leicestershire: inhabited linked scrolls (with pelta and trumpet spiral panels).

Figure 53. Breedon, Leicestershire: a. frieze; b. lion panel.

b

a

b

c

Figure 54. a and b. Breedon, Leicestershire: friezes;
c. South Kyme, Leicestershire: panel.

scroll with short curled tendrils enclosing rounded berry bunches and with round scooped leaves is paralleled in Byzantine metalwork. At its grandest one can compare the bronze doors of St Sophia, of the ninth century (Dalton 1961: fig. 391); or at a more modest level, the plant with rounded scooped leaves is found in jewellery (Ross 1965: no. 33, p. 32 and pl. 26). It is also characteristic of some Carolingian scrolls in the Palace school of manuscripts which are strongly influenced from East Christian art, such as the Coronation Gospels of the Holy Roman Empire, f. 76v (Braunfels 1965: pl. 36). The crossed medallion scroll is also found at Bawit (Torp 1971: pl. 31). The flower with round scooped petals remains a popular motif in the southern English art province. However, the scooped rounded leaf is only found on the Breedon scrolls and is more clearly linked with European and East Christian art. Its ultimate inspiration is to be found in Iranian art. As Dalton noted, heart or pear-shaped leaves are old Persian motifs (Dalton 1961: 70 n.12). Such leaves also found their way into textiles, such as the seventh-century silk of St Calais which is considered to be Byzantine but reproducing Sassanian themes (*Les Trésors des Eglises de France:* no. 244, pl. 6). At a later date such rounded hollow leaves seem to have established themselves as a motif among the Avars, and Cincik has argued that from that area, after Charlemagne's conquest of the Avars and the subsequent Christianization of their territory, such motifs are found in manuscripts such as the Cuthbert Gospels (Cincik 1958: 44-60). He also makes the interesting point that Charlemagne, after his victory over the Avars in 796, distributed the curious treasures he had taken as loot to monastic houses in his kingdom and to client and friendly secular rulers. Among them was Offa, who received an Avaric hatchet, a sword, and two Syrian silk interwoven mantles (Cincik 1958: 52-5). Cincik puts forward the plausible but unprovable supposition that 'The woven textiles presented to King Offa probably carried such elements of artistic style ornamentation which we also find in Cuthbert's Gospel and on the donated Avaric sceptre jar in the monastery of St Maurice d'Asaune'. Certainly there seems to have been a revival of interest in ancient Persian and Coptic motifs in the late eighth, early ninth century in Eastern Europe, and it is from that area that the taste for exotic birds and beasts may have been transmitted to England.

The birds at Breedon fall into several types. First, the round-headed type with a short crest and inset tail which appear as inhabitants of scrolls (fig. 50) and which can be paralleled in Coptic textiles; then birds with long sinuous necks and curving beaks whose heads sprout a long curling plume, found in processions divided by stiff stalks (fig. 51). They are closely paralleled on the Ormside cup, a piece discovered in a ninth-century grave in Cumbria, which also contains its own menagerie of exotic beasts (Bruce Mitford 1960: fig. 63). The speckled cocks and hens of the third type are the most remarkable, since they appear almost completely emancipated from the scroll background. It remains as a slight vestige, still with its hollow heart-shaped leaves. Such birds with displayed wings or tails which spray out in plumes are found on Byzantine capitals of the sixth century as at Parenzo (Dalton 1961: fig. 20), but also appear in the manuscripts of the Palace school in the spandrels of arches, or in Insular contexts as in the Book of Kells, f.67r. These emancipated fowls have no development in Anglo-Saxon sculpture, however. I exclude, as not related, the stiff portrait birds of crosses such as that from Brompton, Yorkshire (Collingwood 1907: figs. f, g, h, i, p.301).

The beasts appear equally varied and original. As inhabitants of the trumpet scroll volutes there are winged lions and centaurs. Both types could ultimately derive from Eastern textiles but both types also have a popularity elsewhere in English sculpture. In the north the small winged creatures on the Hoddam cross head are an obvious parallel, as Clapham realized (1928: 231 and pl. XXXVI, figs. 2 and 3). However, there is also the lugubrious winged lion at Dacre, Cumbria, treated in the heavy 'Roman' manner of the North, just as the Otley griffins are quite unlike the lively Midland creatures (Kendrick 1938: pl. XCIII and XCI). Centaurs too are found on Northumbrian crosses at Cundall, Melsonby and Nith Bridge, with a strange later development at Nunburnholme, and in all these crosses one finds birds with paired animals and small figures in architectural frames (Kendrick 1938: pl. LXXXVIII; Brown 1937: pls. XC-XCIII; Cramp 1970: plates 41-8).

The running hound-like creature which appears twice in the Breedon friezes is paralleled in manuscripts such as the Stockholm Codex Aureus, or Royal I E VI, f. 4a (Kendrick 1938: pl.LXVI). Moreover, the *schema* whereby the small panels of inhabited scrolls or animals are combined with abstract ornament such as the straight-line key patterns or the curving pelta type is also reminiscent of the layout of these manuscripts. The procession of stiff leonine creatures with leafy tails (fig. 52b) or the panel with the lion (fig. 53b) is less usual in manuscripts. These heraldic creatures have something in common with the leonine figures on such Merovingian manuscripts as the Laon Orosius, Paris Bibl. Nat. Lat. 12168 or the St Augustine Quaestiones (Braunfels 1965: pl. 21). However, the facial types are quite different from the Frankish or English manuscripts. The long necks and cat-like faces of the stiff processions of quadrupeds and the lively back-scratching group are, like the horsemen with their bows and lances, clearly linked with the textiles of the Christian East (Dalton 1961: chap. 10). In fact it is difficult to find a convincing parallel for the horsemen or crouching spear man in any other medium, and the muscular tense figure of the spearman (Clapham 1928: pl. XXXIV, fig. 3) even reproduces something of the style of these fabric designs.

There is one other group of lively narrative figures within the friezes - a small vintage scene. These lively prancing people have no parallels in Anglo-Saxon sculpture, although there is a fragment from Ingleby, now at Repton, which has a more static figure of a grape-picker with his bag and wearing a pointed Phrygian cap (Routh 1937: 32-4, pl. 16A, B, C). Routh saw the likeness to the Breedon style but did not think the plant on face B could be of that date. However, it is not unlike the plants at Breedon.

There are in addition at Breedon more monumental figures of relief carving which have to be considered alongside similar reliefs from Peterborough, Castor and Fletton. First there are a very worn pair of figures without haloes set in rather a squashed position within a squareheaded frame (fig. 55). They each clutch a plant spray with a hollow pointed leaf in their right hands and the one on the left holds a book in his left. They stand on tiptoe, heads inclined one to another. The one on the left is bearded with long waving hair, the one on the right has shorter hair which shows the ears. The drapery clearly shows the shape of their legs and arms. There is a loose fold over each arm and the hem folds undulate in sharp V lines. These draped figures are not like any of the others at Breedon, but their plant scrolls link them with the friezes, as does the deep undercutting of the background. Despite the very worn condition of these figures, the way in which the loose drapery folds project in another plane from the figures is very impressive and it is possible to see some of the

a b

Figure 56. Fletton, Huntingdonshire: a. figure panel of a saint; b. figure panel of an angel *(photograph: David Wright)*.

Figure 55. Breedon, Leicestershire: paired figures.

minor folds and the upper arms and ankles which show a very considerable cutting technique.

When compared with the pair of figures from Fletton, each in his own wall panel but with round-headed arch, the difference in carving technique is remarkable. Each Fletton figure stands on tiptoe as does the Breedon pair, and there is similarly an attempt to show the body through the drapery, though not so successfully. The deep undercutting is replaced by light grooves and although the hem lines and the loose folds have the same formula they are more inert. The figure holding a scroll (fig. 56a) is haloed, has tight curling hair and drilled eyes: the drapery folds are lightly incised.

The angel (fig. 56b) holding a tri-lobed staff in his right hand and holding up his left in salutation, has a similar facial type. His drapery however has more close-massed, branded folds and a wide 'sash' around the waist. This type of drapery is found on two other Breedon carvings. The first is of a bearded saint whose right hand is held up in blessing and whose left holds a book (fig. 57a): the folds of his drapery are in close massed grooves, crossed by a 'sash' effect at the waist. His eyes are drilled, but much of the detail of his features is lost. However, he is clearly of the same physical type and wears the same drapery as a figure from Castor which is rather more deeply carved and sits under a plant arcade (fig. 57b). This type of plant arcade which we have noted in the friezes of the birds at Breedon is found also in the solid stone shrine at Peterborough known as the Hedda stone. It is unfortunate that the Hedda stone is so worn that details of features and drawing are impossible to recapture (fig. 57c), especially since its repertoire of Christ with cruciform halo, Mary with her veiled face holding her lily and the ten apostles, some bearded, some beardless, seems to have the complete repertoire of the Breedon, Castor and Fletton models. It is possible that the Breedon figure and the Castor were part of a sarcophagus since they both obviously belong to a series of figures. It is also possible that the decorative formula was derived from antique sarcophagi since both architecture and plant frames are known on these (Hubert 1938: pl. XXIX a and b).

Possibly slightly later but with the same type of drapery is another Breedon figure, this time set in a clearly architectural frame of a double arch supported on cushion-like capitals and bases (Clapham 1928: pl. XXXVII, fig. 1). The figure is half-length. The head is draped in a veil like the Mary figure on the Peterborough shrine though without a halo, but the Breedon figure is holding its right hand in blessing and holding a book like an apostle (fig. 58a). It is possible that the artist's facial type was confused by these masculine attributes in the Mother of God, but there seems to have been an increased devotion to Mary in the late eighth, early ninth century which is reflected not only in sculpture but also in literature. There is a long list of customary Marian feasts in the poem *De Abbatibus* (Campbell 1967: 37-9, lines 460-9); Mary is also prominent and similarly veiled in the Book of Kells, f. 7v; other sculptural examples are the Hovingham slab (Collingwood 1907: 337 and fig. on p. 334); and the Dewsbury cross (Collingwood 1915: 163-4 and figs. d, e), both early ninth century. It may also be significant that the church at Breedon is dedicated to St Mary and St Hardulph.

The type of banded drapery found in these carvings has parallels on the Continent in a manuscript with strong Eastern links, the Corbie Psalter, in which in places it is combined with drapery with the sharp V-shaped hemlines and where the shape of the legs shows through, as on f.IV. The repertoire of ornament, with figures wearing pointed Phrygian caps, with peltas and fantastic beasts and cupped capitals, has been seen as showing a strong Eastern influence, linked perhaps with Bishop George, formerly of Ostia, who was Bishop of Amiens from 770-800. Corbie had close Insular links, and the Eastern characteristics noted in so many of the friezes and plaques could be explained by a common West European interest in the East at this period. The Insular links of the Corbie Psalter have been discussed in relation to the Book of Kells by Françoise Henry (1974: 215-6) and also by Jean Porcher (Braunfels 1965: 54-73).

At Fletton the panels are accompanied by friezes as at Breedon (Clapham 1928: pl. XL). However, the repertoire of inhabitants is much more involved and enmeshed in the background plants. A small human figure stands between two cat-faced creatures, grasping their tails which have dissolved into complicated scrolls. Below, birds merge with scrolls, and as the most original development, the pelta pattern is animated to become the interlinked wings of bats. Finally the human effigy has diminished to half figures or busts which form part of the pattern. Two figures of haloed angels, their faces notably like the one full length slab inside the church, merge into the background of peltas and bats wings. Another frieze has one female and two male busts (Clapham 1928: pl. XL, fig. 3) under a plant arcade which has lost the stiff solemnity of Breedon and developed into fine flourishes. There is also a fine wiry bush scroll, and a flat panel of stiff acanthus which reminds one of late eighth-, early ninth-century manuscripts such as a Gospel book in Paris, Bibliothèque de l'Arsenal 599, f. 16a.

A similar development, or relapse into old Insular tricks, is seen on the roof of the Hedda shrine, with paired birds in bush scrolls and cat-faced bipeds with tails enmeshed. These are likewise found on the Brunswick casket (Smith 1925: 236 and fig. 2), and the base of a cross shaft at Castor, and have their own development in later English art (figs.62 and 63 on pp.230-1). I see no reason in the light of Clapham's arguments and the parallels with eighth- and ninth-century manuscripts in England and on the Continent to convince me that any of the sculpture so far discussed must belong to a later period than the early ninth century. They could all be near in date but I would place them in an internal chronology: (1) Breedon friezes and panel with the saints, also possibly the two strange figures at Peterborough with the staffs in one hand and ? leaves in the other, who stand beneath a date palm and wear pointed Phrygian caps (fig. 58b). (2) Breedon saint and female bust with banded drapery, and the Castor slab (Clapham 1928: plate XLI, fig. 3). (3) Fletton friezes and two panels of angel and saint. (4) The Hedda stone. (5) The Castor cross and allied developments such as the Brunswick casket.

There are, however, two further fragments at Breedon which some would consider later: the massive angel figure in the tower (fig. 58c); and three fragments of what I take to be a sarcophagus (fig. 59). The angel figure's frame, stance, drapery, all differ from those discussed so far. The frame has a round arch set on rounded cupped capitals, very like those from the Book of Cerne Evangelist portrait frames (see Chapter 12, fig. 67). Unlike those surrounding the Virgin which have similar bases and capitals and rounded shafts, they support the rounded capitals on flat pilaster-like features and stepped bases. The figure of the angel steps firmly outside the architectural frame. He blesses with his right hand and holds a trilobed rod in his left. His curled hair is bound in a filet. The figure is heavy and the drapery folds are bold and tubular with complex crumpled hemlines. At his feet are two stiff plants with scooped leaves and ball flowers. He is the only one of the figure

a

Figure 57. a. Breedon, Leicestershire: part possibly of a sarcophagus *(photograph: David Wright);* b. Castor, Northamptonshire: part possibly of a sarcophagus *(photograph: David Wright).*

b

Figure 57. c. Peterborough, Northamptonshire: Hedda stone *(photograph: Courtauld Institute of Art).*

Figure 58. a. Breedon, Leicestershire; wall panel, bust of the Virgin Mary *(photograph: David Wright).*

Figure 58. b. Peterborough, Northamptonshire: two figures, possibly bishops, beside a palm tree *(photograph: Courtauld Institute of Art).*

Figure 58. c. Breedon, Leicestershire: wall panel of an angel.

sculptures whose eyes are not drilled. The heavy parallel folds, which nevertheless connect organically with the hem pleats, are not comparable with the drapery of the tenth century and later and one is not certain how closely the style of this piece is dependent upon its model, perhaps an early Christian ivory. It seems a strange mixture of the antique and of the late ninth century.

The other fragments (fig. 59) I would consider to be part of a box sarcophagus which probably had 12 figures around its sides. They are separated by strange pilasters whose capitals again remind one of the architectural frames of the Book of Cerne, while the ornament of diamonds and pellets on the pilasters is paralleled in the Cuthbert Gospels, Paris Bibl. Nat. Cod. Lat. 1224, f. 18a, as the decoration for an arch. All of the figures are shown in semi-profile and running with a tiptoe movement. The pilasters, like those of the angel slab, are set on stepped bases. Side 1 (fig. 59a) which is complete, encloses the arcade in a plain wide moulding on the left, and a narrow one on the right. It depicts three figures: two figures seem to carry scrolls and one a book. Their heads are haloed, their hair long, and they are dressed identically with a looped drapery fold across the body. This, like the legs which show in profile through the drapery, conveys movement. On side 2 (fig. 59b), three similar figures process to the right. All seem to carry books. The figure on the right is dressed as the figures on side 1. He has a bald head and forked beard, and might represent St Paul. The other two figures are dressed differently in what looks like an overgarment of which the frill hem is about at calf level (cf. the drapery on the early ninth-century book cover from Lorsch (Lasko 1972: pl. 25). The central figure wears a headdress which may be that of a bishop: busts of ecclesiastical figures at Crofton and Collingham and full-length figures at Dewsbury and Halton wear a similar type of headdress (Collingwood 1927: figs. 64, 87, 90, 92). Finally there are two figures on a broken panel who process in the opposite direction (fig. 59c). One carries a book, the other perhaps a scroll. They have the same facial type as the rest but the drapery is too worn to determine details. I see no reason, despite the difference of stone, to date this sarcophagus much later than the other Breedon pieces, perhaps in the mid-ninth century.

It is possible that the tradition of combining panels of animal ornament, abstract ornament and plant scrolls had an earlier basis in the east Midlands, as the panel from South Kyme testifies (fig. 54c), and it is equally possible that this East Anglian material derived from a tradition of early eighth-century Northumbrian art. Nevertheless in the ninth century it is the Midland area which is the donor to Northumbria in introducing new forms and styles such as the Hovingham sarcophagus with its groups of delicate figures set in plant arcades (Collingwood 1907: fig. p.334).

However, there seems to be a parallel and earlier link between Northumbria and the Peak District in the field of cross sculpture. The Peak District crosses, I have already stated, would be later than the Breedon friezes, but they are, as Kendrick pointed out, clearly linked with Northumbria (Kendrick 1938: 164). These monuments are to be found at Bakewell, Eyam, Wirksworth, Sheffield and Rugby. Bakewell, with 41 fragments of both crosses and sarcophagi or tombs, may have been the centre for the school. We will, however, leave out of the discussion the pieces which belong with the later Staffordshire/Derbyshire group with debased Anglian vinescroll and interlace or Anglo-Viking patterns such as the ring chain, and merely note that there are the remains of three stone sarcophagi: one with rows of close packed standing figures; one with panelled scenes on roof and walls as at Wirksworth

(Kendrick 1938: plate LXVII, fig. 2); and one merely the roof with animal ornament (fig. 60a). Such a tradition of stone shrines or sarcophagi may have started with Breedon or Peterborough.

The crosses, however, are clearly linked with Northumbria. In form they are rectangular in section, with cross heads like the complete one at Eyam, of a squat shape with rectangular arms and a roundel at the centre. At Bakewell there is a crucifixion at the top of one broad face, which extends into the lowest arm of the cross head, not using the head to form a crucifix as at Rothbury in Northumberland (Collingwood 1927: fig. 94). This seems to be transitional between the older position confined to the cross shaft and the crucifix head which developed in the ninth century and became dominant in some areas, particularly Yorkshire, in the tenth/eleventh centuries.

Another feature of these cross heads is the prominence given to angels. At Eyam (Routh 1937: plate XIV) there is a three-quarter bust of an angel in the centre of the cross head where elsewhere one might expect Christ in Judgment, as at Hoddam (Clapham 1928: plate XXXVI, figs. 2 and 3) and Easby (Longhurst 1931: plate XXVII, fig. 4). The apocalyptic nature of the figure is emphasized by trumpet-blowing angels in the arms. At Eyam, Bakewell (the standing cross) and Bradbourne (a fragment in the church) appear half-figures of angels with drapery in thin tubular folds and carrying trefoil rods. This plethora of angels is also a link with the Midland friezes and panels.

At Bakewell and Eyam one of the broad faces has figure scenes under round headed arches, with the columns standing on the capitals of the frame below as a base: the capitals are formed by a double or triple ring moulding (Routh 1937: plates IIB and XIVB). A difference is that at Bakewell some of the figures are full-length and half turned. Bradbourne has both square-headed and arched panels and both full- and half-length figures, and here the scenes occupy both broad faces of the shaft. It is difficult to be conclusive about the differing drapery of the carvings since all the crosses are so worn. At Bakewell, below the crucifixion scene are two full- length figures turned towards each other, with quite fine drapery folds, interpreted by Routh as an Annunciation, and below again a seated figure perhaps playing an instrument or holding a rounded object (fig. 60b). The figure may be winged. Beneath this again is a group of one large and two small figures and at the foot of the shaft is a single figure with ?wings or birds on his shoulders. At Eyam the top of the shaft is missing, and the two remaining panels each contain a single frontal three-quarter-length figure. That at the top may be a female figure with a book-satchel, like Nunburnholme in Yorkshire (Collingwood 1927: fig. 152S). The drapery folds are loose and crude. The figure below holds a horn-shaped object or a scroll. The shaft below is occupied by three interlace roundels.

At Bradbourne, on one face most of the panels are too worn to identify, but there was one arched and two square-headed panels above a crucifixion scene with the sun and moon above the cross and the spear and sponge bearer below. On the opposite face are the remains of five panels. The third one down is worn almost smooth, but the rest of the top four have pairs of three-quarter-length block figures like Collingham, Yorkshire (Cramp 1970: pl. 47, figs. 2-3). In the lowest panel is a figure holding a book or book satchel and with two objects, possibly birds, above his shoulders. The whole programme reminds one of the St Andrew Auckland cross, Durham (Collingwood 1927: fig. 50). The east side of the

a

b

c

Figure 59. Breedon, Leicestershire: a-c. three fragments of a sarcophagus.

a

Figure 60. a.Bakewell, Derbyshire: fragments of two sarcophagi; b and c. Bakewell, Derbyshire: cross shaft *(photographs: National Buildings Record)*.

b

c

Bradbourne cross, which perhaps is more slab-like in section than the others, has fine symmetrical tree scrolls. There is no real fruit and each terminal ends in a drop leaf. At the base is an archer. The west side has a spiraliform scroll, each volute enclosing a vestigial berry bunch or a drop leaf. From the trumpet bindings sprout paired leaves.

On the broad faces opposite those with the figure carving at Eyam and Bakewell is a heavier spiraliform trumpet scroll. At Bakewell (fig. 60c) this encloses a small irregular berry bunch and from each volute drops a single leaf, while at Eyam there is a more crowded programme with triple berry bunches and a three element drop leaf.

The fragment from Rugby of which part of three faces survive is more like Bakewell than the others (Cotterill 1935: 475 and pl. 75v). On one broad face is a three-quarter figure holding a book and below under a round-headed arch is part of the figure of an angel. On one side is a simple spiraliform scroll enclosing a rosette berry bunch from which falls a single drop leaf. On the other is an inhabited scroll in which a single bird perches uneasily, as does the quadruped at the top of the shaft at Bakewell. Scroll formations such as these are considered to be an evolved type in the Northumbrian series, as for example at Lancaster, Heysham and Halton, and in a slightly different form at Ilkley. The tendency of the Bradbourne scroll and the heavier Sheffield scroll (Collingwood 1927: fig. 93) to change shape is also seen as a late (i.e. ninth-century) feature in the north.

Were, however, these Peak District crosses, which share with crosses in Lancashire and south-west Yorkshire the figures (busts or three-quarter length) under arches, derived from something like the Otley type, which I have discussed at length elsewhere (Cramp 1970), or was there a period fashion for architectural frames neither Northumbrian nor Midland? The same feature appears in manuscripts such as the Book of Cerne, and in the Breedon group. The only feature of the Peak District crosses which cannot be paralleled in the Northumbrian series is the horse and rider found on the head of the cross at Bakewell (fig. 60c), and this could be a significant link with Breedon. Kendrick is also possibly right in seeing a common denominator for the crowded scenes at Wirksworth and Bakewell and those on the Dewsbury crosses (Kendrick 1938: 164-5). Certainly the Wirksworth sarcophagus has close stylistic parallels with fragments at Bakewell, and despite its antique iconography (Cockerton 1962) could be an offshoot of the Bakewell school.

It would seem then that in the late eighth century contacts with Eastern art and the Continent resulted in the introduction of new forms - the sarcophagus and the round shaft - and new icongraphy of single and paired figures in architectural settings. Such work is found in Northern Mercia and southern Deira, where we may note the Mercian style of delicate figures under leaf arcades on the Hovingham sarcophagus and the Masham round shaft, while the Derbyshire round shaft is linked in style with the later Peak District crosses. The Peak District type scrolls and linear figures under arches also find their way together with Mercian paired beasts, to Ilkley, Yorkshire. These Peak District crosses have some debased derivatives in the Viking period: the spiraliform scroll at Bakewell itself, while the rickety arched frames and the insubstantial paired figures, continue in the Staffordshire/Cheshire series in the tenth century, at Checkley and Ilam. It is interesting also that Bakewell shares the late Yorkshire types of scroll found at such places as Leeds (Collingwood 1915: figs. pp. 212-13). It seems, however, that there was originally an independent

Northumbrian link with the west Midlands, the old territory of the Hwicce. One must remark for this area the independent early links with the Northumbrian church - for example in the mid-seventh century King Osric elected a visiting Northumbrian, Oftfor, as bishop of the tribe to succeed Bosel (Bede, HE, IV, 23, 409-10). Moreover, some have supposed the Hwicce royal family to be of Northumbrian stock.

Although they have not survived, it would seem that there were earlier Insular traditions of art in the west Midlands on to which the Midland styles we have been discussing were grafted. For example, at Gloucester on a stone from St Oswald's priory (fig. 61a), we have an undulating plant scroll with a simple volute with an elaborate leaf flower in the Bewcastle tradition, and in the lowest volute a bird which leans forward to peck at the front. A winged creature on the upper volute strains forward upwards to grasp at the plant. The angular outlines of the creatures are rather Midland in character, but this is more like Northumbrian work than the inhabited scrolls from the Bakewell school.

The long curling leaf flowers of the west Midland scrolls are also found on the Lechmere headstone from Hanley Castle (Kendrick 1938: pl. LXXXI), where they surround the edge of the stone and on the face spring from the pediment of an encircled four-armed cross of west Midland type. This scroll-like form of the cross has been seen by Talbot Rice as Byzantine in origin (1952: 89). However, the figure on the other face is, as Kendrick pointed out, like the Peak District group in having a gaunt skull-like face. The drapery folds are flatter and more incised in technique than the Peak group, and this stone could be a generation later.

Similar figures are found on the cross shaft at Newent, Gloucestershire (Kendrick 1938: pl. LXXVII, fig. 1). Here we have the figures of Adam and Eve standing behind a tree whose trefoil leaves are very Breedon-like. Moreover the plant at Adam's feet is also reminiscent of the plant at the feet of the large angel at Breedon. A further link with the Leicestershire site is to be seen in the iconography, for on a cross shaft at Breedon (fig. 61c) which is later than the friezes there is a combination of Adam and Eve and the Sacrifice of Isaac, both of which scenes are found on the Newent cross (see also Abbott 1963-4: 20-2 and pls. I and II). The long-legged animal with cat-like face on a long neck, at Newent, is also possibly derived from the Breedon creatures (fig. 51b). However, it may be a period fashion, since the form of the cross with a wide binding, and the arcades with tiny figures under them could, like the animal, be paralleled in southern Northumbria (see above, p. 218).

There does, however, develop in the west Midlands a style which seems to be influential throughout the ninth century, not only in sculpture but in metalwork and manuscripts. The earliest examples of this style would seem to be the Cropthorne cross head and the Acton Beauchamp slab (figs. 61b and d). The cross head is of the Northumbrian double-cusped type. It is decorated with animals and plant scrolls and outlined with a double cable and a pelleted base. The plant scroll has incised trumpet bindings, rounded trefoil leaves and round buds. On one face (fig. 61b) it terminates at the top in an animal head with a rounded punched eye and a down-curving slit mouth. Such detached animal heads on scrolls are found in English and Continental art of c.800, as for example at Mustair (fig.61e), and on the metal objects from Lunde, Hordaland, Kaupang and Bjørke, which Egil Bakka dates to the eighth rather than the ninth century (Bakka 1963); and in manuscripts such as the Cuthbert Gospels. The animal figures on the Bjørke mount are particularly like the Cropthorne dog figure. On the transverse arms are canine quadrupeds with

a

b

c

d

e

Figure 61. a. Gloucester: cross shaft; b. Cropthorne, Worcestershire: cross head; c. Breedon, Leicestershire: tenth-century cross shaft; d. Acton Beauchamp, Herefordshire: slab; e. Mustair: detached animal heads in scroll.

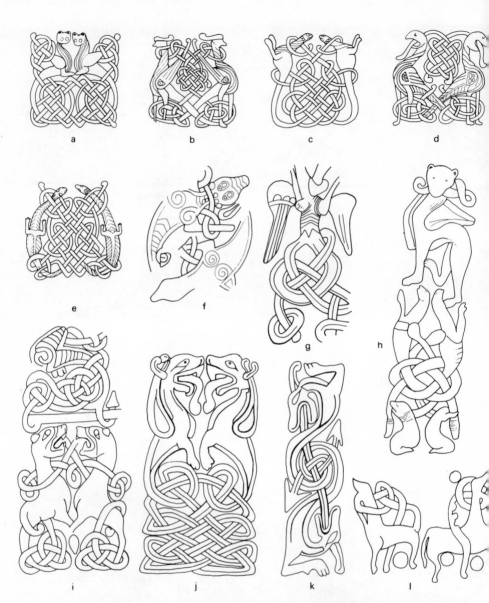

Figure 62. a–e. the Brunswick Casket; f. Gloucester, St Oswald's Priory; g. Breedon, Leicestershire; h. Melsonby, Yorkshire; i. Gloucester, St Oswald's Priory; j–k. Elstow, Bedfordshire; l. Desborough, Northamptonshire.

Figure 63. a. Otley, Yorkshire; b. Newent, Gloucestershire; c, d. Breedon, Leicestershire; e. Moulton, Northamptonshire; f. Breedon, Leicestershire; g. Gloucester, St Oswald's Priory; h. Elstow, Bedfordshire; i. Derby, St Alkmund's.

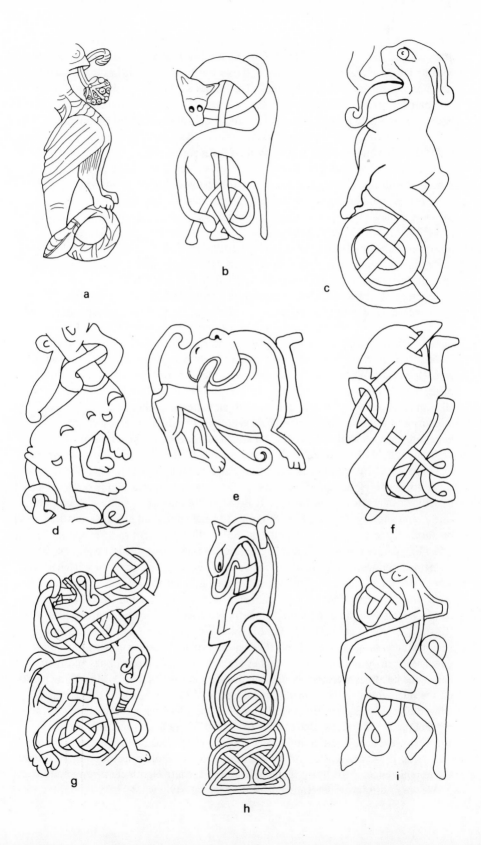

a

b

c

d

e

f

g

h

i

pointed ears, punched eyes and squared-off jaws. Their tongues are evolved into interlace and their tails are curled up. In the lower arm is a rampant winged creature with its tail developing into interlace and its front foot raised. It has the same head type and a plant scroll meets the wing. The bodies are lightly outlined and divided into hatched areas which quite skilfully emphasize the shape of the creatures. On the back there is a hole in the centre and around it are three birds and an animal. In the top arm is a bird with a plume ending in a round tassel and a tail ending in a veined leaf. On each transverse arm are two similar birds surrounded by a spray of plant scroll which grows from a rounded root. The plant scroll and the bird are hatched. In the bottom arm of the cross is a rampant beast with body patterning.

This is so incredibly like the Acton Beauchamp shaft (fig. 61d) that one wonders if they could have come from the same workshop, if not from the same hand. The bird in a volute at the base whose plume terminates in a flat leaf with prominent lobes and veins, the collar, the outlining of the bodies, the large hooked claws, are all paralleled at Cropthorne. There is a slightly later development of this style at Wroxeter, Shropshire (Kendrick, 1938: pl. LXXX, fig. 2).

These creatures are probably nearer their Continental than their English counterparts. The animal types can be paralleled in the Gelasian Sacramentary, and the division of the body into patterned blocks can also be seen in North Italian and Spanish carving c.800, as for example at Sta Maria de Quintanilla de las Vinas (de Palol and Hirmer 1967: pl. 10). This style of body patterning, then, affects south-west Mercia and Wessex. At Gloucester on a second cross from St Oswald's Priory, birds, leonine quadrupeds (fig. 62i) and sprawling beasts (fig. 62f) are patterned and take on a new savagery which spreads, with an increasing schematization of the creatures, to Colerne, Wiltshire, and Steventon, Hampshire: with, by c.900, increasing interest in the serpentine creatures as opposed to the quadrupeds.

In the east Midlands and Northumbria the repertoire of paired beasts, single bird, or rampant quadruped remains smooth-skinned or with minor markings throughout the ninth century (see fig. 63) and merges into the first Anglo-Viking styles. If we merely consider the Midland group: at Breedon itself is a cross shaft with on one side a rampant dog-like creature with tail and head enmeshed in leaf scrolls (fig. 63d); on another side a dog-headed biped (fig. 63f) with a drop-leaf tongue; and on a third side a long-necked beast with head curled in. On the fourth side is a complex changing interlace. These creatures can be seen becoming increasingly flattened and schematized. For example, although still carved in relief the leaping dog-like creature under the horse and rider on the Adam and Eve cross at Breedon (fig. 63f) is losing its individuality in the dominating triquetra interlace. At Elstow, Bedfordshire (fig. 62j), St Alkmund's, Derby (fig. 63i), and Moulton (fig. 63e), the creatures become increasingly flattened and take on the typical Danelaw posture with one paw raised stiffly in salute. Their bodies are outlined with incised lines and their head type becomes increasingly anonymous. Despite the pair of Anglo-Viking beasts on the side, which could be readily paralleled in York, the heads of the pair of winged bipeds at Elstow (fig. 63) still have something of the old rounded form, and parallel the Breedon cross shaft in the formula of three beasts and one interlace panel. However the St Alkmund heads of birds, beasts and reptiles begin to merge (Kendrick 1938: pl. XCVII) and by the time of the Desborough stone (fig. 62l) only the reminiscence of the lively Midland beasts of the late eighth century remains.

We see in this latest development of the Mercian style what I have attempted to show throughout this paper: regional responses to period fashions with the type of response dependent on an accumulation of influences. I have shown elsewhere the tenacity of Midland fashions of plant scrolls and of figural panels at Barnack (Cramp 1975). However, that is another story. Mercia had much to give King Alfred's court in Wessex, but by the tenth century, with a few notable exceptions such as the Wolverhampton column, English art had split into two regions and two social levels. The crosses of the Midlands and Northumbria become merely folk art divisible into small regional groups to which it would be inappropriate to apply any wide-reaching socio-political label.

ACKNOWLEDGMENTS

I am grateful to Miss E. Coatsworth for her helpful discussion of the Bakewell group of crosses, and to Dr R. Bailey for drawing my attention to the references to Marian feasts in the *De Abbatibus*. I am also grateful to Donald Farnsworth and Colin Roper for providing photographs of Breedon; to Dr David Wright for figures 56, 57 and 58a; to the Courtauld Institute for figures 57c and 58b; and to the National Buildings Record for figures 60b and c. I would also like to thank Miss Yvonne Brown for the drawing of figures 62 and 63.

REFERENCES

Abbott, R., 1963-4. 'Some recently discovered Anglo-Saxon carvings at Breedon-on-the-Hill', *Transactions Leicestershire Archaeological and Historical Society, 39:* 20-3.

Bakka, E., 1963. 'Some English decorated metal objects found in Norwegian Viking graves', *Årbok for Universitet I Bergen, Humaniske Serie,* 1963 No. 1 (Bergen - Oslo).

Bede (*HE*), *Ecclesiastical History of the English People,* ed. B. Colgrave and R.A.B. Mynors, 1969.

Braunfels, W. and Schnitzler, H. (ed.) 1965. *Karl der Grosse* III, *Karolingische Kunst* (Dusseldorf).

Brown, G.B. (ed. E.H.L. Sexton), 1937. *Anglo-Saxon Sculpture,* The Arts in Early England, VI, ii.

Bruce Mitford, R.L.S., 1960. 'The Lindisfarne Style in Metalwork' in T.D.Kendrick *et al., Evangelium Quattuor Codex Lindisfarnensis,* II (Olten-Lausanne).

Campbell, A.(ed.), 1967. *Aethelwulf. De Abbatibus.*

Cincik, J.G., 1958. *Anglo-Saxon and Slovak-Avar Patterns of the Cuthbert Gospels.* Series Cyrilomethodiana I (Cleveland and Rome).

Clapham, A.W., 1928. 'The carved stones at Breedon on the Hill, Leicestershire, and their position in the history of English art', *Archaeol., 77:* 219-40.

Cockerton, R.W.P., 1962. 'The Wirksworth Slab', *J. Derbyshire Archaeol. and Nat. Hist. Soc., 82:* 1-20.

Collingwood, W.G., 1907. 'Anglian and Anglo-Danish sculpture in the North Riding of Yorkshire', *Yorkshire Archaeol. J., 19:* 267-413.

Collingwood, W.G., 1915. 'Anglian and Anglo-Danish sculpture in the West Riding of Yorkshire ... ', *Yorkshire Archaeol. J., 23:* 129-299.

Collingwood, W.G., 1927. *Northumbrian Crosses of the Pre-Norman Age.*

Cotterill, F., 1935. 'A pre-Norman cross-shaft at Rugby', *Antiq. J., 15:* 475.

Cramp, R., 1970. 'The position of the Otley Crosses in English sculpture of the eighth to the ninth centuries', *Kolloquium über Spätantike und Frühmittelälterliche Skulptur,* ed. K. Milajcik (Mainz).

Cramp, R., 1972. 'Tradition and innovation in English stone sculpture of the tenth to the eleventh centuries', *Kolloquium über Frühmittelälterliche Skulptur,* III, ed. K. Milajcik (Mainz).

Cramp, R., 1974. 'Early Northumbrian sculpture at Hexham', in *Saint Wilfrid at Hexham,* ed. D. Kirby, 115-40.

Cramp, R., 1975. 'Anglo-Saxon Sculpture of the Reform Period' in *Tenth Century Studies. Essays in Commemoration of the Council of Winchester and Regularis Concordia,* ed. D. Parsons, 184-99.

Dalton, O.M., 1961. *Byzantine Art and Archaeology (*New edn, New York*).*

Henry, F., 1974. *The Book of Kells.*

Hubert, J., 1938. *L'Art Pre-Roman* (Paris).

Kendrick, T.D., 1938. *Anglo-Saxon Art to A.D. 900.*

Lasko, P., 1972. *Ars Sacra: 800-1200.*

Longhurst, M., 1931. 'The Easby Cross', *Archaeol., 81:* 43-7.

de Palol, P. and Hirmer, M. (trans. A. Jaffa), 1967. *Early Medieval Art in Spain.*

Ross, M., 1965. *Dumbarton Oaks Collection. Catalogue of Byzantine and Early Medieval Antiquities.*

Routh, T.E., 1937. 'A corpus of the pre-Conquest stones of Derbyshire', *J. Derbyshire Archaeol. and Nat. Hist. Soc., 11:* 1-46.

Smith, R.A., 1925. 'Examples of Anglian art', *Archaeol., 74:* 233-54.

Talbot Rice, D., 1952. *English Art 871-1100.*

Talbot Rice, T., 1975. 'Animal combat scenes in Byzantine art', *Studies in Memory of David Talbot Rice,* ed. G. Robertson and G. Henderson.

Torp, H., 1971. 'The carved decoration of the North and South Churches at Bawit', in *Kolloquium über Spätantike und Frühmittelälterliche Skulptur,* II, ed. K. Milajcik: 35-41 (Mainz).

From the Land of the Scythians, 1973-4. Catalogue: *Metropolitan Museum of Art Bulletin, 32* pt 5 (New York).

Les Trésors des Eglises de France, 1965. Catalogue: Musée des Arts Decoratifs (Paris).

HAZEL WHEELER

12 Aspects of Mercian art: The Book of Cerne

The Book of Cerne (Cambridge University Library MS LI.1.10) is an illuminated manuscript produced somewhere in Southern England, one of a group usually distributed by art historians somewhere between Canterbury, Lichfield and other non-Northumbrian centres. Cerne consists of the four passion narratives, each headed by a line of decorated text, and beginning opposite a portrait of the appropriate evangelist and his symbol. These are followed by a collection of hymns and prayers, a selection from the psalter, and finally what Kuypers describes as 'an apocryphal dialogue between Adam and Eve *in limbo patrum'* (Kuypers 1902: ix). There are two references in the book to one ÆDELUALD EPISCOPUS; one an acrostic, the other attributing to him the abridgement of the psalter. An Old English gloss, in a Mercian variety of speech, was added to part of the manuscript, and is dated by Sweet to the ninth century (Sweet 1938: vii, 1974). If we accept this date it gives us the choice of two Bishop Ædelualds, one of Lindisfarne 721 - 40, the other of Lichfield 818-30. Evidence in favour of the former consists of Irish elements in the prayers, and the inclusion of three prayers attributed to Alchfrid the anchorite, whose floruit appears to be in the second half of the eighth century (Levison 1946: 295-301). On the other hand the Mercian gloss, the spelling of Ædeluald with an *e* rather than an *i*, and the general similarities of palaeography and decoration to those found in southern England (Sisam 1933), and indeed according to some in Mercia (Kuhn 1948: 626), all argue for the Bishop of Lichfield. His dates too would suit the existing manuscript's decoration. There is of course the possibility that the references to the bishop have been copied, along with the prayers, from an earlier manuscript. It could even be that the Bishop of Lichfield commissioned a copy of his namesake's collection of prayers, but this is speculation.

These inscriptions cannot be used as decisive evidence of either date or provenance of this manuscript.

For evidence of provenance one looks to the larger sculpture, simply because it is too heavy to be portable, though we should remember that the sculptors, like the scribes, retained the use of their legs. An extremely eclectic style existed throughout the country in the eighth and ninth centuries, drawing on elements of the classical, Byzantine, celtic and germanic art traditions: trumpet pattern in Lincolnshire, interlaced animals in the heart of Pictland. It is the occurrence of uncommon elements that may provide us with the art-historical evidence of regional schools and styles.

In Cerne there is one example of a human head being used as a decorative motif (f. 91v; see fig. 64a), and one of a centaur (f. 3, Wilson 1974: pl. IIIb). Both these figures are uncommon in southern English art, though human figures are also found in the British Museum Bede (MS. Cotton Tiberius CII), and in the Rome Gospels (Biblioteca Apostolica Vaticana MS. Barberini lat. 570). It occurs too in the later, probably Alfredan manuscript, the Durham Ritual (Durham Cathedral Library MS.A. iv.19). In Hibero-Pictish art, however, the use of anthropomorphic decoration is not uncommon, and we find it in the Book of Kells (Dublin, Trinity College Library MS.A.1.vi) and on Pictish sculpture. The centaur is of course classical in origin, but does not appear in those manuscripts which are more firmly linked to Canterbury: the Vespasian Psalter (British Museum MS. Cotton Vespasian A.1) and the Codex Aureus (Stockholm, Royal Library). Much nearer to home is the sculptural parallel of the Breedon, Leicestershire, carvings with human figures (Clapham 1928: XXXII,1, XXXIII,1, XXXIV,3), centaurs (pl. XXXIII, 2) and mounted warriors (pl. XXXI, 1,3), the last again a motif more usually attributed to Pictish work.

In three manuscripts, Cerne, the British Museum Bede, and a gospel fragment also in the British Museum, MS Royal I.E.vi, we find vine scroll where in some cases the expected fruit or leaf is replaced by an animal head. One does not expect to find vine scroll, normally a sculptural motif, in manuscripts at all, though it also occurs in a more traditional form in the Rome Gospels (f.11v., Rickert 1954: pl. 12). The animal-headed variety is also found carved on a cross-head at Cropthorne, Worcestershire (Kendrick 1938: pl. LXXX). It does not occur at Breedon, though the tight and regular volutes of some of the Breedon vine scroll is similar in structure, each roundel containing one motif (Clapham 1928: pl. XXXII, 2). Animal-headed vine scroll can be found on Coptic textiles (Wulff and Volbach 1926: pls. 28, 103), and Carolingian ivories (ivory tablet in Munich Museum, Brønsted 1924: 91, fig. 77), and one of these may be its source. On the other hand it could easily have developed independently from inhabited vine scroll, though perhaps such a development might have been expected in Northumbria, rather than Mercia.

Another unusual element in Cerne is the use of small single animals as verse stops in the psalter (fos. 88-98). This usage also occurs in the Rome Gospels (Henry 1967: pl. V), the Book of Kells (pl. F), and in the later Durham Ritual (fos. 2, 7, 15).

Animals form by far the largest part of the decoration of Cerne, but then they are a major element in the art of every region in Britain at this time. The details of the animal type, however, with its round eyes, domed forehead, snub snout, and little round ears (even on birds) (figs. 65, 66), may be more closely placed. Where the Cerne animals have a body, they are often winged, and body or no, they frequently snap and

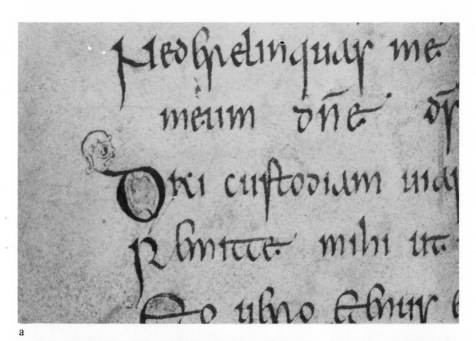

a

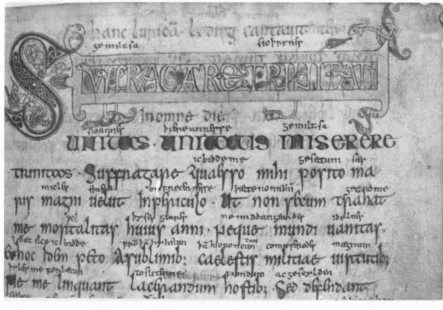

b

Figure 64. The Book of Cerne: a. human-headed initial; b. decorated text with biting beasts *(Syndics of Cambridge University Library).*

Figure 65. The Book of Cerne: animal-headed initials *(Syndics of Cambridge University Library)*.

a

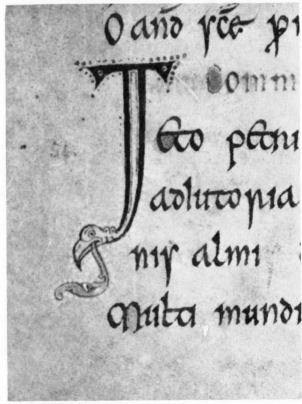

b

Figure 66. The Book of Cerne: a. animal-headed initial; b. bird-headed initial *(Syndics of Cambridge University Library)*.

bite (fig. 64b). Almost identical animals can be seen in the British Museum Bede, and in Royal I.E.vi (fig. 68). Biting, writhing beasts, not quite of the same form, are also found in the Rome Gospels. Again, the manuscripts which surely must belong to Canterbury, the Vespasian Psalter and the Codex Aureus, have quite different animals. In sculpture it is once more at Breedon that we find round-faced, round-eared, snub-nosed creatures with round drilled eyes.

The British Museum Bede, the Royal I.E.vi and Cerne are very like to each other indeed, and the Rome Gospels is related to these three. But Cerne and Royal I.E.vi are similar not only in decoration, but also in their evangelist portraits. These two manuscripts alone have evangelists in roundels, set in the centre of an arch, below which appears the appropriate symbol: in Cerne full-length, taking up most of the space below the arch; in Royal I.E.vi half-length, in the tympanum, with decorated text below in the main body of the arch. Moreover, the details or comparison between the two Luke portraits are very close indeed (Rickert 1954: pls. 16, 17). The position of the two bulls' forequarters are identical. There is the same strong curve of the breast, bent forelegs, ridge of hair down the back and between the horns, the same treatment of eyes and nostrils, and curved folds of skin on the knees; though in Cerne these are uncoloured vellum, whereas in Royal I.E.vi the whole bull is a more naturalistic brown. The wings and halo are drawn in just the same way. Moreover the hindquarters of the bull in Cerne, as also of Mark's lion, are so inept, in comparison with the forequarters, that one suspects that no model was available for them. The similarities between the two manuscripts are such that one is strongly tempted to follow Rickert in suggesting that Royal I.E.vi was the model for Cerne (Rickert 19b4: 25). If this is not the case, then they must share a common model, of which Royal I.E.vi is a faithful copy, not only in detail but in size. For this book is only a fragment of a complete bible, and the size of its pages are three times that of Cerne. Here then is the reason for this almost unique arrangement of evangelist over symbol, that two of these huge pages should not be given up to ornament, since room was available for the decorated text heading below the arch. Cerne, with no reason to restrict itself spatially, has employed the whole of the arch, by using full-length symbols, with wings, halo, and book, in the Hiberno-Saxon style.

The size of Royal I.E.vi's pages may explain the need for this unusual layout, but it does not explain how the artist composed it. Wormald has pointed out that the half-length bull is similar to that in the Luke portrait of the sixth-century Italian Gospel Book, the St Augustine Gospels (Wormald 1954: 10), known to have been in England by the late seventh or early eighth century, and at Canterbury by the eleventh century, and this or a similar manuscript probably provided the principal model for the symbols. The evangelist busts in roundels are more difficult to place. There is what seems to be an Insular tradition of busts of apostles above canon tables, sometimes preceded by a bust of Christ in a roundel, making 13 in all (Nordenfalk 1963). They occur earlier in the spandrels of arches, as in a set of sixth-century Greek canon tables (British Museum Additional MS.511), but in Insular examples they are set on the apex of the arch. There are two sets in the Maeseyk Gospels and one in Trier Cathedral Library MS.61, a work of many scribes, one of whom was English. Canon tables also frequently display the half-length evangelist symbols in the tympana of the arches, as in Maeseyk, Kells and the Rome Gospels. A set of canon tables, combining the beasts, and busts in roundels, as at Maeseyk, may well have provided the ultimate model for the Royal I.E.vi and Cerne arrangement. 'Why then,' it may be asked, 'does not this arrangement appear in the canon tables of Royal I.E.vi?' The answer lies in the size of the book. A full set of canon tables with apostolic busts spans 12 or 13 pages. In Royal I.E.vi, however, the canon tables are completed in five pages. Whatever the precise details, the links between the evangelist portraits of Cerne and Royal I.E.vi are as strong as those between their decoration.

If we look in further detail at the evangelist portraits in Cerne (only one of the original set survives in Royal I.E.vi), we find Matthew, 'in angelic guise' beneath his arch (Kendrick 1938: pl. LXVIII). This may be compared to sculptural representations of full-length men under arches at Peterborough on the Hedda stone (Kendrick 1938: pl. LXX), at Castor (*ibid.,* pl. LXIX), Fletton (*ibid.,* pl. LXXIV), on the Lechmere stone (*ibid.,* pl. XXXI), and at Breedon (Clapham 1928: pl. XXXIX), almost all standing tip-toe, with the same frozen and conventional drapery folds, all facing forward. The arches too, especially at Castor and Breedon, show the same foliate capitals from which the arch grows, rather than springs, as are found on Cerne's Mark portrait (fig. 67).

There are elements of Cerne that are not so closely paralleled either in the other three Midland manuscripts, for such I take them to be, or in Midland sculpture: the massive use of red dot background in the portraits, unlike its very restrained use in Royal I.E.vi (Wilson 1963: pl. V); the calligraphic treatment of the portraits, more like the Durham Cassiodorus (Durham Cathedral Library MS.B.ii.30, Rickert: 1954: pl. 10A) than Royal I.E.vi and certainly most unlike the modelled portraits of the Canterbury manuscripts.

Yet there is in Cerne and in other Midland products a strong Continental influence: purple pages in Royal I.E.vi and purple backgrounds to the decorated text in Cerne; the cloudy background to the Luke portrait in Royal I.E.vi; the massive angel beneath his insubstantial arch at Breedon (Clapham 1928: pl. XXXVII, 2; and fig. 59c above). To date this group of manuscripts and sculpture more closely is largely a matter of guesswork. Among dated metalwork, the comparisons are too few. The Æthelswith ring, dating 853-88 (Wilson 1964: 6) certainly carries a beast of the Cerne type, but we do not know how long this form might be current. It is a developing motif in later Anglo-Saxon art. D.M.Wilson has tried to date Royal I.E.vi, which he sees as the latest of the manuscripts, by the similarity of its animal ornament to that on certain objects from the Trewhiddle hoard, deposited c.875 (Wilson 1964: 25-7). But the animals of the manuscript (fig. 68) are much closer to Cerne and the British Museum Bede, and indeed to the Æthelswith ring, than to the Trewhiddle beasts with their bodies almost turned to foliage, their square snouts, long ears and eyes on strings. The only real likeness is in their speckling, which is also present in the birds at Breedon (Clapham 1928: pl.XXXII, 1), and this need not be derived from metalwork.

Royal I.E.vi, the British Museum Bede and Cerne must be very close in date: they share the same motifs and their differences are qualitative rather than typological. A date in the early ninth century would suit them all. They are all dominated by the dome-headed, catty, snub-faced beast, whose later development in Midland sculpture is exemplified on the stones from St Alkmund (Kendrick 1938: pl. XCVII) and the Church Wilne font.

Figure 67. The Book of Cerne: portrait and symbol of St Mark *(Syndics of Cambridge University Library).*

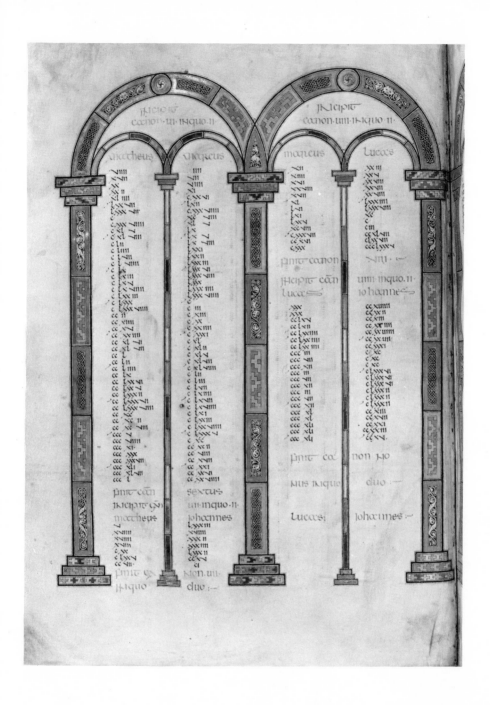

Figure 68. MS. Royal I.E.VI. Canon tables with animal and other ornament *(reproduced by permission of the British Library)*.

REFERENCES

Bronsted, J., 1924. *Early English Ornament* (London and Copenhagen).
Clapham, A.W., 1928. 'The carved stones of Breedon on the Hill, Leicestershire, and their position in the history of English art', *Archaeol.*, 77, 219-38.
Henry, F., 1967. *Irish Art during the Viking Invasions 800 - 1020 A.D.*
Kendrick, T.D., 1938. *Anglo-Saxon Art to A.D. 900.*
Kuhn, S.M., 1948. 'From Canterbury to Lichfield', *Speculum*, 23: 591-629.
Kuypers, A.B. (ed.), 1902. *The Prayerbook of Ædeluald the Bishop, commonly called the Book of Cerne.*
Levison, W., 1946. *England and the Continent in the eighth Century.*
Nordenfalk, C., 1963. 'The Apostolic Canon Tables', *Gazette des Beaux Arts*, 6th series, 62, 17-34.
Rickert, M., 1954. *Painting in Britain in the Middle Ages.*
Sisam, K., 1933. 'Cynewulf and his poetry,' *Proc. Brit. Acad.*, 303f.
Sweet, H., 1938. *The Oldest English Texts.*
Wilson, D.M., 1964. *Catalogue of Antiquities of the later Anglo-Saxon Period.*
   i. Anglo-Saxon Ornamental Metalwork 700-1100 (British Museum).
Wormald, F., 1954. *The Miniatures in the Gospels of St. Augustine.*
Wulff, O. and Volbach, W.F., 1926. *Spätantike und Koptische Stoffe* (Berlin).

Index

9826